'Sets your heart racing... **thrilling**'
Elly Griffiths

'A terrific **twist-filled** crime thriller'
B P Walter

'Dark, twisting and captivating. **The very essence of the just-one-more-page thriller**'
Will Carver

'Wood gets better with every book. **I couldn't let go** of this tragedy of loss and deception from the moment I picked it up'
Alex Marwood

'A **twisty**, gripping read takes us inside the mind of a perverted serial killer. It **pulls no punches**, and the final scenes come as a real shock'
David Young

'Immersive and **darkly devious with sly twists** and a compelling protagonist'
Neil Broadfoot

'If you like your crime books **intense, character-driven** and with regular punches to the gut, this is for you'
Louise Swanson

Michael Wood is a freelance journalist and proofreader living in Newcastle. As a journalist he covered many crime stories throughout Sheffield, gaining first-hand knowledge of police procedure. He also reviews books for CrimeSquad, a website dedicated to crime fiction.

twitter.com/MichaelHWood
facebook.com/MichaelWoodBooks

Also by Michael Wood

THE SEVENTH VICTIM

MICHAEL WOOD

One More Chapter
a division of HarperCollins*Publishers*
1 London Bridge Street
London SE1 9GF

www.harpercollins.co.uk

HarperCollins*Publishers*
Macken House, 39/40 Mayor Street Upper,
Dublin 1, D01 C9W8

This paperback edition 2023
1
First published in Great Britain in audio format
by Audible Originals 2020
First published in ebook by HarperCollins*Publishers* 2023

A catalogue record of this book
is available from the British Library

ISBN: 978-0-00-861854-4

This novel is entirely a work of fiction.
The names, characters and incidents portrayed in it are
the work of the author's imagination. Any resemblance to
actual persons, living or dead, events or localities is
entirely coincidental.

Printed and bound in the UK using 100% Renewable Electricity
by CPI Group (UK) Ltd

MIX
Paper | Supporting
responsible forestry
FSC™ C007454

This book is produced from independently certified FSC™
paper to ensure responsible forest management .
For more information visit: www.harpercollins.co.uk/green

For Tom Witcomb

Part I

1996

Chapter One

The school bell hadn't finished ringing before the doors were thrown open and a crowd of excitable children fled the building. The parents who had been patiently waiting, chatting among themselves in hushed tones, were suddenly assailed by a barrage of noise as the youngsters saw them and charged.

'Mum, Mr Price wants to see you first thing tomorrow morning. Sally Peterson said I hit her at lunchtime but I didn't.'

'Mum, I didn't eat all my sandwiches because Dad put beetroot on them. He knows I hate beetroot.'

'Mum, can I go around to Martin's for tea?'

Standing in the doorway of the 1950s redbrick building, Sam Blackstock waited silently, looking for his mother. He stood on tiptoes, looking over the heads of the other children. She usually waited by the gate but, today, she wasn't there. He scanned around – maybe she was talking to another of the mothers – but he couldn't see her anywhere.

'Mr Appleby, I can't find my mum,' Sam said to his teacher.

'Don't worry, it's only just turned half past. She'll be here soon.'

'Mr Appleby,' a call came from behind him. 'Ruby's had an accident again. She won't come out of the toilets.'

He almost swore but managed to bite his tongue. 'Shouldn't Mrs Pratt see to her? I can hardly go into the Girls' toilets.'

There was a ripple of childish laughter from dawdling children.

'Mrs Pratt went home at lunchtime with her trouble again.'

'Right,' he said, blowing out his cheeks. 'Sam, if your mum doesn't turn up soon, go and wait in the office for her.' A flustered Mr Appleby made his way back into the school, leaving Sam on the steps, alone, looking hopelessly for his mother.

3:35pm

Teresa Blackstock looked at her watch. She was late. She was very late. She always made sure she was at the school gates no later than 3:25. When the appointment came through for the job interview, she knew it would be close getting to the school on time to collect her seven-year-old son, but she was convinced she would make it. She should have arranged for someone to pick him up, just in case. Alice would have taken him back to hers. She only lived around the corner. Why hadn't she asked Alice?

Sitting on the bus, stuck in traffic, drumming her fingers hard on her bag, chewing the inside of her mouth in frustration, she silently begged and pleaded to any god who would listen to make the traffic move quicker. She kept looking at the time on her watch. Surely, that wasn't another minute gone by already.

Sam was a sensitive boy. He had withdrawn into himself since his dad died. He clung to Teresa, rarely going out to play with his friends in case he came home to find her gone, or worse. She had promised him that she would always be there for him; he had nothing to worry about. Now, the thought of her special little man standing alone in a rapidly emptying school playground filled her with horror. She could picture his pale face, eyes wide and wet with tears as he realised he had lost another parent.

3:37pm

It didn't take long for the schoolyard to empty. Once the children had filled their parents in on the kind of day they'd had, they were led away. The school day was over with. It was time to go home.

The silence returned.

A bitter wind came in from the coast and Sam shivered as he stood alone in the middle of the yard. He should go back into the school, and into the office to wait for his mum, but he didn't want her to turn up and not see him there. He looked around. There was nobody about.

Sam, seven years old, three feet tall, blond hair, blue eyes, scuffed shoes, fading black trousers, bitty navy-blue sweater, and in need of a haircut, stood perfectly still and waited. And waited.

A fine rain started to fall. He zipped his jacket up and headed over to the bike sheds for shelter. He stood in the corner and kept peering out so his mother would see him when she came through the gates; if she came through the gates.

A minute went by. Then another. He looked to the car park and saw teachers leaving for the day. Mrs Malinowski headed for her Punto with a plastic box filled with books to mark. Mr Spencer limped to his Land Rover. Sam didn't like Mr Spencer ever since he gave him one hundred lines for pushing Sophie Bishop. Then, Mr Appleby left. He almost called out to him, but Mr Appleby ran to his car as he wasn't wearing a coat and the wind and the rain were getting heavier. By the time Sam had opened his mouth, Mr Appleby had started the engine and was reversing out of his parking space.

Then, while continuing to wait under the shelter of the bike sheds, Sam saw an old football someone had left. Despite the rain, he went over to it and started dribbling with it, anything to keep warm. He flicked it up, tried to head it, but it went wide. The minutes ticked by as he practised his skills. There was still no sign of his mother.

'Sam?'

He stopped at the sound of his name being called. He looked over to the gate, but there was nobody there.

'Sam. Over here.'

Sam turned in the opposite direction and saw a man standing by the rear entrance nobody used except during fire drills. Sam kicked the ball back to the bike sheds and ran over to the man.

'Hello, Sam. Sorry I'm late. Your mum called me from a phone box. She said she's going to be a bit late and you're to come and join Wesley and me at Burger King and she'll meet us there.'

Sam looked up at the tall, thin man. He had dark-brown floppy hair and kept flicking his head whenever it flopped in front of his eyes. Sam frowned. 'It's me, Jonathan. I'm Wesley's older brother. Remember the Nativity play last year? I was the one filming.'

The penny dropped and Sam smiled as he recognised him.

'Mum said I shouldn't go off with strangers.'

'It's lucky I'm not a stranger, then.' Jonathan laughed. 'Come on, it's freezing. I'll buy you a nice big burger to warm you up.'

3:40pm

The doors of the bus opened and Teresa jumped off and burst into a run. Her bag kept falling off her shoulder, and she was wearing the wrong shoes for running in but she didn't care. She charged along the uneven pavement, the cold air biting at her face, stinging her eyes, making a mess of the hair she had spent an hour styling to make a good impression at the job interview.

She turned the corner and saw the school up ahead. Already the yard was empty and the car park only had two cars in it. She pushed the iron gate open and stopped, looking around for her son. He wasn't there. There was nobody there. She looked at her watch.

'Sam!' she called out. Her voice echoed back to her. '*Sam!*' She shouted louder.

Walking further into the schoolyard, her eyes wide and darting in every direction, she was looking for his dark jacket.

She passed the bike sheds and went around the side of the school and there he was, by the back gate.

'Sam!' she called out once more.

Sam turned to look at his mother and stepped towards her, but the man he was with made a grab for him. Sam screamed at the shock and tried to wriggle free but he was no match for the six-foot-tall man looming over him.

'*What the hell are you doing?*' Teresa called out as she ran towards them. 'That's my son. Let him go, now!'

By now, the man had Sam under his arm and was turning to leave the schoolyard. Teresa, almost upon them, grabbed her bag and threw it. It hit the man in the head and, briefly, he lost his balance, dropping the boy, who turned and headed in the direction of his mother.

Teresa grabbed the man by his coat and pulled him back into the schoolyard. Then, kicking the back of his knees, he fell to the ground; at which point, she leapt on him and sat on his back, making sure he was unable to move.

'Sam, run into the school and get one of the teachers. Tell them to call the police. *Now!*'

Sam turned and ran as fast as his little legs could carry him.

'You have chosen the wrong kid to mess with this time, you pervert,' Teresa spat into the man's ear. She had no idea she was sitting on one of the most prolific serial killers England had ever known.

Chapter Two

'I should have dropped him. As soon as I heard his mother shout his name, I should have dropped him and run. But I didn't. I couldn't. Did you see him? All that soft blond hair, those blue eyes. He was so sweet, so beautiful. I wanted him. I had to have him.'

Jonathan Egan-Walsh sat in Interview Room 3 at Skegness Police Station. He saw no point in denying what he had been caught red-handed doing.

Sam's mother had sat on him as two teachers ran out of the school to see what was going on. They called the police and he waited on the concrete – Teresa on top of him – for almost twenty minutes, until the police arrived. He kept looking up at the seven-year-old, and dreaming, wishing, hoping he had that little boy in the back of his van.

'He stood out from all the others, you see. You should have seen him at lunchtime. All the other kids were running around playing, laughing, but he was always on the sidelines. He looked so incredibly sad. Children shouldn't be sad. They need looking after. They need someone to show them love and happiness.'

Across the table sat Detective Sergeant Alan Weeks and

Detective Constable Sarah Daley. They tried not to look disgusted as the twenty-eight-year-old opposite delighted in telling his story. Alan had children of a similar age to his would-be victim. It was painful to listen to his confession.

Ten miles away, on the outskirts of Skegness, surrounded by terraced houses with no front gardens, boarded-up shops and abandoned cars, a tired-looking block of flats stood tall. The once-white façade had long since faded, cladding crumbling, window frames grimy, graffiti etched into the smoke-damaged fire door.

Two police vans pulled up outside the main entrance and out poured the uniformed officers.

The door to the foyer was unlocked and they made their way up to the top floor. A key taken from Jonathan Egan-Walsh was used to unlock his front door and a team of crime-scene officers dressed in white over their suits entered the flat.

Detective Inspector Caroline Turner struggled to get into the suit, before looking into the flat from the hallway. In the corner was a neat pile of newspapers so high they looked ready to topple over. She swallowed hard against the smell of strong cleaning fluid: bleach, disinfectant and cheap furniture polish. Whatever was found in this flat was not going to be good. The first newspaper she picked up was an edition of the local, the *Skegness Standard*. It was three weeks old. There was also a copy of the *Evening Chronicle* from Newcastle, *The Scarborough News*, the *North Norfolk News*, all of which were several weeks and months old, and local newspapers spanning the country among the other piles.

The hallway was carpeted in a cheap grey cord, the outline of the floorboards underneath showing through. On the walls either side were pictures of bleak landscapes and coastlines. One of them depicted a cottage in the middle of nowhere with an angry sky looming down upon it, the famous clock tower on the Skegness seafront drawn in pencil. The artist obviously had talent, but there was something sad and dark about them. Trying to work it out, Caroline suddenly realised what it was: there were no people in any of these scenes. In reality, there always seemed to be people on the pier, walking by the clock tower, and on the beach, even in the depths of a harsh winter. But in these pictures, Skegness, a thriving seaside town, was made to look abandoned, forgotten, lost in time. Caroline shivered. The artwork displayed in people's homes reflected their personality. Turner worried what the rest of the flat would reveal about Jonathan Egan-Walsh's state of mind.

Slowly, she made her way into the living room, where the main hive of activity was taking place. The room wasn't large. The oversized window on the far wall should have acted to bring the outside in and open the space up, but the amount of furniture, the grime on the windows, the half-closed Venetian blinds made the room smaller, claustrophobic. It was a depressing room. There was no happiness here.

A large veneer wall unit was cluttered with cheap ornaments and framed photographs; more bleak landscapes. Caroline headed straight for it and studied the faded pictures.

'Ma'am.' She turned and saw a white-suited DC standing in the doorway of a bedroom. 'You're going to want to see this. There're clothes in the bedroom.'

'There usually are,' she replied.

Caroline headed into the bedroom and looked at the worried faces of two officers standing in front of an open cupboard. She turned to see what they were looking at and felt her heart sink.

The fitted cupboard had floor-to-ceiling shelves, eight of them in total, all full of items of clothing: baseball caps, T-shirts, polo shirts, trainers, sweaters, bags, socks, pants, shorts, coats. They were all carefully placed where Jonathan could stand and admire them at any time he wished. The clothes were all far too small to belong to the man they had in custody. These belonged to children. These were trophies.

She took in the array of bright colours and, with glove-covered hands, reached out and picked an item at random and unfolded it. A blue sweatshirt with a picture of Spider-Man on the front. Something countless young boys had in their wardrobes. Her throat tightened.

'Ma'am, I recognise this,' said PC Lacey, stepping forward, holding a blue knitted sweater in her shaking hands. 'Do you remember Stuart Phillips? Disappeared in March a couple of years back. He was wearing something just like this on the day he went missing.'

'I'm guessing there was more than one made,' Caroline said with a raised eyebrow.

'No. This was handmade by Stuart's grandmother. His mother was in pieces when she described what he was wearing. It was the last thing her mother made before she died: a blue sweater with a white trim on the collar. It's this one. I know it is,' she said with determination, gripping the sweater tight in her gloved hands.

'OK …' Caroline swallowed hard and looked back at the cupboard. 'Was Stuart found?'

'Yes, ma'am. He was found in a shallow grave seven months later.'

'Wrapped in a white sheet?'

'Yes, ma'am.'

'Shit,' Caroline said under her breath. Once again, she looked back at the cupboard. Why did Jonathan have a sweater belonging to a dead child in his bedroom? How many of these items also belonged to dead children?

'Bag everything up.' She looked down and noticed she was still holding the Spider-Man sweatshirt in her hands. She folded it neatly and placed it gently on the bed. 'Everything will need to be tested. I want this entire flat combed. Lacey, go back to the station and get me the files on every missing child and unsolved murder of a child we've got on our patch.' With that, Caroline quickly left the room. She needed some fresh air. She needed to go home and hold her seven-year-old son.

––––––––––

Back at the station, Jonathan's 1990 white Ford Transit had already been impounded. The bodywork was in poor condition, the cab a mess of food crumbs and empty packets, the back empty apart from a few blankets thrown inside. Setting to work discovering what, or who, had been inside this van, Forensics had a long night ahead of them taking it apart.

––––––––––

Weeks and Daley took a break from interviewing Jonathan once Caroline had the files of six young boys from their area in her hands. Five had been found murdered in the past five years, one was still missing.

Caroline briefed her officers and retreated to the viewing room, her heart beginning to thud in her chest. She looked through the glass at the young man sitting alone. He was playing with his fingers, his eyes travelling around the room. Was it possible she had a killer of six young boys in her station?

The door opened, and Weeks and Daley returned to the interview.

'Jonathan, before we continue, are you sure you don't want a solicitor present?' Daley asked.

'I'm sure,' he said, shrugging.

'Jonathan,' DS Weeks began, clearing his throat, 'do you know who Finlay Maynard is?'

Jonathan, stick-thin, prominent cheekbones, beady eyes and thick wet lips, looked up to the ceiling. 'Sandy hair. Blue eyes. Freckles. His two front teeth just starting to grow back. He had a scar on his left knee from when he fell onto glass,' he said wistfully.

Weeks and Daley exchanged glances.

'Do you know what happened to him?'

'I know what the newspapers *say* happened to him,' he replied, a smile spreading across his lips.

Caroline shook her head in disgust. He was enjoying this.

'Go on,' Weeks prompted.

'He was playing on the beach near Skegness Pier with a friend and the friend's family. He became separated from the party and was never seen again. He was found about three months later in woodland just off Greenfield Lane in Aby.'

'How do you know so much about him?' Daley asked.

'It was in the papers. I'm interested in local events.'

'What about Tobias Carver?' DS Weeks asked.

'Tobias Carver,' Jonathan mused. He repeated the name several times, rolling his tongue around the words as if he was savouring a fine wine. 'Nine years old, I believe. He disappeared on 18 September 1993 and was found 14 April 1994. I'm very good with numbers and dates,' he added, leaning forward.

'Did you know Tobias Carver?'

'There was a lot about him in the newspapers, local and national. His parents even appeared on the television. I would think the whole country feels like they knew him. He had a twin sister, enjoyed football, didn't like maths, and had a lisp. Am I correct?' he asked with a wide grin revealing his stained, crooked teeth.

DC Daley recoiled in her seat. The walls of the interview room were closing in, her flesh crawled. 'Why do you remember so much about him?' she asked.

'Like I said, I'm interested in local events. As we all should, detective.'

'Do you know where he went missing from?'

'Yes, I do.' He fell silent, sat back and folded his arms.

'Would you like to tell us?' Weeks prompted.

'He was playing with friends in a park. They were playing football. When he'd had enough, the game broke up – it was his ball, and he went home.'

'He never made it home.'

'No, he didn't.'

'Do you know what happened to him?'

'Yes.'

Weeks and Daley looked at each other.

'Go on …'

'He was found buried in a shallow grave in woodland, wrapped in a white sheet. He was naked. There were signs of sexual intercourse and strangulation.'

'How do you know all that?' Weeks asked, leaning across the table.

Jonathan copied his stance. Quietly, he said, 'Detective, everything I'm telling you is in the public domain. It was in all the newspapers and on the TV news. There is absolutely nothing I'm saying that anyone else in the country couldn't say if they took a close interest in what was going on around them. You have nothing on me.' His voice was calm, almost soothing. He was enjoying himself.

———————

Standing in the viewing room with her arms folded, DI Caroline Turner's blood ran cold as she listened to Jonathan calmly recite what had happened to all of the missing and the dead.

'Peter Wright went missing on Saturday, 16 May 1992,' Jonathan said, sitting back in his seat again. 'His mother was so distraught at the police press conference that the detective spoke for her. Peter had breathing problems and often had to use an inhaler, but he hadn't taken it with him on the day he went missing …'

'You're laughing at us,' Caroline said to herself.

'He was found the day before Christmas Eve 1992. It was a Wednesday.'

Caroline had seen the worst people had done to each other many times in her career, but never once had she met someone as warped as Jonathan Egan-Walsh. He was revelling in his telling, yet knew the police couldn't do anything, as he was correct: everything he was saying was in the public domain. To a court, he would seem bizarre for having such a keen eye for detail, but it wasn't enough for a conviction.

She couldn't listen to it any more. She stormed out of the viewing room, threw open the door to the interview room and slammed it behind her.

Jonathan looked up at her and froze.

'I'm Detective Inspector Caroline Turner,' she began. Weeks stood up from his seat and allowed his boss to sit down. 'I've been to your flat, Jonathan. I've been in your bedroom. I've seen your … collection, shall we call it.'

Jonathan sat wide-eyed, his gaze fixed firmly on Caroline, but didn't say anything.

'We will be testing each and every item found,' she. 'We will be asking the parents of the boys we have as Missing Persons or who have been found dead to identify them; and, if they do, I'll be charging you with their deaths … with their murders. We've already impounded your van and judging by the state of it, I'm guessing that will tell us a great deal about the people you've come into contact with. Do you have anything to say?'

Jonathan's bottom lip began to wobble as his gaze burned into Caroline. Feeling uncomfortable, she turned to look at Daley, who frowned. Before Caroline had entered the room, Jonathan had impressed them with his knowledge. He'd sat straight and tall. Now, though, he was shrunk in his seat, looking afraid.

'Jonathan, are you hearing what I'm saying?' Caroline asked.

A tear fell from his eye, slowly slipped down his face and

landed on the table. The room was so silent that the quiet plop of the tear was picked up by the recording equipment.

'Jonathan?'

He closed his eyes tight and rocked back and forth in his seat. 'You're not real,' he said quietly.

Chapter Three

THE COLLECTOR JAILED FOR LIFE

Serial killer, Jonathan Egan-Walsh, dubbed The Collector, was jailed for life yesterday at Leicester Crown Court.

Egan-Walsh, 28, was found guilty last month of murdering thirteen young boys between the ages of six and nine. All but one of his victims – Zachery Marshall – has been found.

Sentencing him to serve a minimum of twenty-five years, Mr Justice Brownlee delivered a long and scathing attack on the child killer.

'Throughout your four-week trial, you have sat, unresponsive in the dock, as evidence of your crimes has been revealed in terrifying Technicolor. You have put the grieving families of your victims through torment and reduced a jury to tears so you could revel in your despicable crimes.

'The fact you haven't revealed the whereabouts of one of your victims shows the contempt you have shown for the loving family you so mercilessly destroyed. It is because of this that I shall be recommending to the Home Secretary that you die in prison.'

Egan-Walsh, dressed in a pale-grey suit, stood with his hands behind his back as he listened, impassive, to the Judge's remarks.

Throughout the 26-day trial, Egan-Walsh remained blank-faced and, on occasions, aloof, as he gazed around Courtroom 3, taking in his surroundings. When shouts and jeers came from the public gallery, Egan-Walsh's expression was unchanged. As he was taken down, he glanced up at the public gallery and nodded at the crying relatives. He descended the steps to an angry tirade from the crowd, which had to be brought to order by the Judge.

Outside court, Detective Inspector Caroline Turner of Lincolnshire Police gave a short statement to the waiting press, flanked by tearful parents. She said, 'The trial may be over, the families may have received the sentence they wanted, but the agony continues. Nothing will bring back their sons, and they will live with the knowledge of what Jonathan Egan-Walsh did for the rest of their lives. However, they can heal without fear as justice has been served today.'

In a separate interview, DI Turner said, 'Even though Jonathan Egan-Walsh has been sentenced, this is far from over. His disturbing collection contained hundreds of items and there are missing children all over the country. There are a number of police forces wanting to speak to him. And I shall continue to interview him until he reveals the whereabouts of Zachery Marshall. There is no doubt in my mind, Egan-Walsh is responsible for more deaths, and I am making it my duty to uncover the true number of his deplorable crimes.'

Egan-Walsh now heads to Wakefield Prison, where he begins his life sentence. One of Britain's most prolific serial killers is behind bars. The exact number of his victims may, sadly, never be known.

The Collector's Victims, Pages 6 & 7.

Daily Mail, Wednesday, 2 October1996

WHOLE LIFE TARIFF FOR THE COLLECTOR

Jonathan Egan-Walsh will never be released from prison, the Home Secretary said yesterday.

After reviewing his sentence, Jack Straw said, 'Jonathan Egan-Walsh is one of this country's most heinous murderers. He's up there with Myra Hindley and Ian Brady. He was convicted of killing thirteen boys, but who knows how many more he killed. He should die in prison.'

Last week, Egan-Walsh, 29, launched his second appeal after the first one was turned down by the Court of Appeal.

Upon hearing the news of his whole-life tariff, Martha Wright, mother of seven-year-old Peter who was killed in 1992, said, 'This is the icing on the cake. When he was sentenced to life, I always knew there would be a time when he was released. I'm pleased the Home Secretary has seen fit to make sure he rots in prison for the rest of his life.'

Sun, Monday, 18 August 1997

WHERE ARE OUR SONS?

A letter to serial killer Jonathan Egan-Walsh, signed by 18 parents of missing boys, was sent to his solicitor yesterday in the hope of finding out what happened to their sons.

Egan-Walsh, 31, was sentenced to life in 1996 for the murder of thirteen boys. He has never revealed the whereabouts of one of those victims, Zachery Marshall, and it is believed he may have killed many more.

Late last year, it was revealed that some parents with missing boys around the country have identified clothing in Egan-Walsh's collection as belonging to their children. Now, anxious parents are petitioning the killer, and his solicitor, to reveal the whereabouts of their sons.

Diane Marshall, son of Zachery, who disappeared from Skegness aged seven in January 1993 said, 'We don't care about another trial. We know what he has done and we all just want our sons back so we can bury them and mourn. If he thinks we're just going to go away, he can think again. I will not rest until I find out what he did with my Zachery.'

Mr Egan-Walsh's solicitor, Henry Fitzroy, declined to comment.

Independent, Friday, 12 November 1999

Chapter Four

The following are extracts from *The Collector* by Alex Frost.

Violent Beginnings

Life did not begin well for Jonathan Egan-Walsh. On the second anniversary of his parents' marriage, 4 August 1967, his mother, Gillian Egan, had expected to be treated to a night out. She waited for her husband to return home from work to their two-up two-down mid-terraced house in Walker Street, Skegness. But by ten o'clock that evening, sat on the floral, second-hand sofa in her best frock, Gillian resigned herself to the notion her marriage was not to be celebrated that year.

When John did eventually arrive home, he was drunk – Friday was payday; John had a pocketful of pound notes; and, as soon as the hooter sounded in the leather factory, he and his colleagues had headed straight to the Golden Eagle across the road. As usual, John had been the last to leave, and had only left then because his money had run out.

Gillian was still waiting for him in the living room. She heard the crash of dustbins, the swearing as he failed to find his key and the hammering of his fists on the door to be let in. She was tempted to leave him outside to sleep on the doorstep, but his knocking grew louder. Next door, had three-month-old twins, and on the other side was an elderly couple. She didn't want to upset them, so opened the door to find John leaning against the wall.

Statements from both sets of neighbours filled in the gaps as to what happened on that night. Gillian's voice was heard first: an explosion of frustration as she lambasted her husband for forgetting their anniversary.

John's reply was muffled. The argument continued. Furniture was broken. It was a little after midnight when silence fell.

Gillian later told her mother that she had gone to bed, leaving her husband to sleep on the sofa. She was woken by a sweaty palm clamped over her mouth, her husband looming over her, saying, 'You wanted to celebrate, and this is what couples do on their anniversary. Satisfied now?'

It was only when Gillian described to her mother what had happened that she realised she'd been raped. She had tried to push John off her, squirmed as he tore her nightie, prised her legs apart and forced himself inside her. She had tried to scream but his hand remained over her mouth. She couldn't move. John, seven inches taller and four stone heavier, was too powerful for her. All she could do was lie there with her eyes tightly closed and pray it would be over soon.

She said the attack didn't take long. As soon as he was finished, he rolled off her and was snoring within minutes. For Gillian, the suffering was just beginning. She was sore and in great pain for weeks.

John was sheepish the following morning and that night returned from the football early with a bunch of flowers and a cheap bottle of wine. From Gillian's point of view, the marriage was over. She couldn't stay married to a selfish drunkard rapist. She wanted a loving, respectful husband, a man she could have children with. John definitely was *not* father material. Gillian needed to find the strength to break away and that wouldn't come while she was recovering. She endured her husband's half-hearted apologies, having him lie next to her in their second-hand bed, share meals, and trips to the pub together, until, five weeks after the assault, she discovered she was pregnant.

Gillian had always wanted to be a mother, and now she would be – however distant from her dream the reality was.

When Gillian told John, he ordered her to get rid of it immediately. He felt great shame and remorse at what he had done. Gillian's mother recalled how John had spent days pleading his case. He did not want to look at his child and see his one night of madness reflected in its eyes. But Gillian was adamant. She was having this baby and he would have to live with his guilt. That night, John left with a few meagre belongings in a plastic carrier bag. It was the last Gillian Egan ever saw of him.

Gillian went into labour a month early on the top deck of the Number 27 bus. It made the newspapers. The bus company was keen to use the event for publicity, to show how their staff were prepared for any eventuality that occurred on their transport. At the time, Gillian enjoyed the limelight, but, once she saw a photograph in the paper of her sitting on the top deck cradling her baby, the reminder of its conception set in. She was a smiling, beaming mother in the pictures. Her story was one of happiness and gratitude to the strangers who had helped to deliver her baby. But when Gillian looked down at the quiet baby in her arms, all she saw was evil.

What chance did a child have in life when he was a creation of cruelty?

First Known Victim

Jonathan Egan-Walsh had named himself. Born *John* Egan in 1968, he was named after his father – a cruel decision by his mother, and a permanent reminder of his violent father. What prompted

Gillian to give him his father's name may never be known. We can assume that she had no love, no emotion for this child, as she had none for her estranged husband. Friends and neighbours had noticed a decline in her mental state by the time the baby arrived.

Following Gillian Egan's death, John moved in with his grandmother, Elizabeth Walsh, who lived in a more upmarket part of town. He soon began to call himself Jonathan, and once he had ingratiated himself with the locals, he double-barrelled his surname, taking the name of his guardian. He legally became Jonathan Egan-Walsh, changing his name by deed poll, on his eighteenth birthday – a present to himself.

Jonathan was eager to leave his grandmother's home. As much as he enjoyed the stability she provided, he was also keen to taste freedom and independence.

At the beginning of 1989, Jonathan, aged 21, worked in the kitchens of a factory peeling vegetables, washing dishes, mopping the floor and, occasionally, serving the workers their meals. It wasn't a challenging job and not one he enjoyed, but the money was good and the people were friendly. He told one co-worker he hoped to be living in his own place before the beginning of the new decade. Why the rush? Nobody knew.

Jonathan worked hard. He volunteered for overtime and saved more money than he spent. His grandmother commented to friends at the time that he was a model grandson. Neighbours said he was a credit to the strict upbringing she had given him following his difficult start in life.

True to his word, Jonathan moved out of his gran's house in November to his own flat in Bishop's Court, a ten-minute bus ride away from his only surviving relative. Elizabeth Walsh was now in her sixties, and her health, due to a lifetime of heavy smoking, was rapidly deteriorating. Breathing and mobility issues meant that she never saw Jonathan's flat but he often visited her, collecting shopping for her and cleaning her home. Right up until

Jonathan's conviction, Elizabeth's friends and neighbours were in disbelief that Jonathan could be a murderer.

On Sunday, 3 February 1990, seven-year-old Danny Redpath disappeared from a playing field in Seahouses, Northumberland. He had been staying with his aunt and cousins for the weekend with his older brother, Josh. Following a typical childhood argument, Danny had stormed off. Josh, who was with their two cousins Kevin and Malcolm Whittaker, watched and laughed as his brother had headed back to their aunt's, head down, kicking stones as he went. The three ten-year-olds didn't want a seven-year-old hanging around with them.

It was another two hours before the three older boys had arrived home. Josh's aunt, Beryl, asked where his brother was. When it was revealed he should have been home hours ago, panic set in, and a search was launched.

Beryl stayed at home with the boys while her husband, Richard, called on a few neighbours to trace the various routes from the park to the close where they lived. Their search was fruitless. There was no sign of Danny anywhere.

Police were called but a search was not conducted until daylight the following morning. By that point, Danny Redpath had been missing for more than eighteen hours.

Door-to-door enquiries in the built-up area went on for several days.

Fingertip searches of the park and nearby woodland revealed nothing. Appeals were printed in the local press and put out on radio and television. It was as if Danny had left the park, turned right and disappeared off the face of the earth.

Almost five months later, on Wednesday, 20 June, Albert Prosser was walking in the woods next to the park when he noticed an area of disturbed ground. His dog wouldn't leave the area alone and began barking and scratching at the ground until his digging revealed a white sheet. Albert bent down and removed the loose earth. He pulled at the sheet and fell backwards when a child's hand flopped out.

The naked body of Danny Redpath had been carefully wrapped in a white sheet and placed in a shallow grave in woodland that had already been searched by police officers several times in the months since Danny had been missing. The child had been strangled. He had been subjected to prolonged sexual abuse and his body had been thoroughly washed before being buried.

It was a tragic crime, and a senseless act. Jonathan Egan-Walsh's reign of terror was just beginning. On the day Danny had been found, Jonathan was innocently wheeling his wheelchair-bound grandmother around the supermarket as if nothing had happened. Less than a month later, he would claim his second victim.

THE COLLECTION

The forensic evidence against Jonathan Egan-Walsh was non-existent. Each of the twelve bodies of the boys had been thoroughly washed before being wrapped in a white sheet and buried. There were no hairs, no fibres, no skin cells, nothing to link any of the victims to their killer. The only piece of hard evidence was the collection of items Jonathan kept in his flat.

When Detective Inspector Caroline Turner and her team had first entered his home, they had no idea who they were dealing with. 'The collection', kept neat and tidy, included trainers, T-shirts, caps, coats, jackets, jeans, tracksuits, socks, pants, gloves, scarves, shorts and jumpers – all of which belonged to boys. Unfortunately, they had all been washed, ironed, carefully folded and preserved.

Every single item was sent to be forensically tested. The majority came back clear. There was nothing linking the items to the children – no hairs and no skin samples. There was nothing relating to Jonathan on any of them, either. That is, all but one: a T-shirt with two minute traces of blood on its collar. It was this T-shirt became key in convincing a jury that Jonathan was a very clever, and very devious, killer.

The blood was a match for DNA taken from family members of seven-year-old Zachery Marshall – the child who had never been found. Questions were raised: why was there blood on the T-shirt? How did the T-shirt come to be in Jonathan's possession? He either couldn't, or wouldn't, answer.

The parents of the missing and the dead were put through the torturous task of visiting the police station and going through every single item to find something that belonged to their child. It was a long and painful process, which took its toll on the investigating officers who witnessed parents break down once they'd found an item that linked Jonathan Egan-Walsh to their son.

Josie Simms, mother of seven-year-old Mark Simms who disappeared in November 1994, said, 'When I went into that room and saw a huge boardroom-type table covered with all those children's clothing, I started to cry. I couldn't help it. I'd been briefed by the police about what to expect but nothing prepared me for what I *actually* saw. Part of me wanted to grab at the clothes, to find something belonging to my Mark, and part of me wanted to run away screaming.

'I remembered exactly what Mark was wearing on the day he disappeared. It was emblazoned on my memory. I was looking for a pair of light-blue jeans, a pair of red Adidas trainers, a dark-blue hooded sweater and a grey T-shirt. I found them all. There was a lot of underwear on the table but I couldn't bring myself to look at it. I felt sick. My mum came with me for support. I don't think either of us ever recovered from that day.'

One thing that never made sense to the police was the amount of items Jonathan Egan-Walsh had in his flat compared to the number of victims. For example, there were thirty-seven jumpers;

yet, DI Turner and her team were only aware of twelve boys known dead and one further missing, and not all of them had been wearing jumpers when they disappeared. Where did the other items of clothing come from? Who had they belonged to? Just how many boys had passed through Jonathan's home?

Zachery Marshall disappeared on 10 January 1993. He has never been found. However, there is a link between Zachery and Egan-Walsh. They are distantly related and saw each other, occasionally, at family parties.

When his parents, Diane and Nick, went to the police station, they were shocked by what they found.

The Marshalls had already seen the T-shirt with the specks of blood and had identified it as belonging to Zachery, but there were more items for them to look at.

DI Turner said, 'Diane was in a worse state than all the other mothers I had met during this investigation. The others all knew what had happened to their sons. They'd been returned to them, buried, and they had a place to go to and grieve. For Diane and Nick, they were living in limbo. It didn't take Diane long to find the items of clothing Zachery was wearing on the day he went missing. What happened next was something none of us were expecting.

'As Diane picked up a pair of jeans, something caught her eye further down the table. She picked up a red sweater, looked at the tag, and immediately broke down. She identified the sweater as belonging to Zachery but knew he wasn't wearing it on the Sunday he disappeared. Diane had noticed it was missing weeks before and thought Zachery had misplaced it. Upon scouring the table more thoroughly, Diane found twenty-two more items of clothing not only belonging to Zachery, but her other son, Marcus.

'We questioned Nick and Diane carefully. We needed to know if Jonathan had been in their house, and, if so, when, and how many times.

'Jonathan was the nephew of Nick's sister. They didn't know

him well, and, as far as they could recall, Jonathan had only been in their house on two occasions. Had he stolen all twenty-two items of clothing then, or had he gained access to the house while the Marshalls were away from home?

'Interviewing Jonathan again, he remained silent on the subject of the Marshalls, and we still have no idea when or how he took the remaining items. What was clear, was all the grieving relatives would have to come into the station again and see if they recognised any more items of clothing. We always thought Jonathan had chosen his victims at random, but had he been stalking the boys and their families? Had he been in their homes and stolen items before stealing their sons? Again, it is a question we still don't know the answer to.'

I spoke to Jonathan on many occasions during the writing of this book. The only time he was truly animated was when he was discussing his collection. It was something he was proud of. He admitted to spending many hours in the bedroom, standing in front of his open cupboard, marvelling at what he had accumulated over the years. He told me how he would hold items against his naked body, breathe in the scent, and feel the softness of the fabric. He didn't seem bothered about his loss of freedom and liberty, but he missed his collection.

FORENSIC EVIDENCE

Despite the many items of clothing in Jonathan's collection identified by grieving parents, it is not known how many children he killed. He has never admitted to any of his crimes and, with most clothing being mass produced, it cannot be known for certain if the clothing identified genuinely belonged to the missing children.

Because of a lack of evidence, and lack of a confession, Jonathan could have got away with his crimes. Nobody knows when he began his killing spree, but it is possible he started long before his first known victim, Danny Redpath, in 1990, and that he became complacent – leading the police to forensic evidence linking him to six of the thirteen boys he was eventually found guilty of killing.

A stray hair, a speck of blood and a trace of skin samples were all found in the back of Jonathan's Ford Transit van. All three samples belonged to three different boys: Thomas Richards, Finlay Maynard and Danny Redpath. A unique handmade sweater found in Jonathan's collection belonged to Stuart Phillips. There was even a fine strand of Stuart's hair buried deep within the wool fibres. Two specks of blood on a T-shirt belonged to Zachery Marshall, and a traffic camera had picked up Jonathan's van on Tuesday, 26 December 1995, just off New Road in Fritton. Gareth Packman's body was discovered nearby just four days later.

By this time, DI Caroline Turner had amassed information on a total of thirteen boys – twelve of whom had been killed and a thirteenth, Zachery Marshall, who was still missing, presumed dead. The recovered bodies had all been washed, carefully wrapped in a white sheet and buried in a shallow grave. DI Turner convinced the CPS that, despite the lack of forensic evidence, Jonathan Egan-Walsh was guilty of the crimes against these boys, *including* Zachery. She had risked her reputation and career by doing so, but persevered and was vindicated when the jury returned a 'guilty' verdict, finding Jonathan guilty on all *thirteen* charges.

A CHANGE IN THE LAW

Six years into Jonathan's life sentence, the House of Lords ruled that the Home Secretary should no longer be able to increase minimum sentences administered to prisoners by trial judges, as it was incompatible with Article 6 of the European Convention on Human Rights – the right of a convicted person to have a sentence imposed by an independent and impartial tribunal.

At the time of this ruling, more than seventy prisoners were currently serving a sentence in which the Home Secretary had intervened, including that of Jonathan Egan-Walsh. Although he still had nineteen years of his original sentence left to serve, he had instructed his solicitor to launch an appeal to have it reduced to twenty-five years, as set by his trial judge. Jonathan wanted to be eligible for parole in 2021, when he would be 53 years old, still a relatively young man.

The families of Jonathan's thirteen victims were up in arms. They had set up a support group, and its members were unanimous – Jonathan should never be released.

The appeal process was a long one and Jonathan's case was strong. Since being sent to HMP Wakefield in 1996, Jonathan had been a model prisoner: he had studied English Literature with the Open University, achieving a First Class Honours degree; and attended many workshops and courses, including First Aid, which was put to good use when he saved the life of an inmate who suffered an epileptic seizure in the prison library.

However, due to the fact that Jonathan had never admitted to his crimes nor shown any sign of remorse for his victims, or even revealed the location of the body of his suspected seventh victim, Zachery Ethan Marshall, the Court of Appeal judge stated that Jonathan Egan-Walsh should remain in prison for the rest of his natural life, a decision that was backed by the European Court of Human Rights the following year.

Any hope he had that he would be released one day was gone. It took him a long time, but Jonathan eventually accepted his fate. He would die behind bars.

Part II

2017

Chapter Five

Diane Marshall had a busy day ahead of her. She had her shift at the coffee shop until one o'clock, then she was meeting Martha Wright at two to finalise the plans for the weekend retreat. It was anybody's guess how long that would go on for. Then she had to dash home, quickly shower and change, and go over to her mum's house to take her out for a birthday meal. With luck, she should get some time to herself at about midnight.

She slurped the last of her tea and placed the mug in the sink to wash when she returned home. It was only eight thirty in the morning, yet it was already warm outside. She smiled at the photograph of an eight-year-old Zachery looking at her from the sideboard – the boy who never grew up.

'See you later, Zachery,' she said, blowing him a kiss.

Sitting on the bus, Diane tried to read the free newspaper but couldn't concentrate. She wasn't interested in the new female Doctor Who, or Roger Federer winning Wimbledon for the eighth time. She closed the paper and placed it on the seat in front of her.

She looked around at her fellow passengers: people going into work, students going to school and college: a mixture of ages, sexes, colours and religions – all with the same blank expression … Another day … Another week.

The bus stopped and a harassed-looking woman in her thirties got on pushing a pram. Either side of her were two other children, both under ten. She struggled to pay her fare as she juggled with her handbag, the pram and lunchboxes. One of the children, a boy with blond floppy hair, sat on the seat in front of Diane. She looked at him and immediately thought of Zachery. She often looked at young boys and thought of her eldest child, even though he would have been 32 by now.

The coffee shop was more of a tearoom. It was an independent tucked in the corner of the busy High Street. Most of the elderly clientele were not interested in an extra-hot, double-shot, skimmed latte and gluten-free snacks. A cup of tea and a slice of home-made chocolate-chip cake was more than sufficient for the customers of Little Spoon.

When Zachery had disappeared, Diane had been working as a deputy head teacher. She took a leave of absence and eventually resigned her position.

By the time Diane was ready to go back to work, everything had changed. She and Nick had split up, the relationship with her youngest son, Marcus, was fractured, and she had been out of work for almost ten years.

She had tried to teach again, becoming a substitute teacher. Her first assignment had been in a secondary school teaching maths for the final two weeks of the summer term following the instant dismissal of the former teacher for reasons that were never fully explained. At the end of her first day, though, Diane had felt physically drained. Everything seemed to have doubled in speed since she last taught. It was too much. She attempted a second day but had to leave at lunchtime and never returned.

Since the autumn of 2003, Diane had been working at Little Spoon on a part-time basis. It wasn't a career. It wasn't well paid and it wasn't what she had hoped she would be doing as she reached her sixties. However, it was manageable. That was the main thing.

That year had marked the tenth anniversary of Zachery going missing. It was also the first time Diane wrote to Jonathan Egan-Walsh in prison. The investigation into finding her son had been shelved. There was no new evidence and it seemed Jonathan had no intention of revealing the location of his makeshift grave. Diane had written to her MP on numerous occasions and the MP had written to Jonathan in prison on her behalf. Jonathan never wrote back. She petitioned the prison, the police force, the Home Secretary, the Justice Secretary, anyone she could think of who could possibly help in getting Jonathan to reveal what he had done with her son's body. There was only one option left: she would have to write to Jonathan herself. A personal, hand-written letter.

It pained her to sit at the dining-room table and think of something to write. She didn't want to sound desperate or pleading, even though she was, just in case he found this exhilarating and led her up the garden path. She knew she wouldn't be able to cope with the humiliation. After several false starts, she wrote what she hoped was a perfectly acceptable letter. It was direct, yet conversational.

Diane waited two months before admitting that she wouldn't be hearing from Jonathan, but she refused to let his silence deter her. She would get through to him eventually. She didn't care how long it would take. She wrote to him again in the summer and then around Christmas. Her letters all went unanswered.

Diane made a plan. She would write to him around the anniversary of Zachery's disappearance every year. She would also send Jonathan a card on his birthday in March and at Christmas to keep her, and Zachery, always in his mind. She didn't care how long it took, she would find out what happened to her son.

At one o'clock on the dot, she finished work at Little Spoon. Although the work was repetitive and the conversations with the customers were the same – the weather, whatever was on the front pages of the tabloids, last night's *EastEnders* – Diane enjoyed it. It was easy and her colleagues were pleasant. They knew her history, but they had all been working together long enough not to tiptoe around the subject of her missing son.

Diane swapped one coffee shop for another, sitting in Costa with a medium latte in front of her, watching the staff go about their business. They called themselves *baristas*. Diane called herself a server. They seemed pleasant enough, and they smiled, but it didn't appear to be sincere. It seemed to lack the personal touch she and the other women of Little Spoon offered. It wasn't her preferred meeting place but it was a central point for Diane and Martha.

'Sorry I'm late. I broke a heel coming out of the library. I had to go home and change. I've only had those shoes a fortnight.'

Martha Wright slumped down in the seat opposite Diane and let out a huge sigh. She had a battered cardboard folder in her arms, which she slapped down onto the table. She looked tired. At forty-seven, Martha was the youngest of the mothers who had lost their children at the hands of Jonathan Egan-Walsh. Once the court case was over and Jonathan was sentenced, Martha coped with her loss, her grief, by setting up Thirteen, a support group for the parents and families of the thirteen boys Jonathan had abducted and murdered.

In the early days, there wasn't much of a turnout to the meetings. Relatives seemed to want to keep their grief, their anger, to themselves. It was only when Martha arranged for a counsellor to visit her home and offer advice that people began to see Thirteen as a positive step forward. The only people who knew how they were feeling were other mothers, other fathers, who were going through the same emotions. Together, they talked, they cried, they hugged, they offered support, and they helped, when the rest of the world had moved on and the story had disappeared from the front pages.

Diane joined forces with Martha and, together, they came up with new ways they could all help each other. Every summer, the pair organised a weekend retreat for the parents only. Martha had found a gorgeous country hotel in Derbyshire that gave them a good rate on bedrooms and the conference room for a three-day weekend. Martha and Diane organised the events, talks by some of the parents, specialised grief counsellors, exercises in relaxation, massage and organised walks through the countryside. Everyone involved said they looked forward to it. It helped. It was life-affirming.

Despite being an active member in Thirteen, Diane always felt like a fraud when she joined the other parents. Although they still grieved for their lost children, they had moved on with their lives. They went on holidays, celebrated Christmas, laughed and cried like every person up and down the country. Diane didn't. She wasn't grieving as she didn't have anyone to grieve for. Zachery was missing. He was somewhere, and not where he should be. It was this limbo she was living in that made her feel like an outsider.

'Can you believe we've been doing this for ten years?' Martha asked.

'Time seems to pass more quickly than it used to,' Diane said, looking out of the window as a mother and father walked down the street holding the hands of a young boy. They were happy and laughing as they lifted the boy up and let him swing his legs.

They sat and discussed plans for the next excursion, Martha sharing gossip on the other members of the group – the tally of parents who'd separated had now reached eight.

'What about Nick? Is he coming?' Martha asked.

'I haven't asked, but I doubt it.' Diane shrugged. 'He's moved on. He's married with two more kids.'

'But Zachery is still his son. He should come along.'

Diane looked at Martha who was obviously waiting for her to elaborate. 'I'll ask him,' she said, though she doubted she would.

'Good.' Martha took a bite of her muffin and a huge swig of coffee to wash it down with. 'Have you heard from *him*?'

Jonathan's name was never mentioned unless it was absolutely necessary. 'No. I'm not likely to, am I?'

'Are you still writing to him?'

Diane nodded. 'I'll never stop.'

'There's a new book just come out about lifers in British prisons. He's mentioned.'

'I can't read any more books about him.'

'It doesn't go into much detail. I think some of it was ripped from *The Collector*. Speaking of which, I had an email from the author a couple of weeks ago,' she said, rummaging through the full folder to find it. She took out a crumpled sheet of paper. 'Alex Frost. He says he's interested in doing a follow-up, this time focusing on Thirteen. I've said I'll bring it up at the retreat.'

Diane didn't seem to be listening. 'You know, I used to love reading crime fiction. I can't do that now. Whenever a missing child is mentioned I immediately think of Zachery. It's no longer entertainment or escapism. It's reliving the horror.'

Martha reached across the table and placed a warm hand on top of Diane's.

'I know it must feel like you're on your own, but you're not. You've got us. You know that, don't you?'

Diane offered a weak smile. 'I know. Thank you.' *I am completely alone, though,* she thought.

Chapter Six

D iane was soaking in the bathtub. The water was hot and deep. The bubbles covered every inch of her body and the aroma of lavender and jasmine helped her to relax and unwind. The tea-light candles dotted around the room flickered and Diane could feel her body sink further into the water.

Once Jonathan's trial had concluded, Diane had fallen into a pit of depression.

She couldn't cope with not knowing where Zachery was, having hoped Jonathan would reveal his location while in court, but he hadn't, and once he'd been sentenced, that seemed to be the end of it. Case closed. Diane was left to stumble around in limbo.

One evening, she had run herself a bath and stepped in. There was no calming candlelight or relaxing bubble-bath that time, just a tub of hot water.

She had lowered herself into the bath. The hot water was soothing and she soon felt herself slip down in the tub. Closing her eyes, she'd sunk below the surface.

It was obviously not *her* time to die, though: Nick and Marcus had arrived home early because the football match they'd gone to see had been abandoned due to a waterlogged pitch. They heard the sound of running water and went upstairs to investigate. The carpet on the landing outside the bathroom squelched underfoot. Nick knew something was wrong. He kicked at the locked door until it crashed open and found his wife unconscious, submerged beneath the water. He dragged her out of the bath and began performing mouth-to-mouth, screaming at his son to dial 999 between breaths. They saved her just in time.

Nick and Diane's relationship began to break down soon afterwards. Nick considered her suicide attempt to be selfish, when they still had six-year-old Marcus to look after, despite Diane's protesting that it hadn't been a legitimate attempt, just a lapse of concentration. Marcus was confused about why Zachery was no longer with them. He needed the support of them both to help him through this difficult time. How could she dismiss his feelings like this?

They argued most nights. Nick had wanted to move on, but Diane seemed unable to face her grief and anger, her frustration and despair. He wanted to clear Zachery's bedroom, believing it would be better for Marcus if they remembered Zachery how he was: happy, smiling, funny.

In early 2000, Nick had announced that he'd been seeing another woman, for several months. He wanted a divorce. Diane didn't cry. She didn't beg him to stay. She apologised to him and gave him a hug as he left the house with his suitcase. She had always known the marriage would end in divorce once Zachery had disappeared, but she hadn't wanted to be alone. Even though they had been sleeping in separate rooms for the past four years, it was comforting knowing Nick was still in the house.

Once Nick was settled with his new girlfriend, Marcus asked if he could move in with his father. This time, Diane *did* cry. She had failed her only surviving son. He should have been her main priority, yet she had allowed her grief to consume her and destroy everything she valued: her husband, her son, her life.

By the end of 2000, as the eighth anniversary of Zachery's disappearance loomed, Diane was alone. She knew that if her life was in danger again – either accidentally or from a genuine attempt to end her suffering – there would be nobody to save her this time. She now realised that her previous brush with death had been an unconscious cry for help. She didn't really want to die, she just wanted the pain to go away.

Diane sat at her dressing table wearing her dressing gown. It was her mother's 79th birthday and she had booked them a table at an Italian restaurant in town. She looked at her reflection in the mirror as she styled her hair. Her mouth turned down at the edges, and her eyes drooped. There was no sparkle, no twinkle, they were cold and full of sadness. Her entire face gave the impression of a woman defeated by life. She looked down at her array of make-up. It would take more than a bit of lipstick and eyeliner to make her look like the life and soul of the party.

She turned away from the mirror in disgust and picked up her iPhone. She selected Nick's number and took a deep breath before calling. As much as she wanted them to have a normal adult relationship, she couldn't help but feel bitter and angry at how he was getting on with his life while she wasn't. She hadn't wanted to mention the retreat but knew it would eat away at her if she didn't.

'Nick, it's Diane,' she said, trying to sound upbeat and positive.

'What's wrong?' he asked in a flat monotone.

'Nothing. Why?'

'You only usually ring when something's wrong.'

Diane rolled her eyes. The past three conversations she'd had with her ex-husband had been while Diane was drunk and crying. 'There's nothing wrong. I met with Martha Wright today. We're booking the retreat for August. I wondered if you wanted to come.'

Nick sighed. 'You know the answer to that, Diane.'

'I thought you might have changed your mind.'

'I haven't.'

'Nick, it's not helpful to bottle up your grief.'

'I haven't bottled up my grief,' he said, raising his voice. 'I've spent years grieving for Zachery. I think about him every day. I miss him, but I'm at a place in my life where I need to focus on what's happening now. I don't want to go to some bloody retreat and bring it all up again.'

Diane bit her lip to stave off the tears. 'Right, I'll let Martha know,' she said quietly. She felt hurt at Nick's ability to build himself a new life. Hurt or jealous? She wasn't entirely sure.

'You do that. Are you going to ask how Marcus is?'

'I was going to, yes, after we'd discussed the retreat,' she lied. She took a deep breath. 'How is he?'

'He's fine. He and Greta came over for a meal last night. She's looking bigger every time I see her.' Diane wondered if that was a dig that he was seeing their son and daughter-in-law more than she was. 'She's got a few months left to go. They're having a boy, by the way, did Marcus tell you?'

Diane could taste blood as she bit down hard on her lip. 'No. He didn't.'

She couldn't remember the last time she had spoken to Marcus.

'He asked if I would mind if they call him Zachery. I thought it was a nice tribute.'

'Yes. Very nice,' she said, struggling to hold back the tears. 'I've got to go now, Nick, it's Mum's birthday. I'm taking her out for a meal.'

'Oh. Wish her happy birthday from me,' he said, without meaning it.

'I will.'

There was an awkward silence as neither of them knew how to end the conversation.

'Take care of yourself, won't you?' Nick asked, seeming genuinely concerned.

'And you, Nick. Look after your girls, too.'

He ended the call before Diane could say anything else. Not that she could. If she had tried to say anything else, a torrent of tears would have erupted. She threw the phone onto the floor and slumped down on the bed, her crying echoed around the empty room. She had nobody to stifle her emotions for any more. Who cared if she screamed and wailed long into the night? She remained on the bed, staring up at the ceiling through blurred eyes for what seemed like hours.

The letterbox clattered as the evening paper dropped through the door. The sound snapped her out of her reverie. There was still plenty of time to get ready.

She wasn't due at her mother's house until seven o'clock. It was only half past five. A coffee, a few biscuits, and a scan of the paper would distract her from the inevitability of trying to hide her lines and wrinkles.

The story was tucked away on page seven. She had been sitting at the kitchen table for fifteen minutes reading about roadworks, the Mayor opening a new school and a celebrity she had never heard of cancelling their show at the local theatre. If she'd known there was a story about Jonathan Egan-Walsh in the paper she would have gone straight to it.

So, he was dying. A terminal illness, she'd read. Diane wasn't sure how she felt about that. Did the man deserve to die at the age of forty-nine, or should he live to be in the record books as Britain's longest-serving prisoner?

The realisation hit her like a smack in the mouth. The doctors had given him six months to live. So … she had six months to find out where her son was buried – or the secret of the location of her oldest child's body would die with the man who killed him.

Chapter Seven

Jonathan Egan-Walsh
HMP Wakefield
Love Lane
Wakefield
WF2 9AG
18 July 2017

Dear Jonathan

I read in the local newspaper last night that you have terminal cancer.

I am very sorry to hear this. You're still a relatively young man. I hope you are not in too much discomfort.

I assume you can guess why I am writing this letter to you. I know doctors get diagnoses wrong occasionally, but if you do only have six months left to live, time is running out for me to find my son.

You know where he is. I know you do. This is your one chance to do the right thing. Please, Jonathan. Please end my pain and tell me where my boy is.

Kind regards,
Diane Marshall.

Mr L. Minnow
Branagh, Miller and Associates
95–103 Algitha Road
Skegness
PE25 2AG
18 July 2017

Dear Mr Minnow

  My name is Diane Marshall. I am the mother of Zachery Marshall, who disappeared on Sunday, 10 January 1993. Your client, Jonathan Egan-Walsh, kidnapped and murdered my son and buried his body. I have been campaigning for more than 20 years for Jonathan to reveal the whereabouts of his body so that I can give him a proper burial and have somewhere to visit. I write to Jonathan on a regular basis but, as yet, all of my letters have remained unanswered.

  I read in the newspaper yesterday that Jonathan has been diagnosed with terminal cancer. The doctors, as I am sure you know, have given him six months to live. I beg you, Mr Minnow, to please ask your client to tell me where he has buried my Zachery. I need to know where he is. If Jonathan dies, he takes the location of Zachery's grave with him. I don't think I can live knowing I'll never find him.

  I await your reply.
  Yours faithfully,
  Diane Marshall.

Branagh, Miller and Associates
95–103 Algitha Road
Skegness
PE25 2AG

15 August 2017

Dear Mrs Marshall

Thank you for your letter dated 18 July. I apologise for the delay in my reply. As I am sure you can imagine, Jonathan Egan-Walsh has been undergoing many tests in regard to his illness and my contact with him over the past few weeks has been limited.

I have had many meetings with Mr Egan-Walsh over the years and your son has been the subject on many occasions. Each time, my client has, unfortunately, remained silent over his whereabouts.

Following your letter, I requested a meeting with Mr Egan-Walsh at Wakefield Prison. I showed him your letter and he stated for the first time that he has received many letters from you over the years. Once again, he denied any knowledge of what happened to your son and stated categorically that he has no information of his whereabouts.

I am sorry not to have better news for you. However, I am in contact with my client on a regular basis and I shall endeavour to keep asking about what happened to Zachery. Should I receive any information, I shall, of course, contact you immediately.

Kind Regards,

Lachlan Minnow

Chapter Eight

Wednesday, 6 September 2017

'Every time I pick up a newspaper or turn on the news I keep expecting to see a story telling me Jonathan has died. I'm not sure how much longer I can carry on like this, Mum.'

Diane was sitting in the centre of a busy floral sofa, holding a mug of tea firmly in both hands. She visited her mother on a regular basis, to help clean the house or take her shopping, or, like today, to have someone to talk to, someone who understood her and allowed her to open her heart.

Hannah Bridges was a small woman of five foot three inches. She was slim and beautifully turned out. Her thick white hair was cut short and neatly styled. She dressed for comfort but always looked elegant, and the touch of make-up she wore was understated yet brightened up her face. She didn't look 79. She'd been diagnosed with Parkinson's disease but, so far, only suffered very mild symptoms. She kept herself active by going for walks with either Diane or neighbours of a similar age.

'You'll carry on, because that's what mothers do,' Hannah said.

'I'm not a mother. I've lost Zachery and I've failed Marcus,' she chastised herself.

'You haven't failed him, Diane.'

'I have. You should see how things are between us when we meet. It's like two strangers trying to think of something to say at a bus stop.'

'You need to work at it, Diane. He's about to become a father. Use that to wipe the slate clean. Be a good grandmother. Be a good mother.'

Diane nodded. 'You're right. I've neglected him long enough. This is the perfect opportunity to start again. I'll offer to babysit or help out any way I can.'

'Good,' her mother said with a smile. 'You know what young people are like these days; they have to go back to work as soon as the cord's been cut. You could help then. What does she do? Why can I never remember that poor girl's name?'

'Greta.'

'Greta. That's it. Unusual name. You don't get many girls called Greta.'

'She's a research scientist at the university.'

'There you are, then. I've no idea what that means but I'm guessing she'll need to get back to it as soon as she can.'

'You're right.'

'Of course I'm right.'

Diane fell silent as she reflected on the mess she had made of her family.

She thought of Marcus, but every time she pictured him she couldn't help but think of how Zachery might look now. She had tried on many occasions to call her son, ask to meet, repair their shattered relationship, but every time she picked up the phone she had to force herself not to call him Zachery. As much as she wanted her only surviving child back in her life, she knew it was impossible.

Hannah looked on, staring into the strained face of her

daughter. 'Getting on with your life doesn't mean you'll forget Zachery, Diane.'

'I know.'

'It's called life. It's for the living. It's for you, Marcus, Greta and the baby. When you're dead, you'll be with Zachery again.'

'Do you really believe that?' Diane asked, looking at her mother.

'I have to. I'm nearly eighty. I have very few friends left. I'm the only family member left of my generation. I miss your dad on a daily basis and he's been dead thirty years next summer. It's the thought that we'll be reunited soon that keeps me going, that helps me get out of bed in the morning.'

'I wish I had your faith.'

'It's inside you, Diane. You just need to look for it.'

'I lost my faith when I lost Zachery.'

'Faith is never lost. We're all tested so we know how strong it is. I've been through so much in my eighty years. I had three miscarriages before I had you and Maria. Then your dad died in that crash. Then Zachery was taken. Then I had to have my breasts removed. It's all a test. Each time, my faith has been stronger. When I die, I know I'm going to see your dad and Zachery again. I might even get my boobs back,' she said, looking down at her chest.

Diane laughed. She took her mother's hand.

'What if I die never knowing what happened to him?'

'It will be tragic. You should know what happened. You should have somewhere to visit. But when you die, none of that matters, because you'll be together again for eternity.'

Diane leaned over to the coffee table and pulled a tissue out of the box.

She wiped at her eyes.

Her mother took a deep breath. 'Diane, I've been writing to Jonathan in prison since we found out he was dying.'

'What? You never said.'

'I know. I didn't want to say anything in case I didn't get a reply. I didn't want to build your hopes up.'

'Has he replied? Have you heard anything?' Diane asked, wide-eyed.

Her mother shook her head. 'I don't know why I thought he would listen to the grandmother. I should have known some people can't be reasoned with.'

'He's a bastard. A heartless, senseless, evil bastard,' Diane said through gritted teeth. Her bottom lip wobbled. 'You tried. I appreciate that. It's more than Nick's done.'

'Have you heard any more from that group you were in touch with?' her mother asked, referring to a team of students at the university studying archaeology.

'Yes. They said they can't afford to give up any more of their time for free. That private detective looked into one of those ground-penetrating radar machines but you should see how much they cost to hire. I can't afford that. I've already maxed out all my credit cards when I paid that farmer to let me dig up his woodland. I'm sure he ripped me off, too.'

'Can I help?'

'No, Mum, I'm not having you giving me any more money. It's not fair.'

'It's just sitting there in the bank. It'll all come to you, anyway.'

'You'd better not let my sister hear you say that.'

'Maria doesn't need my money. You've seen the size of that place they've got in Australia. She'll understand if I say it's to help you find Zachery.'

'No, Mum. You might need it yourself.'

'What do I need money for? I'm hardly likely to be going on any cruises any time soon.'

'I thought you said you wanted to visit Australia again.'

'I did. But then I think of how long the flight is and it puts me off. You know how I hate flying. Are you staying for your tea?'

'No. I'd better get back.'

'What for?'

Diane stopped in her tracks. 'OK. I'll stay.'

Hannah smiled. 'Good. You can peel the potatoes.'

After their tea, they watched television together and emptied the biscuit barrel. They chatted about nothing, had a laugh when Hannah told the story of the time she and Diane's father went on holiday together for the first time : camping in North Yorkshire during one of the wettest summers Britain had endured. Diane decided to stay at her mother's for the night.

By midnight, Diane was in the spare room, wide awake, staring at the ceiling. The room was airy and clean. She was warm, wrapped in fresh sheets. She considered reading some of the Bible on the bedside table, but decided against it. It had been years since she'd read from the Bible. There was nothing in it to give her any comfort. Her mother's words about her faith being hidden echoed around her head. Was that true? She doubted it. If God was testing her, surely the test should be over with by now. It had been almost twenty-five years since Zachery disappeared. How much longer was God planning on torturing her like this? And why her? Why were other people not having to endure such agony for a quarter of a decade?

She turned over to look at the bedside table. There was no photograph of her seven-year-old boy looking at her, as it would be at home. She threw back the duvet and jumped out of bed. There were a few photos of Zachery in the side pocket of her handbag. It was comforting having him with her as she went about her daily routine. She took them out and propped them up against the base of the bedside lamp, climbed back into bed and wrapped the duvet around her. She kept the light on and laid on her side, staring deep into the pictures of her smiling son.

She closed her eyes and a small smile appeared on her lips. There was Zachery on the swings in the local park, giggling away as she pushed him higher. Then she saw Zachery and Marcus on Christmas morning in their pyjamas, tearing off the colourful wrapping paper of the mound of presents in front of them. Their eyes beaming, smiles wide, as they failed to contain their excitement.

Then, the darkness descended, and the smiles faded. She saw Zachery riding his bike and Jonathan Egan-Walsh stepping out from behind bushes, grabbing him, placing a hand over his mouth to stop him from screaming, throwing him in the back of his van, locking the doors and driving off to God knows where to do unspeakable things to him. She pictured him in the back of the van as it drove at speed, crying, begging, pleading to be let out, screaming for his mum.

Jonathan never told the court where he had hid the children while they were alive. His neighbours never saw him with any kids. Diane squeezed her eyes tightly shut as she imagined some underground bunker with no electricity, freezing cold and damp. Was Zachery kept chained up, starving and thirsty? Was his only contact with people when Jonathan visited to use him for his own sick pleasure? Did other people come, too? Did Jonathan prostitute Zachery to other disgusting perverts who enjoyed having sex with children?

Diane tossed about in her sleep as the nightmares took hold once again. She saw Jonathan, his ugly, evil face, his malevolent grin as he loomed down over her petrified son. She pictured his giant, calloused hands caressing her son's smooth naked body. Zachery must have been so scared. He was eight years old. He didn't know about the evils of the world, he was too young for that, yet he was experiencing them at first-hand. A disturbed, sick predator was using her son for his own barbaric pleasure. The bastard.

Presumably, Zachery had been strangled like all the other boys. When Jonathan had finished with his victim, when he had grown bored with him, or had ruined him sufficiently, his limp naked body was thoroughly washed and carefully wrapped in a white sheet and once more placed in the back of Jonathan's van, driven out into the middle of nowhere and dumped in a shallow grave. Why was he different to the others? Why had the other twelve been found? Had he dug Zachery's grave deeper for some reason? Had he buried him in a place people didn't go? Had Zachery been alive when Jonathan buried him and he had somehow managed to dig himself free? If so, did that mean he was still alive? Traumatised from being subjected to vile sex acts and buried alive, had he blocked everything out? Was he suffering some kind of amnesia and didn't know anything about who he was or where he was?

'*Zachery?*' Diane screamed and sat bolt upright in bed. The bedroom was bright and her mother was sitting on the edge, holding her hand. 'Mum?'

'You were screaming in your sleep.'

'I was having a nightmare.'

'I guessed as much.' She took a tissue from the box on the bedside table and began dabbing at Diane's sweating forehead.

'What was I saying?'

'You were just calling out Zachery's name. Do you have these dreams often?'

'They've been more frequent since I found out Jonathan is dying.'

'Oh, sweetheart.' Her mother leaned forward and hugged her youngest child. 'I wish I could take the pain away from you.'

Diane cried into her mother's bony shoulder as she held on tight. Suddenly, she was sixteen again and crying over Robert Fisher dumping her for Vanessa Calvert because Vanessa said she'd have sex with him and Diane wanted to wait. Hannah had comforted her daughter then, too. Now they were in the same position, in the same bedroom, more than forty years later.

'You don't realise how everything changes when a tragedy like losing a child happens,' Diane said as she sat at the kitchen table.

It was three o'clock in the morning. Diane and her mother had been talking for an hour on the bed before her mum said she was getting cold and wanted a drink. They both went downstairs in their dressing gowns to make a cup of tea. When Hannah opened the fridge door for the milk, she saw the packet of bacon on the shelf and suddenly, she craved a bacon sandwich. She was frying the bacon while Diane was buttering the bread.

'They don't tell you on those crime dramas that you lose your friends, do they?' Diane continued. 'I see Margaret McCrery sometimes, but we used to walk our kids to school together *every* day. She would come over to my house for coffee or I'd go to hers. We were very close.'

'I remember.'

'Now, we don't even look at each other. I saw her in the supermarket a few months back. She's got grandkids now. She was with her Daniel. He's put on some weight, I tell you. He's practically bald, too, and he's only the same age as Zachery would have been. I wonder if Zachery would have been bald.'

'I doubt it. Marcus isn't bald. Neither is Nick. The tomato sauce is in the top cupboard.'

'He's got his own business, Daniel. He was in the paper for taking on some apprentices. He's done very well for himself.'

'Zachery would have done, too. Marcus certainly has.'

'You'd think people would come together when you lose a child. You wouldn't think it'd make you a social pariah. I used to have a lot of friends,' Diane said, resting her head on her hands.

'You still do. Look at those women you work with. You often say you've had a laugh.'

'That's different. They're colleagues. I wouldn't invite them round for a party.'

Her mother made the bacon sandwiches and placed one in

front of Diane, then sat opposite her at the table and took a small bite.

'People are scared of grief. They don't understand it and they're frightened of saying the wrong thing, so they keep away,' Hannah said.

'All I've wanted is for someone to talk to, someone to listen to me talk about Zachery.'

'From their point of view, it makes them look at their own child's mortality. Nobody wants to think about their child dying, but once it's happened to someone they know, that's what they do. By staying away from you, they're ignoring what could possibly happen to their own child.'

'When did you get so knowledgeable about grief?' Diane said, picking at her own sandwich.

'I've read plenty of books about it over the years. I could give lectures.'

'We should invite you to our retreats,' Diane said, smiling now.

'You seemed brighter this year when you came back. It must have done you some good.'

'It did,' she smiled at the memory. 'We had some lovely long walks in the countryside. And Martha's doing a massaging course. She was practising on me. She's got healing hands. It's a shame it doesn't heal what's going on in here,' she added, tapping her temple. 'What am I going to do about Jonathan, Mum? He's probably only got a few weeks left, if that.'

'I'm all out of ideas, Diane,' Hannah said, wiping up a dollop of tomato sauce from her plate and licking her finger.

'I'm going to lose him, aren't I? I'm never getting him back.'

There was nothing to be said between mother and daughter. As much as Hannah didn't want to admit it, it seemed that Diane was right. They were never going to be bringing Zachery back home.

Part III

2018

Chapter Nine

Thursday, 11 January 2018

BBC BREAKING NEWS

Jonathan Egan-Walsh, convicted of murdering thirteen boys
in 1996, died in Leeds General Infirmary yesterday from
cancer. He was 50. More to follow.

Diane, sitting in her usual seat on the bus, closed the newspaper
on her lap, and fished inside her coat for her iPhone. The BBC
news app caused the world around her to stop turning. All
background noise faded and she stared at her phone until the
screen went blank.

That was it, then. He was dead. The secret he had kept for
twenty-five years had gone with him to the grave. She would
never find out where her son was buried.

Her eyes widened. She went back to the BBC News app and

read the brief story. He died yesterday. Yesterday was 10 January. Yesterday was the 25th anniversary of Zachery's disappearance. The bastard had died on the exact day he had kidnapped her son!

Diane felt sick. She felt hot. She needed to get off the bus. *Now!* She stood up and barged past the person sitting next to her. The bus was packed and she had to fight her way to the front. Every time she came to a bell, she pushed the button and shouted for the driver to pull over.

The doors opened and Diane practically fell onto the pavement. The cold morning air stung her face. She pushed by three people waiting to get on the bus and entered the bus stop. She bent over, opened her mouth and vomited. She was sure someone asked her if she was all right, but she couldn't concentrate on anything. She kept retching, her body was trying to expel everything she'd eaten but there was nothing left, just dry heaving. Eventually, she stopped.

Diane looked up. The bus had gone. So had the people. There was just one old lady with a trolley looking at her.

'Are you all right, love?' she asked.

'No. No, I'm not,' she replied, digging around in her handbag for a tissue.

Diane staggered away from the bus stop. There was no way she could face going into work now. Diane Marshall, fifty-eight years old, and all she wanted was to be hugged by her mother.

Hannah must have seen her daughter zigzagging up the road, because she opened the front door before Diane reached the garden path. She held out her arms and Diane fell into them. She was crying and didn't stop for hours.

'He's gone, Mum,' she said. They were on the sofa. Diane's head was on her mother's lap and Hannah was stroking her hair. 'Even though he didn't reply to my letters, I always thought that, eventually, one day, he *would* tell me where he'd buried Zachery. While he was alive, I had that to cling onto. Why couldn't he have found God like a lot of prisoners do? He would have confessed. He would have told me everything. Now he's dead, that's it. There's nothing left. He's gone. Zachery's gone. And there's no way I'm ever going to get him back.'

Chapter Ten

There was no funeral service for Jonathan Egan-Walsh. There was nobody to arrange one and nobody to attend. Even the most sympathetic of vicars would have found it difficult to say something warm and pleasant about the killer of thirteen young boys.

From Leeds General Infirmary, Jonathan made his final journey under the cover of darkness to a local funeral director, where he was cremated in a cardboard coffin without ceremony. The ashes were poured into a simple tin urn and placed into the trust of Lachlan Minnow, Jonathan's solicitor. He had no idea what to do with them, so took them home and placed them on a shelf in his spare bedroom.

Diane Marshall took some time off work from Little Spoon. Jonathan's death had hit her hard. She had become adept at going through life with a painted-on smile and feigning polite conversation with customers, but she had always had something to cling onto. Not Now, though. Now, it was all over. There was nobody for her to write to to find out where Zachery was buried. There was nobody for her to lobby and plead with. Her life was empty.

In the days following Jonathan's death, she received many visitors and phone calls from the parents in Thirteen, all of them expressing their regret and sadness. Everybody took it as read that this was the end. While their words were sincere and spoken from the heart, Diane felt she was being placated; a member of their group who didn't really belong was suffering another setback and needed to hear a few kind words. She couldn't wait for them to leave.

Nick didn't call. She hadn't expected him to, but she would have liked a text or something to acknowledge he was thinking about her. Three days after Jonathan died, there was a knock on the door. It wasn't late, but it was pitch-black outside and, at first, Diane was reluctant to answer. However, the knocking continued, so, hesitantly, she put the security chain on and opened the door a crack. Standing on the doorstep was her son, Marcus, a look of sadness on his face, a baby in his arms.

Diane's face lit up immediately. She quickly closed the door, took off the chain and flung the door open.

'Marcus, what a lovely surprise!' she exclaimed, beaming. 'What are you doing here?'

'I've come to see you, Mum. I thought you'd like to meet your grandson.'

She placed a hand on her chest, swallowing her emotions. 'Yes, sorry. How lovely. Come in,' she said, remembering her manners. 'Is Greta not with you?'

'No. She's tired. I thought I'd give her a break.'

Diane closed the front door and followed her son into the living room. He stood with a big smile on his face, though, she noticed, it didn't reach his eyes. He was obviously proud of his first-born child, but there was an air of sadness surrounding the whole event. She looked at Marcus lovingly, but couldn't help but think of what Zachery would look like now, had he lived. Would he be tall, broad and handsome? Would he have had a shock of dark wavy hair, stubble and glasses?

Diane couldn't take her wide eyes from the small child in his arms.

'Mum, I'd like you to meet your first grandson – Zachery Nicholas Marshall.'

Diane's bottom lip quivered. 'Oh, Marcus,' she said, fighting back the tears, 'that's beautiful.' She wasn't pleased with the choice of middle name, however.

'Would you like to hold him?'

'I'd love to.'

Diane sat down on the sofa and, carefully, Marcus placed the sleeping child in her arms. 'Blimey, he's not light, is he?' she said, smiling through the tears.

'He was eight pounds three when he was born and he's put on a few pounds since.'

Still smiling, Diane looked up at her son. 'I'm sorry, Marcus. I should have come round to see you when Greta first had him. I just …'

'Don't, Mum. You don't need to. I understand.'

She looked down at her grandson then back up at her son, who also had tears in their eyes.

'Mum … I'm sorry,' Marcus said. His voice was soft.

'Sorry? What for?'

'I've seen on the news about Jonathan dying. I'm guessing he never got in touch, to tell you where Zachery was.'

'No, he didn't.'

Marcus shook his head, an array of emotions flitting across his face: anger, upset, sadness, frustration. 'I wish there was something I could do,' he said, fighting back the tears.

Diane had looked down at her grandson. She was bewitched by him already. 'There's nothing we can do,' she said. Then, looking back up at her son: 'We lost the battle. And now the war's over, we've lost that, too.'

'Mum—'

'You know,' Diane interrupted, 'your gran keeps telling me life is for the living. As much as I wanted to believe her, I never did. Now, seeing wee Zachery, here, it all makes sense ...' She smiled. 'This is what life is about.'

Marcus joined his mother on the sofa and placed an arm around her shoulders. 'Can we start again?'

'Of course we can,' she replied, smiling through her tears. Zachery started to wake up. He yawned and stretched and made a gurgling noise. 'He's got your nose, Marcus.'

'Do you think?'

'Absolutely.' The baby, now fully awake, looked directly up at Diane. He looked puzzled as he studied her, before a small smile spread across his little face. 'He's got Greta's blue eyes. Oh, he's a beautiful, Marcus. You must be *so* proud.'

'I am. Shall I make us a cup of tea?'

'I'll do it.'

'No, let me. You get to know your grandson.'

Marcus went into the kitchen, leaving his mother alone with little Zachery. He closed the door behind him. He knew what his mother would be saying, and he didn't want to hear it.

'Hello, Zachery,' Diane began. 'You're a beautiful little boy,' she said. Her voice was low and broken with emotion. 'You're going to have so many people to look after you. There's your mum and dad, and me and my mum as well. We're going to spoil you rotten, and rightly so.' Zachery started fussing so she altered her position so she was cradling him more tightly. 'When you're old enough, I'll tell you all about your uncle Zachery. He would have loved you. We won't let anyone hurt you, little one. All you're going to know is love and kindness, Zachery.' A tear fell from Diane's eye and landed on the baby's face.

She didn't wipe it away. 'My little boy, Zachery,' she said.

By the end of January, Diane had resigned herself to the fact she would never find the final resting place of her eldest son. She had several long talks with her mother, in which she cried her heart out at her agony. Hannah had told her to keep praying, and that it didn't matter where we ended up in this life, since we would all be reunited in the next.

Diane had been seeing more of Marcus and Greta, and their relationship was developing into something akin to mother and son once again. She looked after baby Zach whenever the new parents needed some time to themselves. Greta was planning to return to work by the summer and Diane volunteered to babysit. It had taken twenty-five years, but, finally, Diane was moving on with her life.

One thing she could never get used to, though, was coming home from work to an empty house. She unlocked the front door and stepped into the hallway. As soon as she closed the door behind her, the outside world died away and she was alone again, surrounded by heavy silence. Clocks ticked, the fridge hummed – she could hear every sound of the house settling – floorboards creaking and the distant buzz of the TV on standby. These were the sounds of loneliness and, even after fifteen years of coming home to an empty house, she didn't like it.

Diane didn't watch much television, but it was always on from the moment she arrived home until the time she went to bed – it gave the house a feeling of occupancy. It was background noise, and it was comforting. She was in the kitchen preparing her evening meal when a knock came on the door. Wiping her hands on the tea towel, she went to answer it. Standing on the doorstep was a very tall man in a dark-grey suit, carrying a briefcase in one hand and holding an umbrella aloft with the other, sheltering himself from the rain.

'Mrs Marshall?' he asked in a pure Yorkshire accent. He didn't attempt to hide it, despite dressing like a Harley Street consultant with his designer suit, expensive shoes and manicured nails.

'Yes ...?' Diane answered enquiringly.

'I'm Lachlan Minnow,' he replied.

'Oh ...'

'Jonathan Egan-Walsh's solicitor. You wrote to me?'

'Of course,' she realised. 'Sorry. What can I do for you?'

'I was wondering if I could have a word, in private, perhaps?'

'Of course, do come on in. Let me take that for you,' she added, as he lowered his umbrella.

Lachlan Minnow stepped over the threshold, ducking as he did so. 'Nasty weather,' he said.

'Yes. I got home just in time, it seems. Go on through,' Diane pointed to the door to the living room, before putting his umbrella in the kitchen. When she returned, she found her guest looking at the framed photographs of her two sons.

'Is this Zach?'

'Zachery. Yes.'

'And your other son?'

'Yes. Marcus. They were inseparable when they were small. Sorry ... Mr Minnow, why are you here?'

'Ah. Do you mind if I sit down?'

'No, of course not,' she replied, pointing to an armchair.

The solicitor sat down. He placed his briefcase on his lap, then opened it and took out a cardboard folder.

'As you know, I was Jonathan Egan-Walsh's solicitor for the last six years of his life. He didn't really need one, so my duties were very light. Once he became ill, he contacted me more often to arrange what happened to his belongings when he died. Obviously, he didn't have much to leave. However, there were the items he had in his cell that he'd accumulated over the years. While prison officers in Wakefield were going through these items, they came across a sealed brown envelope, which stated it shouldn't be opened until after his death. Upon doing so, we found a few more envelopes inside it, including one addressed to me, and one to you,' he said. He opened the folder and took out a small white envelope.

Diane's eyes widened. 'What's in it?'

'We don't know. It's addressed to you.'

She couldn't take her eyes off the envelope. It was thin. It looked empty. She took a deep breath. Was this his confession, telling her where he had buried her son? Was she finally going to find him after all these years? As much as she wanted to snatch the envelope from the solicitor's hand, she didn't dare move. Her heart pounded in her chest, her mouth dried and she was visibly shaking.

'Mrs Marshall, are you all right?'

'I don't know. I don't know if I want to read it,' she answered, sitting down on the sofa.

He placed it carefully on the coffee table. 'I can leave it with you, if you like? You can read it in your own time.'

'I don't know if I want to be on my own or not.'

'Would you like me to read it?'

Diane took a deep breath. 'No. I'll read it first. Will you stay?'

'Of course.' He smiled, leaning back into the armchair.

Diane stared at the envelope, then quickly picked it up. Despite its appearance, it felt heavy and hot in her hands, as if whatever magic or poison was inside was already leaching into her skin. She looked at her name written in block capitals in messy handwriting. The paper was cheap. She turned it over, used her thumb to open it and pulled out the single sheet of thin paper that was inside.

---

22 September 2017

Dear Mrs Marshall,

Thank you for your letters over the years. I've received many letters, mostly from admirers, and more marriage proposals than I can remember. But they were just words on a page. The photos were nice, some were bloody filthy, but they're not the same as seeing a person in the flesh. I've never known the writer's accent, how they smelled, how they cried. Your letters were different. When I read them, I remembered you from the courtroom. You were sat in the public gallery next to your husband, your face pale, your lips so tightly pursed they were almost white. You wore a pink blouse for the sentencing. It was tight. Revealing. I've never forgotten that.

As you will no doubt have read, I have recently been diagnosed with bowel cancer and the doctors have said I will be dead within six to eight months. I always assumed I would take that news badly, but I have found having a time limit put on my head quite peaceful. The end is in sight.

Once I have finished writing this letter, I shall hide it in my cell and leave instructions for my solicitor, Lachlan Minnow, to send it on to you after I've died. I'd give him it now but I don't trust solicitors.

He'd probably sell it to a tabloid, and I don't want you to know about this letter until I'm ready.

I am writing to you because I understand you have been living in pain since your son disappeared and I think it is important that you learn the truth.

I am a killer. I am guilty of all the crimes I was convicted of, except one. I did not kidnap your son, nor did I kill him. I know we were only distantly related, but I counted you, and Zachery, as family. I would never have hurt any member of my family.

I honestly cannot recall how many boys I killed, but I do know that I had no contact with your son at all when he went missing. I did not kill Zachery Marshall. Strangely, I feel quite guilty having taken credit for whatever happened to him for the past 25 years.

I am sorry for the anguish you have suffered over the years but I hope you can take something from this letter. I truly hope you find your son.

Yours faithfully
Jonathan Egan-Walsh

Diane's eyes were filled with tears that refused to fall. She gripped the letter firmly with both hands.

'Mrs Marshall?' Lachlan asked.

'He didn't do it,' she whispered.

'I'm sorry?'

'He didn't kill my boy. That's why he never said where he'd buried him, because he didn't know. He didn't do it.'

Chapter Eleven

Diane got rid of Lachlan Minnow and read the letter again, and again, absorbing every word. When the solicitor had turned up on her doorstep and told her of the letter, she thought she was finally going to find Zachery's body. She'd be able to bring him home, have a funeral, and have somewhere to go on his birthday and at Christmas. She should have known Jonathan wouldn't give up any information so readily. He would more likely have given her some bizarre cryptic clue, to continue his sick, twisted mind games from beyond the grave.

What she hadn't expected was to hear he wasn't responsible for Zachery's death in the first place.

Or was that a mind game, too?

'Shit!' Diane cried out. She jumped up from the sofa and went over to the cabinet to pour herself a large drink. She only had vodka and wine in the house as that was all she drank these days. Her mind was racing, her heart was pounding. She couldn't make sense of anything.

Diane emptied the glass of vodka in a single gulp. She looked back at the coffee table, saw the single-page letter and hated it for what it represented. Had the past twenty-five years been wasted? She needed some air.

She threw open the kitchen door, went out into the back garden, and breathed in a lungful of cold air. Slowly, she began to calm down. Her muscles began to loosen as the tension ebbed away. She leaned against the wall of the house, staring at the tree she had planted, her only memorial to the son she had lost. A strong gust of wind shook her from her reverie. She returned to the warmth of the house, the horror of the letter, and thought of what to do next.

The decision was too monumental for her to figure out for herself. Diane needed advice. She decided to call her mother, but every time she started dialling, she hung up. This wasn't something that could be talked about over the phone. Besides, her mum would want to see the letter for herself, not have her daughter read it out. She put a coat on, carefully put the letter back in its envelope, grabbed her car keys and headed for her childhood home.

'Diane, what's wrong? You're as white as a sheet,' her mother said on opening the door.

'Mum, I need your help. I don't know who else to turn to.' Diane didn't wait to be invited in. She pushed passed her mother and went straight into the living room. The television was on loud. Diane picked up the remote and turned it off.

'Mum, sit down. I've got some news.'

'Oh, God. It's not bad, is it? I've had enough bad news to last me a lifetime. You know Alice who cuts my hair? She was mugged at knifepoint last week. In broad daylight. She was—'

'Mum. Please,' Diane interrupted. 'Here. Read this,' she said, shoving the letter almost in her face.

'What is it?'

'Just … read it.'

'Pass me my glasses.'

Diane waited impatiently while her mother struggled to take

the paper out of the envelope. She unfolded the letter and began reading, her eyes moving slowly along the lines of writing. Diane remained standing. She looked at her mother's face, trying to read her expression. Was she shocked, disgusted, surprised? There was nothing there. Diane bit her bottom lip in frustration.

'Well …' she said as she finally reached the end.

'What do you think?' Diane prompted.

'I think that man is a complete bastard,' she handed the letter back to her daughter. 'Here, take it.' She seemed relieved to get it away from her.

'Well, yes, I know, he could have told me all this years ago. But, what do you think? Do you think I should take it to the police?'

'The police? Why?'

'They can reopen the case.'

'Oh, Diane. Surely, you don't believe it.'

'Why not?'

'You know what he's like. He's a killer. He could have owned up to what he did as soon as he was arrested, and not put any of you through the torment of a trial, but he didn't. He lapped up the attention. That's what this is, more attention seeking.'

'But he's not seeking attention – because he's dead,' Diane said, slumping into the sofa.

'He doesn't have to be alive to get attention. His name is going to live on for ever. He's going down in history as one of the world's most depraved and sadistic killers: Jack the Ripper, Myra Hindley, Fred West, Harold Shipman and Jonathan Egan-Walsh. He's just making sure his evil lives on. The best thing you can do, Diane, is burn that letter.'

Diane visibly deflated. It wasn't what she wanted to hear from her mother. She was hoping she'd see this as a ray of hope, a step closer to finding Zachery and bringing him home.

'Diane,' she said, leaning forward and placing a hand on her daughter's lap. 'You need to move on.'

'I can't.' Diane jumped up. 'I've tried, and I can't. Could you move on if it was me or Maria who'd been killed?'There was no answer to that.

'Before you do anything, you need to speak to Nick.'

'*What?* Why?' Diane looked shocked by the suggestion.

'Because he's Zachery's father.'

'He stopped being a father the day he walked out.'

'No. He stopped being your husband. He never stopped loving Zachery or Marcus.'

Diane didn't say anything. She walked further away from her mother, over to the French windows, and looked out into the darkening garden.

'You know I'm right, Diane.'

'And what if he says the same as you?'

Her mother shrugged. 'The letter's addressed to you. It's your decision and I'll stand by you, but you need to involve others who are affected by it.'

'When did you become so wise?'

'Wise?' she chuckled. 'I've never been called that before. Parenting is the hardest job in the world. You feel like you should know all the answers, but you don't. I'm in my eighties, and I'm still making it all up as I go along.'

'You're seventy-nine.'

'Same thing.'

Diane gave a half-hearted smile and returned to the sofa. She held out her hand for her mother to take. She looked down at the two hands. Hers was rapidly ageing. Her mother's was dry, liver-spotted, the skin as thin as paper with bulging blue veins showing through.

'I want my son back,' Diane choked back the tears.

'I know you do. I do, too.'

Diane didn't sleep much that night. She spent the hours of darkness tossing and turning. As her eyelids grew heavy and she found herself relaxing into a slumber, her mind jolted her awake. On a chair in the corner of the room, sat her handbag. Inside the bag was the letter. She kept looking at the bag. She could almost see the letter through the leather, such was the powerful radiance it gave off.

First thing the next morning, she called Little Spoon and said she was sick and wouldn't be going into work today. As soon as she hung up she knew she'd made a mistake. It would have been a welcome distraction, serving coffee and cake, chatting with the regular customers, having a laugh with the staff. For a few hours, she could have forgotten all about Jonathan's letter and lived a normal life.

The day dragged on. She ate breakfast but didn't taste it. She couldn't face lunch and every cup of tea tasted foul. At half past four, she left the house and drove to Barrett International, where her ex-husband worked. Talking about their dead son in a poorly lit car park in the middle of winter wasn't ideal but Diane knew Nick wouldn't want her at his house, not with Beth and his daughters within earshot. She could have invited him over to her house, their house, but she doubted he would come. They needed to be on neutral ground.

The second the clock hit five, the doors opened and people began to file out. She sat up, eyes firmly fixed on the exit, and waited. Eventually, Nick appeared. He seemed taller than she remembered, and he was thinner, too. He wore a navy-blue suit, which hung lifelessly from his shoulders. He dragged his feet along the tarmac to his car. Diane whipped off her seatbelt and opened the door but didn't go any further. The headlights from a passing car danced across his face and Diane saw the sadness etched on him. He looked old, tired, defeated. A car park was no place for such a heavy conversation.

Diane kept well back as she followed Nick's Citroën Picasso

home. She no longer cared how Beth would feel, or if she took offence at Diane turning up unannounced; this was important. Besides, Beth was a contributor to the breakdown of her marriage. She would have to deal with those consequences for the rest of her life. Diane and Nick had history. And unfinished business.

Diane parked away from the semi-detached house and watched as a normal happy family drama played out before her. The living-room light was on and the curtains left open, showing everyone who went past a glimpse into their perfect lifestyle. As soon as Nick entered, his face changed. He smiled. He hugged his young daughters and chatted, animatedly, to his wife. She poured him a drink. They laughed. It was almost sickening. Diane grabbed her bag from the front passenger seat and left the car, slamming the door behind her. She took long strides to the house. She wanted to look confident, determined, so walked with her back straight and her head held high. She no longer felt any animosity towards Nick for leaving her. She was a capable, independent woman, and didn't need a man in her life. She decided she was showing him the letter out of common courtesy. Not for his approval.

She rang the bell and stood back from the door. She felt nervous all of a sudden, but there was no turning back.

The door was opened by Beth. The smile she had prepared to greet her guest fell from her face as soon as she saw who it was. Diane smiled.

'Good evening, Beth. Is Nick home?' she asked.

'Er … he is,' she said, glancing over her shoulder.

'May I speak with him, please?'

'Er … well, I'm not …' she trailed off.

'Beth, there are much better things I'd rather be doing right now than standing on your doorstep in the cold. However, this is important, and I would like to speak to my *ex*-husband,' she said firmly, emphasising the 'ex'.

'Of course. I'll just get him.'

Beth walked away, leaving the door slightly ajar. Diane angled her head and sneaked a look into the hallway – laminate flooring, family photos on the wall, a vase of flowers on an Ikea table by the door. She rolled her eyes. Very pedestrian. Characterless. Not a style Nick would have liked when they were together.

Suddenly, the door was pulled open and Nick looked down at his ex-wife.

'Diane. What are you doing here?'

'I need to talk to you.'

'Now?'

'Yes.'

'Can't it wait?'

'No, it can't.'

He gave a heavy sigh. His eyes darted from side to side as if searching his mind for something to say. 'Fine. OK. What is it?'

'Really? We're going to do this on the doorstep?'

'I don't know what *this* is.'

'Nick, I've had a letter from a solicitor. It concerns Jonathan Egan-Walsh and our son. Now, are you going to invite me in so we can discuss this like civilised adults, or are we really going to chat on the doorstep so you can protect your precious Beth and her perfect life?'

Diane had no idea where that tirade had come from, but she enjoyed it. In her head, she could actually hear her mother cheering her on.

'Fine. Come on in,' Nick relented. He stepped to one side and allowed Diane to enter. 'Go through to the kitchen,' he said, pointing to the end of the hallway.

The kitchen was straight out of a magazine: brightly lit, surfaces clear, everything clean and shiny. It was obvious Beth didn't work, if she could maintain such an obsessive level of cleanliness with two young children.

Nick followed her into the kitchen and closed the door firmly behind him. 'OK, come on, then. What is it?' he asked quickly.

'I'm fine, thanks. No, it doesn't matter, I don't want a drink,' she said, a heavy sarcastic tone to her voice. She pulled out a pine chair and sat at the kitchen table, slamming her bag down heavily on it. She pulled out the letter and offered it to Nick.

'What's this?' he asked, not taking it from her.

'I want you to read it. Don't worry, it's not a summons or anything. You're not going to compromise yourself by putting your fingerprints on it,' she replied, rolling her eyes at his behaviour.

Reluctantly, he took the letter, and remained standing while he read it. As Diane had done while her mother had read it, she tried to find some unconscious reaction from Nick by studying his face, but there was nothing there. His lips moved slightly as he read, but apart from that, she couldn't guess his thoughts.

'Oh,' was all he said when he'd finished.

'Is that it?'

'What do you want me to say?'

'I'd like an opinion.'

'Well, it's rubbish, obviously.'

'Why obviously?'

'Of course he murdered Zachery. Why else would he have had all those items of his clothing in his home?'

'But he doesn't deny killing the twelve other boys. Only Zachery.'

'That's because the others were found.'

'But there was no forensic evidence.'

'There was the blood on his T-shirt.'

'We don't know how it got there. It could have been from an old nose bleed. You know he used to have them from time to time,' Diane said, clutching at straws.

Nick threw the letter down onto the table and squeezed the bridge of his nose. 'I can't believe we're going through this again. Diane, Jonathan killed Zachery. He was a sadistic, manipulative killer. He's written this so he can increase your torment. He probably died with a smile on his face.'

Diane took a deep breath. 'I'm taking this to the police,' she said, picking the letter up and folding it carefully.

'What?'

'They need to see it. I'm going to show it to them and ask them to reopen Zachery's case. They have Cold Case units these days.'

'Diane, if you show that letter to the police, they'll laugh you out of the station. They're not going to reopen the case on the basis of a letter from a madman.'

'This is more than a letter. It's a confession, something the police don't have. He's saying he killed the other boys but that he didn't kill Zachery. If he didn't kill Zachery, then his killer is still out there and needs to be caught.'

'You're being ridiculous. The most sensible thing you can do is to burn that letter and get on with your life.'

'That's what you'd do, is it?'

'Yes.'

'Well, some of us can do that, can't they?' She put the letter in her bag and stood up.

'What does that mean?' he asked, hands on his hips.

'When life gets hard, when they're faced with something they can't control, they run away, find someone else, start afresh.'

'That's not what I did,' he said. His voice was harsh but low.

'Really? That's what it looks like to me,' she said, looking around her at the perfect kitchen. 'You screwed up with one family so you went out and got yourself another one.'

'They are not a replacement. I love Beth, and my two kids.'

Diane's eyes widened as she fixed Nick with a deathly stare. She walked up to him. They were toe to toe.

'You have four children, Nick. You'll always have four children.' She looked him up and down. 'I'll see myself out.'

The tears came before she reached the car. She knew either Beth or Nick would be watching her from the living-room window. She didn't want them to see she'd crumbled. She bit her bottom lip hard to stave off the tears until she performed a three-point-turn and left the avenue. Once she was clear, she parked up and cried, although she had no idea why.

There were two people against Diane going to the police and only one for – herself. However, the letter was addressed to her so the final decision belonged to her. She was going.

First thing the next morning, she drove to the police station and asked the bemused-looking woman on the front desk for someone senior in CID to talk to. She almost asked for DI Caroline Turner until she remembered she was no longer on the police force.

Diane was told to wait in Reception, which she did. It was almost twenty minutes until someone called for her. In that time, Diane had wondered if she was doing the right thing. Each time she questioned her actions, she went over the conversation with Nick last night. Of course she was doing the right thing.

This wasn't about Nick and Beth or even her. This was about Zachery.

'Mrs Marshall?'

She looked up at the mention of her name. 'Yes.'

'DC Bryce. How can I help?'

'DC? I asked to speak to someone senior.'

DC Bryce was a young woman in a smart suit that was a size too big for her. Her haircut was neat and severe. Her face was smooth and heavily made up, as if she was trying to look older. She didn't have a wrinkle or a line on her face. Diane wondered if she was even twenty yet. She certainly didn't look it.

'My boss is currently in a budget meeting. If you'd like to tell me what your query is, I can pass it on and we can go from there.'

'OK,' Diane reluctantly agreed. 'Is there somewhere private we can talk?'

'Of course. Follow me.'

Diane was led into an interview room. She told DC Bryce who she was, all about Zachery and how she had written to Jonathan Egan-Walsh on many occasions over the years. Then, she produced the letter. DC Bryce gave it a cursory glance.

'So, what is it you're asking?'

'I want you to reopen the case,' Diane said firmly.

'What case?'

Diane rolled her eyes. 'The case into finding who killed my son.'

'Mrs Marshall, that case is closed,' DC Bryce said in her most watered-down sympathetic tone.

'No, it isn't,' she said, jabbing her finger hard into the letter.

'If there was any new evidence, then we would look into it, but ...'

'There's your evidence,' Diane interrupted, stabbing at the letter again.

'I'm afraid it isn't. Jonathan Egan-Walsh enjoyed playing mind games. He was a manipulator. This is just another example of his depraved mindset.'

'No. You don't know him ...'

'I studied the case extensively during my training,' DC Bryce said, almost smugly.

'You studied it? Oh, how exciting for you.' Diane jumped up and snatched the letter. 'Well, I *fucking* lived it!' she shouted before storming out.

She got in the car, stalled it in her haste to pull out of the parking space, started it again then drove at speed. She had no idea where she was going but she needed to be as far away from the madness of reality as she could get. Why would nobody believe her? More importantly, why would nobody help her?

Jonathan Egan-Walsh hadn't killed her son. She didn't care

how she was going to do it, but she was going to find the killer herself.

Diane was on the open road, breaking the speed limit, when the thought struck her. She slammed on the brakes and picked up her phone from the passenger seat. It was a long shot, but she went into Google and searched for former Detective Inspector Caroline Turner.

Chapter Twelve

I've been told I have terminal cancer. The parents of Thirteen will be pissed when they read about it in the papers. No life sentence for me. This is almost the perfect ending. They wanted me to rot in here, languish in my dotage. Well, thank you very much, cancer, for allowing me to give them a big fuck you to their life sentence.

I've decided to write a mini autobiography. It's not a confession, more of a detailing of my journey. I hope, when it's found and read, someone will take something from it. I don't want any of those bastard psychiatrists with their tweed jackets and their self-righteous indignation getting their paws on it, though. But, if they do, it won't help them to understand me. They're looking for a key to unlock my brain, to find out how disturbed and diseased I am. They're in for a shock, as I'm more normal than they are.

I can remember each and every one of the boys I met. I know when and where I met them, and even though I had them for only a short period of time, I knew more about them than their parents did.

The first boy I met was called Danny Redpath. He was seven years old and lived in Seahouses on the Northumberland coastline. A beautiful part of the world. Lovely beaches. It was on the beach when I saw Danny with his older brother, Josh, and his mother. It was a bloody cold day. At first, it warmed me to see a mother braving the elements to allow her children to play, but the more I watched, the more I saw what the Redpath family was really like. Josh was a little shit towards Danny; pushing him over, throwing the ball too hard so it would hit him, tossing the Frisbee far so Danny wouldn't be able to catch it. His mother laughed as she watched them 'play', but I could tell Danny was unhappy. He hated his brother. He probably hated his mother too for allowing it to happen. I followed them home.

I kept going back to their home in Seahouses. The more I did, the more I saw of the bullying Danny had to put up with from his brother, the neglect from his mother. The little lad seemed lonely and alone in the world. He needed someone to show him a better kind of life, someone to hold him, to make him feel wanted. Loved.

He was practically handed to me. His mother abandoned him and his brother with a family member, and Danny and Josh, along with two cousins all went out to play together. Danny was younger and the three older boys didn't want him around. They were picking on him for ages until Josh spat at his brother and told him to piss off home. Those were his exact words. They were laughing as Danny left.

I've often wondered what happened to Josh. Did he blame himself for Danny's death? It was his fault, after all. If he'd been any kind of a big brother, he would have looked after him. However, it all benefited me.

Once I'd taken him, and I was looking at him close up, I could see how special he really was. He had short chocolate-brown hair, large brown eyes and pale skin. There wasn't a mark or a blemish on him. He was brand-new. Totally unspoiled. There was, however, one small problem – he wouldn't stop crying.

I'd have thought he'd have been pleased to be away from his vile mother and his horrid brother, but he kept saying he wanted to go home. If he enjoyed being in that house so much, why had he been practically begging me to release him from such a torment? Mixed messages.

I gave him a drink of warm milk. I had to put something in it to calm *him down. Eventually, the crying stopped, and I was able to talk to him properly. I explained to him why I'd taken him, that his mother didn't deserve him. A child was a precious gift. She obviously didn't want him. But I did. I'd look after him.*

I'd love him.

Chapter Thirteen

When Jonathan Egan-Walsh was sentenced to life in prison in 1996, Caroline Turner hoped she could forget about him. The Home Secretary had intervened and said he should never be released. There should be no reason she would have to see his smirking face ever again. Following the court case, she had spent some time on a Spanish beach with her husband and son doing absolutely nothing. She loved it. Once back at work, she fell into the same routine of chasing killers, drug dealers, abusers and rapists. A killer like Jonathan came along very rarely in Britain, thank goodness. Fingers crossed she would never face another case like it. It would take time, but she could eventually move on and start to enjoy life again. Unfortunately, the investigation into more potential victims always kept the case at the forefront of her mind. She often received a phone call from a DI in a different part of the country asking if they could have access to Jonathan's collection. Why people thought Caroline was the authority on the Egan-Walsh case was beyond her, but she was always the go-to person. Eventually, she was able to train her mind to leave Jonathan in her work life. At home, she was a wife and a mother. Jonathan couldn't get to her there. Then, the letters began arriving.

After a year in prison, Jonathan had written to her, asking her how she was, if she was missing him, and how her son was doing at school. She burned the letter in the police-station car park and washed the ashes down the drain. Another letter came. Then another. She told her boss, who made a complaint to Wakefield Prison. From then on, Jonathan's mail was vigorously checked before it left the prison.

Caroline thought she had won, until another letter arrived. The postmark was smudged, but it was written in Jonathan's hand so he had somehow managed to smuggle it out of prison. This letter was more personal. He asked if her son looked like her and began to describe how beautiful he must look and how he wished he'd met him while he was still a free man.

Caroline couldn't finish reading the letter. It had made her feel sick. She wanted to destroy it but knew it needed to be evidence for any punishment Jonathan should face. She handed the letter over to her boss, glad to be rid of it, but no amount of hand washing could get the feeling of repulsion off her.

As a result of the smuggled letter, Jonathan had all his privileges removed and was not allowed to send a single letter, not even to his grandmother, whose health was rapidly declining. However, Jonathan was devious, and he managed to get notes of well-wishing to his only surviving relative, as well as stomach-churning missives to DI Turner.

There was a clamp-down at the prison and everyone associated with Jonathan had their mail thoroughly checked before it was sent out. The letters eventually stopped. Caroline, with help from a police psychologist, was able to put it all behind her and move on.

In 1998, Caroline's son, Dylan, scored a hat-trick in the East Yorkshire U12 Challenge Cup Final. His team, the East Coast Juniors, went on to win 4–1 and Dylan was awarded Player of the Match. The story made the local paper, and the main photograph accompanying the article featured Dylan being held aloft by his teammates. His beaming smile said it all. It was the proudest day of his life.

Three days later, a package was delivered to Caroline's house. Inside, was a replica of Dylan's football kit. There were stains on it, which were revealed to be Jonathan Egan-Walsh's dried semen. Caroline never told her son, or her husband, of the package, but suggested they move house on the pretext of wanting a larger garden.

The letters stopped being delivered to her home, but they continued to arrive at her workplace. The stress of waiting for something to land on her desk started to affect her work, and her health. She lost weight, stopped sleeping, and developed an intense paranoia, which gave her the urge to lash out whenever she sat across from a smirking accused. In early 2000, she handed in her resignation and left the police force for good. The job she had loved had become tainted. She hated the sight of the building as she pulled into the car park every morning. She hated her office and her colleagues. Jonathan Egan-Walsh had claimed his fourteenth victim.

Post-resignation, Caroline opted for a complete change in career and set up a dog-walking business. She bought a Land Rover, kitted out the back to fit up to six dogs at a time, and advertised her services. It was an instant success. There was something about her being a former detective that people found reassuring, and it wasn't long before her books were full and she had a waiting list.

Caroline was driving to the coast at Ingoldmells South with two Labradors, a Jack Russell and a German Shepherd puppy in the back of her car. The German Shepherd was a new customer. She had only taken him out twice before, both times on his own. This time, he had company, and, judging by the noises he was making, he was enjoying his new friends. She pulled up and jumped out of the car.

It was windy. The dark-grey clouds were low and it was threatening to snow. There had already been a shower of sleet this morning. Wrapped up in thermal underwear, waterproof trousers, a fleece sweater and a big waterproof jacket, Caroline put a beanie hat on over her head and put the jacket's hood up. She pulled on her thermal gloves and went to the back of the car. She opened the door and all four dogs stood impatiently, tails wagging, itching to get out.

They were each attached to the car by a short leash so they couldn't jump over the back seats into the front of the car and cause a crash, or escape out the back as soon as she opened the door (she had learned this the hard way). First, she unhooked the adult Labradors and they jumped down and stayed by her, using her body as a windbreak. The Jack Russell, unleashed, followed suit.

'Right, then, Max, you've seen the others do it. Are you going to behave like them?' The black German Shepherd tilted his head to one side when he recognised his name. One ear was pointing up, the other had flopped over. She smiled at him. He was a handsome pup. She unhooked him and he jumped down, excitedly running around her legs, and the other dogs.

Fortunately, the wind wasn't strong enough for the beach to have to close, so she was able to take them off their leads and let them have a long run on the sand. Caroline threw tennis balls for them to chase and the fastest brought it back. Max the German Shepherd hadn't learned the rules yet, so often continued to run once he'd caught the ball.

Caroline was enjoying the bracing air as the wind whipped around her. Her cheeks were red where the icy sleet had hit her. Up ahead, she saw a figure standing at the bottom of a set of steps leading to the beach. It was difficult to make them out from this distance, but he or she seemed to be staring straight at her.

Caroline looked around but they didn't have a dog with them. Whoever it was, they were on their own.

Back at the Land Rover, Caroline wiped the dogs down before allowing them to jump back into the car. Once secured, she closed the door and headed for the driver's side when she saw the figure from the beach again. It was definitely a woman. She was stood in the doorway of a café looking over at Caroline, watching her. Caroline stared back.

'Can I help you?' Caroline shouted above the wind.

The woman stepped forward. She was sensibly dressed in walking shoes and thick trousers. The jacket was waterproof but it didn't look very warm. She didn't have anything covering her head either, so her hair was plastered to her head. She was soaked and windswept.

'Are you Detective Inspector Caroline Turner?' the woman asked.

Caroline's face dropped. 'No, I'm not,' she said firmly. She opened the car door and was almost inside.

'Sorry. Just Caroline Turner, then?'

'Who are you?'

'I didn't think you'd recognise me. It's been more than twenty years. I'm Diane Marshall. I'm Zachery Marshall's mum.'

Caroline leaned forward and squinted. 'Oh, of course it is. I'm so sorry I didn't ...'

'It's OK. Like I said, it's more than twenty years. It's a long time. Look, is there somewhere we can talk?' she said as she shivered following a strong gust of wind.

'As you can see, I'm not in the police any more. I can't help you with anything,' Caroline said.

'Please. I wouldn't ask if it wasn't important.'

Caroline looked at the back of the car. All four dogs were lying down, tired from their run. 'I can probably spare about ten minutes or so.'

They walked awkwardly over to the café next to the car park.

It was a typical twee seaside tearoom with plastic red-and-white gingham tablecloths, net curtains up at the window, and driftwood decorations on the wall.

'What would you like?' Diane asked.

Caroline looked at the menu board. 'I'll have a cappuccino, thank you.'

Caroline chose a table by the window so she could keep an eye on her car, and the dogs. The rough weather was keeping people away from the beach so the café was empty, and Diane soon returned carrying a tray of hot drinks and cake.

'I didn't know if you were hungry, but, well, we can always find room for chocolate cake, can't we?' Diane gave a nervous laugh.

'Thank you.' Caroline took a sip of her drink and she felt herself beginning to thaw. 'How did you know where to find me?' she asked.

'Well, I looked you up on the Internet, saw your Facebook page and looked at your Friends list. Max, the German Shepherd you have in the back of your car, he belongs to a friend of mine – Rita. She said you usually bring the dogs to the beach.'

'Oh,' Caroline said, impressed with her detecting skills.

'Is this what you do now, dog walking?' Diane asked.

'Yes. I've been doing it for a while. It's stress free, it keeps me fit, and I'm home at a reasonable hour every night.'

'When did you leave the force?'

'Sorry, what did you want to see me about?' Caroline asked, not wanting to get dragged into retelling her history.

'I'm guessing you know that Jonathan's dead.'

'Yes,' Caroline replied quickly.

'Not long after he died, his solicitor came to see me. Jonathan had written me a letter.'

Caroline's eyes widened. Diane picked up her bag from the floor and rummaged inside.

'Did he tell you where he—'

'No. Would you like to read it?'

Caroline looked down at the small white envelope Diane had in her hands. She swallowed hard. It took her a long time to take the letter. She read it quickly. Then read it again.

'Is this genuine?' Caroline asked.

'What do you mean?'

'I mean, are you absolutely sure Jonathan wrote this?'

'I hadn't thought. What do you think?'

'I don't know what to think, to be honest. Jonathan never confessed to any of the killings, we had very little forensic evidence. We rested all our hopes on his collection. Thank goodness the jury were on our side. It helped that Jonathan came across as a complete psychopath. He manipulated right, left and centre from the word go. He was a very clever man and knew exactly what he was doing. I genuinely believe he was shocked when he was found guilty.'

'But with so little evidence, how could you assume Zachery was one of his victims?'

'Because ... he fitted the victimology, and he had all of those items of clothing in his flat belonging to your son.'

'But you didn't have a body. Didn't that tell you he wasn't among his victims?' Diane's voice rose slightly in frustration.

Caroline leaned forward on the table. 'He buried his victims. We weren't supposed to find them.'

'But you *did* find them. You found twelve.'

'And they were all found by accident – dog walkers, joggers, kids playing in the woods. That's how they were all found.'

'But ...'

'Diane, Jonathan was a manipulator. He taunted me from his prison cell. He attempted to—' She stopped herself. 'He was one of the reasons why I left the force. He loved playing mind games. I don't believe what he is saying in this letter is the truth,' she said, pushing it back across the table.

'I've lost count of the amount of times I've read it, and the more I do, the more I think he's telling me the truth.'

Caroline looked out of the window. It had started to snow.

Diane said, 'Look, you say he's a manipulator, and that kind of person likes an audience. He likes to see people suffering. If that's the case, he would have sent me this letter years ago, so I could have begged and pleaded with him. He would have delighted in seeing this letter printed in the newspapers, the case reopened, knowing he was getting further coverage. Doesn't the fact that he's waited until he's dead add credence to this?'

'I don't know,' Caroline said, not wanting to make eye contact.

Diane searched through her bag again. 'I've made you a copy of the letter. I've put my number on the back. Read it again, in your own time, then let me know what you think. Please.'

'Why have you come to me? I'm not in the force any more. There's nothing I can do.'

'I want your opinion. Is there a chance I could have the case reopened?'

'You really need to ask the police that.'

'I have.'

'And?'

'I spoke to a DC who looked like she was on work experience. She said the letter doesn't count as new evidence.'

'She's right.'

'But it is proof,' Diane said in a loud, frustrated tone.

'What does Jonathan's solicitor say about all this?' Caroline asked, avoiding her question.

'He said that at no time did Jonathan ever confess to his crimes or deny that he killed Zachery. He was as shocked as I was.' She took a sip of her coffee, looking at Caroline over the top of her mug. 'Is there anything you can do?'

'Like what?'

'I don't know. Use your influence or something.'

'I don't have any influence. I'm just a dog walker.'

'You must still know people on the force.'

'I haven't kept in touch with anyone. That's all behind me.'

'I'm sorry, but I don't believe you. You were in the police for a very long time. It's not just something you can walk away from.'

'Diane, I—'

'Caroline, please, I'm begging you.' she interrupted. 'I need your help with this. You're my last hope. I don't have anyone else to turn to. I can't just toss this letter aside as if it didn't exist. Maybe Jonathan is having a final laugh, but I need to know for sure.'

The silence grew. Caroline looked out of the window again, watching the snow fall more rapidly. She saw her car, the German Shepherd in the back, his tongue lolling out. This was her life now, but it wasn't as fulfilling as she told everyone.

'Leave it with me,' she replied, reluctantly. 'I'll have a think.'

That seemed to be enough to placate Diane. She smiled. 'Thank you, Caroline. I really do appreciate it.'

'I'm not promising anything.'

'No, of course not. Thank you, though.'

'I'd better be getting off.' Caroline took a last sip from her coffee cup then stood up. She hadn't touched her cake.

'Don't forget this,' Diane said, holding out the photocopy of the letter.

Caroline took the letter and placed it in her pocket without looking at it. 'I'll be in touch.'

Caroline left the café and hurried to the car. The snow was falling heavier but it wasn't settling as the ground was too wet.

'Sorry about that, boys,' she said to the dogs in the back.

As she pulled away, she looked into the café but the window had steamed up so she couldn't see if Diane was still sitting at the table. In the rear-view mirror, she saw Max lift his head up. His tongue was lolling out, one ear up, one ear down. She smiled and, not for the first time, wished she was a dog ... not a care in the world.

Chapter Fourteen

Caroline couldn't sleep. She lay awake, staring at the ceiling, next to Jamie, her snoring husband. The green digits on the alarm clock changed to 1:00AM. She sighed, threw back the duvet and swung her legs out of bed. There was no need for her to be quiet, Jamie would normally sleep through the Apocalypse.

She peeled back the curtains to look outside. The snow hadn't amounted to much. By early evening, it had turned to freezing rain. The sky was now clear and an infinite number of stars filled the black void. It was a peaceful view which looked out over the coast and the North Sea. In the silence, Caroline could hear the muffled sound of the sea breaking onto the shore. She wanted to go outside, get in the car and drive. It was times like this where she wished she had a dog of her own.

The box room next to Caroline and Jamie's bedroom was a dumping ground for what they had accumulated over the years. Most of it belonged to Caroline and was a reminder of her former career. A career she had been proud of, and one she was reluctant to let go.

There had been many cases that had affected Caroline, but the Egan-Walsh case had consumed her, and stayed with her long after he was convicted. He wouldn't allow her to rest, as he taunted her from his prison cell. Now, as she stood amongst the boxes and filing cabinets, just thinking about him made her blood run cold.

Was it possible that Caroline had overlooked something in the hunt for Zachery Marshall? She was convinced he was one of Jonathan's victims; all the signs were there. He fitted the victimology and his clothes were among Jonathan's sick collection. There was just one difference: Zachery Marshall had never been found.

Caroline had not worked on the original investigation when Zachery disappeared in 1993, but she had included Zachery in her case against Jonathan. It was obvious to her, and her team, that there were many more victims waiting to be discovered, so they set about trawling Missing Person reports for anyone who matched the range of victims they already knew about. Zachery was one such boy. When Nick and Diane Marshall had identified many items of clothing as belonging to their son, that was all the evidence they needed.

Another missing boy to add to Jonathan's growing list. At the time, she was one hundred percent convinced Jonathan was Zachery's kidnapper.

Now, doubt was settling in. As she opened a box and began unloading files she found a well-thumbed paperback of *The Collector*, the chilling and detailed account of Jonathan's crimes written by journalist Alex Frost. She had met Alex on a number of occasions while he was writing the book, and he had interviewed her at length. He was a thoughtful, intelligent man, and his book was incredibly accurate about the details of the police investigation and Jonathan's version of events. Alex was the only person Jonathan had spoken to about the crimes and the journalist had visited him in prison many times.

Caroline made herself comfortable, sitting on the floor with crossed legs, and opened the book. She was looking for something, anything that would convince her Jonathan was responsible for Zachery's disappearance. She needed to be right. If she was wrong, she would relive the investigation all over again, and, even though he was dead, she didn't want Jonathan Egan-Walsh back in her life.

Chapter Fourteen was titled 'Interviewing The Collector'. It had been a long time since Caroline had read the book but she remembered this chapter. It revealed, in his own words, the origins of Jonathan's strange collection, his reasoning behind it, and what he could recall about where he found the items.

She speed-read the chapter until she came across Zachery's name for the first time:

… I didn't think of them as belonging to Zachery when I found them. I didn't make the connection. To be honest, I don't remember where all of my collection came from, but some stick in the mind, and finding what turned out to be Zachery's clothes is emblazoned on my memory. I can close my eyes and I'm back on that coastal path again.

It was strange, as they seemed to have been placed there. If it wasn't the middle of winter, I would have thought a child had stripped off to go swimming in the sea. I even looked around to see if a child was nearby waiting to collect them. When I saw nobody was around, I took them …

The room lit up and Caroline jumped. She turned around to see her husband standing in the doorway. He looked like the walking dead with his drooping eyes, his creased pyjamas and the dressing gown hanging off his shoulders. His grey hair was sticking up in all directions.

'Bloody hell, Jamie, you scared the life out of me.'

'What are you doing?'

'I couldn't sleep.'

'I thought you said you were going to leave this? You said over dinner you would forget about it.'

'I know,' Caroline sighed. 'I couldn't sleep, though. Diane Marshall needs answers.'

'Then let her go to the police for them.'

'She's been. They won't help her.'

'So, doesn't that tell you something? If the police won't help, there's obviously nothing anyone, including you, can do. Maybe this letter really is Jonathan's final twist of the knife.'

'And maybe it isn't.'

'You've changed your tune since dinner.'

'I know. Listen to this.' She looked back to the paperback and read from it. '"When I spoke to Jonathan about each of his thirteen victims, there was no sign of emotion. His face remained passive, his stare was blank. However, whenever Zachery Marshall was mentioned, I noticed a look of regret in his eyes." See? What does that tell you? I mean, why didn't I pick up on this before?'

'What's to pick up on? The bloke killed thirteen boys. He doesn't know the meaning of the word regret.'

'His face obviously altered for Alex to notice. And, I've just been reading about Jonathan saying how he found Zachery's clothes. All through questioning, all through the trial, he said he couldn't remember where or when he found them. So, how come he could when he was interviewed by Alex Frost? Was he lying to him or to us?'

'Don't get involved, Caroline. Please,' Jamie said.

'I can't just leave this.'

Jamie sighed. The look on his face told his wife he wasn't happy with her revisiting a dark time in her life. Back then, he feared for her mental health as she battled against the manipulative killer. His worry lines had returned. 'Hang on a minute, wasn't he distantly related to Zachery?'

'Yes.'

'There you are then. His face altered because he knew this

victim. The others he didn't, so they were just victims, playthings for his own sick pleasure. He actually knew Zachery before he disappeared. That's why his face altered. Maybe that's why he remembered where he found the clothes too, because he knew who they belonged to. I think you're reading far too much into this, Caroline.'

'I don't think I am,' she said with less conviction. 'Jamie, what if I got it wrong? What if Jonathan didn't take Zachery Marshall?'

'Don't do this to yourself,' he said, stooping down to her level, his knees clicking in the process.

'Jamie, I risked everything to send that man to prison. I put my neck on the line to make sure those families got justice for what he did. I had to fight every step of the way to get Zachery Marshall included in the case. The CPS wanted me to drop it but I stood my ground because I knew he'd killed him too. But what if I got it wrong? There could be someone out there who thinks he's got away with murder. Maybe he's done it again, too. I need to correct that mistake. I can't let it go until I know for sure.'

Caroline wiped away a tear. Jamie tried to hold her but she pushed him away. The window didn't have any curtains as the room was used just for storage. Caroline went over to it and looked out at the blackness. All she saw was her tired reflection staring back at her through the black mirror.

'I need to see Diane. I need to speak to Alex, too.'

'Caroline, don't let Jonathan back in our lives. Remember what happened last time. Remember what happened at the prison. I'll never forget that phone call I received from your DCI. I don't think I could go through all that again.'

She took a deep breath. 'I know what happened but it's different now. Jonathan is dead. He can't hurt me again,' she said, already feeling the tightening knot in her stomach.

Chapter Fifteen

D iane was taken aback to find Caroline Turner standing on her doorstep.

Caroline offered a weak smile. 'Can I have a word?'

'Yes. Of course. Come in.'

The atmosphere between the two women was heavy as Diane showed Caroline into the living room and offered her a coffee.

Alone in the living room, the detective within Caroline came bubbling to the surface and she had a look around at all the photographs on the walls. They were mostly of Zachery and his brother, Marcus, in happier times. Caroline couldn't help but smile as the young children grinned at the camera while they made sand castles on the beach, or, wearing matching Christmas sweaters, tore open large presents.

Here, though, there was a heaviness about the house. It was as if sadness was leaching out of the walls and suffocating everyone who lived in it. The beige sofa and neutral carpet made the room look as though any colour that had once been here had long since faded away.

Caroline went towards the kitchen and stood in the doorway. The kettle clicked off but Diane didn't notice. She was leaning against the sink looking out of the window. Her eyes were filled with tears and one escaped, sliding down her face. She didn't wipe it away.

'The kettle's boiled,' Caroline said.

Diane snapped out of her reverie. 'Oh, sorry, I was miles away.'

'Is something wrong? Has anything happened?'

'No. It's just ... opening the door and finding you on my doorstep. It took me back to the first time you knocked on my door.'

That time, in 1996, she had arrived, as DI Turner, to inform Diane that items of clothing similar to what Zachery was wearing when he disappeared three years previously had been found. 'I'm sorry. I was going to phone but I thought it was best said face to face.'

'You've found something out?' Diane asked, looking up quickly as she made the coffee. A hint of hope appeared on her face.

'I'm not sure. To be honest, I don't know what to believe.'

'Oh. Shall we take these through?'

Caroline stepped out of the way as Diane headed back into the living room carrying a tray with two mugs of steaming coffee and matching milk jug and sugar bowl.

Caroline sat down. She added the tiniest drop of milk to her coffee then breathed in the strong aroma. She took a sip. The injection of caffeine was just what she needed.

'Diane, have you read *The Collector* by Alex Frost?'

'Half of it. I couldn't bring myself to finish it.'

'Alex interviewed me at the time of writing it. It's a very comprehensive account.'

'He interviewed a few of the parents, too. I was asked but didn't want to.'

Caroline fished in her bag and pulled out the paperback. 'I was looking through it again in the early hours of this morning.

There's a section about Jonathan's collection. Alex asked him about it on many occasions and he always said he couldn't remember where he found the items of clothing. However, he remembers where he found Zachery's, as they stood out. He thought they'd been placed there.'

'Purposely?'

'I don't know. From when I interviewed him, he said he found items in hedges or on park benches, where you'd expect children to leave things behind. We never believed him, though, simply due to the amount of items he had. The ones from your son were found, or so he said, on a coastal path where people don't usually go.'

'That doesn't make sense. How does it account for the items of clothing Zachery wasn't wearing that he had in his collection?'

Caroline thought for a while before shrugging.

'Besides,' Diane continued, 'if he's saying he found what Zachery was wearing in a pile, isn't that just a flimsy excuse for why he had the clothing? You can't believe someone would just leave a whole pile of clothing out in the open, especially clothes that had blood on them.'

'Well, we have to remember how much of a manipulator Jonathan was. So, either he was lying, or the clothing was planted there for someone to find and assume Zachery had been taken.'

'I don't know what you mean,' Diane said, shaking her head.

'By the time Zachery went missing, there were already six other boys missing nationwide. Four of them had been found, naked, wrapped in a sheet. We already knew that whoever had killed these boys had either kept the clothing as a trophy or discarded them somewhere. Perhaps, if Jonathan didn't take Zachery, whoever did was using Jonathan's crimes as a cover-up.'

'So, you don't think Jonathan took Zachery?' There was a look of hope in Diane's eyes.

Caroline sighed. 'I really don't know what to think,' she said, running her fingers through her hair. 'On one hand, there's enough to suggest Zachery was taken by someone else, but then I remember what Jonathan was like throughout all the interviews I conducted with him when I went to see him in prison. I remember what a lying, manipulative, vicious bas— Sorry.' Caroline took a deep breath and another slug of the strong coffee, as her emotions were getting the better of her.

'We don't know what it's like, do we? I see this from a grieving mother's perspective, you see it from a detective's point of view, and neither of us takes the other into account,' Diane said with a hint of a smile. 'I always imagine the police to be strong and objective, maybe a little cold, but you're not, are you?'

Caroline bit down hard on her bottom lip. 'This case ruined me. I didn't last long in the police force afterwards. I was a wreck. I got out just in time.'

'It's not just the thirteen victims Jonathan claimed, it's the families, friends and everyone involved who felt it,' Diane said. She allowed a silence to grow between them. 'My husband left me.'

'I know.'

'He's married again with two more children. Part of me hates him for being able to get on with his life while I haven't.'

'What about your other son?'

'Marcus? He's just had a child of his own,' she said with a proud smile. She leaned over to a small table with picture frames on it of varying designs and sizes. She picked one up and handed it to Caroline. 'That's my grandson, Zachery.'

Caroline flinched at the name. 'He's beautiful.' She smiled. 'How are things with you and Marcus?'

'Our relationship isn't great, but it's getting better. I can't believe this: twenty-five years later and we're still feeling the fallout.'

'Diane, I'm going to be honest with you: I don't think the police will reopen Zachery's case on the basis of Jonathan's letter.'

'They more or less said as much. Can't you do something?'

'I'm not in the force any more.'

'No, but surely you still know people. Couldn't they look into it on the sly?'

'Diane, I haven't kept in touch with anyone. I cut all ties when I left.' She thought for a while, all the time looking down at the photo of baby Zachery.

'There is one avenue we *can* explore.'

'Go on.'

'The journalist, Alex Frost,' she said, picking up the battered paperback. 'He was the only person Jonathan spoke to while he was in prison. Alex knows the case inside out, from both perspectives. Also, he can ask the questions you and I can't.'

'Do you think he'd help us?'

'I don't know. It's worth asking.'

'He'd use what he finds out to write another book, wouldn't he?'

'Possibly. He is a journalist, after all,' she said with a slight smile. 'But we might get some answers. We might even find Zachery.'

'That's all I want.'

'Would you like me to give him a call?'

Diane thought for a moment before taking a deep breath. 'Yes,' she said firmly. 'Can I show you something?'

'Of course.'

Diane stood up and motioned Caroline to follow her out of the room. She headed for the dining room but, before opening the door to enter, she turned back to look at Caroline.

'Before I let you in, I don't want you to think anything bad of me.'

'I won't,' Caroline said with a frown.

Diane opened the door and stood to one side to allow Caroline to enter first.

The dining room was not being used for its intended purpose. On the far-side wall, a huge map of the local area had been erected. The locations where all six local boys had disappeared were marked, along with where the five bodies were found. On the opposite wall were smaller maps of where the seven boys who didn't live locally disappeared from, and where their bodies were found. The dining table was covered in piles of paper, reports, newspaper cuttings, statements. It looked like the nerve centre of a Missing Persons organisation.

The faces of the thirteen boys looked down at Caroline, making her feel uncomfortable. She closed her eyes and was immediately transported back more than twenty years to when she was in the middle of the investigation to find whoever had taken and murdered these innocent children. She opened her eyes to find her vision had blurred with tears. Her mouth dried. She felt the pain, the heartache, the sleepless nights, all come flooding back.

'I know this makes me look like an obsessive person, but I just thought there might be some kind of pattern.'

'Pattern?'

'Yes. To where the bodies were found. Look here ...' she went over to the wall displaying the boys who disappeared from elsewhere around the country. 'The first victim, Danny Redpath, went missing on 3 February 1990, in Seahouses. He was found on 20 June, buried in woodland near Wooler. The same thing happened to the second victim, Neil Morris. He disappeared on 13 July 1990, in Scarborough, and was found on 18 November, buried in woodland near Pickering. Both victims were found further inland from where they went missing. I've used this information, and information taken from other victims, to try and gauge where Zachery may be buried.'

Diane stopped talking when she saw the blank look on Caroline's face.

'You think I'm obsessed, don't you? Nick thinks so, too.'

'No, I don't think you're obsessed at all. I think if I was in the same position, I'd have done exactly what you've done. You want to know what happened. Twenty-five years is a long time.'

'Too long. I know everything there is to know about the victims – the dates they went missing, the dates they were found. The names of their parents, brothers and sisters, places they enjoyed going to, what items were found in Jonathan's sick collection. I suppose I am obsessed. This is what drove Nick away. I was in this room more than I was anywhere else. He said I should just let it go, but how could I?' Her voice was breaking. 'Every time I think I should move on, I just picture Zachery lying in a shallow grave, people walking over him, not realising he's just below their feet. Maybe I've walked over him and didn't know about it. I can't move on while I know he's in an unmarked grave.'

Caroline looked at the damaged, broken woman in front of her. 'Do you have anyone you talk to about all this?'

'Thirteen helps, the support group we set up. We all get together on a regular basis to listen to each other, help if we can, offer advice. I talk to other parents online around the world who have missing children. That helps sometimes, especially at night, when I can't sleep. My mum listens, too.' She pulled out a chair at the dining table and sat down. 'I lost all my friends, thanks to Jonathan. They were all sympathetic at first. They couldn't do enough for me – helping with Marcus, bringing round meals and such – but, eventually, they expect you to move on and, when you don't, well, they stop calling. They don't know what to say. If I can just find where Zachery is, I can mourn and move on.'

Chapter Sixteen

I loved and cared for every one of the boys I met. They were friends, and I enjoyed their company. Unfortunately, like all friendships, they didn't last, and before long, it was time to let them go home.

Danny Redpath had developed a trust in me. When I gave him something to eat or drink, he took it without question. He knew I was looking after him.

When he said he was cold, I brought him a thicker sweater. When he was tired, I allowed him to sleep. I asked him what he'd like to eat one evening. I'd never asked him before, and he looked surprised. He asked for something from Burger King. I went out and found a drive-through. When I brought it back, his eyes lit up. It was like a feast. I've never been a fan of fast food, but he enjoyed it. Afterwards, we played a game of snap. I let him win a few times and he actually laughed. That was a heavenly sound. In the evening, I gave him his usual glass of warm milk. This time, I'd laced it with a barbiturate. He drank the milk and snuggled down under the duvet to go to sleep. He said goodnight to me – the first time he'd done that.

When his breathing slowed, I put my hands around his neck and squeezed as hard as I could. I kept my eyes closed while I was doing it. I didn't want to see his expression if he woke as I crushed the life out of him. When I looked at him, he still looked as if he was sleeping, but his breathing had stopped. He looked at peace. He'd had a lovely evening, but that was all over now.

I ran a warm bath and carried Danny over to it. I washed him carefully. I shampooed his hair and clipped his nails. I emptied the water and allowed him to dry naturally in the bathtub while I got the sheet ready.

I placed Danny in the centre of the white sheet and wrapped him up tightly, securing it in places with duct tape. I carried him down the stairs to the van and placed him in the back. Then, I took him home.

As Danny was my first friend, I hadn't planned where to take him. I drove back to Seahouses, but there wasn't anywhere I could find that was suitable. Eventually, I found some woodland in a place called Wooler. I would have liked him to have been closer to home, but this would have to do.

There is a knack to burying a body. I wanted Danny to go home to his mother and brother. I wanted them to have him back, so he needed to be found, but not straight away. I dug a shallow grave, a couple of feet deep, and carried Danny's limp little body to the hole. I placed him gently into the ground, said goodnight, and began to cover him. I didn't feel sad. I'd had my time with him. Now, the trick is not to pack the soil too firmly. He needed to be found by a dog walker or kids playing around digging in the soil with sticks. I stood back and examined the grave. It was obvious something had been recently buried.

Someone, or something, would be curious enough to start digging.

I went home and kept an eye on the news. He was found twelve days later.

By then, I already had my eye on a new friend; Neil Morris. I'd been watching him for a couple of weeks. He was being bullied at school. He was so incredibly sad but he had such a beautiful face. I couldn't wait to see him smile.

Chapter Seventeen

Alex Frost sat behind the wheel of his ancient Volvo in a motorway lay-by as life passed him by at 70 miles per hour. His stomach grumbling had forced him to detour an hour into his tedious journey home and he'd bought a pathetic-looking burger from a dirty man in a converted ice-cream van. Back in the car, he took one bite and quickly spat it out. He looked at the grey piece of meat between the soggy bap. Whichever animal this burger had come from was certainly one Alex had never heard of. He found a warm bottle of water in the glove compartment and rinsed his mouth of the offending meal. He had a rule that he would never eat anywhere that had spelling mistakes on the menu. Why hadn't he stuck to it?

He should have been home hours ago. He had been at HMP Wakefield, interviewing a couple of prisoners about having a whole-life tariff and how they felt about never being released from prison. What did it do to their mental health, their faith? If there was no hope of returning to society, how could they function normally from day to day?

It was a feature he'd been commissioned to write by the *Guardian* and an area he was more than expert in. The staff at

Wakefield Prison knew him well and were always happy to help when he called, asking for permission to interview officers and prisoners.

Once his work was complete, he'd headed for the motorway and the long drive back home to London. With each mile driven, he felt his heart sink and the dark sadness of his home life in the capital swept over him again. 'Home.' He ran the word around his head. Home is where the heart is. Home is where you're welcomed with open arms and loved by the people you live with. He pictured his wife, bedbound, helpless. She, too, was a prisoner serving a life sentence, trapped in her own body.

The smell from the burger was making him feel sick. He picked it up and left the car in search of somewhere to dispose of it. Holding it at arm's length, he dropped it into a bin. It landed with a plop, on top of many other half-eaten burgers.

Freezing rain was starting to fall. It was always colder in Yorkshire than it was in London and he never seemed to be dressed appropriately for the weather. He shivered as he made his way back to the car. Once back inside, he switched on the engine and turned up the heater, ready for the now three-hour drive back home. However, he was just about to drive off when his mobile beeped, signalling an incoming email. Any excuse to delay his journey; he turned the ignition off again and picked up his phone.

It took him a while to remember where he knew the name Caroline Turner from, but when he read the subject line, 'Jonathan Egan-Walsh', it all came flooding back. He couldn't hide his smile. He'd had a feeling he would hear from someone following Jonathan's death. He was somewhat surprised it was ex-DI Turner, though.

He read through the email quickly. The prospect of new information, the thought of an updated version of his bestseller *The Collector* was almost too much to bear. He read through it a second time, more slowly this time. Returning home was going to have to wait.

When Alex had first contacted Jonathan Egan-Walsh, in early 1999, he was surprised to hear back. For as long as he could remember, he had wanted to write a True Crime book, and had often written to serial murderers in prison asking if they wanted their story told. Most of the time, his letters went unanswered. On a couple of occasions, he'd met with the prisoner and told them his plan for the book, only to have them stab him in the back and write the book themselves.

Either Jonathan Egan-Walsh wasn't bright enough to come up with that idea himself, or he couldn't be bothered to write a book. So, after six months of letters, where Alex laid down his plan for the book, Jonathan had agreed to a face-to-face meeting in Wakefield Prison. Alex had driven up from London the day before and spent the night in a nearby hotel. On the morning of their first meeting, he'd been nervous and excited in equal measure. The first thing Alex did was to have Jonathan sign a contract saying he would tell his story only to Alex, who would be his official biographer for the duration of the time it took for the book to be written and released. Jonathan didn't seem to have a problem with that.

All their meetings went well, Jonathan eager to have his story committed to paper. He told Alex he was excited at the prospect of, not only people in Britain reading about him, but also by the thought of someone in a swanky New York apartment, or a country house in Sydney, or an estate in Pretoria doing so, too. There was a disturbing twinkle in his eye at the thought of his becoming not famous, but infamous.

The book had sold well, his publisher having had won a three-way auction for the rights and the *Daily Mail* paying an extortionate amount for the serial rights. The book had peaked at Number Two in the *Sunday Times* bestseller list and stayed in the Top Ten for twenty-four weeks. It was translated into more than thirty languages and sold to over a hundred countries. It won six top awards, and Alex was inundated with invitations to give talks at events and lectures at universities on the mind of a serial killer. His diary was booked a year in advance as he travelled the world.

When Jonathan died, he had newspapers and magazines from around the globe asking him to write a piece for them. Most of the articles he wrote were the same, with just enough re-jigging of sentences and changes of adjectives to make each one sound original. Little effort was required, and the cheques came rolling in. Now, it seemed he had the chance to write an updated version, or, if Caroline Turner's email was correct, a different story entirely. Could it possibly be true that someone had been using Jonathan's killings as a mask to cover up their own murder, or even murders? As Alex reversed out of the parking space, with a satisfied smile on his face, he was already thinking of titles for his next book.

Alex arranged to meet Caroline the next day at a coffee shop in the centre of Skegness. He'd spent the night at a Premier Inn on the outskirts of the town. If he was to stay longer, he'd find somewhere with a bit more character.

He didn't want to be the first to arrive, but he was eager to learn more details than her email had provided, and he arrived twenty minutes before the agreed time. He'd never been to Skegness before. He pictured it as being a stereotypical northern seaside town; a fish-and-chip shop on every corner, so-called gift shops selling smutty postcards and cheap plastic tat. Looking around as he walked to the coffee shop, he had no idea if he was right, as everything was closed. Bright lights from an amusement park flashed and he was right about the fish-and-chip shops.

He hadn't given the weather a second thought. He had no idea it would be so bracing. The strong wind was deafening as, wherever he went, he could hear the waves crashing on the coastline. The northern winter was harsh, hence the reason for the closed tourist attractions. Even the seagulls seemed quiet.

He ordered himself a cappuccino and sat in the corner of the coffee shop. He took his iPad out of his tatty briefcase and turned it on. With his back to the wall, there was no chance of being overlooked.

He logged into the webcam he had rigged up in the corner of the master bedroom at home and the picture came to life. The main feature was a hospital bed. A woman was hooked up to all kinds of feeding tubes and heart-rate monitors. His daughter entered the room carrying a bowl of water, a towel slung over her shoulder. He picked up his phone and dialled.

'Hi, Shona, it's Dad.'

'Hello, Dad.' Shona turned to the webcam and waved. 'How are things?'

'Fine, thanks. How's your mum?'

'She's OK. She had a bit of an uncomfortable night. I think there was a blockage in one of the tubes and she couldn't breathe properly. She panicked a bit, but she's fine now.'

'Are you sure? Do you need me to come home?' he asked out of duty rather than genuine concern.

'No, it's fine. The nurse came in this morning and checked her out. She says she's doing fine. I called Jan last night. She's coming round later when she's finished work and she's going to cut Mum's hair.'

Alex smiled. 'That's good of her. Nothing too drastic, though. You know what your mum was like with her hair.' His smile dropped. He hated it when he spoke about his wife in the past tense, as if she was dead. She wasn't dead. He could see that. She was in bed breathing in and out like a normal person. Normal? There was nothing normal about Melanie Frost. There hadn't been for more than ten years.

'Dad, are you all right?' Shona asked as the silence continued.

'Yes, I'm fine. Just thinking about something.'

'Are you sure you want to get dragged into all this again?'

'All what?'

'You know *what*,' she said, not wanting to say Jonathan's name in front of her mother.

'It's not about him this time, it's about one of his victims, or maybe not one of his victims.'

'Promise me you'll step away if things turn freaky again.'

'I promise. I'm going to go now, Shona. Caroline will be here soon.'

'Will you be back tonight?'

'I don't know. It depends how this meeting pans out.'

'Tomorrow, then?'

'I don't know. I'll let you know.'

'But you only took enough clothes with you for one night away.'

'I know. Don't worry about me, Shona, I'll be fine.'

'I do worry about you, Dad. You've been saying you're fine for years and I'm still not believing you.'

Alex gave a chuckle. 'Shona, I'm eating properly, I'll buy clean underwear, and I'll even wash behind my ears. Satisfied?'

Shona let out a deep sigh. 'I suppose. Promise me you'll take care.'

'I will. I promise.'

Alex ended the call but continued to watch his wife for a few minutes longer. It pained him to see her like that, lying in bed, unable to do anything for herself. A shell of the woman he married. Every time he looked at her, he saw the power Jonathan had to affect the lives of everyone he came into contact with. Melanie hadn't even met Jonathan and her life had been ruined by him. One thing Alex left out of the obituary articles was the fact he was happy Jonathan had died. He just wished he'd had the guts to kill him himself when he had the opportunity.

Chapter Eighteen

'Are you sure about this? Do you want me to come with you?'
'No. I'm fine.' Caroline laughed.

'I'd feel happier if you'd tell me where you're going,' Jamie said.

'Why? So you can sit in the corner with a newspaper held up with two eye-holes cut out?'

'I'm worried about you.'

'Jamie, I'm meeting a journalist, not a suicide bomber.'

Caroline was sat at her dressing table putting on a bit of make-up and trying to do something with her hair. She stole a glimpse out of the window. It was raining and a strong wind was blowing. It didn't matter what she did to her hair, the wind would ruin it within seconds of stepping out of the front door. 'What about your dogs?'

'I only had two to walk today and I've asked Sharon to do it. She doesn't mind.'

'What about me?'

'What about you?' she asked with a chuckle. She turned around to face him.

Jamie was sitting on the edge of the bed, still in his dressing gown, a heavy frown on his face.

'Well, we could have done something today. Gone for a walk or something.'

'You hate walking.'

'Only by myself. I don't mind when I've got some company.'

'We can go another time, when the weather brightens up. I need to do this, Jamie.'

'Will you promise me something?'

'What?'

'Promise me you won't let this destroy you.'

'I promise,' she said, going over to him and kissing him gently on the forehead. As she left the bedroom and headed for the stairs, she tried to remember the last time she had lied to her husband. It was probably the last time Jonathan Egan-Walsh had invaded their lives.

Caroline found Alex Frost watching something so intently on his iPad that he didn't see her approach. He had aged dramatically since they'd last met. She wondered if she had changed much in the past decade. Probably. Most definitely.

Alex had a thick mound of grey hair and a pallor to match. He looked gaunt. His suit was heavily creased, the cuffs of his shirt were frayed, his shoes scuffed, and his nails were bitten to the quick. The only thing missing from the resemblance to a stereotypical hack was a cigarette sticking out of the corner of his mouth and a fug of smoke around him.

'Alex.'

He looked up with wet eyes. For a brief second, he had the look of a man in the depths of depression. When he registered his visitor, a smile spread across his face.

'DI Turner.'

'It's been a while since I've been called that,' she said, smiling.

'Sorry. Caroline. Lovely to see you again.' He stood up and kissed her on both cheeks, then stepped back to look at her. 'I don't think you've aged a day.'

'You're joking, surely. I look terrible.'

'Rubbish. Now, what can I get you?'

Caroline sat and looked over to Alex as he stood in the queue waiting to be served. He really did look like a shadow of his former self. She had read a few of his articles, and his *Wikipedia* page said he was on a lecture circuit talking about lifers in prison. Was he living in hotel rooms out of a suitcase? That would age anyone.

'Here you go,' he said, placing a tray carefully on the table. 'Remember all those years ago when we'd go out for a coffee? You had two choices – tea or coffee. Now look what we've become,' he said, nodding at the large mocha and cappuccino in front of him. 'There's no such thing as a simple black coffee any more.'

'You're showing your age,' she said, laughing.

'I remember this little café near the paper on my first job. You could smoke and you got a coffee and a bacon roll for less than a pound.'

'I don't think you can buy anything for under a pound these days.'

'So, what have you been up to since you turned your back on the police force?' he asked, taking a sip of his cappuccino and sitting back in the comfortable chair, crossing his legs at the knee.

'Not much, really. I've moved house a couple of times and set up a dog-walking business.'

'Really?' He frowned. 'That's a bit of a difference from being in charge of CID.'

'I wanted something completely different, something undemanding.'

'I still can't believe you left the force. I would have put money on your being Chief Constable one day.'

'Getting attacked in prison changes your outlook on life.'

'Oh, God, I remember now. Caroline, I'm so sorry.'

'That's OK,' she smiled painfully. 'You adapt and move on. How about you? Still freelancing?'

'Best kind of journalist to be,' he said with a smile that was obviously false. 'I've written a couple of books.'

'I've seen. You've done very well for yourself. Lecturing, too, I understand.'

'It pays the mortgage,' he shrugged.

'How's the family?'

'Well, you heard about Melanie, I suppose?'

'Yes, I did. Jonathan ruined quite a few lives, didn't he? How is she?'

'The same as she was ten years ago. There'll be no improvement.'

'It must be difficult for you,' she said, leaning forward and placing a hand on top of his.

'It is, but I'm not home much these days. It's Shona who deals with the lion's share. She's Melanie's full-time carer. I don't know where I'd be without her. Anyway,' he said, snapping out of his melancholy, 'your email was very intriguing. You have new information, I gather.'

Caroline picked up her handbag from the floor and pulled out the photocopied letter Diane Marshall had given her. 'Read this,' she said, handing it over.

As Alex read, his eyes widened.

'I want to say he's lying,' Alex said.

'So do I.'

'You don't think so, I'm guessing.'

'No. He was a manipulator. A man like him, he wanted an audience. Why wait until after his death to reveal this kind of information? If this had been known while Jonathan was alive, it would have been front-page news, and he'd have loved it.'

'Agreed.'

'So, he's telling the truth?'

'It's possible. What does Diane say?'

'She wants the case reopened.'

'Naturally.'

'Alex, you should see her house. She's got maps of where all the victims were taken and found. She's got information on all thirteen of the children, stuff even we didn't know about.'

'She's not moved on?'

'She's been fighting for more than twenty-five years to find her son. She has nothing else.'

'She had another son, didn't she? And a husband? What do they think?'

Caroline let Alex know how Zachery's disappearance had led to the complete breakdown of Diane's family. 'All she's clinging onto is the hope she'll find Zachery.'

Alex shook his head. 'She's not still hoping she'll find him alive, is she?'

'I really don't know.'

'What do you want me to do?'

'You met Jonathan. You spoke to him at length. He trusted you. Do you think he's telling the truth?'

Alex took a deep breath. He bit the inside of his cheek while he thought long and hard about the content of the letter. From a journalist's point of view, he would love for what Jonathan had written to be the truth. He could take this to a publisher and he'd be able to write his own cheque. From his own *personal* point of view, he hoped it was a lie. Melanie and Shona would not want him going through the case all over again.

'It's certainly his handwriting,' he said, unable to take his eyes from the letter. 'As to whether he's telling the truth … I remember asking Jonathan, several times, about how he got the items for his collection. Each time, he said he couldn't remember, that he just found the items lying around, but the clothes of Zachery Marshall stood out to him, as they seemed to have been placed. At the time,

I thought he was playing with me. Zachery was still missing, so he could say anything. But when you put it all together, it does make sense.'

'What was Jonathan's alibi for the time Zachery went missing?'

'Hang on.' Alex took his iPad out of his battered satchel and began flicking through his files. 'You'll not believe the amount of crap I've got stored on here.' he smiled. 'Here we go, Alibis.' He skim-read the document. 'Zachery Marshall disappeared on Sunday, 10 January 1993. At the time, Jonathan said he was in Robin Hood's Bay.'

'That's miles away. Did anyone verify that?'

'I don't know. No offence, Caroline, but shouldn't that have been your job?'

'I didn't work on the Zachery Marshall disappearance. The first I knew about Jonathan was when he was arrested in 1996.'

'Who was the senior investigating officer on the Zachery Marshall case?'

'The SIO ...?' Caroline thought for a moment. Then, her face suddenly dropped. 'Oh, my God. It was Finnian Atwood.'

'Not a fan?'

'He was a chauvinist. He didn't like any woman officer above the rank of DC, so he obviously hated me,' she said with a pained smile. 'He always had the same officers on his team, and they were all men. It was like a private members' club.'

'Do you think he'll talk to us?'

'I don't know. I'm not even sure he's still alive.'

'Any way, we can find out?'

'You're the one with the iPad.'

Alex logged on to the Internet, and, with his two-fingered typing, set about searching for something about 'Finnian Atwood'.

'There's an article here from 2005 about his retirement. He was a DCI by then. There's something here about a Veronica Atwood doing a sponsored abseil for a dementia charity from 2009. Hang on ...' He clicked on a link to a fundraising page but it had expired. He then clicked on a link to a Facebook page for Veronica Atwood. He turned the iPad around to show Caroline. 'Did you ever meet Veronica? Is this her?'

Caroline leaned forward to study the profile picture. 'I met her once at a Christmas party. She knew some filthy jokes, but she'd had a few by then.' she smiled. 'It could be her. Does Finnian have a Facebook page?'

'Not that I can find.'

'Maybe he's died.'

'I'll send her a message. Fingers crossed.'

Caroline studied him as he typed. 'You've got that look in your eye again, Alex. You're loving this, aren't you?'

'I can almost smell the CWA Gold Dagger award,' he replied, grinning.

'You'll help, then?'

'Of course.' He clapped his hands together. 'Can you recommend a suitably shitty hotel?'

'Are you kidding? This is Skegness. The place is full of them.'

Chapter Nineteen

'Bloody hell, it looks like my office when I was writing *The Collector*,' Alex Frost said upon seeing Diane's dining room for the first time.

Caroline Turner had been wondering if introducing the two was a mistake. The opening handshake was cold, the conversation stilted and awkward. It was painful to witness and Caroline sank into an armchair, cringing as Alex defended his book while Diane criticised him for not focusing on all the victims and spending too much time looking for a reason behind Jonathan committing his crimes.

'I couldn't read all of it,' she said. 'It was all Jonathan this, Jonathan that. I didn't want to know his so-called excuses.'

'The reason True Crime books sell is because people want to understand why a criminal does what they do. All of his victims were killed and discovered in the same way. It would have been an incredibly dull book to have thirteen chapters identical apart from the names.'

'*Dull?*' Diane spat.

'I know you, and the rest of the families, wouldn't have seen it that way, but a book is entertainment. Even a True Crime book has to entertain.'

'My son's life is not entertainment.'

'Which is why I didn't focus on the victims, but on the perpetrator.'

'I hardly think a serial killer could be classed as entertainment, either,' Diane said, looking to Caroline for support.

'Mrs Marshall, I'm here because Caroline asked me to meet you. I'm here because I wrote the book on Jonathan Egan-Walsh and may be able to help. If – and it's a big if – there is the possibility of another book, then, of course, I'll write it.'

'I don't want my son exploited.'

'I know journalists have a bad reputation in this country, but I would never use your son to sell more copies. Like I said, if there is a book here, or a feature, or an article, it will be sensitively written and with your co-operation.'

'Diane,' Caroline sat up in her seat. She decided she needed to jump in to save the situation from going around in circles. 'I'm the last person to defend a reporter, but I've never met a man like Alex in the whole of my career. He's not an exploitative hack. He writes with heart, and humility.'

Caroline could feel Alex's eyes burning into her but dared not meet his gaze for fear of embarrassment. If Diane wanted to know the truth behind Jonathan's letter, then Alex was her only hope.

'I'm sorry,' Diane said. 'I'm just a bit sceptical. Part of me wants the truth but another part of me is scared of uncovering something I may regret.'

'Diane, I'm not going to lie to you,' Alex said. 'If Jonathan wrote the truth in his letter and he did not have anything to do with your son's disappearance, the odds are that it is someone you know very well. This is not going to be easy for you, or your family.'

The atmosphere in the living room intensified. Caroline looked around at all the photographs on the wall, of a happy, smiling

Zachery Marshall looking down on them. She wished there weren't so many. She could feel him pleading, begging with her – not to find him, but to stop this right now, to end the pain his mother was about to go through.

'Diane, maybe we should show Alex your information.'

'Right.'

Diane stood up and left the room. Caroline instructed Alex to follow. At the dining-room door, Diane paused, her hand on the handle. Once she allowed Alex inside there was no going back. This was the final point where she could ask Alex to leave. From this moment, everything would change. She took a deep breath and pushed open the door.

Alex stood in the centre of the room, marvelling at the detailed information Diane had accumulated over the years. On the dining table, there were thirteen box files, one for each of Jonathan's victims. She had spoken to all the parents and families to get information on the dead boys, where they were when they disappeared, where they were found, what they were wearing, who their friends were. It was more detailed than the initial criminal investigations.

'The more I think about Jonathan's letter and look at what I've gathered, the more I think someone else took Zachery.'

'What do you mean?' Caroline asked.

'Look here.' Diane went over to the wall that had the seven nationwide victims on it. 'The first victim was Danny Redpath. He went missing from Seahouses and was found between Chatton and Wooler. That's roughly fourteen miles from where he disappeared. It's the furthest distance of all the victims. Each one after that was found closer to home. Now, I've been searching for Zachery on my own over the years. I've used my own money to dig up private fields, waste ground … What?' she asked as she looked up at Alex.

He was biting his bottom lip. 'It's the first time I've seen detailed maps of where they went missing and where they were subsequently found. I should have done this when I was writing the book. I would have seen it more clearly.'

'Seen what?' Caroline asked.

'One of the things that always bothered me was where Jonathan kept his victims before he buried them. His neighbours never saw him with any boys, which suggests he had another location where he kept them. Looking at these maps, once he'd killed them, he took them home. He returned them to their families, or as close as he safely could.'

'What does that mean?' Diane asked.

'He wanted them to be found,' Caroline jumped in.

'Agreed.' Alex nodded. 'When each of the boys was found, they were in a shallow grave, yet they were carefully wrapped up in a white sheet. The bodies had been thoroughly washed. They'd been well fed while they were held, and looked after. Ignoring his crimes for a moment, he had genuine feelings of care and protection for his victims.'

'But he raped and murdered them,' Diane said with disgust.

'I know. But from Jonathan's point of view, he was loving them.'

'That's not love.' Diane folded her arms tightly across her chest.

'It's not what we call love, no, but Jonathan cared for each of his victims. He loved them in his own way.'

'I think I'm going to be sick.'

'I'm sorry, Diane, none of this is going to be easy listening, but it's the truth. I've spoken to Jonathan about this. I've spoken to psychologists and therapists and they've all said the same. If Jonathan was simply committing an act of evil, he would have cut the bodies up, there would have been bruising, broken bones, but there wasn't. He looked after them. He cared for them. When he killed them, he carefully wrapped them in a white sheet. He buried them somewhere close to home, where they would be found. He wanted them to be returned to their families.'

'So, the reason I haven't found Zachery is because he didn't bury him, because he didn't take him in the first place?' Diane asked with wide-eyed optimism.

Alex and Caroline looked at each other. Neither of them wanted to give her false hope.

Diane took a deep breath. 'So, what's the plan of action, then? Where do we go from here?'

'We need to re-examine Zachery's case,' Caroline said. 'Hopefully, we're going to speak to the original investigating officer, Finnian Atwood.'

Diane flinched at the mention of his name.

'You didn't like him?' Alex asked.

'It wasn't a question of *like*. The man had no compassion. It was like we were an inconvenience. The longer the case went on, the more annoyed he became. I'd phone him up and he'd practically shout at me – as if I was disturbing him for no good reason. I saw him at the police station on the day I came to identify some of Zachery's clothing, just after Jonathan had been arrested. He looked straight through me as if I was a complete stranger. He should have done more.'

Caroline and Alex exchanged glances but neither of them said anything. They allowed the silence to grow.

'Is there anything you need me to do?' Diane eventually asked.

'There is, actually,' Alex said. 'I need you to think. I need you to go back to when Zachery disappeared and remember every single detail. Was anyone hanging around who you didn't recognise? Did anything strange happen in the days and weeks leading up to his disappearance? Was anybody different towards you or your family after he went missing? Make a list of everyone who was involved, who came to visit you, even if it was just to express how sorry they were. Can you do that?'

'I've been doing that for twenty-five years, reliving it all. Every time I close my eyes, I see Zachery cycling down the road. He was so happy to have got his first bike that Christmas. It was all he'd been asking for, for months. I can still hear the song that was playing on Classic FM. I've never been able to listen to Verdi since.'

'I think the three of us should be able to find out what happened to Zachery. I'd stake my reputation on it,' Alex said.

'I just want to bring him home. That's all.'

'You will do. I promise.'

———

'Should you have done that?' Caroline asked, as she and Alex made their way to the car.

'Done what?'

'Promised Diane you'll bring her son home.'

'Every case can be solved, Caroline. As a former detective, you should know that.' He leaned on the roof of the car and lowered his voice so as not to be overheard by any nosy neighbours. 'I am more convinced than ever that Jonathan Egan-Walsh did not kill Zachery Marshall.'

'How can you be so sure?'

'Because of Diane's research. Jonathan returned his victims home. If he'd killed Zachery, he would have left him somewhere he would have been found. The fact he hasn't been found is evidence enough.'

'Maybe he just buried him in an isolated place,' Caroline shrugged.

'He wouldn't have done that. You've seen the locations of where all the victims were found. They were meant to be found. Like Diane said, the reason we haven't found Zachery Marshall is because Jonathan didn't bury him.'

With a heavy frown, Caroline pulled open the front passenger door and lowered herself into the cold. As Alex got in beside her, she said, 'You don't think …? No,' she dismissed her own thought.

'What?'

'Nothing.'

'You were going to ask if I thought Zachery Marshall might still be alive, weren't you?'

Caroline sniggered. 'You're a bloody good journalist, Alex.'

'Award-winning,' he smirked. 'You said it yourself.'

'True. So, come on then, what's your answer? Do you think Zachery Marshall could still be alive?'

Alex's smile dropped. 'When a young child goes missing, there really is only one logical reason behind it. If that's the case, then, by now, he won't be alive, anyway. He would have been sold, handed around to all kinds of people like nibbles at a party, and then discarded.'

'We can't allow Diane to get her hopes up that Zachery might still be alive, then.'

'I don't think she is doing that. She just wants his body back, that's all.'

'She's watching us,' Caroline said.

Alex looked up and saw Diane standing at the living-room window. She stood with her arms firmly folded across her chest.

'She looks so lost,' Caroline said.

'That's probably her usual look,' he said, reversing slowly out of the driveway. 'Give her a wave.'

She did and Diane waved back.

'Poor woman.'

'I've got the strange feeling that if we do uncover the truth, it's not going to be the closure she's looking for,' said Alex.

Caroline didn't say anything. She sat back in the passenger seat and frowned as she thought of the horrors they were possibly going to uncover.

Jamie was not going to be happy with this.

Chapter Twenty

'Why do they always give nursing homes such patronising names?' Alex said, looking up at the sign for Sunny View Rest Home.

Sunny View was on the coast of Skegness, overlooking the North Sea. In the middle of February, with dark clouds looming, angry waves crashing against the shore, and freezing rain battering the windows, there was more than a hint of irony in the name.

'Tell me about Finnian Atwood,' Alex said as he reversed into a tight parking space.

'The bloke was a glory hunter. He had a good record for solving cases and he made sure everyone knew it. That's probably why he was annoyed with Diane constantly calling him. He couldn't solve the case and didn't want to be reminded of it.'

'If the case went cold pretty quickly, was he the type of person to pass it down to the lower-ranking officers and move on?'

'Definitely,' Caroline said firmly.

'You wouldn't get away with that these days.'

'Thankfully, the likes of Finnian Atwood no longer exist in today's policing. At least, I hope they don't.'

The heat inside Sunny View was oppressive. The radiators were turned up to nuclear and there wasn't a hint of fresh air from anywhere.

A harassed-looking nurse led them down a corridor once they'd introduced themselves. Veronica Atwood had kindly told the staff they would be coming. As they headed for Finnian Atwood's room, Alex looked into the others they passed – the residents were slumped in their beds or in armchairs; they looked as if life had already left them.

He had visited a few similar places in London. They had been brighter than Sunny View, airier, but there was still the underlying sense that it was the final point people came to before the inevitable. He had immediately made up his mind that Melanie would stay at home, where she belonged. He and Shona would care for her. He couldn't put her in one of those places to be forgotten and ignored.

The nurses introduced Alex and Caroline to Veronica Atwood, who was already in her husband's room, and quickly left. 'We've met before, haven't we?' Veronica asked Caroline.

'Once or twice.'

'I thought so. Your hair's shorter now. It suits you.'

Veronica was a small woman and had to crane her neck to look up at her visitors. She had soft white hair, and her eyes sparkled, but her permanent smile showed someone who was obviously keeping strong for the sake of her husband.

'Finnian,' she spoke loudly as she turned to her husband, who was sat at a table doing a jigsaw. 'There are a couple of friends who've come to see you.'

Finnian Atwood eventually turned in his seat. He was bald. His face was a map of extruding veins and broken capillaries; a bulbous nose sat between drooping, vacant eyes. Caroline hardly recognised him.

'Ben? Sarah? I haven't seen you for years.'

'No, sweetheart. Ben and Sarah are in Canada. Ben's our son,' she said to Caroline. 'They're coming over in the summer. Finnian, do you remember Caroline Turner? She used to work for you, at the police station.'

'Caroline?' he asked, looking back at his visitors.

Caroline stepped forward. 'Nice to see you again, sir,' she said loudly. 'I've come to ask you a few questions, if that's all right?'

'Not under arrest, am I?' He laughed loudly.

'No, nothing like that. I want to talk to you about one of your cases.'

'You'd better sit down then, love.' He patted the seat next to him. 'Erm …' He pointed at his wife.

'Veronica,' she instructed him.

'Yes, I know,' he said, annoyed. 'We'll need tea and biscuits.' Veronica smiled and quickly left the room, relieved to have a break.

'She fusses. It gets on my nerves,' he said.

'She cares about you,' Caroline replied.

'She makes a good cake, so I can't complain,' he said, laughing slightly. 'So, you want to talk about one of my cases. I doubt I'll be much use. Bloody mind's fucked.' Caroline stifled a smile and looked up to Alex.

'Mr Atwood, I'm Alex Frost, I'm a writer. Do you remember Zachery Marshall?' Alex stepped forward as he spoke, holding out a hand for him to shake. It wasn't accepted, so he moved it away.

'You're one of those scabby reporters, aren't you? I can smell you a mile off.'

Caroline laughed. 'Sir, do you remember Zachery Marshall?'

'Remember?' He picked up a piece of his jigsaw and began to scour the half-completed puzzle of Buckingham Palace. 'Remember,' he said again. 'I'm asked that a lot. Do you remember our wedding day? Do you remember that holiday to Greece? I remember more than *she* thinks.'

Caroline looked in her bag and took out a photograph of

Zachery. She placed it on the table next to the jigsaw. 'This is Zachery Marshall. He disappeared in January 1993. He was seven years old.'

With shaking hands, Finnian picked up the photo and held it lightly in his thick fingers.

'Zachery Marshall …' he said quietly. 'We never found him.'

'That's right. He's still missing.'

'We found his bike,' he said after a long moment of thought.

'Yes, you did,' Caroline said, a hint of surprise in her voice. 'His bike was found while you were looking for another boy who had gone missing.'

'In a sewer pipe.'

'Yes. That's right.'

Finnian smiled. 'I remember.' He looked to both his visitors in turn as if seeking praise at remembering. 'I didn't like his father,' he said, his smile dropping.

'Zachery's?'

'Yes. I didn't like him. He told me something. In secret. Asked me not to let his wife find out.'

'What did he tell you?'

'I don't know. There was something wrong. He was away from the house for too long.'

'Who was? Nick Marshall?'

'Don't keep asking me questions,' he snapped. 'Let me think. And don't crowd me. *She* does that. I need space.'

Caroline leaned back in her seat and looked over at Alex, who shrugged. They all remained in silence, waiting for Finnian to elaborate. He looked down at the photograph still in his hand.

'Is this Ben?'

'No. That's a little boy who is missing.'

'Ben's missing? Do the police know?'

'Perhaps it would be better if we left,' Alex said.

At that moment, Veronica came in carrying a tray with a teapot and four mugs on it. As soon as Finnian saw his wife, he jumped up out of his seat.

'Veronica! Ben's missing. You need to call the police,' he said, panic rising in his voice.

'I'm sorry. I think we may have said something,' Caroline tried to explain.

'That's OK.' Veronica put the tray down. She took the photo from Finnian's hand and handed it back to Caroline. 'Leave him with me. I'll sort it out.'

'I'm really sorry.'

'Don't be. He gets like this sometimes.'

'What are they saying?' he asked, getting upset. 'What's happening? You need to phone Ben ...'

Quietly, Caroline and Alex left the room, listening to Finnian Atwood's sad, urgent pleas to find his son as they went. Neither spoke as they walked back down the hallway , heading for the exit.

'He's not the Finnian Atwood I knew all those years ago. It's sad,' Caroline said when they were finally back in the car, her voice breaking. 'What do you think he meant when he mentioned Nick?'

'I don't know,' Alex replied with a sigh. 'I don't think we can take anything he said as gospel. He might have got things mixed up with another case.'

'Do you want to go for a drink?'

'Only if it has a high-alcohol count.'

With that, Alex started the engine, which spluttered into life. He drove slowly down the gravel drive. They passed the sign as they were leaving.

'Sunny View, my arse,' Caroline said.

Chapter Twenty-One

Alex Frost didn't plan on going home for the foreseeable future. The commute between London and Skegness would take up a large part of the day, time he could spend interviewing Diane, members of her family, and trying to get to grips with the original investigation. Surprisingly, a couple of the bigger hotels in the town were full. Being February, Alex thought he'd have had the pick of the best rooms. Not so, however: there seemed to be a number of conferences and events taking place in the seaside town. The Majestic had a room for him, though. He braced himself as he followed the route on the satnav.

Alex had spent the majority of his working life staying in hotels. Usually, if a place was called The Grand or The Palace, it was anything but. His theory was proved right again when he pulled up outside The Majestic. The Victorian façade had taken the brunt of the bad weather the East Coast had thrown at it over the years. Crumbling rendering, tired-looking windows, and a bird-shit-covered roof. If Google had brought up a hotel called The Complete Dive, he would have booked a suite there.

The foyer of The Majestic was straight out of the 1950s. Mustard-coloured carpet, gaudy flock wallpaper, built-in reception desk in dark mahogany. The smell was fusty and damp. Every surface was cluttered with seaside tat. This was the hotel of the damned.

He signed in, accepted the key from the sullen young girl behind the desk and made his way up the three flights of narrow stairs. The red, yellow and green carpet had worn thin in places. Generic pictures had been added to the walls to try to brighten up the place, but they were failing, miserably.

Surprisingly, his room was cosy. The bed was large and looked comfortable. It had a clean smell and the décor wasn't as busy. The en suite was modern and there was plenty of storage space. It may not be majestic, but he was sure he'd have a good night's sleep beneath the thick duvet. Alex always kept an overnight bag in the boot of his car, should he need to stay over on any story he was working on. As he opened the case, he found a few crumpled shirts, a change of underwear and a bottle of whisky. There wasn't enough here to last him for long. He'd need to go shopping; for clothes as well as alcohol.

Once settled in, Alex met Caroline for a few drinks. They talked about anything other than Zachery Marshall, or their own lives. Alex suggested they go for a bite to eat. However, Caroline quickly made her excuses and said she needed to get back home to her husband. Alex wasn't in the mood to go back to his hotel room just yet. It was still early evening, though it was pitch-black outside, and so he found a quiet corner in a pub, ordered a large portion of shepherd's pie and chips, ate it with a couple of pints of lager and half-watched a football match showing on the big screen.

Back in the hotel room, full from his dinner, he opened his laptop and video-called his daughter. The laptop was on the table over the bed and the screen was filled with an image of his smiling daughter and the blank expression of his wife, whose eyes were open. She was awake, just not responsive.

'Hi, Dad. How's your day been?' Shona asked, perky and jolly as usual. She always liked to have a positive attitude around her mother as she thought it helped her condition.

'It's been good. Productive,' he lied. He didn't bother asking how her day had been. It was the same every day.

'That's good. Do you think you'll be able to find out what happened to Zachery Marshall?'

'I don't see why not. Any mail?'

'The usual bills. Where are you staying?' Shona asked, leaning in and looking at the room behind her father.

'The Majestic.'

'Oh. What's so majestic about it?'

'I haven't found that out yet.' he smiled. 'What are you reading to your mother tonight?'

'We're still on *Little Women*.'

Alex smiled. 'She loves that book.'

'I was never bothered about the classics until I started reading them to Mum. They've grown on me.' She leaned forward, closer to the camera. 'Are you looking after yourself?'

'Don't I always?'

'Have you eaten?'

'Yes.'

'Healthily?'

'Of course.'

'You're a liar, Dad.'

'Kiss your mum goodnight for me, will you?'

'I always do.'

'I love you, Shona.'

'Love you, too, Dad.'

Alex closed his laptop and leaned back on the bed, trying not to cry.

Jonathan Egan-Walsh was back in his life, in one form or

another. Writing *The Collector* may have been a turning point in his career, bringing him fame and wealth, recognition and respect, but it had come at the cost of the one thing that he would give everything up for – his wife.

Diane spent the afternoon going over the day her son disappeared, minute by minute. She had written everything down, sometimes her hand scribbling faster than her thoughts. She wrote until she couldn't grip the pen any longer. Then, she fell, exhausted, onto the sofa and cried. She cried for the son she had failed to protect, the life she had lost and the people around her she had ignored.

The phone rang. It was Marcus. The conversation was difficult and there were more silences than words spoken. He invited her over for a birthday tea he was having for Greta at the weekend. Before she could reply, he told her Nick and Beth weren't going to be there. He just wanted his mum and grandmother there, if they could make it. Diane said she could.

As much as Diane was pleased Marcus was back in her life and they were rebuilding their relationship, she still found it difficult to talk to him. At the back of her mind, she couldn't help but wonder what Zachery would be doing now if he was still with them. She ended the call, making some excuse about potatoes boiling. She realised she had been tense while talking to her younger son. Why was that? Why couldn't she relax around her own son? She hated herself for destroying the family.

After her evening meal of a bowl of soup (she had no interest in cooking a big meal just for one and mostly lived on tins), she called her mother for their usual nightly chat.

'We've been invited to a birthday tea.'

'Whose birthday?'

'Greta.'

'Things *are* looking up,' Hannah replied, a smile in her voice. 'Will *he* be there with her?' she asked, meaning Nick and Beth.

'No.' Diane smiled. 'Would you like to go halves on a present?'

'What do we buy her?'

'I don't know. I don't really know the woman.'

'Well, she's just had a baby, how about something relaxing to put in a bath?'

'Good idea, Mum. I'll pop into town tomorrow and pick something up.'

'Make it look expensive but don't go mad.'

Diane paused. 'I had Caroline Turner around here this morning. She brought Alex Frost with her – you know, the writer of that book about Jonathan.'

'Oh … yes.'

'He was asking some difficult questions.'

'He's going to, it's his job.'

'Mum.' Diane's mouth dried and she swallowed hard a couple of times. 'What if someone else took Zachery? What if it's someone I know?'

'We'll cross that bridge when we come to it.'

'But—'

'Don't let this eat away at you, Diane,' her mother interrupted. 'Until we know the facts, there's no point in getting yourself tied up in knots.'

'You're right.'

'Of course I'm right. I'm your mother.'

Diane smiled. 'Thanks, Mum.'

'What for?'

'For listening.'

'Don't be silly. Now, what time are you collecting me tomorrow to go shopping?'

'You want to go with me?'

'Of course. It'll me good to get out.'

Diane smiled. She wished her mother goodnight and tried to

relax in front of the television, but there was nothing worth watching. She sat through *Newsnight* without listening to a single word. Her mind was elsewhere. She closed her eyes tight and found herself standing at the window looking out on a bright but cold January afternoon. Zachery, wrapped up against the winter elements, cycled down the road. Before he reached the bottom, he turned and waved at his mother. Diane opened her eyes and tears fell.

Exhausted, she locked up, closed all the curtains and headed up the stairs. Once at the top, she turned around and went back downstairs and into the dining room. She found what she was looking for straight away – the paperback of Alex's *The Collector*.

Diane read until the small hours of the morning, until her eyes wouldn't stay open any longer. She had only read the odd chapter before, and promised herself she didn't want to know about Jonathan's life and any excuses he offered as to why he committed his crimes. However, if Jonathan didn't take Zachery, there was no harm in her reading about him now. She read of his violent start to life and his appalling childhood without an ounce of emotion.

This was no longer a book about Zachery's kidnapper. It was simply a book about a serial killer.

————————

Caroline lay awake. Next to her, Jamie was sleeping. She didn't tell him about visiting Finnian Atwood. She had complained about him on a daily basis when he was her boss. Instead, over dinner, she had told her husband about the conversation between Alex and Diane, how the grieving mother's extensive research into the thirteen victims had given Alex a new understanding of Jonathan's crime. That seemed to placate him, and the conversation had soon petered out.

While they had been snuggled up together on the sofa after

dinner, watching something Caroline had no interest in, Jamie had asked if she was going back to dog walking tomorrow.

'Not tomorrow, no. Sharon's taking over for a bit. I'm helping Alex out.'

'How? What can you actually do?' Jamie asked, turning the volume on the television down a notch.

'I can help, advise, from a police point of view.'

'But you're not a detective any more.'

'I know. But I can point him in the right direction.'

'The bloke's been a journalist all his life. If he doesn't already know the right questions to ask, he never will.'

'It's not as simple as that. I arrested Jonathan. Between us, we've got the complete story on him.'

'But you said you thought Jonathan hadn't killed Zachery Marshall. You didn't work on his disappearance, so why are you getting involved? You've no loose ends to tie up.'

Caroline couldn't answer that. He was right.

The question consumed her as she had had her nightly soak in the bathtub before having climbed into bed next to her husband and pretended to sleep.

She was still trying to answer his question – why was she so involved in the search for Zachery Marshall? The answer was obvious, though one she wasn't prepared to admit – she really did miss being a detective. She would give anything to be a serving officer once again. Unfortunately, every time she thought about it, she was back in that prison interview room, alone with Jonathan Egan-Walsh, her back against the wall, his hand around her throat, and the life being squeezed out of her body.

Chapter Twenty-Two

The second meeting between Diane and Alex didn't have the same dark, icy atmosphere as the first. In fact, when Diane opened the front door to find Caroline and Alex on the doorstep, she welcomed them with a warm smile.

'I've been baking. It's not something I usually do but I thought we could do with some comfort eating over coffee.'

Alex stood in the doorway to the kitchen and his eyes fell on the very rich-looking chocolate cake on the table. He was visibly drooling.

'That looks lovely,' Caroline said. 'I wish I had the knack of baking. You should see how my scones turn out. I could use them to build a rockery,' she said, laughing.

Alex and Caroline sat at the kitchen table while Diane made coffee. She seemed to have perked up since their first meeting and Caroline worried that she was looking to Alex to offer a miracle, and find Zachery.

'Diane, can you take me through everything that happened on the day Zachery went missing?' Alex began, taking his notepad and files from his satchel. 'I want to know about everyone who visited the house, any phone calls, anything strange or out of the ordinary you remember.'

Diane settled the tray of coffee on the table, served three generous slices of chocolate cake to her guests, then pulled out a chair and sat down. She didn't speak until she had poured them all a drink. 'I was going through it all yesterday after you left, minute by minute. It was a Sunday. It was bloody cold, too.' She gave a nervous laugh. 'We'd had some snow the night before but it hadn't amounted to much. I remember Zachery being very disappointed when he woke up. He was expecting us to be snowed in, I think. Anyway, Jacqui and Bryn Jones, who lived next door, came round about ten o'clock-ish. They had a football kit for Zachery to try on.'

'Why was that?' Alex asked as he scribbled shorthand notes in his pad.

'Oh. Well, Bryn was manager of the local under-ten football league and Zachery was starting training with them at the end of the month. He wasn't much of a football fan, but Nick was. Still is … I assume. A few of Nick's friends had sons who were in the team and Nick thought it would be good for Zachery to join, too. You know, help him mix with other boys, build up his confidence.'

'Did Zachery have difficulty making friends?'

'No. It's just … well, sport gives you self-esteem, doesn't it? Zachery was sometimes quiet. He needed bringing out of his shell more. Besides, we were quite close with Jacqui and Bryn. They were a lovely couple. Bryn was a huge football fan and he liked to get the community involved. It just seemed natural that Zachery would join.'

'Did Zachery say that he wanted to join?' Alex asked.

'No. He never really spoke about it.'

Alex and Caroline exchanged glances. The reporter quickly scribbled something down.

'How long were Jacqui and Bryn here for?'

'I'm not sure. Me and Jacqui were in the living room with a cup of tea, having a gossip. Time flies when you're having a laugh, doesn't it?' She smiled.

'Where was Bryn?' Caroline asked.

'He was upstairs with Zachery. He was helping him try on his kit – you know, making sure he had the right sizes and everything he needed.'

'How did Zachery seem once Bryn and Jacqui had left?' Alex asked, pausing in his note taking to take a sip of coffee.

'He was fine. What are you suggesting?'

'Nothing. I mean, if Zachery didn't really want to play football, did he feel pressurised into doing so, or was he excited by it?'

'He wasn't excited but there was no pressure. If he didn't want to play he didn't have to. He just accepted it. It was another thing to do.'

'Did you see Bryn and Jacqui any more that day?' Caroline asked.

'No.'

'Do they still live next door?'

'No. Bryn's from Wales, originally. Well, he would be, wouldn't he, with a name like Bryn Jones,' Diane laughed. 'They moved back there.'

'When?'

She puffed out her cheeks. 'I can't remember, a long time ago.'

'Was it long after Zachery had disappeared?'

'I don't know. Time didn't seem to have any meaning back then. The days seemed to just run into each other. He disappeared in the January, and before you knew it, Christmas was around again.'

Alex was about to say something, but Caroline placed a hand on his arm to stop him.

'Diane,' Caroline said, leaning forward. 'Think hard: when did Jacqui and Bryn move back to Wales?'

'In the summer,' she said, eventually, swallowing hard. 'About August, I think. My sister moved to Australia that summer and I think it was round about the same time.'

'Seven months after Zachery went missing? Did they say why they were moving?'

'I can't remember,' she said, shaking her head. 'They'd never mentioned it before, I'm sure.'

'Do you still keep in touch with them?'

'No. We lost contact. You do, don't you?'

'How long after they moved was it before you lost contact?'

'I know we received a Christmas card from them that first year. I don't remember after that.'

'Diane, I think I'd like to speak to them,' Alex said, pen poised.

'You don't think …? I mean … What are you saying?' Diane stuttered, agitated. 'I knew Jacqui and Bryn. You don't think they had anything to do with Zachery going missing, surely?'

'I don't know what to think, Diane. I find it strange that a man who you say was so involved in the local community, the local football team, would suddenly up and leave like that.'

'It might not have been suddenly. Everything's a blur around that time,' she said. A heavy frown had formed on her face.

'Had they ever mentioned returning to Wales?' Caroline asked.

Diane pushed the small plate with her untouched slice of cake on it to one side, a look of panic appearing on her face. 'No. I mean … I don't … They were in this house all the time. They sometimes took the boys to the beach with them.'

'Diane, calm down,' Caroline said. 'Alex and I, we deal with the disturbing side of people all the time. We could be reading too much into this. Couldn't we?' she asked Alex.

'That's right. There's no need to stress yourself until we have all the facts. This is lovely cake, by the way. Now, what else happened that day? Did you have a Sunday lunch?' Alex asked, quickly moving on. He and Caroline would have a private word later about Jacqui and Bryn Jones.

Diane's face brightened up. 'Yes, we did. I always did a big lunch for Sunday, especially in the winter. Nick and the kids loved it. Zachery was only small but he could certainly eat. I don't know where he put it. His plate was often piled high – Yorkshire puddings, mashed potatoes, and he loved his veg. Not many kids do, but Zachery did. Cauliflower was his favourite.'

Caroline smiled as she watched the grieving mother relive a final happy memory. 'And Zachery went out on his bike afterwards?'

'Well, he was always the last to leave the table. I often used to sit there with him while he finished. Marcus wolfed his food down and then went into the living room to watch telly. I remember Nick was disturbed a couple of times during lunch.'

'In what way?'

'The phone rang a couple of times. It was one of his friends from work at British Gas,' Diane said with a heavy frown. 'I can't remember his name. He came to the house a few times. He seemed like a nice young man,' she said, looking down into her coffee cup.

'What did the children make of him?'

'Zachery said he was weird. Nick didn't like that.' She half-smiled at the memory.

'Why did he come to the house? Were they friends as well as work colleagues?,' Caroline continued. 'If they worked together, he would have seen him there.'

'They worked in different departments,' Diane said.

'So, Nick and this other man wouldn't have had any reason for their paths to cross at work?' Alex asked.

'I'm not sure,' Diane replied. Her frown was getting heavier again.

'So what linked them together? Why did they see each other out of work? Did they go to the same gym, football club, pubs?'

'I don't know.'

'When was the last time you saw this man?'

'I don't know,' Diane said, rubbing at her worry lines. 'Look, why are you doing this?'

'Doing what?'

'It seems like everyone who came into this house is some kind of criminal who you're trying to cast a shadow over,' Diane said loudly.

'Diane, I'm trying to get a picture of Zachery's last movements.'

'No, you're not. You're casting aspersions on people I knew, people I liked. You're twisting everything to make everyone seem like they had a motive. Who are you going to accuse next? My mother called on that Sunday. Is she harbouring some dark secret, too?'

'Look, why don't we all have a break and calm down,' Caroline said. 'I think we're in danger of allowing our emotions to get the better of us.'

Diane pushed her chair back and stood up. She walked over to the window and looked out into the back garden. There was a stiff wind blowing. The bare branches of a tree were tapping against the window. She had meant to cut it down a long time ago. Every winter, the leaves blew off and it got more wearisome to tidy them. With her arms folded tightly across her chest, she turned around to look at Caroline and Alex. 'I'm sorry. I shouldn't be taking any of this out on you. I know you're only trying to help. It's just … it's not easy.'

'We understand, Diane, and you have nothing to apologise for,' Caroline said.

'Diane, have you cleared out Zachery's bedroom?' Alex asked.

'No. That was what first set Nick and me apart. He wanted to throw things away and I didn't. There was always that thought at the back of my mind that he would still come home.'

'Would it be OK for us to go and take a look?'

'What do you think?' Caroline asked quietly.

Diane had shown Alex and Caroline to Zachery's bedroom before leaving them alone to go back down stairs. The room was clean and tidy with an underlying fusty smell. It was decorated in various shades of blue. The single bed was neatly made with a matching Spider-Man duvet and pillowcase. On top of the chest of drawers were cars and trucks made out of Lego. There was one single poster on the wall, of Garfield and Odie.

'Typical boy's bedroom,' Alex said.

'I meant about downstairs.'

'Oh. Well, that Bryn Jones fella certainly needs looking into. I reckon he was up here alone with Zachery for a good half-hour or so, maybe even longer. It doesn't take that long to try on a football kit. And why couldn't he have just asked Diane what size he was? She would have known.' He spoke in hushed tones just in case Diane was listening. 'People connected with the Marshalls seem to have moved away quite quickly, don't they?'

'Are you thinking about the sister and brother-in-law?'

'Yes. Do you have siblings?'

'No. I'm an only child.'

'I have one of each. If one of their children had disappeared and needed my support, I would not have moved to the other side of the world.'

'True. Also,' Caroline pushed the bedroom door to and lowered her voice further so she couldn't be overheard. 'When Diane got upset, she accused you of casting aspersions on people she knew, people she liked. She didn't call them friends. I don't think she was as close to her neighbours as she likes to make out.'

'Maybe not.'

'And what about this friend of Nick's?'

'We need to track him down, too. Maybe he did have a connection with Nick that Diane didn't know about, but that doesn't explain why Zachery thought he was weird.' Alex went over to the window and looked out at the view. 'I mean, it could be perfectly innocent, maybe he didn't know how to interact with children, but everything's heightened in a case like this, isn't it?'

'So, that's three lines of enquiry we've found already. Not bad for a morning's work.'

The view from the window was directly above the kitchen and looked out onto the back garden and the expanse of field beyond. 'Caroline, when you arrested Jonathan, and you realised there was a familial link between him and Zachery, did you just assume he was responsible?'

Caroline closed her eyes and took a deep breath. 'I think I did. The main angle we worked on was the collection of clothing Jonathan had in his flat. We contacted all the parents of missing children and had them come and identify them. Diane and Nick Marshall found Zachery's clothing among the hundreds of items he had.'

'So, you didn't go looking for Zachery?'

'It had been three years. The original investigation had uncovered no leads at all. To all intents and purposes, he was dead and buried. We just hadn't been able to find him. I interviewed Jonathan on numerous occasions. I asked him several times what he had done with Zachery Marshall and he never replied.'

'Because he didn't know.'

'I didn't know that at the time. From my point of view, we had his killer, his kidnapper, in the cells. It would have been a waste of resources to look into the case again. Besides, Jonathan had clothes Zachery had been wearing on the day he went missing, and some had blood on them. What else were we to think?'

'I'd really like to look at those files.'

'I can't help there, I'm afraid.'

'I know. But perhaps there is something you *can* help with. Do you know anyone in the Wales police force?'

'Actually, I do. One of my old DCs moved to Wales when she was promoted.'

'Do you think she'll help us find Bryn Jones?'

'I can ask. We're friends on Facebook.'

'OK. Well, you look into that and I'll go and have a word with Nick Marshall.'

'I really hope that's a dead end. For Diane's sake.'

Alex decided not to call on Nick Marshall while he was at home. It would be easy for him to slam the door in his face if he didn't want to talk. Instead, he decided to catch him where he worked, Barrett International. Arriving in good time, Alex parked in the company's car park and waited for five o'clock to arrive.

He sent a text to his daughter, checking in, asking how she and her mother were, and was relieved to hear that Melanie had had a good night. The health-care nurse was there, letting Shona have a much-needed break.

Alex hated leaving Shona at home to look after her mother alone while he was out researching stories. It was no way for a woman in her twenties to be spending her days, looking after her severely disabled mother, but what was the alternative? Alex didn't like the thought of a stranger looking after his wife, and the press was full of horror stories of so-called home help abusing or stealing from their patients.

Melanie wasn't expected to live to a ripe old age. A minor illness could lead to serious, potentially fatal consequences. In his weaker moments, he felt it would be a blessing, but for whom? He thought he knew Melanie, and that she would hate to spend the rest of her life like this, but he often wondered what would happen to him and Shona when she was gone.

It started to snow. Nothing heavy, a light flurry. Alex felt cold and turned the heating on. He looked around his ancient Volvo. He wondered how it managed to start every morning, and always thanked a god he didn't believe in when the engine burst into life. He needed to upgrade, but the money he made went into Melanie's care and paying for Shona to have some kind of a social life.

He read through his emails. Nothing interesting, a few offers of a story from a couple of national newspapers, but by the time he had travelled to wherever he needed to be and taken off his overnight stay, he would be lucky to come out with fifty pounds. He politely declined their offers.

From his satchel, Alex took out the notes he had been making about Zachery's disappearance. After today's session with Diane, he was more convinced than ever that Jonathan Egan-Walsh was not responsible for Zachery going missing. There was definitely a book to be written there. He was sure he could get an advance from a publisher. That would come in very handy. Also, he could write a revised edition of *The Collector* with the new information he'd received. The question was, who kidnapped Zachery Marshall and what happened to him? At the moment, Diane's former next-door neighbours were his front runners. He needed to get his hands on the original police case files. He wondered what they had said in their statements during the original investigation.

He typed Caroline's name into a search engine. He couldn't get his head around the fact that Caroline had entirely cut herself off from her old life. He still had sporadic contact with people he'd worked with, going back thirty years or more. The first story to come up was, unsurprisingly, about Jonathan Egan-Walsh. It was slim pickings. There was very little about her. One tiny story on her retirement from the *Skegness Standard*, which gave away very little. He remembered hearing about her being attacked in prison but, surely, she wouldn't have allowed something like that to decide her future. Why had she retired at fifty-two? Burnout? Forced out? Or did the reason lie within the Jonathan Egan-Walsh case?

———————

Diane's mind rarely switched off at the best of times and, since Caroline and Alex had entered her life, it was permanently whirring. She washed up the dishes her visitors had used and, while she was in cleaning mode, decided to give the kitchen a good blitz. It was what she did when she needed to clear her head. As she sprayed kitchen cleaner on the cupboard fronts and vigorously wiped them down, she thought about her ex-neighbours, Bryn and Jacqui Jones. They had always seemed a friendly couple – kind, welcoming, would do anything for anyone, always happy and smiling. Suddenly, those smiles seemed more sinister, hiding a multitude of possible dark deeds. She hadn't thought of them for years and wondered where they were now, and, wherever they were, had any other boys gone missing?

The phone rang in the living room, and Diane jumped. Her phone rarely rang. If it wasn't for her mother, she would have had the landline taken out years ago.

'Hello?' she asked cautiously upon answering.

'Mrs Marshall?'

'Yes.'

'My name's Delilah Thomas. I'm a reporter for the *Sun* newspaper. We've had a call from someone who says Jonathan Egan-Walsh wrote you a letter telling you he didn't kill your son. Is this true?'

'Where did you get that from?'

'I'm afraid I'm not at liberty to say at the moment.'

'In that case, I'm not at liberty to say anything, either.'

'Mrs Marshall, I'm sure you want to find your son. If it turns out Jonathan had nothing to do with his disappearance, then talking to us may help. We could put out an appeal. Someone could come forward with new information.'

'I'm sorry. I'm not talking to you.'

'If Jonathan didn't take your son, do you think the perpetrator could be someone closer to home?' Delilah asked quickly.

'What?'

'The majority of people who are kidnapped, or killed, tend to know the person committing the crime. Do you think a close friend or a member of your family was involved?'

'I'm hanging up now.'

'Mrs Marshall, is it true your husband—'

Diane slammed the phone down. The room around her began to spin and her vision blurred as the blood felt as if it was draining from her body. She was so angry and shocked. Who had told the newspapers? Alex wouldn't have, as he'd want to write the story himself, and Caroline definitely wouldn't have done so. Nobody else knew.

She sat down in the armchair and put her head in her hands. She wanted to cry, to scream and shout and break something, but she couldn't. She was numb.

———————

A little after five o'clock, the doors of Barrett International started opening and people began to file out. They were all dressed in dull sensible colours of navy blue, grey and black. Wrapped up against the winter elements, they made their way to their cars or the bus stop, each of them with the same life-beaten expression on their faces. Alex didn't know what he would do if he had to be an office monkey; probably open one of the windows on the sixth floor and jump out.

Although visibly older, he recognised Nick Marshall straight away. He had looked up his photograph on the Internet. The last time his picture had appeared in the press had been at Jonathan's sentencing. In the photograph, Caroline Turner was standing on the steps of the court reading out a statement, the other relatives of the murdered boys behind her. Just over her left shoulder were Nick and Diane Marshall. Diane hadn't changed much over the years. Her hair was the same style. She was thinner, had more lines on her face, but she was recognisable. Now, looking up out of the murky windscreen, Alex saw Nick Marshall head in his direction.

Nick was tall – at least six feet, if not a couple of inches more – his dark hair rapidly thinning, and he had the look of a man in need of a good night's sleep. His eyes were heavy, as were the bags beneath. He dragged his feet along the concrete as he headed for a Citroën Picasso.

'Mr Marshall?' Alex said, getting out of his Volvo as the man passed his car.

Nick jumped and quickly spun around. 'Yes.'

Alex held out his hand. 'Hello, you may not remember me, I'm Alex Frost. I'm a freelance journalist. I wrote—'

'I know who you are, Mr Frost,' Nick said, looking down at the proffered hand but keeping his own deep in his pockets.

'I'm working with your wife on a letter she received from Jonathan Egan-Walsh. I'm assuming you know about it.'

'Yes. I don't know what it's got to do with you, though.' His attitude was as cold as the weather. He tried to get past Alex but the journalist quickly blocked him.

'Your wife contacted me and asked me to look into it.'

'And where do I fit in?'

'I'd like to ask you a few questions, if I may, about the day your son disappeared.'

Nick let out a heavy sigh. Even in the stiff breeze, Alex caught the smell of strong coffee on his breath. 'I have been over and over the day of Zach's disappearance many times. I relive it on a daily basis. I really don't want to do this again.' He pushed past Alex and headed to his car.

'Mr Marshall, do you remember a young man you used to work with while you were at British Gas? Diane couldn't remember his name. He came to the house a few times,' Alex said, trotting behind him to keep up.

'Jason?' Nick asked with a heavy frown on his forehead. 'Jason Brown. What about him?'

'He phoned you during Sunday lunch on the day your son disappeared. He called a couple of times, Diane said.'

'Yes. So?'

'Who was he?'

'Someone I worked with.'

'You were more than colleagues, though, weren't you? You were friends.'

'Yes.'

'What did you have in common?'

'What? What's that got to do with anything? What are you trying to say?'

'Mr Marshall, there's no need to be so defensive. I'm trying to find out what happened on that day. Now, this Jason Brown called you twice on a Sunday. Why was that?'

'I'm not talking about this.' Nick unlocked his car and climbed in behind the wheel. He tried to close the door but Alex put himself in the way.

'Mr Marshall, *please* talk to me. Where's Jason Brown now?'

'I've no idea. I left British Gas shortly after I left Diane.'

'Was Jason still working there at the time?'

'Yes, he was.'

'Did you stay in touch?'

'I don't recall. Probably not, as we're not in touch now.'

'So, you weren't close friends?'

'No.'

'But close enough for him to visit your house, call you up on a Sunday? Close enough for your sons to think he was weird.'

'What's Diane been saying to you? Look, I don't know what you're getting out of this, but you, and Diane, are not involving me. It's been twenty-five years, for fuck's sake! Zachery's gone. He's dead. Jonathan killed him. She should move on and leave it alone. Now, please, move away from my car.'

Alex realised he had no choice but to step out of the way. At which point, Nick got in his car, slammed the door shut and drove out of the car park.

Alex watched the Citroën disappear. Why was Nick so easily riled at the mention of Jason Brown? He wondered what the basis was for their friendship, and thought of his own friends, not that he had many. Caring for Melanie and working away so often left little time for friends. The ones he did have could mostly be classed as work acquaintances – his editor, a couple of freelance journalists – but he'd never been to their houses. That was the question that needed answering: why did Jason go to Nick's home on a Sunday? And was it merely a coincidence that it just happened to be the same Sunday Zachery disappeared. He shivered at the mention of the c-word – he was a journalist, he didn't believe in coincidence.

As Alex made his way back to the Volvo, a small smile appeared on his face. He was already filling his head with questions and potential suspects. This was what he lived for. The thrill of the unknown. There was going to be no easy solution to this case. So much for just a couple of days in Skegness. Maybe he should think of relocating here.

Diane was halfway up the stairs when the phone started ringing. It had been ringing on and off all evening with reporters wanting to ask her questions about whether Jonathan took her son. How had they found out about all this? She was tempted to ignore it but when she saw it was almost eleven o'clock, she decided to answer. A journalist wouldn't be calling at this time of night. Surely, they'd all be in the pub by now. She smiled to herself.

'Hel—'

'It's Nick.'

'Oh. Nick. How—'

'What's going on?'

'What are you talking about?'

'I've had that Alex Frost waiting for me outside work, asking questions. What have you said?' Nick's voice was low but threatening. The sound of the wind was heard clearly in the background. Had Nick gone outside to make a clandestine phone call so his precious Beth couldn't hear him?

'I told you I'd be looking into that letter, Nick. Alex interviewed Jonathan. He knows the case inside out.'

'Do you have any idea what you're going to do?'

'Find out the truth, hopefully.'

'You already have the truth.'

'I don't have my son back,' she said, gripping the phone firmly, her knuckles almost white. 'I will do everything in my power to bring him back home.'

'And what about everyone else? What about me and Marcus and the baby?'

Diane breathed a heavy sigh. 'I'm sorry if this is going to cause you the odd sleepless night, Nick, but I'm doing this for myself.'

'You're a selfish bitch, Diane. Drop this now before it goes too far,' he threatened.

'We're not married any more, Nick. You can't talk to me like that now.'

She slammed the phone down and fell against the wall of the

living room. She was shaking. Alex had been right. Digging this up after all these years was going to upset a lot of people. For a brief moment, she wondered if she should go on with it, but then her gaze landed on a framed photo of her missing son, lit by the brilliant moon peeking through a gap in the curtains. Of course she was doing the right thing! Zachery needed to come home. Nick could go to hell, as far as she was concerned.

Chapter Twenty-Four

'Are you going to work today?'

Caroline rolled her eyes. She was sat at the dining table, nibbling on a slice of granary toast and sipping a coffee. She was dressed, but not in her dog-walking clothes. She was smart in black trousers and a cream sweater. She was even wearing a touch of make-up.

'Why are you doing this, Caroline?' Jamie asked. He pulled out the chair opposite and sat down. His face was a picture of worry.

'Are we going to have the same conversation every morning? There's nothing to worry about.'

'You hardly said a word to me last night. You're going quiet again.'

Caroline took a deep breath. 'I was chatting to Sarah. She's working in Wales now. She's getting some information for me. Look, Jamie, I need to do this.' She stood up, taking her plate and cup into the kitchen.

Jamie watched her from the living room. 'Promise me you'll not shut me out this time. I want you to tell me how you feel, how you're coping.'

Caroline stood in the doorway. She looked at her husband. His eyes were big and full of tears. He was worried for her. She liked that. It made her feel secure and warm. She smiled at him. 'I promise. I'll tell you everything.'

'Nothing too gory, though.'

Caroline laughed. She walked over to him, sat on his knee and kissed him passionately on the lips. 'I love you, Jamie Turner.'

'I should hope so. We've been married twenty-eight years.'

'You're supposed to say you love me, too.'

'I don't think I'm there yet,' he said, with a twinkle in his eye.

Alex stared at his reflection in the mirror as he finished shaving. It could be the neon tube buzzing above the mirror, but he suddenly thought he looked old, ashen, grey. How much longer could he go on living this lifestyle? He knew the real reason behind being a freelancer: he didn't have to go home. As much as he loved Melanie, he hated seeing her lying in bed every day, unresponsive to everything around her. She would hate it, too; he knew it. Before the accident, Melanie was a lively, energetic woman. She ran half-marathons, she went hiking, she was always on the move, always helping people and smiling. He wondered if she was still alive inside her body or was there nothing left, just a shell of Melanie? If she was alive in there, was she screaming at them, begging, crying, pleading with her husband and daughter to end her life, end her suffering? She wouldn't want to live like this.

Alex focused back on his reflection and noticed the tears pouring down his face. He loved Melanie with all his heart, had done since the moment he set eyes on her at that publisher's party all those years ago. She was engaged to someone else at the time and he had been seeing Daisy Simpson, though it wasn't serious. They'd spent that first night exchanging glances and smiles like love-sick teenagers in a schoolyard. Eventually, Alex plucked up the courage to speak to her. By the end of the evening, they were both smitten.

They arranged to go out for a meal a couple of days later, but Alex knew this was going to be something special, so, the following morning, he went to see Daisy and broke things off between them. She cried. She said she loved Alex, even though they'd only been dating for eight weeks. Alex apologised, several times, before leaving her flat. It was the most difficult conversation he'd ever had, but he knew he was doing the right thing.

Melanie never told Alex how she ended her engagement to Sebastian. He didn't want to know. She told him when she had done it and shed a tear, but Alex was the man for her. They were married within three months of their first meeting, and Shona came along exactly nine months after their honeymoon.

Now look at where they all were. Melanie was in a persistent vegetative state, Shona was her full-time carer, and Alex was avoiding going home at all costs. This was his life. He looked back into the hotel bedroom and felt the anger inside him bubble up to the surface. He had a permanent knot in his stomach, caused by anxiety, worry and stress. He hated himself for neglecting his family. He hated what meeting Jonathan Egan-Walsh had done to his life.

He hated this fucking hotel room.

After a shower, he sat on his unmade bed, towel wrapped around his waist. He looked at his sagging body through the mirror. He used to take care of his appearance. Melanie always looked good, so he felt he should look good, too. Now, he had nobody to impress, so it didn't matter if he put on a bit of weight. His mobile on the bedside table beeped, making him jump. For a brief second, he hoped it wasn't Shona complaining about something but, in fact, it was Caroline, asking him where they could meet. He looked around the untidy hotel room. He couldn't have her come here, and he had no idea where was good to meet in Skegness for them to have a private conversation. He asked her to meet him in the lobby of his hotel. He looked at himself in the mirror again and sucked in his stomach.

The lift doors struggled to open and Alex stepped out. Caroline was waiting for him, a smile on her face. She was wrapped up in a scarf, gloves and hat. He smiled back. He had never realised before how attractive she was. When she smiled she had dimples in her cheeks and her eyes lit up. How old was she again? He quickly did the maths in his head and realised she was sixty, though she looked a lot younger.

'You've never been to the North in winter, have you?' Caroline asked, looking him up and down.

'What do you mean?'

'A thin jacket and Converse trainers. You'll freeze to death. There's a strong wind blowing in off the coast.'

'Oh. Well, I need to go shopping at some point. I haven't got enough clothes with me. Is there anywhere decent around here?'

'Everywhere is decent around here. The North isn't a Third World country, you know. By the way, have you seen the papers this morning?'

'Not yet. Why?'

Caroline went over to a small table in Reception, where several daily papers were fanned out for people to read. She picked up the *Sun*, flicked through the pages until she found what she was looking for, and handed it to him.

'Cast your eye over this.'

'How did they get hold of it?' Alex asked.

'I've no idea. I saw it this morning.'

'I didn't have you down as a *Sun* reader.'

'I'm not.' She smiled. 'I was googling.'

'It could have been one of the prison officers, maybe.'

'Or the solicitor, Lachlan … what was it?' she asked as they headed for the exit.

'Minnow. Maybe. I think he might be worth paying a visit. He visited Jonathan in prison. Maybe Jonathan said something to him about Zachery Marshall.'

'No. Diane told me that Jonathan never said anything about Zachery to his solicitor. Well, nothing that would help us, anyway.'

'I'd love to know what they did talk about,' Alex said. 'What happened to the solicitor who represented him at his trial? What was his name? Strange bloke in a tartan suit.'

'Henry Fitzroy,' Caroline said. 'He died about five years ago. Liver cancer. It turned out he'd been a secret drinker for years.'

'We'll not get any information from him, then.'

'Hmm … I've been thinking about where Jonathan said he was on the day Zachery went missing.'

'Robin Hood's Bay?'

'Yes. Now, it was winter, a bloody cold winter, not many people would have been about. Surely, a bloke in a van would have stuck out.'

'Well, yes, I'm guessing he would have done. But who is going to remember if they were in Robin Hood's Bay twenty-five years ago? Can you remember what you were doing on 10 January 1993? I think we're going to have to draw a line under Jonathan's alibi and concentrate on all the other characters in our drama.'

They left the hotel and stood on the steps. Alex looked out at the North Sea. He felt the chill straight away. The sea looked angry. The dark waters crashed onto the shore, whipping up spray. The sky was grey and overcast. He watched the people as they went about their business. Everyone was wrapped up against the elements. Heads were down, shoulders hunched, getting on with their lives. He wondered if they were going through any personal dramas, any demons causing them sleepless nights. Surely he wasn't the only one.

'I spoke to my old friend in the South Wales Police last night. I told her all about what's going on and she's going to look into Bryn and Jacqui Jones this morning when she gets to work.'

'Sorry?'

'Are you listening?'

'Yes. Sorry, just … that's good. In the meantime, I think we should try and find Jason Brown.'

Alex told Caroline about his meeting with Nick Marshall in the car park last night as they made their way to the hotel car park for Alex's Volvo.

'Why was he being so obstructive?' Caroline asked.

'I'm not sure. He said Diane should move on, but I got the impression he doesn't want it all brought back up. Part of me can understand it. He's married again, he's got two kids, but, at the end of the day, Zachery was his first-born child. You'd want to know what happened to him. I certainly would.'

'So would I. So, what, then, we leave Nick alone for now?' Caroline asked.

'For now, yes. Let's try to track down this Jason Brown bloke and see what that brings up. Also, can you think of a way of talking to Diane's sister in Australia without Diane knowing about it?'

'Not really. Why?'

'I'd love to know why they left England when they did. The *real* reason.'

'You think there's something fishy there?'

'Maybe I'm being paranoid but I like all my boxes ticked before I move on. I know someone at a university in Sydney. She used to teach criminal studies. I wonder if she could help.'

'Worth a call, at least.'

'Can I ask you a question?' Alex asked. They'd reached his car, each standing at either side. Alex was leaning across the roof.

'As long as it's not about me leaving the force.'

'No, nothing like that. When you first met Nick and Diane all those years ago, what did you think?'

'What did I think?' Caroline repeated, slightly taken aback by the question. 'Nothing, really. They were just ordinary grieving parents.'

'You didn't think they might have something to do with Zachery's disappearance?'

'What? No. I mean ... no, absolutely not. We had Jonathan arrested. Besides, if Diane had anything to do with it, she wouldn't have spent the last twenty-five years trying to find him, would she?'

'Nick hasn't been looking for twenty-five years, though, has he?'

'True.'

'Come on, let's go somewhere warm, I'm freezing my nuts off here,' Alex said, getting into the car.

'Turn the heating on.'

'I would if it worked properly. It seems to be on the blink.'

'I thought you were a multi-million-selling author?' Caroline asked, looking around the battered car.

'I am. We've been through a lot together, me and this car. She understands me.'

'I've never understood the relationship a man has with his car. Come on, I'll point you to a great café I know. It'll never win any awards, but they do an amazing full English.'

Alex's face lit up. His mood was beginning to lift already.

Chapter Twenty-Five

I didn't like my first solicitor, Henry Fitzroy. He always looked at me like I was something he'd stepped in. God knows why. If it wasn't for me, he wouldn't have got the fame and fortune he so desperately wanted. Once I was sentenced, I often saw little stories about myself in the news. I knew it was Fitzroy feeding the press. He was as big a leech as they were. I wonder how much they paid him? Probably just enough for him to buy a bottle of Scotch and block out his pathetic life for another night. I was pleased when I heard he'd died. A sad end to a sad man.

Then, in walked Lachlan Minnow. I'll never forget that first meeting. He was young, inexperienced, like a rabbit caught in the headlights, bless him. I'm afraid I allowed myself to have a little bit of fun with him in those early meetings. He was expecting to see a violent child-killing psychopath and I lived up to that description. I gave him lingering looks, nuggets of information that I knew would give him bad dreams. He couldn't get out of the meeting rooms quick enough. When you're in prison for life, you have to get your kicks from somewhere.

Eventually, I warmed to Lachlan. Who'd have thought it would be possible to like a solicitor? Behind those expensive suits and fifty-quid haircuts, I saw a more vulnerable side to him. He reminded me of myself. When I was growing up, I tried to come across as brash and confident. I *used to practise my swagger in my bedroom. But, inside, I was a quivering nervous wreck. Lachlan was the same. I asked him once why he became a solicitor. I could never picture him standing up in a courtroom arguing some poor bastard's case. He said he wanted to make a difference to people's lives. I didn't believe him.*

Lachlan visited me far more than Fitzroy ever did. There was no need for him to, but after my gran died, it seemed there was always another piece of paper to sign, or another document to discuss. I think he was making the most of these visits up. He probably just wanted another story to tell his friends.

One thing I didn't like about Lachlan, however, was that he was a smoker. You could see the yellow stains on his fingers and smell the stale odour on his expensive suits. I never liked the smell of smoke. My gran was a sixty-a-day woman. Filthy habit. I helped Lachlan quit. It took months, but it worked. We became quite close after that. The walls of client and solicitor came down. It was like we were friends. I had a friend. I liked that. I think Lachlan did, too. I imagined him to be quite fake among his colleagues; with me, he seemed relaxed and real. It's funny the way two seemingly completely different people can get on under surreal circumstances.

Chapter Twenty-Six

Once a month, Martha Wright organised a get-together for all the local families who were victims of Jonathan Egan-Walsh and sent a newsletter to all the members of Thirteen. Today, in her living room, Julie Richards, Belinda and Tobias Carver, Susan Phillips and Rebecca Maynard were gathered on the sofas. The coffee had been poured and the doughnuts passed around when the doorbell rang. Martha went to answer it.

'I didn't think you were coming,' she said as she ushered Diane into the house.

'I didn't know whether I should.'

'Why not?'

'Well, things are happening. You've seen the papers?'

'Yes. Look, come on in.'

Martha opened the door to the living room and almost had to push Diane inside. The five parents she knew so well all looked up at her from their seats, sympathetically.

'Diane was just saying she didn't think she should have come today.'

'That's ridiculous,' Tobias said, standing up and giving Diane his seat. 'You're as much a part of this as we all are.'

'Thank you,' she replied with a painted-on smile. 'But what if the reports are true? What if Jonathan didn't take Zachery? I'm not one of his victims then, am I?'

'You've been a victim for the past twenty-five years,' said Belinda, Tobias's wife. 'Whether he turns out to have taken Zachery or not, you've had to live with him in your head.'

'Belinda's right,' Martha said. 'We're not just going to cast you aside. We will help and support you in any way we can, right?' she asked the group.

'That's right. I sent an email to everyone the other day with an idea,' Susan said. 'And everyone agreed. We've set up one of those fundraising websites to raise money to help with the search for Zachery. You know, so you can hire that imaging equipment thing. I looked this morning and we've already passed the thousand-pound mark.'

Diane placed a hand on her chest. 'I don't know what to say.'

'You don't have to say anything. We're all in this together.'

'Now, that money is for you to do whatever you want with,' Martha said. 'Though, if you use it for a holiday, you'd better take us with you,' she added, laughing.

———

'I think I've found him,' Alex said, sitting back in his seat.

He and Caroline were still in the greasy spoon. Their plates were smeared with the remnants of a fry-up, cups had been drained and both felt satisfied after their delicious unhealthy breakfast and a strong cup of builder's tea. Around them, manual workers were fuelling themselves up for the long cold day ahead, working outdoors. Plates were piled high with fried eggs, greasy sausages and beans. Who cared if it was bad for you? This was the food you needed on a freezing day.

Alex passed his iPad to Caroline. 'What do you think?'

She looked at the Facebook page for a Jason Brown. He was a

local man, born in Ingoldmells, which was where Diane lived, and gave his former employer as British Gas. He was now a manager at a small caravan park on the outskirts of town.

'He fits the description,' Caroline said. She clicked on his profile photo. He was bald, with a heavy build, and squinted against the sun into the camera. 'The way Diane was talking, I was expecting Lemony Snicket. He doesn't look especially weird. I wonder why Zachery thought he was. Mind you, kids pick up on all kinds of things, don't they? My son used to cry every time Jamie's brother picked him up when he was a baby. It didn't make him a serial killer – just the butt of many jokes over the years,' she said with a smile.

'You have a lot of fish-and-chip shops here, don't you?' Alex said, staring out of the window at three of them in a row opposite.

Caroline smiled. 'In the summer, this place is buzzing. All those shops will be packed. There'll be queues out into the street.'

'Really?'

'Don't turn your nose up. I bet even Florida looks dead in the middle of winter.'

'I don't think it ever gets this cold in Florida; not for six months of the year, anyway.'

'According to the news this morning, it's going to get worse. There's a cold blast coming in from Siberia. The Beast from the East, they're calling it.'

'Isn't that what they call the fans of the local football team around here?' Alex asked with a smirk.

'Cheeky sod. Look, were you even listening to what I was saying?'

'Yes.'

'Good. Fancy a trip to Chapel St Leonards?'

The caravan park was closed for the winter and looked completely abandoned. Even under *her* thick layers, Caroline shivered as a strong wind blew in from the coast. Alex had put on a beanie hat and a pair of mismatched gloves he'd found in the glove box. They made their way on foot to the site office, which sat in front of a sea of white caravans, all neatly lined up like gravestones.

Alex said, 'I've never understood the fascination with people staying in a caravan. For the majority of the year, they live in spacious houses but, for their holidays, they choose to cram themselves into a baked-bean tin. Where's the pleasure in that?'

'I've had some fun holidays in a caravan. The first one me and Jamie had on our own was very memorable,' Caroline said with a twinkle in her eye.

'Too much information,' Alex joked, before knocking hard on the door of the Portakabin and waiting for a reply.

When one didn't come, he tried the handle. The door was unlocked, so he pushed it open and they both stepped inside. The office was bland – grey, hard-wearing carpet, beige walls, brown chipboard desks. It wasn't welcoming but it was warm, thanks to storage heaters dotted about the room. They both went to one to help thaw the blood in their veins.

A toilet flushed in a side room and a chubby man stepped out. Jason Brown.

'We're shut. We reopen next month,' he said, his local accent strong, as he sat down at one of the desks.

'Jason Brown?' Alex asked.

'Aye.'

'Did you used to work with a Nick Marshall at British Gas? About twenty-five years ago?'

'Who wants to know?' he asked, looking confused.

'Alex Frost, I'm a journalist. I'm looking into the disappearance of Nick and Diane's son, Zachery.'

'And who's she?' Jason asked, nodding towards Caroline, who was now rubbing her hands together to warm them up.

'She's my assistant,' Alex said as he looked back at Caroline.

He gave her a wink. 'New evidence has come to light that suggests Jonathan Egan-Walsh may not have had anything to do with Zachery's disappearance.'

'Oh,' was all Jason said, though his eyes widened and he licked his lips. He adjusted himself on his chair awkwardly.

'Do you mind if we ask you a few questions?' Alex asked, rummaging in his satchel for his notebook.

'I don't know. I'm very busy.'

'Doing what? I thought you were shut. We won't take long. Ten minutes, at the most.'

'Go on, then. If you're quick. I've still got stuff to do.'

'Right,' Alex said, pulling up a chair and sitting down opposite Jason's desk. 'Now, you worked with Nick at British Gas, didn't you?'

'Well, I didn't actually work with him. We were there at the same time.'

'Not in the same department?'

'No. I was a meter reader. I was always out on the road.'

'So, how did you first meet him?'

'Dunno,' he shrugged.

'I understand, you saw him out of work? In what capacity?'

'What do you mean?'

'As friends?' Caroline asked. She was still standing in front of the heater. 'What did you have in common that made you friends?'

'Dunno. We both had a season ticket for Lincoln City.'

Caroline rolled her eyes. 'That doesn't make you best mates, though, does it? I'm guessing thousands of people have got a season ticket for Lincoln City.'

'I wouldn't go that far,' Alex said as an aside with a smile on his face.

'We just got talking one day. We got on.'

'Did you go round to Nick's house often?' Alex asked.

'Sometimes.'

'Why?'

'We were friends. It's what you do.'

'Did he ever go to your house?'

'No. I was only about twenty back then. I still lived at home.'

'Did you ever see Nick's children?'

'Yes.'

'What did you think?'

'About what?'

'About the children,' Alex replied, getting annoyed.

'Nothing. They were just kids. They seemed nice.'

'What about Diane?'

'What about her?' he asked, shuffling in his chair again, which groaned under his weight.

'Jason, you're not giving me much, here.'

'I don't know what you want me to say,' he said, getting flustered.

'Jason, did you ever go to Nick's house when he wasn't there?' Caroline asked.

'What? No. Why would I?' he answered quickly.

Caroline studied him. 'You did, didn't you?'

He looked away. 'I might have done. Once or twice.'

'Why would you do that if Nick wasn't there?' Alex asked.

'Were you having an affair with Diane Marshall?' Caroline quickly asked.

'What? No …' Jason replied with a laugh.

'OK, so maybe "affair" is too strong a word,' Caroline said, stepping forward to the desk. 'But have slept with her?'

'No. Like I said, I was only about twenty. She was in her forties.'

'When Zachery Marshall went missing, Diane was only thirty-three. Jason, did you sleep with Diane Marshall?' Caroline asked. She suddenly felt like she was back in a police interview room.

'Yes!' he almost shouted.

'How many times?'

'I don't know. I didn't keep count.'

'Over how long?'

'I can't remember, honestly. It stopped after Zachery disappeared, though. She said it was her fault he'd gone missing: It was her punishment, like.'

'You were with her, weren't you? On the afternoon of 10 January 1993, you were in the house with Diane when Zachery went out on his bike.'

Jason nodded.

'You're the one who called Nick twice during Sunday lunch. Why did you do that?'

He shook his head in shame and squeezed the bridge of his nose tight. 'I told him there was a problem at work. I'd been working on Saturday collecting meter readings. I'd sometimes go in on a Sunday to submit my readings. I called Nick and said there was a problem with one of the computers. He told me what to do over the phone to fix it. I called him back about fifteen minutes later telling him it hadn't worked.'

'There was nothing wrong with the computer, was there?'

'No. I just wanted to get him out of the house. I told him I couldn't stay. He said he'd pop along after he'd had his dinner to look into it. I parked around the corner and waited for his car to leave the street. I noticed he had one of the kids in the front with him.'

'That would have been Marcus.'

Jason nodded. 'I went round the back of the house so none of the neighbours would see me. Diane was looking for me through the bedroom window. As soon as she saw I was there, she sent Zachery out to play, before letting me in.'

'How long were you there for?' Alex asked.

'About an hour, maybe.'

'Zachery hadn't come back when you left?'

'No.'

'Did you see him at all, as you were driving away?'

'No. The roads were empty. It was Sunday and cold. There was nobody about.'

'Diane said that Zachery thought you were weird. Why would he think that?'

Jason laughed. 'I suppose I was weird. I didn't know how to act when I was around there. I was sleeping with Diane, yet I was in the house acting as Nick's friend. I knew what I was doing was wrong, but, well, you know …'

'It was fun,' Alex finished Jason's sentence. He nodded.

'Where did you go on that Sunday after you'd slept with Diane?' Caroline asked.

'I went straight home.'

'Can anyone confirm that?'

'My mum and dad were at home. Well, my dad's dead now, but my mum will be able to tell you.'

'What do you think happened to Zachery?' Alex asked.

'I don't know. I felt bad, you know, that I was with his mum while God only knows what was happening to him.'

'Did Nick know about the affair?'

'No. I don't think so. He never said, if he did. You're not going to tell him now, are you?'

'To be honest with you, Jason, I don't know what's going to come out in all this,' Alex said, closing his notebook. 'However, I'd prepare yourself for a shit-storm, if I were you.'

———

Alex and Caroline returned to the car in silence. Once they were inside, Alex turned on the heater but nothing happened.

'She'll work in the summer,' he said.

'Well, it's safe to say, I wasn't expecting that,' Caroline said.

'You can understand why she hasn't been able to let go. She's blamed herself for twenty-five years.'

'Why didn't she tell us, though? She knew we'd talk to Jason. She's not daft. Surely, she knew we'd find out about the affair.'

'Maybe she's embarrassed about it.'

'After all this time? Who actually cares? We're not here to judge the state of her marriage. Although, from the way she's spoken, I always got the impression the marriage broke down because of the struggle with Zachery going missing, then *Nick* having an affair. Maybe it all started from this.'

'Perhaps she didn't tell us because Nick never found out about it.'

'Well, it's all come out now,' Caroline said. 'I can't believe she didn't tell us. We're going to have to talk to her about it, see if she's keeping anything else from us.'

'Do you mind if I leave you to have that conversation with her?'

'All girls together?'

'Something like that.'

Caroline laughed. 'You've gone white. You can interview serial killers but you can't ask a woman why she was unhappy?'

'I don't do emotions.'

'Really? I bet your wife loves you.' Caroline smiled.

Alex's face dropped. He looked at Caroline with an icy glare.

'Shit. Alex, I'm sorry. I didn't mean to …'

'No. It's all right,' he said quickly.

'It was a slip of the tongue.'

'I know. Don't worry about it,' Alex said with a painful smile. 'Look, let's get you back to Skegness. You can talk to Diane and I'll do some more digging, maybe buy myself a few jumpers,' he added with a shiver.

With that, he started the engine and pulled away, indicating left towards the dual carriageway. Whenever his wife was mentioned, Alex always felt guilty that he was out living life and working while she was, literally, trapped at home. He always felt the need to call home, see how she was doing. If he were being honest with himself, he knew he really wanted to go back to London, so he could climb into bed next to her and hold her. The only problem was, she couldn't hold him back.

Chapter Twenty-Seven

On her way home, Diane felt buoyed by the Thirteen meeting. She didn't know why she'd been so nervous about attending. She knew these people. They'd been connected for more than twenty years. She should have known they'd be supportive. As she thought of the fundraising they were doing for her, she felt choked up again and wanted to cry, but stopped herself. It was the first time in ages that she felt like she had friends, genuine friends who would always be there for her.

Once home, she flicked on the kettle and decided to make herself a proper meal for tea instead of something out of a can. The landline rang. She went into the living room to answer it, but it stopped ringing before she picked it up. She dialled 1471 but the caller had withheld their number. It was probably a sales call from the Far East; it usually was.

She was back in the kitchen, chopping an onion when the phone rang again. She sighed, wiped her hands, and went into the living room. Again, it stopped ringing before she reached it. Again, the caller had withheld their number. Diane frowned at the annoyance but didn't think anything of it. Ten minutes later, it happened again. And again.

On the seventh time, she had been waiting by the phone, willing it to ring.

As soon as it did, she picked it up.

'Hello,' she said firmly.

There was no reply, but she could hear someone on the other end. There was a faint sound of breathing.

'Who's there?' she asked. 'I know there's someone there, so you may as well tell me who you are.'

Again, there was no reply.

'People like you disgust me. Is this how you get your kicks? You're sick, do you know that?'

The caller hung up. Diane slammed the receiver down. There was a loud bang on the front door, which made her jump. She ran into the hallway and pulled the door wide open but there was nobody there. She went out into the twilight and stood on the doorstep, looking around her. She shivered in the breeze and pulled her cardigan tightly around her. Everywhere was quiet. She couldn't even hear the faint roar of the sea like she usually could. It must be a quiet sea tonight. Lights were on in her neighbours' homes, cars were in the driveways and life was ticking along as normal. She heard childish laughter and saw two young boys running down the alley at the end of the close.

'I know who you are,' Diane shouted. 'I'm going to have a word with your mother next time I see her.'

When Diane was a child, she and her friends used to knock on people's doors and run away. To her, it was fun. Now, she realised just how bloody annoying it was. She closed the door, put on the security chain, shot the bolts at the top and bottom, before returning to the kitchen to cook her meal. The makings of a cottage pie were laid out on the counter but she no longer felt like eating. Whoever had been calling had unnerved her.

A little while later, as she was sitting in the living room with a cup of tea and a packet of biscuits – substitute for her evening meal – half-watching television, the doorbell rang, making Diane jump again. Afraid to answer it this time, she muted the TV, went over to the window and, carefully, peeled back the curtains to look out. She relaxed audibly when she saw Caroline Turner on the doorstep.

'Hello, hope you don't mind me calling unannounced. I'm not interrupting your tea, am I?' Caroline asked, shivering on the doorstep.

'No. I've not even thought of cooking yet,' she lied. 'Come in. I'm just having a cup of tea. Do you want one?'

'I'd love one. Alex's car is bloody freezing. I think I'll still be shivering come summer.'

They went into the living room and Caroline stood in front of the fire to warm herself up while Diane headed for the kitchen to make another cup of tea. While she was waiting, Caroline looked at the photographs on the wall. It was difficult to ignore them, as they were everywhere. Whenever she saw Zachery, she thought of her own son when he was that age. In another universe, Dylan could have been one of Jonathan's victims. She shuddered at the thought. Would she and Jamie have survived such a tragedy, or would they have divorced as Diane and Nick had? She couldn't imagine life without Jamie by her side.

Diane returned with the tea and Caroline sat down on the armchair next to her. She kept her coat on and held the mug firmly in both hands. Slowly, she was beginning to thaw. On the drive over, she had been ruminating how to best broach the subject of Diane having had an affair with Jason Brown. It wasn't the easiest of topics to bring up. In the end, she decided to be blunt and just ask. When she did, Diane almost spat her tea out.

'I should have known this was going to come up. I just hoped it wouldn't, I suppose.'

'It might have,' Caroline said.

'I bet you think I'm a bad mother now, don't you?'

'No, not at all. You had your reasons for the affair.'

'It wasn't an affair. It was just … a fling. It was just sex. There was never any chance of me leaving Nick for him. Jason and I didn't even talk about that.'

'Why did you do it?'

Diane took a deep breath. 'I was thirty-two when we started. I'd put on a bit of weight. Me and Nick had stopped sleeping together and, suddenly, this twenty-year-old is chatting me up. I felt attractive again.'

'Who initiated it?'

'He did. I didn't even try to stop him. He was good looking, fit, everything was firm. It was nice to hold a young body again. He made me feel like a woman. It was just a bit of fun. If I knew what it would lead to, I would never have allowed it to develop like it did.'

'Diane, you can't think you're to blame for Zachery going missing?'

'Can't I? I sent him out on his bike. He didn't want to go because it was cold. I told him to put his coat and gloves on and wrap up warm. I forced him out of the house, so I could fuck a twenty-year-old. What does that say about me? Of course I'm to blame.' She started crying. She held herself firm and began rocking back and forth. 'If I'd been a better wife and mother he would still be alive today.'

Caroline leaned forward and took Diane's hand in hers. She held it tight. 'Diane, we can't live our lives on the basis of what-ifs. We do what we think is right at the time. If we worried about the potential consequences, we'd never leave the house. Nobody could possibly have known Zachery was going to disappear, and it wasn't because you were having an affair. It was just something that happened.'

'I can't believe that.'

'Why not?'

'Because I'm a bad mother. I deserve all this pain. It's my punishment. I'm just sorry that Zachery had to go through whatever he suffered.'

'Diane, if you continue thinking like that, it's going to kill you.'

'Look at me, do you think this is living? I'm waiting until I know what happened to Zachery. Once I know, I can let go.'

'What do you mean?'

'You know exactly what I mean.'

Chapter Twenty-Eight

Jamie Turner wasn't happy. Caroline had arrived home at a decent hour with a shopping bag laden with ingredients, saying she was going to cook him a special meal they could eat together. She spent over an hour in the kitchen roasting a chicken and making Yorkshire pudding and doing the potatoes just how he liked them. Then, within five minutes of sitting down to enjoy the feast, Caroline's mobile had burst into song. She looked at the display and answered, running out of the room without the hint of an apology. For a while, Jamie sat in silence, waiting for his wife to return. After a few minutes, he decided to tuck in. It would be her fault if her dinner went cold and the gravy congealed.

'Guess who that was,' Caroline said as she came into the kitchen after half an hour. There was a distinct spring in her step.

'Your journalist friend?' he asked from the sink as he was scrubbing a saucepan.

'No. Sarah Daley. From Wales. She's got some information for me about Bryn Jones.'

'Really.'

'You don't sound interested.'

'That's probably because I'm not. You said we were going to have a nice meal together. Just the two of us. Then your phone rings and out you go.'

'I'm sorry. Did you eat yours?'

'Yes, I did.'

'Well, there you are, then. I cooked it for you.'

'I thought you cooked it for us.'

'Jamie, you know—' She stopped.

'Go on,' he prompted. Caroline didn't say anything so he continued the sentence for her. '"You know what it's like when I have a case on." That's what you were going to say, wasn't it?'

'No.'

'Caroline.'

'All right, yes, it was. I'm sorry. Look, Jamie, you know how I miss being on the force. I've spent more than a decade walking dogs and this is my final stab at being a detective.'

'How many more times, Caroline, you're not—'

'A detective, I know, but I can still do this. I know I can.'

'What do you expect to get out of this? Do you think the chief constable is going to phone you up and ask you back to investigate cold cases?'

'Of course not.'

'Is that what you want? To be back at the station, working long hours, coming home when it's dark, going to work when it's dark, hardly seeing me? You said you wouldn't let this consume you. You promised me.'

'I can't help it, Jamie. This is what I do.'

'No. You're a dog walker now.'

'No, I'm a detective!' she snapped. '*And* I'm a bloody good one. And I'm going to keep on digging until I find out what happened to Zachery Marshall, whether you like it or not.' Caroline stormed out of the kitchen, slamming the door behind her.

'Caroline, can I come in?' Jamie asked, knocking tentatively on their bedroom door.

'It's your room as much as it is mine,' she said, icily.

'I'm sorry,' he said. 'I'm worried, that's all.'

'How many more times do I have to tell you? There's nothing for you to worry about,' she replied, turning around on the bed to look at him.

'There is. The last time you interviewed someone, you were almost killed. I could have lost you. I don't want that to happen again.'

'It won't.'

'You don't know that.' Jamie sat on the edge of the bed and held out his hand for Caroline to hold. They linked fingers. 'I was so proud of you being in the police force. I never thought about what kind of dangerous job it could be until you were attacked. When you said you were leaving, I was so relieved, I could finally stop worrying. When you set up the dog-walking business, you seemed content. I thought you were happy.'

'I was. I am. But I'm a detective, Jamie. It's in my blood. It's what I love.'

'But what if you get attacked again?'

'I won't.'

'You don't know that.'

'Will you stop saying that?' She jumped up from the bed and went to look out of the window. 'You're right. I don't know what will happen. But if something does, I hope you'll be there to help me pick up the pieces.'

'You shouldn't put yourself in that position in the first place.'

'I'm not going around looking for trouble.'

'You said yourself, you don't know what this is going to uncover. You could get yourself into something you can't get out of.'

'I'm not doing this on my own. I've got Alex, and Diane.'

'Do you honestly think Alex is going to protect you? He's a journalist. He's there to write about it, not get stuck into the action.'

'You don't know him like I do.'

Jamie took a breath. He went to his wife and put his arms around her. 'Caroline, you're not a detective any more,' he said quietly.

'I know. I'm a sixty-year-old dog walker with rapidly greying hair and bunions.'

'Is that what this is about, age?'

'No!' she snapped. 'You don't understand, do you? You're happy to go out and play golf, go to craft fairs at the weekend and spend the evenings in front of the telly, but I'm not. Not for another twenty years, anyway. I may be sixty, but I'm not *dead*.'

'And you think I am?'

'No … Look, this is not about you or me, it's about justice. It's about finding Zachery Marshall. It's about saving Diane from killing herself.'

'And what about us?'

'What about us?'

'Where do we fit into your new life of running around the country trying to solve crimes?'

'It's just this one time,' she said, slowly, trying to get him to understand. 'Once I've found out what happened to Zachery, I'm back walking the dogs.'

'And what if Alex Frost calls you up with an exciting new story he's working on?'

'He won't.'

'You don't know that.'

'You don't understand,' she said, frustrated at not being able to get through to him. She picked up a pillow and removed her nightie from underneath.

'What are you doing?'

'I'm sleeping in the spare bedroom.'

'Oh, don't be ridiculous.'

She grabbed her dressing gown from the bottom of the bed and headed for the door. 'Oh, and another thing, you'll have to feed yourself this weekend because I'm going to Wales.' She left the bedroom, closing the door behind her.

Chapter Twenty-Nine

'Can I be cheeky and ask if I can use your dining room as an office?' Alex asked Diane as he stood on the doorstep with a small bunch of flowers in his hand.

Diane gave a genuinely warm smile for the first time in ages. She took the flowers from him and stepped to one side to allow him to enter. 'Of course you can.'

'Thank you. It makes sense. All the information is here, you have central heating, and I'm getting funny looks from the staff in coffee shops for spending all day in there.'

He went into the dining room and placed his satchel on the floor. He removed his coat, revealing his new clothing. Diane sniggered.

'What's the matter?'

'You've left the tag on your sweater.' She went over to a drawer and took out a pair of scissors. She cut off the tag and handed it to him.

'Thank you. I thought I'd got them all.'

He looked up at the maps, where all the victims were clearly marked. Diane stood behind him.

'The scale of Jonathan's crimes never fails to shock me,' he said. 'How can one man cause so much pain and suffering?'

'I know. You spoke to him more than anyone. Do you think he was born evil, or did he become evil?'

Alex turned to her. 'Wow, that's a loaded question. I'm not sure if anyone can be *born* evil.'

'I'm reading your book, finally,' she said. 'He didn't have the best start in life.'

'No, he didn't.'

'But it sounds like his grandmother loved him.'

'She says she did. But she was also very harsh. She gave him strict curfews, vetted who he could play with. There's a story my editor removed from the book because it couldn't be verified and he was worried about being sued.' Alex pulled out a chair and sat down. Diane did the same. 'When he was twelve years old, Jonathan was caught by his gran performing a sex act on a child of a neighbour. She went ballistic. She hit him, screamed at him, called him every name under the sun. He told her that he'd learned what to do from the man who ran the local paper shop. Jonathan had a paper round there and this man was abusing him.'

'Bloody hell!'

'His gran went round to the shop, all guns blazing, but the man denied it, obviously. But she was convinced that Jonathan's story was true. She just couldn't prove it. The worst part is, when she questioned Jonathan about why he hadn't told her the man was abusing him, he told her it was because he enjoyed it.'

'He enjoyed being abused?' Diane asked, a disgusted look on her face.

'He didn't see it as abuse. The man in the paper shop had told Jonathan it's what people do to each other when they like them, when they have feelings for them. It was the first time anyone had ever told Jonathan they liked him. His father had abandoned him, his mother was dead, and his grandmother was a bit of a cold fish.

This bloke saw his opportunity, saw what Jonathan was missing, and manipulated his way into justifying his actions.'

'But why wasn't any of this brought up at the trial?'

'There was no proof. Nobody else complained about the paper-shop man. What we have to ask is: was what Jonathan did to his victims a continuation of his abuse, or, in his eyes, was he loving them the same way he believed the paper-shop man loved him?'

Diane remained silent. She looked at the map on the wall, at the faces of the thirteen boys looking back down at her.

'I've never been able to understand why someone who is abused would go on to abuse others,' she said, emotion in her voice.

'They don't see it as abuse. Jonathan didn't.'

'But that alone reveals something seriously strange about Jonathan. How many normal twelve-year-olds enjoy having a man more than twice their age perform sex acts on them? It defies belief,' she said, a look of disgust still on her face.

'These adults are incredibly manipulative. We can only assume that this newsagent told Jonathan exactly what he wanted to hear. He made him feel loved, wanted, something that had never happened to him before. That's why he enjoyed it.'

'Heavy stuff,' Diane said to fill the silence that descended. 'Oh, by the way, I've dug out some scrapbooks,' she added, changing the subject slightly, 'I thought you might want to see them.' With that, she went over to the sideboard, took out the books and placed them in front of Alex. 'They're newspaper clippings from the time Zachery went missing and around the time of the trial. I don't know why I saved them. I've never looked at them.'

Alex placed his hand on top of the books. 'Thanks,' he said quietly.

'I'll make us some tea,' she said, then, leaving the room quickly, not wanting to see the banner headlines screaming out of the pages at her.

Alex opened the top scrapbook and began scanning the

articles: SEVEN-YEAR-OLD MISSING. It was a simple headline but, looking back at it after twenty-five years, it packed a punch. One little boy had gone missing, but he was part of a much bigger picture. Whether he suffered at the hands of Jonathan or not, he was involved in one of the most prolific serial-killing cases Britain had ever witnessed.

'Jesus!' Alex said, placing a hand against his chest.

'What is it?' Diane asked, re-entering the room, carrying a tray.

'This photo. I thought it was Caroline,' he replied, pointing to an article after the trial detailing Jonathan's background. 'It's Jonathan's mother.'

'Oh, yes. I never realised that before. Same hairstyle, too,' she said. 'You'll have to show Caroline – she'll hate it,' she added with a smile.

Alex continued to flick through the pages of the scrapbook. The articles became smaller as time went on. Other children went missing, their bodies eventually found. The aftermath of their murder made for more interesting reading than a child who was still missing. Zachery was an unanswered question.

The doorbell rang, making them both jump.

'That'll probably be Caroline. I told her I was coming here.'

Alex went about setting up his iPad and arranging his papers, while Diane answered the door. He heard an animated conversation coming from the hallway before the door was swung open and Caroline charged into the room.

'Why are men complete knobheads?'

'I hope you're not including me in that generalisation.' He said, closing the scrapbook and pushing it to one side.

'No. I'm talking about a retired optician who thinks I should stay at home and wait for him to come back from golf and greet him with a pair of slippers and a cake in the oven.'

'Oh. I didn't realise you'd married a man from the fifties,' Alex said, smiling.

'Neither did I. Since he retired, he seems to have aged twenty years. I'm so angry right now, I could scream.' She looked up at Diane and Alex. 'Sorry, you don't want to hear this, do you?'

'I don't mind, actually,' Diane said. 'It's nice hearing other voices in the house.'

'I'd be careful what you say, Diane. Caroline might ask to sleep in your spare bedroom.'

'You'd be more than welcome.'

'No. I'm sorry. I shouldn't have burst in like this. Anyway, what are you two doing this weekend? Fancy a trip to Wales?'

'Wales? Why?' Alex asked.

'I heard from Sarah last night. She's got some information for us about Bryn Jones. It was too much to go into detail over the phone, so I said I'd pop over.'

'Well, yes, if you think the travelling will be worth it.'

'Excellent. Diane?'

'I'd love to, but Marcus has invited my mum and me over to his house for a meal,' she said, beaming with pride. 'It's Greta's birthday. We're having a sort of party. I don't want to turn it down.'

'No, that's fine. I'm pleased things seem to be working out for you.'

'Well, it's early days. We're on speaking terms, that's the main thing. I've messed up so much over the years. There's a lot of ground to make up. That reminds me, I need to buy her a birthday card. Do you mind if I leave you here?'

'No. Go ahead.'

'Help yourself to anything in the kitchen while I'm gone,' Diane said, scurrying out of the room.

'So, just you and me, then,' said Caroline. 'I'll book us a couple of rooms in a cheap hotel.'

For the rest of the morning, Alex worked on what he was going to question Bryn and Jacqui Jones about, while Caroline searched the Internet for a hotel. On her return from the shops, Diane supplied refreshments, and any information that Alex needed about her former neighbours.

Currently, both were sitting at the dining table. 'When Zachery first went missing, your husband organised a search and got all the neighbours involved. Did Bryn join that search?' Alex asked her.

Diane frowned and bit her bottom lip while she thought. 'I don't know. I was in the house crying my eyes out. I honestly can't remember.'

'Who was in the house with you while the search was taking place?'

'My mum and my sister came over. Geraldine, who used to live on the corner, she came round, too.'

'Not Jacqui?'

'No.'

'Why not?'

'I'm not sure,' she said with a heavy frown.

Alex leaned forward. 'I mean … you saw her earlier that day. You were good friends. Surely, she would have been round here to offer support.'

'Well, I would have thought so, but she didn't. At the time, I didn't think anything of it, my mind was all over the place.'

'That's understandable. I'm just finding them to be a very odd-sounding couple, from what I'm learning about them. Did they have any children of their own?'

'No. I don't think Jacqui could. Or maybe he couldn't. There was a reason why, but I can't remember.'

'Caroline, did you know anything about the Joneses?' he asked, turning round. 'I know you weren't involved in the case surrounding Zachery's disappearance, but it would be really useful to know if either of them gave a statement.'

Caroline looked up from Alex's iPad.

'I don't remember their names coming up in any of the files, and I couldn't tell you whether or not they were interviewed, but I've been in touch with Siobhan Gardner, a DI based at Lincolnshire Police HQ in Nettleham. She's agreed to see me. So, fingers crossed, she'll let me have access to the files.'

Diane looked uncomfortable. 'Are you considering Bryn and Jacqui as serious suspects?'

Alex let out a heavy sigh. 'At the moment, Diane, I don't know. There are just a lot of question marks surrounding them. And I don't like loose ends.'

Diane shivered. 'They were in my home. They babysat my children. It makes me sick just thinking—'

'Diane, until we know anything concrete, don't think like that,' Caroline interrupted.

'You're right. I don't know how you can do what you do every day. You see people at their worst,' Diane said to Caroline. 'Don't you ever wish you were writing a happy story?' she then directed to Alex.

'I was once sent to interview a couple who'd won five million on the Lottery. My editor wanted a piece several months down the line to see how it had changed their lives. Since winning, they'd divorced, he'd turned to drink and practically lost all his money, and she was miserable on her own in a six-bedroom house. Even happy stories can turn sour.'

It was starting to go dark around four o'clock. They decided to finish for the day, so Caroline and Alex could each go and pack a few things ahead of their impending trip to South Wales. Diane asked them to keep her informed then wished them a safe journey as they headed to their respective cars.

'Bloody hell!' Alex exclaimed suddenly.

'What's the matter?' Caroline called back.

'Some bastard's slashed my tyres.'

'*What?*'

It was difficult to see in the poor light, so Alex took a torch from his glove box and shone it on the front-left tyre. There was a huge gash in the side of it.

'Look at that! I only had these put on a few months ago.'

'Shit! We can use mine to go to Wales.'

'That's not the point, though. Who would have done this? And why? You don't know where the nearest garage is, do you?'

'Is there a problem?' Diane called from the front doorstep.

'Alex has had his tyres slashed.'

Diane didn't say anything, but her mind went immediately back to those silent phone calls she'd had the night before.

Chapter Thirty

Peter Wright was found on the day before Christmas Eve 1992. I was pleased with that. His mother had him home for Christmas. For a while, I was beginning to think he'd never be found. I took him in the May and had to take him back in September. I remember watching the news coverage of his mother and father being led into the police station. They were supported by friends and family. I remember thinking at the time that as soon as the news cameras lose interest, they'll move on. Poor Martha and Leon will be left to deal with their grief alone. I wonder what happened to them. Did they split up? Did one of them turn to drink while the other became hooked on anti-depressants? I wish I'd had more of an interest in the fallout. All I did was send poor Martha and Leon a sympathy card, like I did with all the parents. Anonymously, of course.

Christmas 1992 was a strange one. I had lunch with my gran. We watched the Queen's Christmas Message (no talking while it was on). Then we exchanged crappy presents. I gave my gran a Teasmade. She was having problems getting up and down stairs, so I thought it would be nice for her to have a cuppa before getting out of bed in the mornings. She didn't seem too thrilled by the gift. Typical. I can't remember what she gave me.

Afterwards, I left, and went for a drive. I wanted to spend a few *hours with Ed. That wasn't his real name. I had no idea what his real name was. He didn't speak a word of English. He was one of the world's lost children. I found him begging on the streets of Norfolk. He was cold and shivering. I offered to buy him a Happy Meal and asked if he wanted a bed for the night. He couldn't understand what I was saying so I drew a picture of a bed on a napkin. He smiled and nodded, so I took him in the van.*

I had to wash him first. He was filthy. I think he enjoyed the hot water of the bath. He probably hated feeling grubby. I thought I would have to throw his clothes away. They were grimy, heavily stained, torn in places, but they came up fine after a few cycles in the washing machine. I liked his little woolly jumper and his cargo jeans. His parka was proper old-style.

I asked him several times where he was from. He did say but I'd never heard of the place, probably somewhere in Eastern Europe.

He didn't cry the first time. He'd probably been through all this before. How else was a young boy going to survive on the streets of twentieth-century England? He was a good-looking boy, someone was bound to have taken advantage of him before I came along. At least I was offering him food and a warm bed to sleep in and not just a quick hand job in the back of a car.

Unfortunately, that's what put me off Ed. He was used goods. Someone had been there before me. I let him have Christmas and New Year to relax in a soft bed, have regular baths and meals and, then, on 2 January, I drugged him and threw him into the North Sea. I wonder where he washed up, if he washed up. Like it really matters.

Eight days later, Zachery Marshall went missing …

Chapter Thirty-One

Caroline dropped Alex off at his hotel and said she'd pick him up in half an hour. It was enough time for him to have a quick shower, get a change of clothes and pack a bag. She went home to do the same and was pleased to find an empty house. Jamie was probably in a bar with a golfing friend, knocking back the lager and bad-mouthing her to anyone who'd listen.

She left a note telling him where she would be. She didn't want to sound petty, so ended it by telling him to look after himself, that the ham in the fridge would need to be eaten by the end of the weekend or it would be no good, then added a couple of kisses.

Before she left, she stood in the doorway to their living room and looked around. She pictured them both curled up together on the sofa watching a BBC4 Nordic crime drama, or laughing at repeats of *Father Ted*. She loved Jamie. Why couldn't he realise this was something she needed to do? She wasn't being selfish, she was doing what she always did – putting other people first: Diane, Zachery, Dylan. She was doing it so all those demons in her mind would be laid to rest.

Alex was waiting for her on the pavement outside the hotel. He was wearing a new winter jacket and decent walking shoes. His bobbly beanie hat was the same, as were the faded black jeans.

'Nice coat,' Caroline said when he climbed into the car and closed the door behind him. 'You've obviously given the credit card a hammering,' she added with a smile.

'I can put it all on expenses.' He grinned.

'Are you ready?'

'I am. How long do you think it'll take us to get there?'

'Satnav says about four and a half hours, traffic permitting,' she said, pulling out into the main road and heading for the motorway.

'If you want me to take over driving, just let me know.'

'I'm not sure you'll be able to handle a modern car. This has power steering, a heater that works, heated seats, built-in satnav—'

'Yes, all right,' Alex interrupted. 'I don't see any point in getting another car until I have to. Like I said, she's been good to me over the years.'

'Did you contact a garage about yours?'

'Yes. They're going to collect it from Diane's driveway. I'd love to know who slashed my tyres.'

'Probably kids messing about.'

'I never did anything like that as a child.'

'I'm sure you rebelled at some point.'

'I probably did, but I didn't go around destroying other people's property.'

Once on the road, the conversation dried up. Alex sat back in the seat and allowed the heated leather to envelop him. He was comfortable. He could feel himself nodding off.

'What was the tirade all about this morning?' he asked.

'What tirade?'

'Calling all men knobheads. I'm guessing you've had a row with Jamie.'

'He doesn't think I should be doing this,' she said, keeping her eyes on the road.

'Why not?'

'It's a long story.'

'We've got a few hours. Plenty of time to share.'

'Towards the end of my career as a detective, I wasn't the easiest person to live with: I was quiet, moody, I snapped all the time. Looking back, I'm surprised Jamie didn't file for divorce. I think he's worried I'll return to those dark days.'

'You don't have to do this, you know. I've worked by myself practically all my working life.'

'No, I need to do this.'

'Why? You've nothing to prove.'

'I know I haven't. It's just ... I don't know. I can't explain it.'

'What are you wanting to achieve from all this? Do you want Jonathan to be guilty of Zachery's murder, or someone else?'

'I don't know. I want Diane to be able to get an answer. It's not about me.'

'You'll have had other difficult cases in your career. Why has this one drawn you back into the fold?'

'It's unfinished business. There are other victims out there. I know it.'

'But Zachery might not be one of them. If he isn't, are you still going to keep looking?'

Caroline didn't reply. She couldn't.

When Alex realised he wasn't going to get any further, he sat back and looked out of the window. It was fully dark now and the landscape had disappeared. All he could see was his own reflection looking back at him. And from where he was sitting, it wasn't a pretty sight.

The hotel door opened just wide enough to squeeze through. The door was quickly closed and locked. The room was already a mess. The bed was unmade, dirty clothes were thrown into a corner and drawers left open.

From their rucksack, the figure removed two copies of *The Collector* by Alex Frost. With leather-gloved hands, they began tearing pages out of the books and throwing them around the room. By the time they'd finished, pages covered the bed, the carpet and the furniture. The intruder took a marker pen from their back pocket and went over to the mirror by the en-suite. In big block capitals, they wrote: NEXT TIME IT WON'T BE JUST YOUR TYRES I'LL SLASH.

Surveying the wreckage, the vandal went to the door, looked through the spy hole to make sure the coast was clear, left the room, closing the door quietly, and placed the DO NOT DISTURB sign on its handle.

Chapter Thirty-Two

By the time Caroline and Alex arrived in Wales, it was close to 9.30PM – some four and a half hours after they'd left Skegness. They were both tired and hungry, and ached in places they didn't think it was possible to ache. The hotel was generic, bright, airy and lacking in character. It was a world away from The Majestic, though. They went to their respective rooms, deciding to freshen up and then try to find somewhere to go to eat. It was getting late, but they didn't care if it was a Michelin-starred restaurant or a run-down fish-and-chip shop with Health & Safety violations – they just needed food in their stomachs.

The little Italian restaurant turned out to be quite a pleasant, homely place. Deep-red painted walls, framed prints of Italian landscapes and soft lighting. It wasn't too busy, the tables were a decent space apart to allow for private conversation and, most importantly, they were still taking orders. The menu was varied and not too expensive – while scanning it, they both snacked on the complimentary breadsticks, then asked for their starters to be brought to them as soon as possible.

Caroline knocked back her glass of white wine in one gulp and it went straight to her head. Alex was more restrained and stuck to water.

'I can't drink on an empty stomach. It makes me feel sick,' he said.

Caroline was dressed in a white shirt, open at the collar, and smart black trousers. She had her hair down, sitting elegantly on her shoulders. When she had freshened up, she'd added a touch of make-up. Under the glow of the candlelight from the centre of the table, she looked beautiful. She may have hated the lines on her face, but Alex saw character, a life well lived.

Alex had changed into smart black trousers and a white shirt with a dark-grey V-neck pullover on top – all newly bought the day before. He'd run his fingers through his grey hair and sprayed himself liberally with the cologne Shona had bought for him last Christmas. She'd put her mother's name on the gift tag, which Alex thought was a lovely touch. She was always buying him a new fragrance to try whenever she went shopping.

'Nice place this, isn't it?' Caroline said, looking around.

'Yes. You'd think it would be busy on a Friday night.'

'Cardiff are playing at home,' Caroline said.

'That would explain the traffic.'

'Who's the baked brae?' the waitress asked. She had a thick Welsh accent despite her name tag saying *Mesalina*.

They both tucked in straight away, neither of them talking until their plates were empty. They settled back in their seats, now with a glass of wine each, and waited for their main courses.

'What happened to Melanie?' Caroline asked. The question came out of nowhere, but it was obviously one she had been dying to ask since meeting up with Alex again.

A sadness appeared on Alex's face. He looked down into his glass.

'Sorry. You don't have to talk about it if you don't want to.'

'I thought you knew.'

'Only bits of gossip. I don't know the details. Like I said, you don't have to say.'

'No. It's fine.' He looked over Caroline's shoulder and into the distance, as if watching his past play out. He struggled to find the words to begin. 'Do you remember the name Julianne Parker?'

Caroline frowned as she thought. 'It sounds familiar. Remind me.'

'She was engaged to Jonathan Egan-Walsh. When *The Collector* was released, she was fuming that she wasn't mentioned. I'd interviewed her a couple of times but hadn't referenced her in the book. I thought she was weird. *Even* Jonathan thought she was weird, which is saying something. A few months after my book came out, Jonathan broke off the engagement. She contacted me, blaming me for all the attention he was getting from new admirers. She started following me. She even turned up at my home and put a brick through the window. I got the police involved after that, got a restraining order. It didn't seem to matter to her. Like I said, she was seriously obsessed with Jonathan. She kept saying how they belonged together and how I'd broken them up.'

The waiter came over and asked if they wanted any more wine. They realised both their glasses and the bottle were empty so asked for a replacement.

They sat in silence until it arrived and their glasses refilled.

'Go on,' Caroline prompted, hooked by the story.

'I didn't really take her seriously. I just thought she was a lonely weirdo who'd move on to the next serial killer when she got bored. One day, she followed my car – but *I* wasn't driving. I was away at the time, in Liverpool. Melanie had called me that morning to tell me her car wouldn't start and could she borrow mine. I didn't think anything of it. I mean, you don't, do you?'

'What happened?' Caroline asked when Alex stopped talking. He had a faraway wistful look on his face.

'She followed my car until Melanie was on the dual

carriageway and driving at the speed limit, then she rammed into it at seventy miles per hour. Melanie went into the central reservation. The car flipped and landed on the opposite side, where it was hit head-on by a coach.'

'Jesus Christ!'

'I remember the doctors telling me she was lucky to be alive. Now I'm not so sure.'

'Alex, I'm so sorry,' Caroline said, reaching across the table and taking his hand.

'I miss her,' he said, choking back the emotion. 'She's there, but she isn't. All the things I love about her are gone. Her laugh, her smile, her voice, her warmth, they're all gone. She's just a body in a bed that happens to look like my wife.'

'What happened to Julianne?'

'Nothing. We couldn't prove it was her. There were markings from the car on mine, but they couldn't be matched. A burnt-out car was found a few days later but it was too badly destroyed to get anything from it.'

'Then how do you know it was Julianne who did it?'

'Because she phoned and told me.'

'What?'

'It was ages later – I can't remember how long. I was working from home, just crappy stories I had no real interest in, when my phone rang. She said, "You've took my love away from me. I've took yours from you. Now we're even." Then she hung up. I'll never forget those words. I still hear them in my head at times – you know, at night, when I can't sleep.'

'Oh, my God. Another one of Jonathan Egan-Walsh's victims.'

The waiter returned with their main courses and placed them on the table. They both looked at their pasta dishes, but neither picked up their cutlery. Suddenly, their appetites had gone.

'Why are you doing all this, then?' Caroline asked.

'I'm here for the money.' He smiled slightly. 'All my wages go on caring for Melanie. You've no idea how much it costs for machines and tubing, bed-sore cream, nappies, then there's the nurses to pay for who check on her. I pay my daughter Shona, too. She's her full-time carer so she gets a wage. If I can get another book out of this, or a few decent features, then that will help.'

'I'm not hungry any more,' Caroline said, looking down at her meal.

'Neither am I. I could do with another drink, though.'

'Fancy finding a pub?'

Most of the pubs they went in were crammed with football supporters. If they could get to the bar to order a drink, they wouldn't be able to have a decent conversation over the cheering and swearing. Instead, they found a late-night convenience store, bought a few bottles of cheap wine and smuggled them back into the hotel.

Sitting on Caroline's bed, Alex opened the first bottle, and poured them both a mugful of white wine. He drank it and pulled a face at the taste.

'You're not a wine drinker, are you?'

'I prefer a lager. Wine is OK with meals.'

'We should have got some lager.'

'I didn't want you to think you were out with a lout who swigs back Fosters by the can.'

'I'd never think you were a lout,' she said, sitting next to him on the bed. 'Besides, with everything you've been through, you'd be forgiven for necking vodka straight from the bottle.'

'I've done that a few times.'

'So have I, actually,' she said, swigging back her drink and refilling both their mugs. 'I can't believe Jamie, sometimes,' she said, slightly slurring her words. 'I'm sure he thinks I need to ask his permission before I do something.'

'He's worried for you.'

'God knows why. It's not like I'm running after bad guys with a gun in my pocket.'

'He's retired. He was probably hoping for a slower pace of life.'

'Retired,' she said with a shudder. 'I hate that word. Do you know what other word I hate? Pension. It's all downhill from there.' She sighed, stood up and went over to the full-length mirror. 'Is that me in there?'

'Yes.' Alex smiled.

'It doesn't *look* like me,' she said. 'I don't feel *that* old.'

'Sixty isn't old.'

'Try telling my husband that. He wears Argyle sweaters and comfortable slippers. I used to be a detective inspector, for crying out loud.'

'And a bloody good one, too.'

'I'll drink to that.' They clinked mugs and both took a drink. 'I *was* a good detective, wasn't I, Alex?' she slurred, sitting back down on the bed next to him.

'Yes. Look, Caroline, don't think you haven't done much with your life, because you have. How many women were high up in the force when you were a DI?'

'Not many.'

'Exactly. And there are plenty now. You were a pioneer.'

'Do you think?'

'Absolutely. You led the way for more women to enter the force, climb the ladder.'

She thought for a moment. 'You're right. I was. I was a ... what was it?'

'A pioneer.'

'A pioneer, yes. Cheers.'

They slammed mugs again, almost missing, and drained them. Caroline leaned over to the bedside table to grab the bottle. It was empty, so she opened another and refilled their mugs again.

'Alex?'

'Yes.'

'Will you kiss me?'

'What?'

'Jamie and I, we don't any more. The last time he kissed me was on my birthday. And that was probably only because he felt he had to.'

'I don't think we should.'

'When was the last time you … you know?'

'A very long time ago,' he said, trying not to give the answer any thought.

'We could, you know. Two friends, helping each other out.'

They looked at each other. Their faces were inches apart. Caroline put her hand on Alex's lap and leaned in. Their lips gently touched, and their mouths began to open.

Alex jumped up. 'I really don't think we should. We're both drunk. It's not a good idea.'

'You're probably right,' Caroline said, suddenly coming to her senses, reddening with embarrassment.

'Look, I think I should leave.'

'What?'

'I should probably go back to Skegness.'

'But it's late.'

'No. I mean, tomorrow morning.'

'But what about Bryn?'

'You can interview him on your own. Take Sarah with you. I'll go back to Skegness and arrange to talk to Siobhan Gardner.'

'Shit! Alex, I'm sorry. Have I ruined everything?' she asked, wiping tears from her eyes.

'No. Not at all. In another universe, you and I would be all over each other right now, but not in this one.' He held her by the shoulders and kissed her on the forehead. 'You're a wonderful woman, Caroline Turner, do you know that?'

'I do now.' She smiled. 'Thank you for tonight.'

'You're welcome. Now, get some sleep. And, tomorrow, be the best DI Turner you can be.'

She slumped down on the bed and watched as Alex left the

room. She grabbed her handbag from the floor and tipped it up. She grabbed for her purse, opened it and looked at the photograph of her husband with Dylan taken on her son's graduation. 'You are a knobhead at times, Jamie,' she said through the tears. 'But you're *my* knobhead and I love you to bits.'

———

In the room next door, Alex fell onto the bed. He was too tired and too drunk to get changed. His eyes were heavy, and his body ached. He kept thinking of the doctor's words when he first arrived at the hospital: 'Your wife is lucky to be alive.' Was it luck? For the past nineteen years, she had been trapped in her own body, unable to communicate with anyone. For nineteen years, Alex hadn't looked at, kissed, or slept with another woman. Lucky? That doctor was taking the piss.

'I'm sorry, Melanie,' Alex quietly wailed. 'I love you so much, but you really should have died in that crash. It's horrible what we're making you go through. I'm *so* sorry.'

He cried himself to sleep, whimpering over and over that he was sorry, until he eventually succumbed and his eyes closed. In his dream, he and Melanie were strolling, arm in arm, along a sun-kissed beach in southern France. They were happy, in love, and full of life. In all of his dreams, the crash had never happened. They did all the things they planned to do and were still very much in love. It was a shame that when he woke up the next morning, he could never remember any of them.

Chapter Thirty-Three

Alex wasn't sure what woke him up. Usually, after a night of heavy drinking, he could sleep like the dead. Yet, at six o'clock, he was wide awake. Was it guilt or shame that had woken him? His pillow was still damp with tears. His mouth felt dry and he was freezing cold, having spent the night slumped on top of the bed. He dragged himself into the shower, peeling his clothes off as he went, and stood under the cascading hot needles as they injected life into him and washed away the 'car crash' of the previous evening.

He had to admit, he was attracted to Caroline. She was a good-looking woman. She was intelligent, warm and he felt comfortable and relaxed in her company. Or was she just the first woman of a similar age he felt a connection with, a substitute for his bed-ridden wife? He hated how his mind worked. For his job, it was handy to question everything, look at life from different angles and be over-analytical. On a personal front, it was a bloody nightmare.

After his shower, he dressed in clean clothes and dumped yesterday's in his overnight bag. He decided against breakfast and would grab something to eat on the train back to Skegness. He wanted to be out of the hotel before Caroline woke. He didn't want any awkwardness.

As he tiptoed past her room, he stopped to listen. He could hear the sound of industrial snoring. It would be many more hours before she woke. He smiled to himself as he headed for the lift. He should be proud of himself. Last night, he was tempted to cheat on Melanie and he'd turned the offer down. Most men would have jumped at the chance of a night of uncomplicated sex, but he knew, deep down, that if he had slept with Caroline, he would have felt more than a little hungover this morning. He would have felt suicidal for betraying his wife and daughter.

Standing on the platform at Cardiff Central station in the cold morning air was sobering for Alex. He was still in urgent need of a strong coffee and something greasy inside him, but he didn't have time. His train was due. He was tempted to miss it and get the next one. The smell from the McDonald's kiosk was luring him in, but he wanted to get back to Skegness and put this whole episode behind him.

Once he was settled in his seat, and the train pulled out of the station, he looked at his phone. He sent a 'Good morning' text to Shona and read the several texts from Diane asking him how it was going in Wales. Then, he sent a message to Caroline. He deleted it and rewrote it three times before pressing Send. He wanted to make sure it was eloquent, sympathetic, and showed that they were still good friends:

Good morning. Hope you're not too hung over. I've gone back to Skegness. I'm going to try to see Siobhan at some point this weekend. Make sure you give Bryn the third degree when you see him. Thanks for listening last night. It was nice to talk to you about Melanie. Give Jamie a call. Tell him you miss him. He loves

you and he's worried about you. Nothing wrong with that. See
you on Monday.
Lattes are on you, LOL.

'Would you like anything from the trolley?' the woman asked in a soft Welsh accent.

Alex looked up from his phone. 'Oh, God, definitely,' he said with a smile.

———————

By the time the text came through to Caroline's phone, she was already semi-awake and propped up in bed by a mound of pillows. She felt like death. She couldn't remember the last time she had drunk so much. Never again! At the bottom of the bed was a dressing table with a mirror over it. She could see her tired reflection looking back at her, judging her. She looked rough. Her make-up was smudged. Her hair was knotted and sticking up. There was a look of shame in her eyes. She felt more than hungover. She felt disgust and horror at what she had wanted to do last night.

Was she attracted to Alex? She didn't think so. The grief he felt for Melanie had aged him. He had a permanent look of sadness about him, like a basset hound, but without the cute ears. She couldn't believe she had asked him to kiss her. She knew where it would have led. At the time, she would have felt fulfilled, wanted, needed. Neither of them had had sex for a long time. It would have been a passionate, explosive affair. Or it could have been over within half a minute. Either way, she would have felt a hundred times worse than she already did this morning.

She picked up her phone, and, with blurred vision, read Alex's text. It made her smile. Reading between the lines, last night would never be mentioned again – thank goodness! As much as she liked and admired Alex, she had no inclination to see him naked, and shivered at the thought. She decided to call Jamie. When all this was over, they would go away together, somewhere warm, somewhere romantic, somewhere they could rekindle their lost passion. Sixty was the new forty, apparently, and as the phone began to ring, she remembered what she had done on her fortieth birthday and caught her reflection blushing in the mirror.

'I said we'd be there for seven. It's not going to be anything big, just us, Marcus and Greta, and baby Zachery. Apparently, Greta's quite a good cook, so Marcus said she'll put on a nice spread. I did suggest taking a bottle round but Marcus said she's not drinking at the moment, so I bought a fancy box of chocolates, instead. They're handmade. And the box is pretty, I thought.'

Her mother looked at her intently. 'Something tells me you're nervous.'

Diane was sitting on the edge of the armchair. A cup of tea shaking in her hands. Yes, she was nervous, and she had no idea why. It was a birthday tea with her son, daughter-in-law and their new baby. What was there to be nervous about?

Her mother had come for a light lunch – and so Diane could help her with her make-up. Hannah was still in the early stages of Parkinson's, which made her self-conscious about putting lipstick on.

Diane said, 'I just want tonight to go well. No awkward moments.'

'There won't be any.'

'What if I say something?'

'Like what?'

'I don't know. I might put my foot in it. Or, what if I cry when they mention Zachery's name?'

'You won't cry, Diane. Look, you're reading too much into this. It's just me and you, Marcus and ...'

'Greta,' she reminded her mother.

'Greta, yes, and the new baby. It's very informal and relaxed. Now, what present did you buy?'

'As you suggested, I've bought her a basket of things for her to pamper herself with. She's going to have her hands full with a newborn, so I've bought her some relaxing things to put in the bath. I asked Marcus if there was anything she's allergic to, so I've not got her anything that will bring her out in a rash. She should like it. Hopefully ...' Diane stopped herself. Even she knew she was waffling. She picked up her iPhone, looked at the display and placed it back on the coffee table.

'Are you expecting a call?'

'No. Why?'

'That's the fourth time you've looked at your phone in the past hour.'

'Alex and Caroline are in Wales. They're interviewing Bryn and Jackie who used to live next door. I'm a bit worried about what they're going to uncover,' she said, chewing the inside of her mouth. 'I liked Jackie. She was a lovely woman, do anything for anyone. Bryn was the same. What if they had ulterior motives?'

'I always thought they were a funny couple,' Hannah said, looking through the gift basket for Greta.

'You never said.'

The doorbell rang and Diane went to answer it. On her way, she caught a glimpse of herself in the hallway mirror and wondered if she was wearing too much make-up. She opened the door to find her ex-husband on the doorstep.

'*Nick!*' she exclaimed.

'Can I have a word?'

'Er ...' She looked back into the house. Her mother and Nick had never got on, even when they were married. The animosity they had towards each other was even stronger now. 'I'm just about to go out for lunch.'

'This won't take long,' he said, barging past her, entering the house without being invited.

'My mum's here,' she said after him, as a warning, but it was too late. He'd already entered the living room.

'Oh. Hannah. Nice to see you,' he said, icily.

'Nick. How's the child bride?'

Nick rolled his eyes. 'She's called Beth, and she's only ten years younger than me; hardly a child.'

'What do you want, Nick?' Diane asked.

'I want to know what the hell you think you're doing?'

'What are you talking about?'

'I've had reporters ringing me at home, ringing me at work. Beth's had them knocking on the door. People are talking about us behind our back.'

'Well, if you're going to cheat on your wife and abandon your family, you should expect a backlash,' Hannah said with a smug look on her face.

'I'm not talking about that. I'm talking about the papers being full of stories that Jonathan Egan-Walsh didn't kill Zachery. I'm talking about you!' he said, poking his ex-wife in the shoulder. 'Telling anyone who'll listen that his killer is still out there. You've even got a former detective and a sleazy journalist acting as private investigators.'

'Have you quite finished?' Diane asked, folding her arms in defiance. 'First of all, the letter I received from Jonathan was addressed to *me*. What I do with the information is my business. Secondly, yes, I have some people helping me find out the truth because I don't know what to believe, but I need to know for my own sanity. And, thirdly, if you were any kind of a father, you'd be on my side. Don't you want to know what happened to Zachery?'

'*We already know!*' he exploded, his exasperation on show. 'Jonathan kidnapped him and killed him. The police said so.'

'And it's not like the police have ever got anything wrong,' Hannah said.

'Nick, I'm sorry the press are harassing you they're harassing me, too – but this is important to me. You've been able to move on. I haven't.'

'That's not my problem,' he said, his voice lowering.

'I know it isn't. That's why I'm not involving you in this. I'm doing this on my own – for me, and for Zachery.'

'But you're raking everything up,' he said, slumping down into the armchair, almost defeated. 'I'm not sleeping, Diane.'

'Guilty conscience,' Hannah said as an aside.

'*Leave it*, Mum.'

He rubbed his face hard and ran his fingers firmly through his receding hair. 'So,' Nick began, sniffing back his emotions, 'what have they uncovered so far, this crime-fighting duo you've got working for you?'

'They've …' Diane struggled to find the right words. 'Well, they've come up with a few new lines of questioning.'

'Such as?'

'Well, they're in Wales at the moment. They're interviewing Bryn, who used to live next door.'

'Bryn? Why?'

'I don't know. They seem to think he's someone worth talking to.'

'Oh.' Nick sounded surprised. 'Anyone else?'

'I don't know. Look, Nick, if you want, I can keep you informed.'

'I don't know what I want,' he said, slumping further into the chair and folding his arms. He looked like an insolent child being told off for swearing.

'Typical man,' Hannah said.

He gave his former mother-in-law a deathly look. 'I should go,' he said, standing up. He moved over to the door, before turning back. 'Diane, I really think you should think twice about all this. It's not doing you any good. You need to move on.'

'I know I do,' she said defiantly. 'But until I know what

happened to Zachery, I can't. I'm sorry it's distressing you, Nick, I really am, but I can't rest until I have a grave I can visit.'

Nick shook his head and turned and left the house, slamming the door behind him.

Hannah went over to the living-room window and looked out. She watched as her ex-son-in-law, head down, walked slowly to his car, dragging his feet along the pavement as he went.

'You certainly told him,' she said to her daughter with a smile on her face. 'Personally, I'd have added a few swear words.'

'Hmm ...' Diane said. She was standing by the living-room door. Her arms were folded tightly around her chest, a thoughtful expression on her face.

'What?'

'I felt sorry for him,' she said, shrugging her shoulders.

'For him? Why?'

'He looked lost.'

'You mean he didn't get his own way for once.'

'No. It was something else. He looked incredibly sad.'

'Like I said, guilty conscience.'

Hannah went back to the sofa while Diane moved over to the window. She saw Nick sitting behind the wheel of his car. He had his seatbelt on but he hadn't started the engine. Diane couldn't see properly from where she was standing, but she was pretty sure he was crying.

Chapter Thirty-Four

Following a long hot shower, a tearful chat with Jamie, and a hearty breakfast, Caroline felt ready to face whatever lay in store for her. At the back of her mind was still the thought of what could have happened last night, but, hopefully, that would fade in time. For now, she had a job to focus on.

Caroline didn't recognise former DC – now DI – Sarah Daley. They had arranged to meet in a coffee shop and, as Caroline didn't know the area too well, she was running late. She went to the counter, bought her drink and looked for somewhere top sit.

It was busy but she managed to find a table. She sat down and starting scanning around. A woman she didn't recognise made eye contact with her, stood up and made her way across the floor towards her.

'You looked straight at me three times,' Sarah said with a huge smile.

'*Sarah?*' Caroline asked, surprised. 'My God, I didn't recognise you. I'm so sorry.'

'Evidently.'

Caroline stood up, they embraced and Sarah pulled out a chair to sit opposite her former boss.

'I can't believe it, you look so different.' Caroline looked her up and down. The hair was definitely different, it was darker. And she had put on weight, but that wasn't something you mentioned.

'I've put on a bit of weight since having my third,' she said as if reading Caroline's mind.

'*Three* children?'

'Yes. Aaron's eleven. He started secondary school last September. Sean is eight and Alice is five. It was her birthday last weekend,' Sarah replied, beaming.

'Good grief! And you're a DI, too.'

'Yes. There's no stopping me.' She laughed.

'I should hope not. I always knew you'd go far. I want you to be Chief Super, at least, before you retire.'

'So do I,' she said, grinning.

'Is your husband in the force?'

'Tactical Support. We might be moving to London in the next year – he's trying to get into Counterterrorism. I'm not too happy about that, what with us having the kids, and I've made my home here in Cardiff, but he's had his heart set on it for years. Besides, this isn't the kind of job where you stay in one place, is it?'

'Not really.'

'So ... what about you?' Sarah asked her former boss. 'Do you miss the force?'

'Not a bit,' Caroline replied with a fake smile.

'It doesn't sound like it from your messages.'

'Well, there are some cases you can't turn your back on.'

'I know. My mind still goes back to those interviews, from time to time. Do you really think Jonathan's letter is telling the truth?'

'The more we're uncovering, it's certainly beginning to look that way. What can you tell me about Bryn Jones?'

Sarah pulled her bag up from the floor and took out a notepad. She flicked through a few pages. 'You're not going to believe this. That's why I thought it would be better for us to meet up in person rather than do it over the phone. Bryn Jones is currently in Cardiff Prison.'

Caroline almost dropped her mug. 'It's safe to say I wasn't expecting you to say that. What's he done? How long is he in for?'

'Well, he was jailed in 2014 to serve a minimum of fourteen years for historical child sex abuse going back to 1997. Eighteen victims came forward.'

Caroline's eyes lit up. Alex was right to have suspicions about his behaviour.

'What triggered it?'

'He was coaching a football team in 2012 and a child on the team accused him of touching him inappropriately when he was injured. It turns out he was massaging several of the boys on the team but taking it further.' Sarah looked around her and lowered her voice so they couldn't be overheard. 'When this first boy made a complaint to the police, others came forward. He'd been coaching since the mid-nineties and involved with youth community work, too. He only admitted to the eighteen who came forward. I think if more had complained, he would have admitted those, too.'

'Did you know about him living in Skegness at the time of Zachary Marshall's disappearance?'

'No, we didn't. We did put out an appeal for any other victims to come forward, but the ones who did were all within the South Wales area. The thing is, he never volunteered any information. He just went along with whatever we accused him of.'

'Strange.'

'I know. It was like he was waiting to be found out and now that he had been, there was no point denying it. I've arranged for us to visit him this afternoon. My sister-in-law, Daphne, works in the prison. It's being logged as an official visit by police looking into historic sex crimes. I can take you with me.'

'Thank you for this, Sarah. It means a lot.'

'I've also been in contact with Jacqui Jones. She's agreed to talk to you, but she doesn't want you in the house.'

'I can understand that.'

'After this, we're going to meet her in a park close by, if that's OK?'

'Yes. Fine. Are they still married?'

'Yes. She's sticking by him and she visits him as often as she can.'

'I don't think I could do that,' Caroline said.

'I know I couldn't. If I found out my Danny was doing anything like that, I'd chop his balls off,' Sarah said, before draining her cup. 'Right, then, shall we go?'

'I don't want to take up all your free time, Sarah. You can just tell me where the park is. I'm sure I'll find it.'

'You're not. Danny has worked for the last four weekends. I told him, this weekend is my time. He can look after the kids for a while,' she said with a smile.

As they exited the coffee shop, Sarah pulled open the door and allowed Caroline to go through first.

'After you, boss.'

'Not any more, I'm not.'

'Sorry, it's just like old times, isn't it?'

'It really is,' Caroline replied, smiling.

As they started walking down the street to where Sarah had parked her car, Caroline performed a double-take when she caught her own reflection in a shop window. She looked shorter, her face wrinkled. She felt tired and old. No, it wasn't like the old times at all. In the coffee shop, she'd felt like she was in a briefing with a colleague. On leaving, she'd felt like Christine Cagney. Now that she'd seen herself in the window, she felt more like Miss Marple!

The taxi turned the corner and The Majestic hotel came into view. So did two marked police cars, parked haphazardly outside the main entrance. Alex paid the fare and made his way inside. The foyer was full of police officers talking to distraught staff.

'What's happened?' Alex asked at Reception.

'We've had an … incident. Absolutely nothing for you to worry about, Mr Frost,' she said with a strained smile.

'What kind of incident?'

He was pushed out of the way as a team of paramedics made their way through to the lifts, pushing an empty trolley.

'One of the guests died last night,' the receptionist said, quietly.

'Oh. Never a dull moment in the hotel industry,' Alex replied.

Making his way towards the narrow stairs, he ascended slowly, careful not to knock off any of the framed prints on the walls with his overnight bag. Pulling open the door to his floor, he started to walk along the dimly lit corridor just as the paramedics wheeled the trolley out of the room opposite his. There was a white sheet covering the body. Alex squeezed himself tight against the wall to allow them to pass.

Before entering his own room, he glanced in at the open door opposite and saw a noose hanging from the ceiling. He wasn't surprised: The Majestic gave off the vibe of a place where the depressed came to end it all.

Unlocking then pushing open his door, he failed to notice the DO NOT DISTURB. Kicking it closed behind him, he now stood in the middle of his room and looked around, aghast. Who the hell had done this? The room was a mess, pages from a book covered the floor and every surface. He bent down to pick up a page and immediately recognised it as one from *The Collector*.

It was then that Alex turned and saw the threat written on the mirror in permanent marker.

There was only one person who could have done this. His mind went straight to Julianne Parker.

Chapter Thirty-Five

Bute Park in Cardiff, on the River Taff and next to Cardiff Castle, was picture-postcard beautiful. Despite the cold weather that had followed Caroline here, she was enjoying being away from home, where the roads were always busy, the coast was always packed, and there was a permanent wall of noise. Bute Park was the antithesis of Skegness. It was calm, relaxing, and peaceful.

The slight breeze clattered the bare branches together. The birds in the sky could be heard chorusing. This was what Caroline wanted. She could picture herself bringing her dogs here, letting them run through the woodland. She understood why Sarah was reluctant to leave for the bright lights and the twenty-four-seven lifestyle of London.

Caroline was almost lost in her surroundings, so taken was she with the beauty of the setting. She felt like she was alone, strolling through an undiscovered wilderness. She pictured her and Jamie walking through here, arm in arm, ignoring the fast pace of life and taking the time to breathe in the calming influence of Mother Nature.

'There she is,' Sarah said.

Caroline jumped, broken from her reverie, and turned to her former colleague. She had forgotten she was there. 'Who?'

'Jacqui Jones. Purple coat. Two Dalmatians.'

'Oh.'

'Not what you were expecting?'

'No. Exactly what I *was* expecting.'

Jacqui Jones was sitting on the edge of a park bench. She looked tense, her shoulders hunched and knees together, staring straight ahead with a faraway look. Her face was weather-beaten, her dark hair lank and lifeless. She was painfully thin and had the expression of a woman on the verge of tears.

Sarah called out to her, loud enough to make the timid woman almost jump out of her skin. The dogs reacted, too, jumping up from their position at her feet. Sarah thanked her for agreeing to meet them and introduced Caroline to her.

'Beautiful dogs,' Caroline said, bending down to make a fuss over them in turn. 'That's what I do back in Skegness. I have my own dog-walking business.'

'Oh. I thought Sarah said you were a detective.' Her voice was pretty accentless – hint of Yorkshire, a tinge of Welsh, a nod to somewhere else; a woman who was used to not settling in one place long enough to absorb any particular locality.

'I am. Was. I'm retired. What are their names?' she asked, wanting to get off the topic of her retirement. Every time she thought about it, Jonathan Egan-Walsh popped into her head.

'Jud and Prudie,' she replied with a smile.

Caroline looked up at her from where she crouched, stroking the dogs.

'I'm a huge fan of the Winston Graham novels,' Jacqui added by way of explanation.

'I'd have thought you'd have called them Ross and Demelza.'

'I have a cat at home called Demelza. Ross was my previous dog.'

Sarah looked confused, not following the exploits of the Poldarks.

'Do you come to this park often? It's beautiful.'

'Yes. Most days. I come here on my own sometimes, too. It's nice to have a walk, blow away the cobwebs.' Jacqui gave a hint of a laugh. Her face lit up when she talked about herself rather than the reason they were all here. It was as if the real Jacqui was trying to break through.

'Shall we go for a walk?' Sarah asked, filling the silence.

Jacqui and Caroline both stood up. Caroline asked if she could hold one of the leads and Jacqui handed Jud over to her care. The dogs were obviously used to a slow trek around the park, for they didn't pull and kept to the same pace as the women.

'So, you want to talk to me about Bryn?' Jacqui said, her voice lowering, her face paling.

'If you don't mind.'

'What do you want to know?'

'I hope you don't mind me asking, but … why have you stuck by your husband?' Caroline asked.

'What people don't seem to realise about paedophilia is that it's an illness. It's not something you decide to become. Bryn is ill. If I turn my back on him because he's ill, what does that say about me?' Caroline and Sarah exchanged glances.

'I know what you're thinking,' Jacqui said. 'He abused boys. He's scum. I'm a fool to stand by him. But he's my husband and I love him. Would I leave him if he had cancer or depression or AIDS? No, I wouldn't. So, I'm not leaving him while he's like this.'

'As far as I'm aware, there's no cure for people who have these feelings towards young children,' Caroline said.

'No, there isn't. But there is therapy. He's undergoing sessions with a psychologist while he's in prison and a course of cognitive behavioural therapy.'

'What will that do?'

'CBT aims to reduce attitudes, beliefs and behaviours that

increase the likelihood of offences against children,' she said, as if quoting from a medical textbook. 'It's about learning self-control, empathy and social competence, and about changing the person's views on sex with children.'

'So, hang on a minute … let me get my head around this,' Sarah said, looking perplexed. 'Before all this therapy, he believed – and I'm guessing all paedophiles believe – that sex with children is fine, that there's nothing abnormal or disgusting about it?'

'That's right,' Jacqui said without flinching.

'Is the therapy working?' Caroline asked. She saw the look of horror on Sarah's face.

'I think it is, yes. His therapists think so, too.'

'He has more than one?'

'Oh, yes.'

'When you visit him, how is he?'

Jacqui took a deep breath. 'He's incredibly sad. He's full of remorse. He pleaded guilty at his trial. He's accepted what he's done.'

'He was sentenced to a minimum of fourteen years. That's a long time to wait,' Caroline said.

'It's been nearly four already. I can wait. I will wait. He'll get parole. He's doing everything right while he's in prison.'

Again, Caroline and Sarah exchanged glances.

'Have you received any animosity from friends and neighbours?' Sarah asked.

Jacqui stifled a laugh. 'You could say that. I no longer have any friends and I've had to move twice since Bryn's been in prison. These are my family,' she said, nodding towards the dogs.

'It must be a very lonely life for you.'

'Not really. I keep myself busy. I work. I visit Bryn as often as I can. I've got Jud and Prudie and Demelza. I don't need anyone else.' She raised her voice slightly and what she said sounded forced, as if she was trying to convince herself into believing she was happy with the life she was leading.

'Jacqui, when did you first know about Bryn's crimes?'

She shuddered. 'I hate the fact that they're called crimes. He's ill. He couldn't help what he was doing.' There was pain in her voice, as if she had spent her whole life justifying her husband's behaviour.

Caroline felt uncomfortable. Here they were, three women and two dogs. From the outside, they looked like members of the same family taking a stroll in the park with the family pets on a Saturday afternoon. They could be talking about anything in the world – moaning about their husbands, the contestants on *Strictly Come Dancing* – but they weren't. The conversation was dark and heavy. All three of them could feel it.

Jacqui stopped walking. 'I think I always knew. Looking back, it seems obvious now. I must have chosen to ignore it, to turn a blind eye. We moved around a lot,' she said, setting off again. 'We've lived in Rhyl, Edinburgh, Middlesbrough, Brighton. I liked Brighton,' she said wistfully.

'Is that why you left Skegness in 1993?'

'Yes. I couldn't cope with Zachery going missing. He was our neighbour. I liked the Marshalls, I really did. They were a lovely family. They didn't deserve what happened to them.'

'Did you suspect Bryn had something to do with his disappearance?'

She nodded. 'I remember hearing about Zachery going missing. I should have gone round to Diane's, tried to comfort her, offer support, but I couldn't. I waited in that house for Bryn to come home. I needed him to tell me he had nothing to do with it. I needed to see it in his eyes. I felt sick. It was pitch-black when he came home. Nick had stopped him in the road, told him what had happened. As soon as he came in, I laid into him. I screamed at him and hit him. I begged him to tell me the truth, to tell me that he'd had nothing to do with Zachery going missing.'

'What did he say?'

'He told me he hadn't. He said he hadn't seen Zachery since the morning we'd both gone round with the football kits.'

'Did you believe him?'

'Yes, I did,' she said firmly.

'Was Bryn with you on the day Zachery went missing?'

'Only until lunchtime. He was coaching the football team in the youth centre in the afternoon.'

'Why did you move so suddenly if you believed him?'

'Because at the back of my mind I don't think I really did. I knew what he did with boys, but he wasn't a killer. He was definitely *not* a killer.' Jacqui took a crumpled handkerchief out of her pocket and wiped her eyes. 'About a year after he'd been sentenced, he said he'd been talking to his therapist about how understanding I was, and she told him to make sure I knew everything if he wanted me to stand by him. So he did. His therapist arranged for me to sit in on one of their sessions. He poured his heart out to me. I think that was the worst day of my life,' she said, looking far off into the distance.

They walked on in silence for a long moment. Eventually, Caroline asked the question she was most eager to know the answer to. 'Jacqui, did he abuse Zachery Marshall?'

She nodded. 'But only once.' Her voice remained unchanged. She spoke in a general conversational tone. Any feelings she had were obviously deeply buried.

'What about Marcus?' Sarah asked.

'No.'

'Did the police come and interview you and Bryn in 1993?' Caroline asked.

It was a while before Jacqui answered. 'They came to the house a few times. The first time, Bryn was at work. They said they'd come back when he was home and ...' she shook her head. 'I gave them a false time.'

'Why?'

'I needed to keep the police away from Bryn. They would have suspected him. They would have arrested him. Besides, I only had to put them off a couple of times, and I never heard from them again.'

'Didn't anyone question you when you said you were moving?'

'No. I made up some excuse about Bryn's mother needing looking after.'

Caroline took a deep breath. She wondered how Jacqui could stand by a man who abused young boys, who readily admitted it – and even cover for him with the police. Was Bryn so manipulative and controlling that his disturbed mind games were played with his wife, too, or was Jacqui so hopelessly delusional that she truly believed her marriage was a sacred, loving one? 'Did he kill Zachery?' she asked.

'No. Absolutely not,' Jacqui answered quickly.

'How can you be so sure?'

'Because he isn't a killer. He's ill. He's not a murderer. You don't know him like I do. You don't understand,' she almost cried out.

'I'm trying to understand, Jacqui, I really am,' Caroline said.

They came to another bench and Jacqui slumped down onto it. She looked as if all the life had been sapped out of her. 'I told him, when we moved to Wales, no more football coaching, no more youth-centre groups, just get a job and we'll lead normal, boring lives. But he couldn't. He wasn't having therapy then so he didn't know the exercises and the behavioural training.' She blew her nose again. 'He hates the way he is. He thinks he's a freak,' she cried. 'I keep telling him, it's not him, it's his illness.'

'Jacqui, do you have any children?'

'No. I can't have any. I don't mind. I was never the motherly type.' She tried to sound convincing, but it was an obvious lie. She looked up. 'You think I'm crazy, don't you, for standing by him?'

Sarah didn't say anything.

'Actually, I admire you,' Caroline said. 'As much as I love my husband, if I found out he'd done what Bryn has done, I'd have left him long before now. You're a stronger woman than you give yourself credit for.'

Jacqui gave a weak smile. 'I love him. From the moment I first saw him all those years ago, I knew I wanted to spend the rest of my life with him. I meant every word of my wedding vows and I've stuck by them – "till death do us part".'

'What was Bryn like when you met him?' Caroline asked.

A warmness seemed to spread across Jacqui's face as she remembered a simpler, happier time. 'He was perfection. He was like the missing piece to my puzzle. He was what I'd been waiting for, to make me feel complete. He changed my life from that very first day. Do you know, when I've been to visit him, and I'm walking out of the prison, I ache. I physically ache that I'm not going to be seeing him again for another two weeks.'

'Jacqui, when Bryn was a child, did he have any traumas or accidents?'Sarah looked at Caroline with a confused frown.

'How did you know that?' Jacqui asked.

'Just wondering.'

'When he was six, he fell off a swing and landed head first onto concrete. He was in a coma for two days. He still has a slight indentation in the back of his head.' She paused, obviously finding the conversation painful. 'Look,' she said finally, 'do you mind if I go home? I'm not feeling too well.'

'Are you all right?' Caroline asked.

'Yes. I'm just … I have a headache.'

'Would you like us to give you a lift?' Sarah asked.

'No. I've got the car, thanks. Look, I know you're investigating Zachery's disappearance, and I really hope you find him, but Bryn had nothing to do with him going missing. I can honestly say that with my hand on my heart.'

She took the dog lead from Caroline and headed in the opposite direction.

Caroline and Sarah turned to watch her walk away.

'It was nice meeting you,' Caroline called out.

Jacqui waved back but didn't turn around.

Sarah blew out her cheeks. 'Wow, that was an intense conversation. What do you think? Do you really admire her for standing by her husband?'

'No. I think she just needed to hear something positive to make herself feel a bit better. I think, if she was honest with herself, she's regretting she didn't divorce him years ago.'

'Do you think?'

'God, yes. She's incredibly sad.'

'What was that about Bryn having an accident as a child?'

'I was reading something a while ago about paedophiles. There's no direct cause that they can find, but there is a greater probability of a person developing paedophilia if they've sustained a head injury in childhood. Especially one where they have been rendered unconscious.'

'I didn't know that. Do you believe it's an illness, then?' asked Sarah.

'Well, it's all to do with the brain, how it's wired. Whatever Bryn is doing in prison, he's heading in the right direction.'

Jacqui had disappeared around a corner by now so Caroline and Sarah turned and headed back towards the car.

Sarah said, 'Has this answered any questions for you?'

'I don't know. You said Bryn only admitted the crimes that were put to him and didn't volunteer any information, yet he told his wife he abused Zachery Marshall. How many others has he abused while they've been married? In fact, how many has he abused in his lifetime that the police don't know about?'

'Do you think Bryn could have killed Zachery?'

'I do. I don't believe what Jacqui said about Bryn not being a killer. The majority of crimes take planning and attention to detail – bank robbery, fraud – but murder? We're all capable of that. Behind the majority of murders, lies a strong emotion, something we all feel on a regular basis.'

'Heavy stuff.'

'Don't forget, they were next-door neighbours. If he touched him, maybe Zachery said he was going to tell his dad or something and Bryn got scared, thought killing him was the only way to silence him. He's not going to admit murder to a wife who's standing by him, is he?'

'I suppose not. That means he's not going to tell us, either.'

'True. And his therapist won't because of bloody client confidentiality. We need hard evidence. And to get it, we need to find Zachery's body,' Caroline said.

Chapter Thirty-Six

Alex Frost sat on his bed in the hotel room in Skegness. He could hear the sound of police officers going about their business in the aftermath of the suicide in the room opposite. He had picked up the torn pages of his paperback and had attempted to clean the threat off the mirror, but it wasn't shifting. He wondered if he should mention it to the police. He didn't want to report it, for fear of the hotel asking him to leave. Then where would he go? Caroline would probably offer her spare bedroom, but, after last night, that was the last thing he wanted.

The threat had made him think of Julianne Parker, of how dangerous that woman obviously was, and wondered where she could be now. It appeared she still had deep-rooted feelings for Jonathan if she had gone to such lengths to scare him – but why? And why hadn't she shown her face when Jonathan died?

Alex picked up his mobile and called his daughter. It took a while for her to answer and he almost hung up.

'Shona? Where were you?'

'I was in the bath.'

'Oh.' He relaxed. 'How are you? Are you all right?'

'Yes. Fine, thanks. Alice is spending the day with Mum. I've been out with a friend for lunch and thought I'd have a long soak in the bath.'

'Oh. That's good. Are you sure everything is all right, though?'

'Yes. Why wouldn't it be?'

'No reason.'

'You sound strange. What's wrong?'

'Nothing. I ... I think I'm just missing home,' he lied.

'Then why don't you come back? Even if it's just for a day or two? I'm sure Caroline can manage on her own.'

'No. I want to get on top of things,' he said, reading the threat on his mirror again.

'Has something happened?'

'Why do you ask?'

'Because you really do sound weird,' she said.

'I'm probably tired, that's all. Look, Shona, everything's all right at home, isn't it? The alarm is working fine? The window locks aren't broken or anything?'

'Not to my knowledge. Come on, Dad, out with it. I'm not a child any more. What's going on?'

'Nothing. I had a bad dream,' he lied again, 'and it made me worry about you.'

'If you were *that* worried, you'd come home.'

'I know. I will. Soon. Kiss your mum for me.'

He ended the call and threw his phone to the other side of the room. It landed with an echoing thud on the floor. If Julianne Parker *was* back on the scene, who else could be in danger? He only had Shona left. If anything happened to her, if he lost her, he would never forgive himself.

———

Alex didn't like being on his own, yet he felt awkward around people. Even his own daughter's company was too much for him sometimes. Most of the people he interacted with were ones he was interviewing, in the driving seat, leading the conversation. When it came to normal, everyday small talk, he was stymied. He picked up his mobile, rolled his eyes at the cracked screen, and quickly left the hotel room.

The lobby was empty now, just the receptionist reading a magazine. She looked up and gave Alex a nervous smile – a death in the hotel wasn't good for business. He passed through without comment and went out into the open air. It was busy with Saturday shoppers, people meeting up with friends they only saw at weekends. He stood on the steps of the hotel and watched life continue as normal. He wondered if Julianne was among the passers-by. It was more than twenty years since he'd last seen her. She could have changed beyond all recognition in that time. Was that her going into Primark? Was that her in the red with the hood up, feeding a parking meter? Or was she right under his nose? Was she one of the receptionists in the hotel? Had she served him his scalding coffee on the train back from Wales?

He tried to shake the thoughts from his head and went to find his Volvo in the hotel car park, where the garage had agreed to bring it to. He checked the tyres. All four had been replaced and were fully inflated. As he started the ignition and drove out into the bright afternoon, he couldn't help but feel paranoid. Where the bloody hell was Julianne Parker, and just what was she planning?

Thinking about Julianne now as he was driving along brought back everything that had happened to Melanie. Alex remembered the last conversation he'd had with her. It was over the phone. Alex was away, as usual, working on a feature about female killers in prison. His book, *The Collector*, had been out for a few months and he had received praise for his in-depth investigation, yet there had been a bit of a backlash, too – mostly from twisted admirers of Jonathan who thought the book painted him in a bad light, showed him to be a depraved sexual predator, when, according to them, he was just misunderstood. Alex had witnessed many dark and disturbing acts over the years but even he was scared by some of the emails and calls he received from members of Jonathan's fan club.

His wife had called him to tell him that her car had broken down and she was borrowing his. In those days, he travelled to places by train so he could work on the journey. She was going to do some shopping, stock up the cupboards, and she'd seen a dress she wanted to buy for their holiday next month.

That was it. That was the final conversation he had with his wife. It was so uneventful and ordinary. It meant nothing, but it meant the whole world. If he'd known it was the last time he would hear his wife's voice, he would have said something more meaningful, something poignant. She'd ended the conversation by saying she loved him. He hadn't said it back. *Why hadn't he said it back?*

There was a loud beep, which brought Alex out of his daydream. He slammed on the brakes and shot forward in his seat, the seatbelt pulling him back, cutting into his neck.

'It's a red light, you twat!' someone shouted out to him.

Alex looked up. He was on a narrow road with shops either side. The pavements were busy with shoppers going about their business. He'd shut his eyes tight to close the door on his memories. He'd opened his eyes and had no idea where he was or how he had got here. He could have caused a pile-up.

———

Alex found the building he was looking for and pulled up. He looked at the bland façade of Branagh, Miller and Associates. He looked at his reflection in the glass. What a mess. His hair was unruly, his tie was askew, his shirt untucked and creased, and his suit crumpled. He moved away from the solicitors and adjusted his appearance, using the darkened window in the accountancy firm next door as a mirror. He smoothed down his hair as best he could. It was in need of a trim, but that was something else he had been putting off. He just didn't have the time. He straightened his tie and tucked the shirt into his trousers. He took another look at his reflection in the window. It wasn't much of an improvement, but it was the best he could do. Besides, he was a freelance journalist. He was supposed to look dishevelled – the movies said so.

He pushed at the door but it didn't open. Then he remembered, today was Saturday and solicitor's firms didn't open at the weekend. He sighed and dropped his shoulders. He'd have to come back on Monday and hope he could get past the receptionist without an appointment.

There was nothing left for him to do today. He could pay a visit to Diane Marshall, but he wanted to be left alone. He was just about to get back into his car when he saw the bustle of the town centre up the road. He really should explore his temporary home while he was here.

Alex walked along to and through the town centre, past smiling couples arm in arm and happy families with young children. He remembered Melanie and himself taking Shona to Brighton a few times when she was young. The beach was all pebbles rather than the soft sand of Skegness, but it was fun to walk in the shallowness of the sea, eat candyfloss on the pier, buy the usual seaside tat from stalls and gift shops, and be a normal family.

He strolled along the windswept pavements, his hands plunged into his coat pockets to keep warm. Passing the Embassy Theatre, which was so quiet that it looked abandoned, he carried on walking and soon became aware of the town's historic clock tower. Stopping to look up at the structure, he thought about how strange it was seeing such an impressive monument in the middle of a roundabout.

A strong wind from the coast made him shiver. Despite his new fleece-lined waterproof jacket, he was still cold. The sky was a dark, angry-looking grey. Thick clouds loomed over him, blowing across at speed. There was no sign of a break in them, no sun peering through; just a vast, endless expanse of bleakness. *How very apt*, he thought. Alex shuddered and decided to head for the nearest pub. His eyes adjusting to the darkness inside, he walked up to the bar and ordered a pint of lager and a whisky chaser. He took a large slug of lager and knocked back the whisky in one gulp. Straddling the bar stool, he then downed the pint and ordered the same again.

Taking the time to look around at his surroundings for the first time, Alex realised it wasn't exactly welcoming or inviting, but, compared to what was still waiting for him outside, he felt much better off in here. Alcohol always made things seem better.

———————

It was only four o'clock, but it was already dark. The cul-de-sac where Diane Marshall lived was poorly lit. There were three lampposts but only two of them worked, and they weren't very bright. Diane's house was in darkness. Either side, both neighbours had their living-room curtains closed, and there was absolutely nobody about. Cars were parked up in driveways, except for Diane's. She was obviously out. Perfect.

The sound of the brick smashing through the lounge window echoed around the quiet close. Chances are, it wouldn't be long before a curtain was pulled back, a front door opened and someone came out to investigate. Running on tiptoes so as not to make a sound, the vandal ran down the alleyway at the bottom of the road.

Chapter Thirty-Seven

E veryone in Cardiff knew what lay behind the imposing brick wall topped with barbed wire, but that didn't make the sight any less grim and frightening. It was the thought of the type of prisoners residing in HMP Cardiff that caused the imagination to work overtime. Whoever needed such a high wall and razor wire to keep them from polite society was not locked up for just some petty theft. These were hardened criminals, only a stone's throw away from houses and shops.

Cardiff Prison had been refurbished in 1996. New wings had been added to the Victorian structure, and the prison now had the capacity to hold just over eight hundred Category B and Category C prisoners. Currently, it wasn't quite full, but it was the closest it had ever been to overcrowding – as with many prisons throughout the UK.

The sky had darkened with thick grey cumulus clouds and there was a fine drizzle in the air. Caroline looked up at the imposing prison. The last time she had been in one had marked the beginning of the end of her career as a detective. This one had a heavy atmosphere surrounding it – a place of danger, violence and sadness, of lost hope and ruined lives. Caroline took a deep breath. She watched as Sarah strode ahead of her towards the main entrance as if she was out for on a Saturday-afternoon shopping trip. Caroline followed tentatively.

Inside, at Reception, they met Daphne, Sarah's sister-in-law, who signed them in as visitors with South Wales Police at Cardiff Bay Police Station. Sarah's name, rank and car-registration number were entered, and nothing else. To all intents and purposes, she was visiting alone.

Daphne was a woman of formidable stature. She was close to six feet in height and of a solid build. On the journey there, Sarah had told Caroline how Daphne used to be an amateur weightlifter, who, in her spare time, was often found scaling Mount Snowdon. While most people used their annual leave to lie on a sun-kissed beach in Spain, Daphne packed her kitbag and flew to Canada to trek the Rockies.

Once out of Reception, Daphne took the two other women to one side and lowered her voice: 'Now, it's down as an official interview but don't draw attention to yourselves and don't do anything that could invite questions at a later date because of ... well ...'

'Because of me,' Caroline finished her sentence.

'Exactly.'

'That's fine,' Sarah said with a smile. 'We really appreciate this, Daphne.'

'Always happy to help. I'm sure you'll both sign my sponsor form before you leave.,' she said with a slight smile, 'I'm climbing Ben Nevis in the autumn, raising money for deaf and blind children.'

'Of course,' Sarah said.

'Definitely,' Caroline added.

Bryn Jones was in B1, the wing holding vulnerable prisoners. As a convicted child sex offender, he was at risk from other prisoners. Since his incarceration in 2014, he had been attacked three times, and needed to be hospitalised on two of those occasions. He tried not to attract attention to himself. He went about his work without complaint. He visited his therapists and did all the work required of him and never answered back. He was a model prisoner.

Daphne showed them into a small interview room with a table and four chairs secured to the floor, then left to fetch their prisoner. It was similar to the ones Caroline had used when visiting Jonathan Egan-Walsh in Gartree Prison and Wakefield Prison. She wondered if all prisons used the same decorator. All the old negative emotions came flooding back. She thought about that last interview she'd had with Jonathan, the subterfuge he'd planned to get Caroline alone so he could attack her. Suddenly, she felt sick. Her throat began to tighten as she raised a hand to her neck.

'Is everything all right? You've gone white,' Sarah said as she sat down.

'I'm fine. Bit hungry, I think.'

'Well, we shouldn't be too long. Then we'll go and grab a sandwich or something, if you like?'

'Thanks,' Caroline replied, giving a weak smile.

A clock on the back wall ticked away the silence.

'So, Daphne seems quite a character,' Caroline said as she paced around the nondescript room, filling the silence with something, anything to take her mind off being back in a prison.

'Yes, she is. I know she looks frightening but she's a lovely woman. She'd do anything for anyone. Unless you get on the wrong side of her, of course, Then you certainly know about it.'

'I can imagine. Why is she raising money for deaf and blind children?'

'She's got twin girls, they're both deaf and partially sighted.

They go to a special nursery and she helps raise money for equipment and trips out.'

At that moment, the door opened, and Daphne brought Bryn Jones into the room. She didn't say anything. She closed the door and left them to it.

A tall man with cropped grey hair and a weather-beaten face, Bryn walked with his shoulders hunched and his head down. He had the dour expression of someone who had given up on life and the slow gait of a man heading for the gallows. She wondered whether he'd survive another ten years.

Bryn stood with his back to the door, as if awaiting instruction. He was wearing blue jeans and a grey top which showed signs of being through the wash several hundred times. He oozed fear and dejection.

'Hello, Bryn,' Sarah said, standing up. 'I'm Detective Inspector Sarah Daley from South Wales Police. This is my associate Caroline Turner. Would you like to take a seat?'

Without a word, Bryn nodded and shuffled over to the table. They all sat. Bryn seemed to have brought in a heavy atmosphere with him. There was an air of frigidity about him. This did not seem like a man who had abused his position of trust to lure young boys into his trap. This was a man who was petrified of his own shadow.

'Bryn, before we start, I want to say that we're not accusing you of anything here. We just want to ask you a few questions about an event that you were part of. Is that OK?' Sarah asked.

Bryn nodded again but remained silent. He wore a heavy frown which seemed a permanent fixture on his face.

'Bryn,' Caroline began, 'I used to be a detective inspector with Lincolnshire Police. I worked on the Jonathan Egan-Walsh case back in the nineties. Jonathan was imprisoned for the murder of thirteen boys. One of them was your neighbour, Zachery Marshall, from when you lived in Skegness. Do you remember the Marshalls?'He took a deep breath then nodded.

Caroline continued. She spoke slowly and precisely as if talking to someone for whom English wasn't their first language. 'Jonathan died in January and new information has come to light that he may not have taken Zachery Marshall. That's what we're investigating. Now, we're talking to everyone who interacted with Zachery on the days leading up to his disappearance to try and piece together his last known movements. We understand you and your wife visited the Marshalls on the Sunday he went missing. Do you remember?'

Nothing. He sat in complete silence looking down at the stained table in front of him. He played with his fingers. They were long and thick and heavily wrinkled. The nails were bitten down to the quick. They looked red and sore.

'Zachery Marshall went missing on Sunday, 10 January 1993. Can you tell me anything you remember about that day?' Caroline asked.

Still nothing.

'Bryn, remember the Marshalls,' Sarah said, leaning forward and softening her voice. 'They were your neighbours, your friends. If there is anything you can remember then please tell us – for them. Diane and Nick are in torment. They've been searching for answers for more than twenty-five years. We're not accusing you of anything here.'

Finally, Bryn looked up. He licked his dry lips and cleared his throat a couple of times. 'We went round to their house in the morning.' His voice was quiet, hardly above a whisper. His accent was pure Welsh.

'Both you and your wife went round?'

'Yes.'

'What was the purpose of your visit?'

'Zach was joining the football team I coached. I had some kit I wanted him to try on.'

'OK. Where did he try this kit on?'

'In his bedroom.'

'Did you go with him?'

'Yes.'

'Where were Diane and Jacqui?'

'They were having a cup of tea downstairs.'

'Were Nick and Marcus at home?'

'No. They'd gone out in the van before we went round.'

'Did you see the van go?' Sarah asked.

'Yes.'

Sarah briefly looked at Caroline and took a deep breath, steeling herself, before she asked her next question: 'Did you purposely wait until Nick had gone out before you went round?'

Bryn bit his bottom lip hard and nodded.

'So, you and Zachery …'

'Zach,' Bryn interrupted.

'I'm sorry?' Caroline asked.

'He told me he hated being called Zachery. He preferred Zach, but his mother didn't like his name being shortened.'

'OK. We can call him Zach. So, how long were you and Zach up in his bedroom?' Sarah asked.

'About half an hour.'

'Why so long?'

Bryn shrugged. Caroline and Sarah exchanged glances. Neither of them wanted to ask the inevitable questions.

'What did you talk about?' Sarah asked.

'Not much.'

'Was Zach looking forward to playing football?'

'Yes. He said he was.'

'Did anything happen between you while you were alone in his bedroom?' Caroline asked.

Bryn swallowed hard and his breathing grew erratic. 'He fell.'

'He fell? How? Was he hurt?'

'No. He stumbled when he was trying the shorts on. You know, sometimes when you lose your balance on one leg?'

'And what happened when he stumbled?'

'I caught him.'

'And then what?'

'I sat him on my knee and helped him put the shorts on.'

Caroline shifted in her seat. She was growing uncomfortable. Her mouth felt dry and she could feel the prickle of sweat under her arms. 'Did you touch him?' she asked quietly.

Bryn nodded with his eyes tightly closed.

'Where?'

'Down there,' he said, looking towards his own crotch.

'You touched his genitals?' Sarah asked clinically.

He nodded.

'Was he wearing underpants?'

'I'd told him to take them off.'

'Why?'

'The shorts were tight.'

'How did Zachery react when you touched him?' Caroline asked. She'd returned to calling him Zachery, as that was what his mother wanted, not what a child abuser wanted to call him.

'He didn't. I just … felt him. Only for a few seconds. Then I told him to try on a bigger pair of shorts and we left the room. I felt so … sick with myself.' He screwed his eyes tightly closed and looked at the floor.

'Why did you feel sick?'

'Because I knew the family,' he struggled to say. 'I'd promised myself not to … not with anyone I knew.'

'So, it was fine for you to abuse boys as long as you didn't know their parents?' Caroline asked, anger now starting to show in her voice.

'No … it's … that's … not the reason,' he stammered.

'OK. Let's move on,' Sarah said. 'You and your wife left the Marshalls' house and went back home, yes?'

'Yes.'

'What did you do for the rest of the day?'

'We had lunch. Then I went to the community centre for a football-training session.'

'OK. How many boys were there?'

'About twenty or so.'

'Were any parents there?'

'Yes.'

'How long did the training session go on for?'

'About an hour.'

'What happened afterwards?'

'Everyone went home, and I stayed behind to lock up.'

'Bryn, did the boys wear their kit during training?' Caroline asked.

'Yes.'

'And did the boys take the kit home afterwards for their parents to wash?'

'No. Jacqui and I always did it.'

'So, when they'd gone home, you were alone in the community centre with the football kit belonging to the boys?'

'Yes,' he said, looking back down at the table.

'Did you—'

'Yes,' he interrupted, raising his voice slightly.

Caroline shook her head. She had a look of disgust on her face. She could feel her blood boiling. Her clammy hands folded into fists and her knuckles turned white.

Sarah placed a hand on Caroline's arm. 'What time did you get home?' she asked.

'I can't remember. It was dark.'

'When you turned into the road, what did you see?'

'People. So many of them, just walking in the middle of the road'

'What did you think?'

'I don't know.'

'Who told you that Zachery Marshall had gone missing?'

'His dad.'

'What did he say?'

'That Zach had disappeared. He asked if I'd seen him.'

'What did you say?'

'That I hadn't. It was the truth. He said the police had been called but there was nothing they could do as it was dark, so a few of the neighbours were going to search for him. He asked if I'd help.'

'Did you?'

'No. I told him I would, but I just needed to use the bathroom, then I'd join them, but I didn't.'

'Was Jacqui in the house?' Caroline asked.

'Yes. She had a face like thunder.'

'Why?'

'She thought I'd … done something.'

'Did she say that?'

'Yes.'

'What did you say?'

'I told her I hadn't. I swore I hadn't seen him since that morning, and it was the truth,' he said, looking up at Caroline and Sarah. He looked each of them in the eye for the first time.

'What did Jacqui say?'

'We had a massive argument. That's why I didn't go back out to help with the search. She said that we'd have to move again.'

'Why is your wife sticking by you?' Sarah asked.

'Because she loves me,' he said without hesitation. 'She knows I'm ill. She knows I can't help the way I am.'

He slumped on the table, his head in his hands. There was the faint sound of muffled sobbing coming from the wreck of a man before them. Sarah and Caroline allowed him to compose himself before continuing.

'Bryn, did you know Jonathan Egan-Walsh?' Caroline asked after a long silence.

He looked back up and sniffed hard, wiping his nose on the sleeve of his sweater. 'Yes.'

His reply shocked them both. There was no record of them having ever known one another and Caroline had merely asked because Jonathan claimed to have helped in the search for his distant relative.

'How did you know him?'

'He helped out with the football-training sometimes.'

'Was he there that Sunday?'

'No. He only really came on match days.'

'What was his role?'

'He took photographs of the matches, action shots. He was a very good photographer. We'd sometimes sell them to the parents so we could raise money for the club. It wasn't cheap, especially the travel costs for away games.'

'He took photographs?' Caroline asked.

'Yes. And videos, too.'

'What did you think of Jonathan?'

'He was a nice enough lad, a bit quiet.'

'Did you know about his … behaviour towards young boys?'

'Not really.'

'What does that mean?' Sarah asked.

'We had some kit go missing once. I didn't think anything about it. I thought I'd miscounted or something. Then, one day after training, I saw Jonathan put a shirt and a pair of shorts in his bag. He stole them.'

'Did you question him about it?'

'No.'

'Why not?'

He shrugged.

'Did you think he was abusing boys?' Caroline asked.

He nodded.

'And you thought that if you saw that in him, he could see it in you?' she suggested. 'You also thought that if you questioned him about it, he'd raise questions about you?'

'Yes,' he replied weakly.

'Did you think Jonathan had anything to do with Zachery's disappearance?'

'Yes.'

'And you kept quiet because you thought other boys might point the finger at what you had been doing?'

'Yes.'

'So, you sat back and watched the Marshalls go through hell?' Sarah asked, raising her voice for the first time.

'I had no choice.'

'You had every choice,' Caroline said, almost shouting. She didn't care if Bryn was ill or not. He'd had the power to stop Jonathan early into his crimes but had chosen to sit back in silence. 'Jonathan murdered thirteen boys – that we know of – and you could have stopped it. Those deaths are on your conscience, too.' She stood up. 'You may be ill. You may be attending therapy sessions and working towards some kind of redemption, but I hope you rot in here.'

'Caroline,' Sarah warned.

The cold air hit them as soon as they stepped out of the prison building and into the car park. Caroline swayed. She felt lightheaded. She was angry.

'He knew!' she spat. 'He *fucking* knew what Jonathan was up to. He could have stopped it and he didn't.'

'How can Jacqui possibly stand by him? It's beyond me,' Sarah said.

'I don't think I've ever felt so angry as I do right now,' Caroline continued as she stormed towards Sarah's car. 'Whether he had anything to do with Zachery going missing or not, he contributed to making his last day with his family one of pure hell.'

'Come on, let's go for a drink.'

'I don't want a drink,' she said, her hands clenched into fists. Her face was red with rage.

'Well, I do. Come on,' Sarah insisted, almost manhandling her.

At that, they both climbed into the car, Caroline slamming her door behind her. The seething anger was radiating out of her.

'I would sponsor Daphne my entire pension if she would go into his cell and snap his neck for me.'

'I think she'd do that for free.'

Sarah quickly started the engine, put her foot down, and they left the prison behind them. They *both* needed a drink – but not here, not in the shadow of Cardiff Prison. Sarah turned left and headed out of town. She knew a few pubs in the country that would be quiet, even for a Saturday evening. Who cared if she got too drunk to drive home? That's what husbands were for.

Chapter Thirty-Eight

My gran called me and said Zachery had gone missing. I wasn't expecting that. She asked me if I'd go round to Nick and Diane's and help look for him. I couldn't say no, could I?

I didn't know the Marshalls very well. They lived across town from me. We only really met on big family occasions like a wedding or a funeral. They seemed like a nice family. Diane was a bit snooty and Nick didn't talk much, but the boys were lovely. Marcus was the younger one. He was always with his mum or dad, a bit clingy. Zachery was at that age where he was always running off, wanting to explore things on his own. I was the same at that age. Though I'm guessing Diane didn't hit Zachery with a belt buckle like my gran did with me.

So, I went straight round to Nick and Diane's. There was a strange feeling to the close. People were everywhere, dressed in thick clothing, hats and gloves, wielding torches and big sticks. Nick put us all into groups and told us where to go to search. He seemed to know all the places Zachery went to play. Fingers crossed, he'd fallen and was hurt, that's all.

I stood at the side of the road waiting to set off when a car pulled into the close. It was Bryn Jones, the next-door neighbour. Nick ran over to him straight away and, after a brief chat, Bryn parked up. When he got *out of his car, he looked over to me and we made eye contact. We'd had a bit of a row at the community centre earlier in the week. I knew more about him than he thought. I smiled. He looked nervous. I hope he hadn't been touching Zachery. He's my second cousin, or something. I didn't want that fat useless lump touching my family.*

Before we set off in the search, I asked Nick if I could use his toilet. I went into the house and into the living room to see Aunt Diane. She wasn't really my aunt, but I'd called her that when I was younger. She was sitting in the middle of the settee, crying her eyes out. There were a few people around her offering words of comfort, hollow words with no meaning. Nobody saw me.

They were all wrapped up in the excitement.

I crept upstairs and slipped into Zachery's bedroom. He had the poster of Garfield and Odie up that I'd given him. His bed was unmade, so I neatened up the duvet and fluffed up the pillows. His pyjamas were thrown on the bed, so I folded them and placed them under the pillow. Then I went over to his chest of drawers and looked inside. He was quite a small boy for his age. His clothes looked even smaller. I ran my fingers through a few items. I took a T-shirt and a hooded sweater.

In the bathroom, there was a laundry basket. I picked out a few of the smaller items and inhaled their smell. I could tell which ones belonged to Zachery and which to Marcus. I don't know how, I just knew. I put a pair of pants, a pair of tracksuit bottoms and a T-shirt up my sweater, flushed the toilet and went back outside.

While I was searching, I kept getting a hint of a smell from the clothes I had hidden under my jumper. I felt like a police dog tracking a scent. We searched for hours, despite the cold and the dark. We searched the next day, too, and the one after that. We never found him. Not that I expected to.

Chapter Thirty-Nine

'Y ou're not from around here, are you?'

'No. London.'

'I thought so. Nice accent.'

'Thank you.'

'So, are you here for business or pleasure?'

'Business.'

'I'm sure you've got time for some pleasure, too.'

'I don't know about that.'

'Are you staying in a hotel?'

'Yes.'

'How about I come back with you? We can continue getting to know each other.'

'I'm married,' Alex Frost said, holding up his left hand to show his wedding ring.

'So am I,' the dyed-red-haired woman opposite slurred. 'But wedding rings come off,' she added, raising her own left hand to show a finger with a white band where the ring usually was.

'I don't think so,' Alex replied. He was tempted. He was *very* tempted. The woman opposite was relatively attractive under the dim light. She was wearing an incredibly low-cut and revealing top. She kept leaning closer to Alex to show off her biggest assets, hoping to lure him into her trap.

'Come on, you're only young once. Your wife's back in London, that's miles away. She'll never know.'

How right you are, Alex thought. His wife wouldn't know if he took this woman back to his own house and shagged her at top volume in the next room.

Alex drained his pint glass and stood up. 'Thanks for the offer, but, no thanks.' He grabbed his jacket and headed for the other side of the bar. He could hardly believe how restrained he was being: two women had offered themselves to him within twenty-four hours and he'd turned them both down. A testament to how much love he still had for Melanie, even after all these years.

'Stuck-up London wanker,' she shouted after him.

He was about to order another pint when his phone rang. He looked at the cracked display and saw it was Diane calling. He rolled his eyes and realised he hadn't replied to her many text messages. Quickly, so as not to miss the call, he stepped outside into the cold night air before answering.

'Alex, it's Diane. I'm sorry to call you at this time. I know you're in Wales but I don't know what to do.'

'That's OK. I'm back in Skegness.'

'Oh. Thank God,' she said with a deep sigh. 'Look, do you think you could come over?' She sounded upset, frightened, even.

'Yes, sure. Why? Has anything happened?'

'Someone's thrown a brick through my window.'

Alex told her he'd be right over and ended the call. 'Fucking Julianne Parker,' he said to himself as he headed for his car.

By the time Alex arrived, Diane's mother, Hannah, was sweeping up the larger pieces of glass from the living-room carpet. Both women had coats on, shivering against the cold that was blowing through the house. As soon as he entered, Diane ran up to him and hugged him.

'Shit! I'm sorry. I don't know why I did that,' she said, looking embarrassed. She had tear tracks down her face.

'That's OK. Don't worry. What happened? Are any of you hurt?'

'No. We were at my son's for a birthday tea. When we got back we found all this.'

'Did anyone see anything?'

'No,' she said, wiping her eyes with a wet tissue. 'I've been round next door. They heard the smash but by the time they came outside there was nobody about.'

'Has anything been taken? You know, in there?' He nodded towards the dining room.

'No. I've checked.'

'And you've called the police?'

'Fat lot of good they were,' Hannah said, standing up to full height and rubbing her back. 'Nothing's been taken, nobody's hurt, nobody saw anything, so they're not coming out. We've been given a crime number to pass on to the insurance company. I told Diane, take photos of it all on your phone, keep the evidence.'

'That's good. Here, let me do that,' Alex said, taking the broom from Hannah.

'I've called a glazier but they can't come out until tomorrow. Richard who lives two doors down, he works for the council. He's sending someone out to put some boarding up until then. I just don't know who could have done such a thing.'

'*You* do, though, don't you?' Hannah said, studying Alex. 'It's written all over your face.'

'You're good,' Alex said, smiling.

'I may be a doddery old woman with a stick, but I've lived. I've seen things that would make your hair curl. Come on, then, ace reporter, out with it.'

Alex took a deep breath. He told them both to sit down, which they did. The sofa was cold from the night air blowing in. They looked strange, three people sitting in a living room with their coats on, shivering. Alex told them all about Julianne Parker, her relationship with Jonathan Egan-Walsh and what she had done to his wife.

'That's terrible,' Diane said.

'I'm so sorry,' Hannah said, placing a comforting hand on Alex's lap.

'I don't understand, though,' Diane said, looking confused. 'Why would she come back now, after all this time?'

'Because Jonathan's dead,' her mother said. 'Maybe reading about him dying has brought back all those feelings she once had for him.'

'But his name's hardly ever been out of the papers. If it wasn't him appealing then it was about him being beaten up. Do you remember that time he tried to get a film company interested in telling his story on the big screen? He's always tried to keep himself in the limelight. She would have seen all that. So why now?'

'I don't know,' Alex shrugged.

'Shouldn't she be in some kind of an institution?' Hannah asked.

'She *should*, yes,' Alex replied, 'I don't know where she is, though. I will go and see someone at the police tomorrow and ask them if they can find her.'

'Well, shouldn't Diane have protection or something?'

'Mum,' Diane said, rolling her eyes.

'I mean it. This woman sounds dangerous.'

'Would you feel better if I stayed over tonight?' Alex asked. He was hoping Diane would say yes. He didn't fancy going back to his hotel room and having to look at that threat in permanent marker on his mirror again.

'Would you?'

'Of course.'

'Diane, let's go and make a cup of tea, warm us all up,' Hannah said, practically pushing her daughter towards the kitchen.

'What do you think you're doing?' Hannah asked her daughter in hushed tones, closing the kitchen door behind them.

'What?'

'Asking him to stay the night. You don't know him.'

'Yes, I do.'

'For a few days. He could be a sex pest, for all you know.'

Diane burst out laughing before she could clamp a hand over her mouth. 'I doubt it. You saw how he was when he spoke about his wife. It's obvious he loves her. I bet he's not even thought about another woman since the crash.'

'He's a man, Diane; of course he will have. They can't help it. I'm staying, too.'

'What?'

'I'll have the spare room. He can have the sofa.'

'Mother, I'm not a child.'

'And I wasn't born yesterday. Men will take the smallest opportunity to jump on a vulnerable woman – and that's exactly what you are right now.'

'You've been watching too much television,' Diane said, pushing past her mother and going over to the kettle.

'And you haven't been watching enough.'

At that moment, the kitchen door opened, making them both jump.

'Sorry,' Alex said. 'The bloke's come to board up your window.'

'Oh. Good.'

'I've just called Caroline, told her what's happened, and she was telling me about seeing Bryn Jones this afternoon. He's in prison.'

'Prison? What for?'

'Historical sex crimes. He'd been abusing young boys for years in Cardiff since the late nineties.'

'Oh, my God,' Diane said. The tears started to fall again. She placed a hand over her mouth and looked at the floor.

'I never liked him,' Hannah said. 'He always looked shifty to me.'

It didn't take long for the hardboard to be screwed to the window frame, plunging the room into darkness. Even with the light on, it still seemed dark. There didn't seem to be any point in closing the curtains, and they wafted in the slight breeze from the gap between the board and the frame. Despite the fire and the central heating being on, it was still cold, and all three kept their coats on.

Diane broke the silence. 'If it is this Julianne who's doing all this, why is she targeting me?'

Alex frowned while he tried to think of an answer. Diane was right. She was a victim herself. 'I don't know. It doesn't make sense,' he said, finally. 'I can understand Julianne coming back for me, if she thought I was writing another book without including her, or besmirching Jonathan by assigning more victims to him.'

'If it's not Julianne, then who?' Hannah asked.

'The *real* killer!' Diane suddenly said, her face lighting up. 'It's been in the papers about Jonathan's letter saying he didn't kill Zachery. Maybe the real killer has seen that, realised we're getting close and is getting scared. The brick through the window, the tyres slashed, he's trying to frighten us, so we'll back off.' She looked at the expectant faces of Alex and her mother. 'Don't you see what that means? Jonathan really didn't kill Zachery. The real killer is still out there – and he's close. We can catch him and find out where Zachery is.' She looked almost joyful.

Alex exchanged glances with Hannah. If Jonathan wasn't the killer, and the real killer *was* trying to frighten them into stopping their enquiries, the journalist thought, just how far would he go to silence them?

Breaking windows, slashing tyres and breaking into hotel rooms was child's play. If he knew that wasn't working, then he would up his game. How far would he be willing to go to keep his secret?

———————

Lying on the sofa, inside an ancient sleeping bag, his head propped up by sofa cushions, Alex wished he'd gone back to the hotel. He wasn't comfortable, he was freezing cold and there was what felt like a spring sticking into him, whichever position he put himself in. He looked at the time on his phone. It was almost half past one, and he wasn't tired. Or maybe he was, but there was so much whirling around his mind that he couldn't relax and let sleep envelop him.

He couldn't stop thinking about what Diane had said – if it wasn't Julianne targeting them, then it could only be the real killer. Maybe he and Caroline had already interviewed them. But who? Nobody they had spoken to so far stood out as a killer.

He closed his eyes. A headache was beginning to take hold and he wasn't surprised. When Caroline had first contacted him about potential new information surrounding Jonathan Egan-Walsh, and to ask for his help, he'd worried whether he should take it on or not. The journalist in him, the man with one eye on the bank balance, had thought this could lead to another book, more lectures, more money. The human side to Alex's nature, though, thought differently. Jonathan had all but murdered his wife. He was dead ... Finally. If there'd been a headstone to visit, Alex would have happily cracked open a bottle of champagne on it, but that wouldn't have brought back his wife, and the bills for her care would still be piling up. In the end, money had won. So, here he was, camping on Diane Marshall's sofa, being targeted once again by a serial-killer-loving psycho.

He kicked out in frustration. Could Diane be right? Maybe, Julianne had got over her obsession and was living a perfectly normal life with a husband, two kids and a dog. Maybe, they were all being targeted by the real killer. Either way, his life was in danger.

'For fuck's sake, Alex, go to sleep,' he whispered to himself, turning over once again. Still, sleep eluded him, though.

He picked up his phone and went into the messages app. He wanted to talk to Caroline but guessed she would be sleeping by now. He put his phone back down. He squeezed his eyes closed and begged for sleep to take him. Eventually, after counting sheep well into three figures, it did.

On the floor beside him, his phone lit up and vibrated with an incoming text message: *Consider this your final warning.*

Chapter Forty

Alex woke at seven o'clock on Sunday morning. He ached all over, having held himself in a painful position on the sofa. He was cold. So much for the thermal sleeping bag. As he sat up, he saw the reason why he'd been cold all night: the zip had broken, and his legs were exposed. They were so white, they were almost blue. He looked over to the living-room window, saw the boarding, and it all came flooding back. He quickly dressed and went into the kitchen.

'Good morning,' Diane said as she entered the kitchen. Alex was at the table, already on his second coffee.

'You don't mind me helping myself, do you?' He nodded to the plate of toast in front of him.

'No, of course not. I appreciate you staying over. I'm going to make some porridge, if you'd like some.'

'I'd love some, thanks.'

'I've just realised, I thought you were staying in Wales for the weekend. How come you came back?'

'It didn't need two of us,' he said, looking deep into his coffee cup.

'Oh. Did you sleep well?'

'Er ... well ...' he struggled to answer.

'I know. That sofa isn't the most comfortable one in the world, is it? I keep meaning to replace it but I never sit on it. I'm always in the armchair,' she laughed. She pulled out a chair opposite him and sat down. 'Can I tell you something?' She lowered her voice. 'I had a text last night while I was in bed. From Nick.'

'Oh.'

'Yes. He apologised – which isn't like him at all – for coming around here yesterday morning and behaving like he did.'

'Maybe he wants to make amends,' Alex guessed.

'Do you think?' she asked. There was the faint hint of a smile on her face. 'I do hate this animosity between us; but every time I think about him, I just think of all the hurt he put me through, leaving me when I needed him the most.'

'That's understandable. Did you reply?'

'Yes. I just said it was OK, that I understood. He asked if I wanted to meet him for a coffee, have a proper chat.'

'Will you?'

'I've nothing to lose. It might be better, just the two of us. I mean, our paths are going to cross more now that Marcus has a baby. We're bound to bump into each other. It would save a lot of awkwardness. You won't mention any of this to my mum, will you? She'll only launch into one of her diatribes about all men being bastards.'

Alex laughed. 'I hope I'm not included in that.'

'I think you're safe,' she replied, not too convincingly. 'I'll make us that porridge.'

Diane set about making the porridge. She was humming lightly to herself, and there was a spring in her step as she made her way around the kitchen. Alex went back into the living room. He checked his phone for any messages from Caroline or Shona and stopped in his tracks when he saw the threatening text waiting for him.

'Thanks for your number, Julianne,' he said quietly to himself.

Chapter Forty-One

WHO REALLY KILLED ZACHERY MARSHALL?

When serial killer Jonathan Egan-Walsh died from cancer last month, very few people mourned. For one person, Diane Marshall, it ended the 25-year search for her son's body. Zachery Marshall went missing when he was eight years old and was believed to be Jonathan's seventh victim. However, a letter found in Jonathan's prison cell following his death, has given fresh hope for Diane and her family, as the evil child predator has revealed information about her missing son.

Jonathan Egan-Walsh had, at long last, put his hands up and admitted he was guilty of the crimes he was sentenced to a whole-life tariff for in 1996. In the handwritten letter, addressed to Diane, Egan-Walsh categorically denies having anything to do with her eldest son's disappearance. At first, Diane was angry she had spent a quarter of a century begging for the paedophile to reveal the whereabouts of her son. Now, the 58-year-old is starting a new fight to find the truth behind Zachery's disappearance on Sunday, 10 January 1993.

[Continued ...]

After a large bowl of porridge and a long hot shower, Alex left Diane's just as the glazier arrived – telling her and her mother that he would be in touch later. He was on his way for his pre-arranged meeting with Detective Inspector Siobhan Gardner at Lincolnshire Police Headquarters in Nettleham. His phone told him it was only a fifty-three minute journey in light traffic. Traffic was indeed light, but it took him over an hour and fifteen minutes, thanks to his satnav taking him the wrong way down a one-way street.

Eventually, though, he arrived at Police HQ and checked in at Reception; whereupon, he was asked to take a seat until DI Turner could see him. While doing so, he found himself beginning to relax for the first time in days. This was what he was good at: researching, digging for information. He pondered on how many police stations he'd been in during his career, and that they all looked the same. He looked at the crime-prevention posters adorning the walls. If you took them all seriously, he thought, they would make you a nervous wreck and you'd never leave your house. For instance, there was one, laminated, poster on the door leading into the main station, informing visitors that the terror threat level was severe.

At that moment, the nearby lift doors opened, and a heavily pregnant woman stepped out. She was tall with mousy hair pulled back into a severe ponytail. She smiled when she saw her visitor.

'Alex Frost?'

'Yes,' he said, looking surprised at how huge she was. Shouldn't she be on maternity leave by now? he wondered, praying that she wouldn't go into labour while they were chatting. He didn't want to witness that.

'Nice to meet you. I'm DI Siobhan Gardner.' They shook hands.

'I'm sorry I'm a bit late. Sunday traffic,' he lied.

'That's fine. We'll go up to my office. Don't look so worried, I'm not due for another couple of months, yet.'

'Really?' he asked.

'I know. I'm big, aren't I? Apparently, there's only two in there. Personally, I think there's a full rugby team setting up home.'

They made small talk in the slow-moving lift and along the corridor to Siobhan's third-floor office, during which Alex found out she already had one child, a two-year-old named Daisy, and that she had been married for six years to a DCI Duncan Britton. Once in her office, she waddled over to her desk, where a steaming pot of tea, a jug of milk, some sugar and two mugs had already been placed.

Lowering herself into a reinforced chair, she motioned for Alex to take the one opposite. 'It's decaf, I'm afraid. You don't mind, do you?'

The coffee he'd drunk back at Diane's had woken him up, but he would have loved another injection of caffeine.

'That's fine,' he replied with a forced smile.

She poured the tea and handed him a mug, then opened a desk drawer and took out a packet of bourbon biscuits, 'To make up for the lack of caffeine, eh? Help yourself, and to milk and sugar.'

Siobhan was a warm and approachable woman. She had a young-looking face, spoke with a local accent, and a permanent smile that was welcoming.

'Now, you want to know about the Egan-Walsh case? How can I help?' she asked.

'Well, I was hoping for find out about the original investigation into Zachery Marshall's disappearance in 1993.'

'Well, following our earlier telephone conversation, I had the case file brought up from the archives. I'm afraid you're not going to be very happy.'

'Oh?' He stopped dunking his bourbon and looked up.

Siobhan reached across her desk and lifted up a box file. She opened it.

'I've got statements from the family and neighbours. There's information about the search and the registered sex offenders living in the local area who were questioned. Unfortunately, that's more or less all we've got.'

'Really?'

'The case stalled very early on, until DI Turner arrested Egan-Walsh in 1996. Unfortunately, there was very little activity in the three years in between.'

'Why was that?'

'To be honest with you, I have no idea.'

'Is there anyone still working here who was part of the original investigation?' Alex asked, hopefully. He looked out into the CID suite, at the few staff members who'd drawn the short straw to work on a Sunday. They all looked so young. He doubted anyone out there was *even* born in 1993.

'Not at this station, no,' she said, sympathetically. 'Obviously, when Jonathan was convicted, including for Zachery Marshall, our case was filed.'

'Even without having found a body?'

'All of Jonathan's victims were found by accident by passers-by. We don't have the resources to search every strip of land. If further evidence came to light, then, of course, we would take an interest. Until that happens, there's nothing, realistically, that we can do.'

Alex dug around in his satchel for the photocopied letter Jonathan had written to Diane. It was crumpled, so he smoothed it out on his lap as best he could before handing it across the table to Siobhan to read.

'Do you believe this is genuine? That Jonathan is telling the truth?' Alex asked.

Siobhan read it and sighed. 'I never met Jonathan. I don't know what mind games he was capable of playing,' she replied. 'However, after reading the article in the *Observer* this morning, I must admit that there's a pretty compelling case for *someone* – you, maybe? – to take another look,' she added with a smile, before handing the letter back to him.

'Article?'

'Yes. Haven't you seen it?'

'No.'

'Oh.' She looked around her untidy desk for the newspaper but it wasn't there. She struggled to turn around in her chair and, eventually, found it on top of a printer. She flicked through the paper, licking her finger with each turn of the page. 'Here we go,' she said, handing it over.

Alex read the article. It didn't go into much detail and there were no direct quotes from Diane. He wondered where the journalist had got their information from. 'Bloody journalists,' he said, ironically, throwing it down on the desk.

'I've been saying that for years,' Siobhan said. 'I'm pleased to hear *you* dislike them as much as we do,' she added with a friendly laugh. 'Do you mind if I ask you a question?'

'Go ahead,' he said, his eyes still on the offending article.

'Do *you* believe Jonathan's letter is sincere?'

Alex let out a heavy sigh. 'One day, I think it is, yes, another day I think, no, it's one of his mind games. He has manipulated everyone his whole life. I think we will only find out if Jonathan is telling the truth when we find Zachery's body and discover if it's wrapped in a white sheet or not.'

'True.'

'I don't suppose there's a chance of getting the case reopened?' Alex asked, a hopeful look on his face.

'Not on the basis of the letter.'

'So, I really am on my own, then?'

'Sorry.'

'Don't apologise. It's not your fault,' he took a sip of his bland tea. 'Jonathan's collection, where is that?'

'It's in storage.'

'Would I be able to see it?' he asked with the hint of a smile.

Siobhan looked out of her office into the CID suite. The few officers who were about were busy with their heads down, looking at their laptops. 'I think I could take you for a sneaky visit.'

'Thank you,' Alex said with a smile before reaching for another bourbon. 'What happened to Jonathan's flat?'

'It was sold by his solicitors to pay for his court costs, I believe.'

'What about all his possessions?'

'I'm not sure. You'd need to speak to his solicitor about that.'

Alex thought for a while before asking his next question. He was unsure whether he should. Screw it. 'DI Caroline Turner, who secured Jonathan's conviction – did you know her?'

'I wasn't here then. I know *of* her, though.'

'She left the force not long after Jonathan was sent down. Do you know why?'

'I'm not sure I should …'

'I just want to get a feeling for what Jonathan was like as a person from all angles. He ignored Diane Marshall's letters for years, he was manipulating her, giving her false hope. I want to know how he treated other people. It may help me to decide whether his letter is sincere or not, whether or not he was telling the truth,' he said, not quite believing his own rhetoric.

'I can understand that. DI Turner visited Jonathan several times in prison. He was convicted of thirteen murders, but it was believed there were many more victims out there that he was responsible for. There are still plenty of missing boys dating from the time Jonathan was committing his crimes. Anyway, on her last visit to interview him, something happened. He arranged something so he would be alone with Caroline.'

Alex looked on, wide-eyed. His mug was halfway to his mouth. 'What happened?'

'He raped her.'

Chapter Forty-Two

Alex's mind didn't refocus until they were back in the lift on the way down to the basement of the police station. Siobhan cried out.

'What's the matter?' Alex asked, snapping out of his reverie.

'I think the little buggers are trying to kick their way out,' she replied, holding onto her bulging stomach.

'Are you sure you should be at work?'

'I'd rather not be, but I've got a few more weeks left yet.'

The lift doors struggled to open. Alex immediately felt the difference in temperature now they were in the bowels of the police station, several metres below ground level. The lift doors opened, and the darkness beyond disappeared as the strip lights flickered slowly to life. Some stayed flickering stubbornly.

'Be careful,' Siobhan warned, her voice echoing. 'We've got rats down here.'

The room was large but not very high, like an underground car park. Running the full length of the space was floor-to-ceiling metal shelving. Nearly all were full, bursting at the seams with exhibits from cases going back years, decades.

'Do you really need to keep all this?' Alex asked as they walked slowly along the narrow passageway between two units.

'It depends. Once someone has been convicted and the appeal process is over, then, no. However, if there's ever any doubt, or, as in the case of Jonathan Egan-Walsh, there may be more victims out there, we are obliged to keep it for future reference.'

'You genuinely believe there are more victims out there?'

'Absolutely. You should see the Missing Persons list. It's frightening,' she said, caressing her baby bump, protecting her unborn twins.

They walked along the concrete floor, four shoes clacking loudly, resounding off the bare breezeblock walls. Each shelf was coded and alphabetised. Siobhan knew what she was looking for and stopped when she reached it.

'Here we go: "E".'

'Which shelf belongs to Jonathan?' Alex asked, looking up and down at the six-shelf unit.

'All of them.'

'Really?'

'And the next unit, too. He wasn't called The Collector for nothing,' she said with a smirk.

'That's not what I wanted to call it, originally,' he said, defensively, as he made his way along the shelves, reading the labels on the boxes. 'Can I look inside these?'

'Knock yourself out. I'm going to find a chair, my back's killing me. Give me a holler when you're ready to go back up. And mind the rats,' she added as she walked away.

Alex could already taste the dust from the boxes before he even touched them. It was in the air and he was breathing it in. His mouth was dry, his throat scratchy. He needed a drink, and he didn't mean water or coffee, *or* more decaf tea.

He stood back and examined the boxes in front of him. They were coded but it meant nothing to him. He pulled one out at random. It was heavier than he anticipated and it landed on the floor with an echoing thud. He coughed as a cloud of dust blew up in his face, then lifted off the lid and looked inside.

Wrapped in plastic to try to protect them from the rats were small items of clothing, all belonging to the missing and the dead. Alex lifted out a yellow T-shirt with a distinctive red-and-blue geometric print on the front. It was so small, and that made him feel incredibly sad. A boy who fitted this top should have been running around freely, kicking a ball, playing with friends without a worry in the world. Instead, he had come into contact with Jonathan Egan-Walsh, a man who didn't care about the innocence of the young, only about satisfying his own sick pleasure. Alex dropped the shirt back in the box and replaced the lid. He looked at the rest of the boxes with a look of contempt on his face. So many boxes. So many innocent lives lost. At the end of the day, Jonathan was a sick predator of young boys. One less victim didn't make him any different. Alex didn't need to see any more.

On leaving the police station, having thanked DI Siobhan Gardner for her time, Alex wandered aimlessly in the car park looking for his car. His mind was full of Jonathan's victims. There were twelve, possibly thirteen, that they knew of. How many more were out there? Then he remembered Siobhan's revelation about what had happened to Caroline. She was another victim of the depraved serial killer. As was Alex himself. As was his wife, Melanie. He wondered why Jonathan hadn't told him about the rape during their sessions together to research *The Collector*. He had mentioned Caroline on a few occasions but only with regard to the times she had interviewed him about his crimes. Did he regret what he had done or did he not want Alex to see him as a complete monster? This changed everything.

It was a cold, dull day, which seemed to be getting colder by the hour. A heavy dark cloud hung over Lincolnshire and fine flakes of snow had started to fall. He needed to get his thoughts in order before he continued with this. He had been hoping to get a second book out of the investigation, or at least an updated version of *The Collector*, but he liked Caroline. He wouldn't be able to write about her rape, put her through that again after everything she had suffered, but it wasn't something that should be left out. He coughed and could suddenly taste the dust from the basement.

His stomach grumbled but he wasn't in the mood for anything to eat. He felt sick at the thought of Jonathan forcing himself on Caroline and how helpless she would have been.

While he was writing *The Collector*, and researching Jonathan's life, Alex had tried to find something, a scrap of humanity, inside the serial killer. Had his tortured beginning turned him the way he was? Could it be that he himself being a result of a rape had had a profound and disturbing effect on him? Or was he just plain evil? Now, looking back, Alex realised Jonathan had used his neglected childhood as an excuse. All of those sessions they'd had where Jonathan had seemingly poured his heart out – how he had cried when he spoke of the death of his mother and how he would love to know who his father was, the tears for his grandmother dying alone in her flat – were a complete fabrication. Jonathan was vile, evil to the core – and he loved it.

———————

Having located his car, Alex drove back to the hotel on autopilot. He wasn't in the mood for doing any more work. He didn't want to eat or drink. He wanted to be alone with his thoughts. He'd thrown his battered satchel onto the back seat of his Volvo, jumped in, started the engine and turned left out of the police station car park to head back to his temporary home. He suddenly became aware of the distinctive smell of the coast coming through the air vents. Maybe a stroll along the beach would help clear his mind, he thought, despite the freezing temperatures.

Typically, his plan didn't work out and he soon found himself stuck in traffic. He looked out of the window at his surroundings: dated architecture, gaudy signs, shop windows filled with plastic tat to sell to tourists, flashing neon signs that wouldn't have looked out of place in Amsterdam advertising GIRLS GIRLS GIRLS rather than two-penny slot machines.

Family cars full of children were heading for the pier or the arcades. It was far too cold for the beach. Alex looked at the parents' blank faces as they listened to their warring children in the back of their cars, desperate to be entertained. He thought back to his own childhood. There was just him, a mother and father, living in Tottenham, in a spacious flat above an Italian restaurant. They didn't have much money, but he remembered his mother smiling, making his childhood as happy as possible. There were always plenty of presents under the Christmas tree, weekends on the coast at Brighton. Then his mind went to Jonathan and the childhood he'd been forced to endure. But was even that the truth? Had *he* been a pawn in Jonathan's manipulations?

Alex slammed his hands on the steering wheel to release some of the pent-up anger and frustration he was feeling. He hit the horn. The driver of the car in front lowered his window and stuck two fingers up.

Finally, the traffic seemed to thin out and he was soon moving forward once again. Then, forced to stop at a set of traffic lights as they turned red, a Citroën pulled upon his inside.

Glancing over, he spotted Nick Marshall in the driver's seat, but quickly looked away again, not wanting to attract his attention. Then, realising there was a passenger in the car, Alex risked taking another, quick, look. He'd never met Nick's second wife, Beth, so he had no idea what she looked like. However, he knew they had two children together so guessed she would be a bit younger than him – but certainly *not* as young as the twenty-something who was chatting away in the front passenger seat.

When the amber light started flashing, Alex immediately indicated left and quickly changed lanes behind the Citroën, much to the annoyance of the other drivers. He continued to follow Nick's car, taking care to keep well back. He had no idea why he was doing so, other than that something about their meeting the other night had unsettled him. Why was Nick so cagey about his son being found? What was he hiding?

The Citroën indicated left, then, to Alex's surprise, pulled up right outside the hotel he was staying in. Alex did the same, again facing the wrath of the cars behind. He lowered his passenger window and readied his mobile phone to take a photo.

The woman, whoever she was, leaned over to Nick and kissed him on the cheek, then opened the door and jumped out. Quickly, Alex took the opportunity to snap a photo as she did so, and managed to catch what she said. 'Thanks for the lift, Dad. I'll ring you in the week,' she said, loud enough to be heard above the noisy wind.

She was young, her long hair in braids, and Alex realised then that he'd seen her before, on Reception in the hotel on his first day here. Tonight, she was wearing a short skirt and a long sweater. She looked cold against the stiff wind but, Alex thought, obviously preferred to risk hypothermia as long as she looked good.

Alex frowned. He couldn't hear what Nick said in reply but there was no mistaking what his passenger had said.

Chapter Forty-Three

Monday, 26 February 2018

Caroline received a text from Alex before eight o'clock in the morning, asking if he could come over for a private word. She sent him reply straight back, asking if they could meet in a coffee shop, but Alex countered that this needed to be a private conversation. She didn't mind Alex coming to her home, but she was sure Jamie would.

Caroline had arrived home from Wales yesterday evening, around five o'clock, and Jamie had been waiting for her. He'd apologised, and she'd reciprocated. He then went on to say how empty the house had felt while she'd been away. Caroline wondered if that was the basis for his apology – he didn't like being on his own.

Either way, she accepted it. They had a long chat about how the Egan-Walsh case was important to Caroline, how she needed to find the truth about what had happened to Zachery Marshall.

Over a meal cooked by Jamie, they talked more about their lives as they both headed into old age. Jamie's primary concern was that he was frightened of losing his wife. As much as Caroline tried to allay his fears, he still maintained the lost look of a dog left out in the cold.

They had an early night, and, for the first time in years, they made love. It didn't cause much movement on the Richter scale, nor did it rattle the headboard, but it was physical contact and that was what Caroline had been missing. As she lay in his arms afterwards, her head on his chest, she smiled as she as began to drift into sleep. She realised her marriage was more important than anything else, and it wasn't worth sacrificing for closure on the Egan-Walsh case.

The next morning, she woke to an empty bed. The first thing she thought about was Zachery. So much for putting her marriage first. She wasn't bothered that Jamie had risen before her – something he rarely did – Alex's texts reinforced her drive to solve the case. He had information, and she was eager to hear what it was. She just needed to get Jamie out of the house first.

Fortunately, when Caroline descended the stairs, struggling to find the sleeve on her dressing gown, she found Jamie in the hallway wearing his yellow golfing trousers, searching in the cupboard under the stairs for his golf shoes. 'You're going out?' she asked.

'Yes. I'm meeting Frank for a round of golf. I told you last week.'

'Of course you did,' she said, not remembering.

'Did you sleep well?' he asked, taking her by the shoulders and kissing her firmly on the lips.

'Yes,' she smiled coyly.

'I was thinking, why don't we go away? We could rent a cottage somewhere.'

'I'd like that.'

'Not now, obviously. When it gets a bit warmer.'

Caroline visibly relaxed. She was dreading the thought of telling him she wanted to finish working with Alex and Diane before she did anything else. Hopefully, they would be done by the time spring arrived. Hopefully.

Jamie gave her another kiss and left the house. He didn't ask what she had planned for the day; he already guessed. He told her it would be late when he got back so not to do anything special for tea.

As the front door closed, Caroline sighed. It felt like she was having an affair, wanting rid of her husband so she could invite Alex over. She sent him a text then ran upstairs to shower and dress. She was dreading this first meeting with Alex after what had happened in Wales.

———————

Caroline was trying to make herself look decent in the bedroom mirror when she heard Alex's Volvo struggle up the incline of the road. She looked out of the window and watched as he parked on the drive.

Through the half-closed vertical blinds, she could see Alex looked awful. His hair was ruffled, though the strong breeze might have done that; his clothes looked slept in and she was sure he'd aged ten years over the weekend.

'Alex, is everything all right?' she asked, showing genuine concern, having opened the door before he had had a chance to knock.

'Yes. Fine. Why?' he replied, stepping inside.

'You look rough.'

'I feel rough. You haven't got anything to eat, have you?'

Caroline smiled. 'Go on through to the kitchen. I'll make you a bacon sandwich.'

'That would be heaven, thanks. A mug of builder's tea wouldn't go amiss, either.'

So much for worrying about their first meeting after the events in her hotel room. It was like Wales had never happened.

'You're not looking after yourself, are you?' she chided, following him into the kitchen where he sat at the table with a heavy sigh.

'I haven't been sleeping too well the past couple of nights. Someone hanged themself in The Majestic on Friday night.'

'Oh, God. How dreadful. That place is jinxed, I'm sure it is. A woman was murdered there last summer.'

'You didn't mention *that* before.'

'I didn't think you'd mind. You said you wanted a place with character.'

'By character, I meant period features, not a chalk outline on the floor.'

Caroline set about getting the bacon out of the fridge and hunting around for a frying pan. 'So, what have you got to tell me that couldn't be overheard by the people in Costa?'

'It's getting more confusing by the hour.'

'What do you mean?'

He filled her in on his hotel room being trashed, the threatening message on the mirror, the brick through Diane's living-room window and how Julianne Parker seemed to be back on the scene.

'What did DI Gardner say?' she asked, placing a large mug of strong hot tea in front of him.

He took a long sip. 'That's like a hundred-year single malt to me, thank you. I didn't think to mention Julianne to her. I'm not sure what Siobhan would be able to do, anyway, as all I have is her name and the fact she used to live in Coningsby. I have her the phone number from the text but, odds-on, it'll be a burner.'

'Are you worried?'

'Not for me. Slashing tyres and breaking windows is kids' stuff. I'm just worried about how this might escalate. It's you and Diane I'm worried about. You've not noticed anyone hanging around or had any strange phone calls, have you?'

'No. Look … Alex, are you sure you want to continue with

this? No offence, but you're looking tired. Why don't you go home and spend some time with Melanie and Shona?'

'I'm fine, honestly. It's sleeping on Diane's sofa that's made me look like this. You think you're doing someone a favour, and you spend the night with a spring up your arse,' he said with a wan smile. He took another lingering slurp of his tea. He seemed to be perking up with every sip. 'Answer me this: How many children do Nick and Diane have?'

'Two. Zachery and Marcus.'

'And when they split up, Nick remarried, yes?'

'Yes. I can't remember her name. They've got two children together, though, Diane was telling me. How do you like your bacon doing?'

Alex stood up and went over to the cooker. He looked in the frying pan. 'When the smoke alarm goes off, that's when it's ready.'

Caroline pulled a face. 'Bloody hell! You're just like Jamie – cooking the goodness out of everything.'

'Just bacon and toast. Nick's second wife, how old is she?'

'I'm not sure.' Caroline frowned. 'If I recall, Diane said she was a bit younger than Nick. Maybe mid-forties.'

'Have you seen her?'

'No. I haven't even seen Nick since Jonathan was sentenced. Why?'

Alex dug his heavily scratched mobile out of his pocket and scrolled through the photos. 'Take a look at this. Who is she?' He showed her the phone.

'I've no idea. Who is it?'

'That's what I asked you. She works as a receptionist in The Majestic. I saw Nick yesterday dropping her off in town, so I took a snap. She kissed him goodbye and called him "Dad".'

Caroline's eyes widened. 'Nick's kids are young, not even ten, I think. This woman looks to be in her mid-twenties. So, he's got other kids?'

'It proves that he's hiding something. A secret family, perhaps.' Alex replied.

'Why, though?' Caroline asked.

'Let's say she *is* his daughter. Let's say she is in her mid-twenties. She would have been born in the mid-nineties.'

'You think Nick and Diane were both cheating on each other? Bloody hell! What a set-up.'

Caroline took the mug from him and went over to the kettle to make him another. He watched her. He wanted to bring up what Siobhan had said to him yesterday but didn't want to hurt her by making her relive the horror. He was just about to say something when the smoke alarm sounded – Alex's bacon was ready.

Now in the Volvo, Alex filled Caroline in on their plans for the day. They were to visit Lachlan Minnow to find out more about Jonathan's past and what had happened to the contents of his flat. Afterwards, Alex wanted to call on Nick Marshall again, and find out who his mystery lady friend was.

Caroline's phone beeped an incoming text. 'It's Diane. She's asked if we're going over to hers today. She's been texting me on and off all weekend.'

'Yes. I hear from her a lot, too.'

'She's really digging her heels in, isn't she? I can't blame her, though. We seem to be her last hope. Poor woman. I'll tell her we'll call round later.'

As they drove along, Alex stole a quick glance at his passenger. He couldn't help but look for signs of sadness. He wondered why she was getting so involved in this case again after Jonathan had attacked her so violently the last time they met. Surely, she would want nothing more to do with him, or his crimes.

'What's wrong?' Caroline asked.

'Nothing. Why?'

'You keep looking at me.'

'Do I?'

'Yes.'

'Oh. Sorry. Listen, do you want me to drop you somewhere?'

'What? I thought we were going to see Lachlan Minnow.'

'We are. But I can do that on my own if you don't want to,' he said, thinking it may bring back more disturbing memories for her.

'No. I'm interested to know what he's going to say.'

'You're sure?'

'Yes. Look, Alex, what's going on?' she asked.

'Nothing. I just thought that ... Well, you know ...'

'No, I don't know. What are you going on about?'

He paused while he tried to think up a plausible answer. 'I mean, you arrested Jonathan. You got him convicted for thirteen murders. What if he is innocent of Zachery Marshall going missing? That's sort of putting your judgement into question.'

'Not really. We secured a conviction on the evidence we had. Jonathan pleaded not guilty. He never admitted his crimes. We often thought there could be more dead bodies out there he's responsible for.'

'Do you think that's possible?' he asked, wondering if Caroline would echo Siobhan Gardner's theory.

'Definitely. People go missing all the time. It's a sad fact that a lot aren't found. Some don't want to be found, but some are taken, and sometimes we don't find their body. They're forever listed as a "Missing Person".'

'That must be very difficult for the families,' Alex said.

'It is. Look at the way the Marshalls turned out. If only Jonathan had said right from the start he had nothing to do with Zachery going missing,' Caroline said, seething.

'He really got under your skin, didn't he?'

'Oh, look, John Lewis have a sale on,' she said, suddenly, staring out of the window, purposely avoiding his question.

Lachlan Minnow's suit screamed "designer". As did his glasses. As did his heavy ballpoint pen. The cologne he had doused himself with was making Caroline's eyes water. He tried to look young with his trendy haircut, but the eyes never lied. The crow's feet told Caroline he was leaning more towards forty than thirty.

'Thank you for seeing us, Mr Minnow,' Alex began.

'Lachlan, please,' he replied, pointing for them both to sit down in the comfortable leather chairs opposite his oversized desk.

'Lachlan … I'd like to ask you if you know anything about the stories that have appeared in several newspapers in the past week about the letter to Diane Marshall found in Jonathan Egan-Walsh's cell.'

Lachlan's faced reddened, giving himself away. He loosened his tie. 'Ah. I may do.'

'It was you? Why did you do that?' Caroline asked, genuinely shocked.

'A few extra quid in your back pocket?' Alex suggested.

'No. That wasn't it at all,' Lachlan replied, slightly affronted. 'I got talking to a friend about it who happens to be a journalist. I didn't think,' he said, lowering his voice and looking over at the door to make sure it was closed. 'Trust me, we're not friends any more. Look, do you mind telling me exactly why you've come to see me?'

'Yes, of course. What happened to Jonathan's flat after he was sent to prison?' Alex asked. He crossed his legs and waited for the reply, pen poised, notepad balancing precariously on his lap.

'Well, when Jonathan launched his appeals, he needed money, so the flat was sold and the money placed in trust to pay his costs.'

'What about the furniture?'

'That was sold, too.'

'And personal effects?'

'I wasn't at the firm at the time. However, I do know that an inventory was made of all the possessions in the flat and a solicitor went through it carefully with Jonathan. What he didn't want was simply thrown away.'

'And what about the items he did want?'

'They were given to him. If memory serves me correctly, it was just a few photos and books.'

'And what has happened to the items from his cell now that he's dead?'

'Jonathan made a will. He had some money left from the sale of his flat and what he'd earned while working in prison. After our fees were deducted, what was left was donated to charity, as per the instructions in his will.'

'Which charity?' Caroline asked.

Lachlan turned to his laptop and hammered loudly on the keys. 'There were four charities – two local children's homes, the NSPCC and a police charity to help officers injured in the line of duty. All donations were made anonymously,' he quickly added.

Caroline shook her head in disgust. He sexually abused and murdered at least thirteen boys, yet left money to children's charities.

'And his possessions?'

'We have them. To be honest, I'm not sure what we're going to do with them.'

'What are they?'

'As I said, books, photographs, and, also, some letters and drawings. I've looked and there's nothing of any great value.'

'Nothing worth selling to the media,' Alex said as an aside. Lachlan heard him but chose to ignore it. 'Would there be any chance of us seeing them?'

'I don't see why not. They're in the basement, though. Would it be possible for you to come back later this afternoon?'

'He's stalling,' Alex said once they'd left the building and were stood in the street.

'What do you mean?'

'He said there's nothing of value but he's going to have another last look, to see if there's anything he can use to his own advantage before handing it over. If the press doesn't want it, I'm sure some sicko on eBay will be willing to pay good money for a piece of serial-killer memorabilia.'

'What are we going to do now?'

'Nothing we can do until this afternoon. Fancy a walk on the seafront?' he asked.

'Really? It's bracing.'

'I think I'm becoming hardened to the northern winter,' he said with a smile as he zipped up his waterproof jacket.

Wrapped up against the elements, Caroline took Alex along the coastline. The beach was closed due to high winds. Several shops were also closed but the arcades and gift shops were open as usual.

'There's a permanent smell of fish and chips,' Alex said. 'Even when I open the window in my hotel room, I can smell fish and chips. And I keep getting a whiff of candyfloss, too. You could get diabetes just inhaling in this town.'

'You don't like the North, do you?' Caroline asked.

'I do, actually. Melanie and I had a few walking holidays in the Peak District when we were first married. I couldn't live here, though. It feels too much like a holiday resort. I bet you don't see the same people twice.'

Caroline laughed. 'It's the seaside; it's supposed to be like that. Besides, the last time I was in London, it was an hour before I heard an English accent. There were Americans with maps and Japanese taking photos and Australians posing outside Big Ben.'

'That's London for you. Do you get many Americans up here?' he asked, a hint of sarcasm in his voice.

'Can you honestly see people who live in swanky New York apartments slumming it in a caravan in Skegness?'

'Not really. I don't mean to make fun. I'm sure it's lovely in the summer.'

They leaned against the railings, looking out at the angry sea as huge waves crashed on the shore and the spray hit them in the face. Maybe at the height of summer with the sun beating down on the golden sand and the blue sea whispering to the shore, it did look welcoming, but, at the moment, in the depths of winter, with a desolate pier, an abandoned seafront and closed shops, it felt more like a town under curfew.

They walked further along the seafront. Building work on a new parade of shops had been left to the elements, the tarpaulins rattling in the wind. Caroline was talking, pointing out local features, telling him what the council had planned for the future to make sure the English seaside town continued to thrive, but Alex wasn't listening. His mind was elsewhere. He thought back to the person in The Majestic who had hanged themself. He wondered how many others had chosen that hotel to end their life. There were many hotels and guest houses dotted around Skegness. Had they all had a suicide at some point? At this time of year, it was understandable. If your life was meaningless, an out-of-season seaside town was not the place to be.

Alex wondered who would miss *him* if he walked to the end of the pier and jumped into the violent sea below. Melanie wouldn't. She wouldn't even know about it. Shona would, of course, for a while, but he had several insurance policies.

He was probably worth more dead than alive. She could move on, build a new life for herself. He surrounded himself with killers, broken families, death and destruction on a daily basis. What kind of a life was this?

'Do you like the clock tower?' Caroline asked when they reached it at the junction with Lumley Road.

'What? Yes. Very beautiful,' he said, looking up at the structure in the middle of the roundabout.

'It was built to mark Queen Victoria's Diamond Jubilee in 1897.'

'Really? It doesn't look that old.'

'We like to look after things up here.'

Alex's phone beeped the sound of an incoming email. With cold fingers, he fished his mobile out of his pocket. 'Excellent!' He exclaimed. 'It's from a friend of a contact of a contact in Australia,' he said, quickly reading the email. 'She's got a number for Diane's sister.'

'Do you know, it wasn't until I left the force that I realised how cynical the job had made me. Everyone has to have an ulterior motive for their actions. Maybe Maria just moved away for a better life. It's the same for journalists too, isn't it?'

'Maybe. But it's my job to cover every angle and get to the truth. Do you think there's somewhere warm open where we can sit down so I can thaw out enough to type a reply?' he asked, looking around him.

'I thought you were getting hardened to our northern winter,' she said with sarcasm. 'Come on, I'll treat us to some hot chocolate.'

They went into the nearest café they could find. It wasn't until Caroline was being served that she realised this was the same place she and Diane came to on the day Diane had tracked her down on the beach. This was where it all began. She turned around to see Alex perched on the radiator against the wall. He was tapping frantically on his mobile.

On a tray she carried the hot chocolate and muffins over to their table, where he joined her, putting his mobile away.

'This is ... quaint,' he said, searching for the right word.

'You mean old-fashioned and dingy?' she smiled.

'No, quaint. It's typical olde-worlde seaside.'

'Which do you want, chocolate chip or lemon?' she asked, pointing to the muffins.

'Like you need to ask,' he said, snatching the chocolate chip.

'Come on, Alex, out with it,' Caroline said, eventually, while they were tucking into their cakes.

'What?' he asked with a mouthful muffin.

'You've been looking at me funny all morning. I thought we were putting the whole Wales thing behind us.'

'It's not that.'

'What is it, then?'

Alex looked around him, but they were the only customers in the café and the old woman behind the counter was too engrossed in her *Take A Break* to listen to what they were saying. Nonetheless, he leaned forward and lowered his voice.

'When I went to see DI Gardner, she told me what happened between you and Jonathan when he was in prison. Is it true?'

'Is *what* true?' Caroline asked, not making eye contact, suddenly more interested in her drink.

'He … you know … raped you.'

'*What?* No. He did not. Is that what she said?'

'Yes.'

'He didn't rape me. Look, now is not the time to talk about it. *Jesus!*' she said, slamming her spoon down on the table and pushing her mug away.

'Sorry, have I upset you?'

She remained silent for a moment before answering. Her face was a picture of angst and frustration. 'No. I left the force because I couldn't get Jonathan out of my mind. He was always there, constantly fighting for my attention. Whenever a missing child cropped up, I went straight to thinking of him, even though he was in prison and couldn't possibly have anything to do with it.'

'So why are you getting involved now?'

'Because I promised Nick and Diane I would find Zachery for them. I'm doing it for them, not him.'

'But why? It's not your job any more.'

'When I was working on the case, my son, Dylan, was eight years old. When I met the Marshalls, I kept going home and seeing Zachery when I should have been seeing Dylan. I ruined his childhood by being overprotective: not letting him play out without me being able to see where he was, constantly checking up on him, phoning his friends' parents. He now lives in Norway. The first opportunity he got, he left home, moved as far away from me as he could. We have a better relationship now, I suppose, but it's still not great. We're not as close as we should be. I just think that if I can find out what happened to Zachery, all the sacrifices I made would be worth it.'

Caroline turned and looked out of the window. It had steamed up from the heating inside, but through the condensation she could see a blurred image of what lay beyond, and it was a depressing sight. A seaside location in the middle of winter was dreary, dank dead. Despite her rhapsodising to Alex about Skegness, she hated it around here. When Jamie retired, she had planned to bring up the topic of moving somewhere more rural, or maybe abroad. She could easily get rid of her dog-walking business. However, every time she had thought of broaching the subject, she'd remembered that, somewhere in this bleak landscape, Zachery Marshall was waiting to be discovered. She couldn't leave. Not until he had been found and returned to his mother.

Chapter Forty-Four

Thursday, 24 August 2000

Caroline pulled up in the car park at HMP Long Lartin in Worcestershire. It had been a long drive, made longer thanks to roadworks. She looked in the rear-view mirror to check her appearance, making sure she didn't have anything in her teeth, opened the glove box and took out a packet of mints to freshen her breath, then sat back in her seat and waited, sucking hard on the mint, running it around her mouth. She had not been looking forward to this visit one bit.

On the front passenger seat was a pile of cardboard files, each one containing details of a missing boy, from various towns and cities across England. All fitted Jonathan Egan-Walsh's *modus operandi*: the boys were between the ages of seven and ten, and had disappeared without a trace. During Jonathan's incarceration, various police forces had tried to arrange an interview with him, but he had flatly refused. Instead, through his solicitor, he had released a statement, stating that the only person he would talk to would be DI Caroline Turner. She had asked why, but wished she hadn't when she heard the reason: Jonathan said he really liked her. It was the stress the solicitor gave to *really* that sent a chill down her spine.

Her boss hadn't asked her *if* she would like to see Jonathan again; it had been decided that she *would* see him, acting as an intermediary, to try to discover if he were responsible for the eight missing boys these forces had unearthed. The parents of the missing had been to look at Jonathan's collection. Six had positively identified items belonging to their son. And there were many more parents around the country who had missing children who also fitted the victimology. This case would never end. Caroline knew Jonathan would be in her life until she retired, if not longer.

She had spoken to Jamie long and hard before agreeing to her boss's diktat, not that she felt she could easily turn it down – they would make life incredibly difficult for her if she did. So, she had set off for Worcestershire while it was still dark, and as she'd made her way down the motorway, the sun had begun to rise, a beautiful red sky stretching out before her.

Leaving her handbag and phone in the car, Caroline headed to the main entrance. She could feel her white shirt sticking to her back but didn't know whether she was sweating from the heat of the sun or because of her nerves.

She had a twenty-minute wait in Reception, until a member of staff became available to take her to the interview room. Twenty minutes in which to sweat some more, to panic, to worry.

Eventually, a large barrel of a man led her along the sticky tiled floor, up a flight of stairs, along a narrow corridor and through several security doors to the interview room. She had been in rooms like this many times before; the table and chairs were screwed to the floor, the glass in the windows and doors was reinforced and two cameras in the corners of the room recorded everything that went on.

Caroline sat down and placed the files in a neat pile in front of her. She waited, nervously, for the arrival of the man she had arrested and had seen sentenced to a whole-life tariff. Jonathan entered the room five minutes later. As soon as he saw her, he smiled.

'Detective Inspector Turner, what a treat it is to see you once again. I'd shake hands, but ...' he said, raising his handcuffed wrists.

Two prison officers escorted him in and sat him down at the table. One of them stationed himself directly behind the prisoner, the other stood by the door. They were tall, broad men with the hardened expressions of seasoned officers. Nothing would shock these men. They had seen everything there was to see in a prison.

'Jonathan, I've been asked to question you on the whereabouts of eight missing boys. Clothing from six of them has been identified in your collection by their parents.' Her voice was shaking. She had tried to control herself, but her voice let her down.

'Caroline, this is so insensitive. You and I go back a long way. Tell me how you're doing. How's Jamie? How's Dylan? He must be a teenager by now.'

Caroline swallowed hard. She dared not look up from the file she was flicking through. She tried her hardest not to let him see he was having an effect on her, but it wasn't easy.

'The first boy is seven-year-old Shaun Paisley. He went missing in Norfolk on Sunday, 16 July 1994 ...'

'Straight down to business, then, is it?' he interrupted.

Caroline looked up and into his small, smiling eyes. 'We have a lot to get through, Jonathan.'

'Surely, there's time for a little chat first. I don't get many visitors. It's nice to find out what's going on in the outside world.' Caroline remained impassive. 'You're looking well. Have you been on your summer holidays? Let me guess, you and hubby took Dylan to Spain. I bet he looked lovely running on the beach in just a pair of shorts.'

'That will do, Jonathan,' the officer at the door said in a heavy Birmingham accent.

'Caroline and I are old friends, Mr Jarrett. We're just catching up.'

'I am not your friend, Jonathan. Now, are you going to answer my questions, or aren't you? If not, I'm leaving.' Caroline tried to sound strong and authoritative but she couldn't hide the fear in her voice. She was inches away from the killer and, even with the prison officers in the room, she didn't feel one hundred percent safe.

'OK. Show me your files, then, if you're going to get all huffy about it.'

Caroline opened the first file and looked down at the school photograph of a smiling Shaun Paisley. To think the man opposite her had toyed with him, tormented him, tortured him, made her feel sick. She turned the file around and slid it across the table.

'Where did he go missing from, again?' he asked as he licked his lips and looked down at the photograph.

'Norfolk. To be precise, Coltishall in Norwich.'

'When was it, again?'

'Sunday, 16 July 1994.'

'Hmm …' he said, studying the picture. After a few long seconds of silence, he looked up into Caroline's eyes. 'He's a good-looking boy. Cute dimples.'

'Do you recognise him?'

'I'm not sure,' he said, playfully. 'He looks familiar. Actually, don't you think he has a striking resemblance to your Dylan? Same eyes.'

'You've never seen my son,' Caroline said.

'Oh, but I have, Caroline. Believe me, I have,' he said, sitting back in his chair with a smug expression on his face.

Caroline could taste the bile in her mouth. 'Jonathan, please answer my questions. Do you recognise this boy?'

'I don't know. Show me the others.'

Caroline took a deep breath. She opened all the files and took out all the photographs of varying sizes and slid them across the table.

Jonathan held up his hands. 'I can hardly flick through them while I'm like this, can I?' He rattled his handcuffs.

'Can you remove them?' she asked the officer standing directly behind him.

He took a key from his back pocket and leaned down to unlock the cuffs. As he did so, he whispered into Jonathan's ear, 'Try anything, and I'll break both your arms.'

Jonathan smirked. He flexed his wrists and rubbed at them, taking his time. When he was ready, he picked up the photographs one by one, taking his time to look through them all.

'Well?' Caroline asked.

'A couple look familiar, but, well, kids all look the same, don't they?'

'Not really.'

An alarm sounded from outside. Caroline looked up but the prison officers ignored it. 'Is that a fire alarm?' she asked.

'No. There's probably an incident on one of the wings. Nothing to worry about.'

'Are we safe in here?'

'Perfectly,' he replied, smiling reassuringly.

'Probably Thatcher,' Jonathan said. 'He's been threatening to slash his wrists for weeks.'

'Jonathan, back to the photos,' Caroline said.

The alarm continued and the prison officers kept exchanging nervous glances. Caroline looked between the two. The one standing behind Jonathan may have sounded confident when he said she was perfectly safe in here, but now she wasn't so sure. Why couldn't she have broken down on the motorway and had to cancel?

'I'm going to see what's going on,' said the officer by the door. 'Put the cuffs back on him until I get back.'

He left the room, closing the door behind him. The officer behind Jonathan took the key out of his back pocket and leaned down to secure the cuffs. Just as he was about to do so, Jonathan jumped up, grabbed the officer's hair and slammed his head down onto the desk. There was a loud bang. The officer was knocked unconscious. Jonathan threw him to the floor, grabbed at his chair and wrestled with it to tear the screws out of the ground. It seemed to come away *so* easily. The whole time, Caroline watched in shock. He then took the chair over to the door and secured it under the handle.

Caroline dropped to the floor and tried desperately to wake up the prison officer, but he was out cold, blood pouring from his broken nose. She searched on his body for something she could use as a weapon, but she was out of time. Jonathan lunged towards her, wrapped her long hair around his fist and pulled her up from the floor. She screamed.

'I've been waiting for this for a long time,' he whispered into her ear.

He pushed her against the wall and pressed himself up against her.

'Jonathan, let me go. This isn't going to do you any good.'

'I'm in here for life. It doesn't matter what I do. I could rip you open and eat your liver. What can they do, give me another life sentence? Big deal.'

Caroline started to cry.

Using his right hand, he grabbed her by the throat and started to squeeze.

'Don't cry. I'm going to enjoy this. The first time I set eyes on you, I knew I wanted to kill you. I'm a very patient man. I play the long game. I've waited and I've waited and now I'm going to squeeze every inch of life out of you, *mother*.'

Caroline's eyes widened. 'What?' she struggled to say.

From somewhere, Caroline managed to find an ounce of

strength. She brought her knee up to his crotch and pushed him off her. He staggered backwards.

'*You fucking bitch!*'

She kicked him in the crotch, harder this time. He bent over double. She ran to the door, grabbed the chair, with an effort released it from under the handle, then, with as much energy as she could muster, brought it crashing down over his head. '*You disgusting bastard!*' she screamed at him.

Running back to the door, she opened it and screamed for help through the sound of the screeching alarm.

Chapter Forty-Five

'What happened to Jonathan?' Alex asked.

They'd left the café behind them, had decided to go for another walk, and had taken cover in a bus shelter. The weather was against them.

'He was charged with all kinds of things. He'd arranged for a fellow prisoner to start a mini riot so the alarm would be set off, knowing full well one of the officers would leave the room. He'd even had someone loosen the screws on the chair in the interview room. He'd orchestrated the whole thing.'

'Bloody hell! Was the prison officer he knocked out all right?'

'Broken nose and a fractured skull. He never returned to the Prison Service. Not that I can blame him.'

'Did you cause Jonathan much damage?' he asked with a smile, nudging Caroline.

'I did, actually,' she replied, looking smug. 'He had a ruptured testicle and concussion.'

'Well done.'

'Thank you. I was quite proud of myself. There was no way I was allowing that creep to kill me.'

'He had some real mother issues, didn't he?'

'It wasn't until that point that I realised I looked like his mother.'

'Funnily enough, Diane and I noticed it the other day, when we were going through some old press cuttings.'

'When I first walked into that interview room, Jonathan stared at me. He was mesmerised. I had no idea what he was thinking,' she said, shuddering at the memory.

'And he definitely didn't … you know … rape you?'

'No!' she said firmly.

'I wonder why DI Gardner said he did.'

'Chinese whispers, I suspect.'

Alex frowned. 'Mind you, he probably wouldn't have been able to, even if he wanted to. That was one of his main defences, that he was impotent.'

'Total fabrication. He was caught, many times, in his cell, masturbating over pictures of young boys.'

'How do you know?'

'Like I said, I've had Jonathan living in my head since I arrested him. I've had prison officers tell me stories that will make your eyes water. Look, I'm fed up of all this waiting around; let's go back to his solicitor and get that information from him.' Caroline lifted up the collar on her jacket and headed back out into the sleet.

―――――――

Lachlan Minnow had arranged for a pot of coffee for the three of them. The strong coffee aroma mingled with Lachlan's cologne.

'I was right. It's just photos, books, letters and drawings,' Lachlan said as he got up from his desk to retrieve two cardboard boxes from underneath a table.

Caroline picked up a framed photograph from Lachlan's desk and studied it. 'Who's this?'

Placing the boxes on top of the table, Lachlan moved back

towards Caroline. 'My grandma,' he replied. 'She brought me up when my parents died. That was taken on her one hundredth birthday.'

'Really? She doesn't look a day over eighty.'

'I know.' Lachlan smiled. 'She was a very active woman, right up until the end. She was a hundred and two when she died. Remarkable lady.' He took the photo from her and looked at the picture himself with wide eyes, as if seeing it for the first time.

'Lachlan, you knew Jonathan,' Caroline said, sitting down. 'What did you think of him?'

'I liked him.'

Caroline and Alex looked at Lachlan, wide-eyed.

'You *liked* him?' Caroline looked disgusted. 'He murdered thirteen boys, if not more. How could you *like* him?'

'I didn't know him, then. I only saw the Jonathan in prison. He was … personable,' he said. 'He was highly intelligent, well-read. He always helped other prisoners with letters home if they needed it. He even helped me.'

'In what way did he help you?'

'I used to be a smoker – quite a heavy one, actually. I used to get nervous going into courts and I found a cigarette, or three, helped to calm me down. Jonathan helped. He was very supportive,' he said with the hint of a smile.

'But you were solicitor and client.'

'That doesn't mean you can't befriend someone.'

'You were *friends*?' Caroline replied, aghast, genuinely unnerved.

'Well, perhaps not friends.' He looked down at the photograph of his grandmother. 'We … got on well, that's all.'

Caroline tried to think of something to say but she was struck dumb by this revelation. How could anyone claim to be friends with a mass murderer?

'Who wrote to Jonathan?' Alex asked, bringing the conversation back on topic.

'His gran, until she died.' He moved from his desk, away from Caroline, and over to Alex who was standing by the table. He'd already opened one of the boxes. 'They're not the nicest of letters, I must say. She repeats over and over about how disappointed she is in him, how she gave him every opportunity in life and he threw it back in her face. I felt quite sorry for her.'

'Did he go to her funeral?' Alex asked.

'He was supposed to, but he was involved in a fight the day before, so had the privilege withdrawn.'

'Did she have anything to leave in her will, do you know?'

'I don't know. We weren't her solicitors. If she did, she didn't leave anything to Jonathan.'

Caroline came over to the table, though she couldn't take her questioning eyes from Lachlan. He retreated back to his desk and adjusted the framed photograph of his grandmother.

Alex took a tatty brown envelope out of the box. He looked inside and tipped out the contents: photographs. They were all creased or stained in some way. He flicked through them rapidly. Most of them he had seen before while he had been interviewing Jonathan for *The Collector*. There were childhood snaps of him in his grandmother's back garden or on the beach playing with other children. On the face of it, they were innocent photographs, but when you considered what the young Jonathan would grow up to become, they had a more sinister edge.

Caroline stepped away from the table, moving over towards the window.

'Is everything all right?' Alex asked.

'Jonathan as a child; he looks like his victims. I had so many files on my desks of missing children around the country, hundreds of photographs of kids in school uniforms or on holiday, grinning to the camera, just like he's doing there,' she said, pointing to the photos. 'He looks so … sweet.'

'It's hard to fathom how children are going to grow up, what they're going to become.' Alex looked down at a picture of Jonathan on a swing. He was wearing a dark-red T-shirt and blue shorts. His smile was huge. He was enjoying himself. At what age did playing in a park no longer satisfy him and kidnapping and murdering did? It was an unimaginable leap.

There were a few pictures of his grandmother: a small, plump woman with a hardened expression, even when she was showing the approximation of a smile. There were no other photos of family members.

'Are there no photographs of his mother?'

'No,' Lachlan said.

'When I interviewed his grandmother for the book, she showed me an album full of photos of her. Do you know what happened to them?'

Lachlan went over to his desk and took a file out of a drawer. 'I've got a list of everything that was in Jonathan's flat, what he wanted to keep, what he wanted destroying. There is no mention of a photo album.'

'His grandmother's solicitor, he would have gone through all her possessions with Jonathan, wouldn't he?'

'If he was named as next of kin, yes.'

'So, it's likely he asked for the photos of his mother to be destroyed?'

'It's possible.'

'That's harsh,' Alex said, looking over towards Caroline.

'Well, we both know how he felt about his mother, don't we?'

Alex picked up a roll of paper fastened with a rubber band. He took it off and spread the A3 sheets of paper out on the desk. They were pencil drawings of landscapes.

'Wow!' he said, genuinely impressed. 'These aren't bad.'

'He took a few art classes in prison,' Lachlan said. 'I remember him showing me these. They *are* good, aren't they?'

Alex studied one more closely. It showed a large expanse of fields with an isolated house in the middle distance. The sea in the background looked calm and welcoming, certainly not how it looked today.

'Did he draw from anything in particular or are these just random pictures?' Alex asked.

'I don't know. He never said.'

Caroline came back to the table from the window. She looked over Alex's shoulder at the sketches then reached into a box and picked up a sketchpad. She flicked through the pages, seeing half-finished drawings of trees, hands in various poses, woodland.

'Oh, my God,' she said.

'What is it?'

Alex looked at the sketchbook over her shoulder. 'Bloody hell!'

They were looking at a pencil drawing of a young boy. The lines were soft and smooth, each strand of hair had been lovingly drawn. It was beautiful.

'Who is it?' Lachlan asked.

'It's Zachery Marshall,' Caroline replied.

Chapter Forty-Six

A whole-life tariff is a long time to spend in a prison cell. The boredom sets in pretty quickly. I had a job in the kitchens and I went to art classes and I was studying for a degree with the Open University, but I always seemed to have so much free time. Too much free time.

I didn't make friends among my fellow inmates. I don't think the prison authority like you to, anyway. They seem to move you around a lot. I was on remand at Gartree then started my actual sentence at Wakefield, then seemed to go on a tour of prisons throughout the country before ending up back at Wakefield. Never once did I see the outside world.

I enjoyed drawing. I seemed to pick it up quite easily. My first tutor, Geoffrey Pritchard, was a decent bloke. He saw my talent and often left me alone to draw what I wanted while he spent time with the other prisoners showing them where they were going wrong when their vase of daffodils looked like crap. I used to sit in the corner with my pad and my row of pencils and I'd draw whatever came into my mind.

I drew a picture of Caroline Turner's son, Dylan, in his football kit from that photo in the newspaper. I drew him with long floppy hair, *sweat running down his face, his kit tighter than in the photo. That nonce, Clive Moffat, stole that one. I could never get it right again.*

At night, when I was locked up in my cell, I'd spend hours in bed with my sketchbook, drawing, whiling away the long hours. Even after lights out and I was plunged into darkness, my eyes seemed to adjust as I could still see what I was drawing by the scant light that came through the small window. I'd be awake until three or four o'clock in the morning, drawing Danny Redpath, Peter Wright, Kevin Watts and Zachery Marshall. I saved drawing Zachery until it was dark as I could see him in my mind's eye better than anyone of the other boys. All I had to do was close my eyes and there he was. I could spend hours lovingly pencilling in every strand of his hair. Even now, I can picture him running around at family weddings and celebrations. He was a very good-looking boy.

You knew he was going to grow up to be a heart breaker.

My favourite picture to draw was of the cottage my gran used to take me to when I was a child. It was out in the middle of nowhere, overlooking the sea.

It was always cold as the wind used to be so strong there, but it was great to get away from other people and noise for a weekend or so. It was a long walk to the beach and there wasn't really a path, so we often stayed in the cottage all day. Gran would sit there with her puzzle books and I'd read or play with a deck of cards.

It was a simple cottage, only one bedroom with a huge iron bed in it, which I'd have to share with Gran. I didn't mind. She was always so warm.

I wonder what happened to that cottage. It was never mentioned in my gran's will. I bet she sold it. That should have been mine once she'd died. I wanted it. I loved that place. I cherished it.

Chapter Forty-Seven

A lex drove in silence, concentrating on the road ahead. In the passenger seat, Caroline stared out of the window, watching the landscape blur as they broke the speed limit. On the back seat were the two boxes Lachlan Minnow had allowed them to take away. Once he realised there had been drawings of the victims, the solicitor was keen to get them out of his office.

Caroline turned back and looked at the boxes. Her blood ran cold at the thought of the contents. Jonathan had obviously spent hours in his cell sketching from memory the faces of those he'd killed. But why had he drawn Zachery Marshall if he claimed he wasn't one of his victims? Or *was* his letter from beyond the grave another act of his manipulation? Just when they thought they had a handle on this case, they found something that threw them in a different direction.

'Where are we going now?' Caroline asked, eventually, breaking the heavy silence. 'Alex?' she said more loudly when he didn't reply.

Alex eased on the brake and they started to slow down. 'Sorry, I was miles away. What did you say?'

'Where are we going?'

'We're going to see Nick Marshall.'

'What are we going to do about all this lot?' she asked, nodding back towards the boxes.

'Do you have the stomach to go through all his sketches and letters?'

'When I was a detective I wouldn't have batted an eyelid.'

'And now?'

'I don't have anyone to delegate the task to now, do I?' She gave a nervous laugh. 'We'll take them to Diane's, go through it all there.'

'Is that wise?'

'Where else can we go …' It wasn't a question. The only other logical place was her own place, and she didn't really want any of those items in her house. Jamie certainly wouldn't.

Alex turned into the car park of Barrett International and parked close to the entrance.

'What do they *actually* do at Barrett International?' Caroline asked as she unclipped her seatbelt.

'Something to do with communications. I looked at their website and still hadn't much of a clue.'

'So, what's the plan? Are we just going to go in and confront him?'

'I don't see why not.'

Alex took huge strides to the building. He seemed like a man on a mission, full of determination. Caroline had to trot to keep up with him.

The automatic doors yawned open with an ear-piercing squeak. The reception area was unnecessarily spacious with modernistic furniture that looked more like works of art than seats for visitors.

'Good afternoon and welcome to Barrett International. How may I help you?'

The receptionist did not fit in with the designer building. She was close to retirement age, wore a thick mohair cardigan and had glasses on a chain around her neck.

'Good afternoon,' Caroline said with a smile. 'We'd like to speak to Nick Marshall, please.'

'Is he expecting you?'

'No. Could you tell him it's Caroline Turner and Alex Frost? He knows who we are.'

'Certainly. Would you like to take a seat?'

Caroline turned to look at the seating area. She assumed the receptionist meant the mounds of bent Perspex.

'Apparently, it's minimalism,' the receptionist said. 'You wouldn't believe how much it cost, either. I decorated my whole house for less.' She laughed then picked up the phone and dialled a three-digit number.

Caroline joined Alex who was busy reading the company's Mission Statement, which had been painted onto the wall.

'This is all bollocks,' he said in a hushed voice. 'It's just buzzwords.'

'Mr Marshall said he won't be long,' the receptionist called out. 'Can I get you a tea or coffee while you wait?'

'We're fine, thanks.'

Caroline decided not to attempt to sit on the chairs, but flicked through a magazine while they waited.

'Interesting article?' Alex asked.

'It's about the fibre-optic revolution and the global effect on communications transfer.'

'What does that mean?'

'Not a clue. It's not exactly *Cosmo*. I wonder if there's a quiz you can take to find your ideal partner in the business world.' She laughed.

'He's here,' Alex whispered.

Caroline slapped the magazine down on the plastic table as she looked up to see Nick Marshall exit a lift. He smiled at the receptionist but waited until he was almost nose to nose with Alex before he addressed them.

'Couldn't this have waited until after work?' he asked. His quiet tone was seething with frustration.

'I'm afraid not,' Alex said loudly. 'We'd like to ask you a few questions about your private life.'

'Not here,' Nick said, looking around. 'Susan, is there a room free?'

'Number Two. Would you like me to bring in some refreshments?'

'They're not staying.'

With that, he ushered them down a corridor at the side of the reception desk, opened the first door on the right and practically pushed them both in. He followed and closed it firmly behind him.

The room was nondescript and didn't have the fashionable furniture of Reception. Grey carpet tiles, bland Venetian blinds and furniture from Ikea.

This was a room rarely seen by members of the public, it seemed. Typically, the company was all flash on the surface and no substance underneath.

'What's this room used for?' Caroline asked out of curiosity.

'It doesn't matter. What do you want?' Nick asked, still using his quiet, angry tone.

'Can you tell me who this is?' Alex asked, showing Nick the photo he'd taken of the young woman exiting his car.

'Have you been following me?'

'Not intentionally. Who is she?'

'She's a family friend,' he lied, blatantly. 'Her name's Jennifer. I was giving her a lift.'

'Is that why she kissed you on the cheek?'

'She thanked me.'

'So, why did she call you "Dad"?'

Nick's eyes widened. His face paled. He pulled out a chair and sank into it. 'She's my daughter,' he admitted, finally.

'We guessed that much. How old is she?' Caroline asked.

'She's twenty-six,' he said after swallowing hard. Caroline flinched. 'She was born five months before Zachery went missing. Beth's her mother. When she got pregnant, I'd planned to leave Diane but I kept putting it off. Then Zachery went missing and it all just … I couldn't leave.'

'Hang on,' Caroline said. 'Diane told me Beth has two children from a previous marriage. But you didn't leave Diane until 2000 …'

'Jennifer's mine as well.'

'You were living a double life all that time?'

'I couldn't leave Diane. Not in the state she was in.'

'But why did you have two more children? It's a bit of a big age gap, isn't it?' Caroline asked.

'That's none of your business. Look, why do you have to come here and rake all this up? You're not a detective any more, so why are you putting me through all this torment?'

'We're trying to get answers.'

'You have answers. We all know what happened to Zachery. You're just creating tension when there doesn't need to be. This has to stop,' he said, almost pleading.

'We can't stop, Nick,' Alex said. 'We've uncovered things. We're getting closer to the truth.'

'And I think Diane is going to have a few questions now,' Caroline added.

'You can't tell her.' He jumped up.

'Does Marcus know?'

'Nobody knows. You can't tell them,' he said, panic etched on his face.

'Nick,' Alex began, 'on the day Zachery disappeared, you went to the British Gas offices to sort out a problem and you took Marcus with you. What happened?'

'What do you mean?' His eyes were darting from side to side.

'How long did it take you to sort it out?'

'Not long. It turned out one of the computers had been unplugged. Then I went to see Beth.'

'And you took Marcus with you?'

'I said she was someone from work I had to sort out the problem with. I wanted to see my daughter. Oh, God!' he cried. 'Do you think I haven't gone through that day over and over again in my head? If I'd gone straight back home, Zachery might not have gone out on his bike, or I might have gone with him.'

'Nick,' Caroline eventually said, stepping forward. She put a comforting arm around him, 'I really think you need to talk to Diane about all of this.'

'There's no need. We rarely speak.'

'You texted her on Saturday night,' Alex said. 'It's obvious you want to make amends, move on.'

'Nick, you're not to blame for Zachery going missing. You can't not do things on the basis of what may or may not happen. You'd drive yourself mad if you did.'

Nick started laughing.

'What's funny?'

'Saying I'd drive myself mad. I did. I've been seeing a therapist for years. I had a sort of breakdown after Zachery disappeared. I tried talking to Diane but she was in her own little world. I felt like I had to be strong for her and Marcus and I couldn't because I blamed myself. I just lost it. I'm still on tablets now, twenty-five years later. Beth doesn't know. Nobody knows. Sometimes, the girls would come over and there we'll be – me and Beth and the four children, and we're having a meal or laughing and joking, and suddenly, it'll all hit me in the face – Zachery isn't here and it's all my fault.'

'Nick, it isn't your fault.'

'Stop saying that!' he erupted. 'I've had enough of people saying it's not my fault when it fucking is!' He jumped up from his seat, sending it toppling backwards to the floor. 'You weren't there. None of you were there. This doesn't affect any of you. You two can go home at the end of the day, back to your perfect families, and put it all behind you, but I can't. I've lived with this for twenty-five-fucking years … *It's. Killing. Me!*' he screamed. 'So *don't* think you can come in here and pretend to know how I'm feeling, because you don't.'

The room fell silent. Nick leaned back against the wall. He raised his arms behind his head and let out a deep sigh. The sleeves of his shirt fell slightly down his arms, revealing two faint scars on his wrists. He noticed Alex frown and he quickly covered them up.

'I'm sorry,' Caroline said quietly.

'Don't apologise. If there's one thing I'm fed up of hearing after all these years, apart from it not being my fault, it's fucking baseless apologies.'

Caroline opened her mouth to say something but Alex shook his head.

'Look, I think we've probably got enough, here. We'll see ourselves out.'

He grabbed Caroline by the elbow and led her to the door. Once in the corridor, she looked back through the small window in the door.

'Should we just leave him like that?'

'Come on.'

'That was certainly unexpected,' Alex said once they were back in the car.

'If they'd both just sat down and talked, they could have saved themselves twenty-five years of agony,' Caroline said. 'He had an affair. She had an affair. They both blame themselves for what happened to Zachery, but neither is to blame.'

'It's too late now. The damage is done.'

'True. I think they're both too numb from everything that's happened over the years to be hurt any more.' She sighed. 'It's pathetic, though. Why didn't they just talk to each other? Don't couples talk any more?'

'Do you tell Jamie everything?'

'Of course,' she said with a hint of a smile. 'That's what scares him.'

Chapter Forty-Eight

M arcus pulled up outside his mother's house. He didn't worry about parking correctly. He knocked loudly on the door. When it was opened, he gave a small smile then went straight into the living room. He was surprised to see his gran there. He hugged her before launching into a well-prepared speech.

'Mum, this is going too far now. You're uncovering things that someone obviously doesn't want you to know. This is getting dangerous. Car tyres being slashed and now a brick through your window! I think you should call a halt to all of this. What would have happened if you'd been in? What would have happened if Zachery had been here?'

'If Zachery was here none of this *would* be happening.'

'I meant my son,' Marcus said, his jaw tensing.

'Oh, sorry,' Diane said, her face reddening with embarrassment.

'I knew it. You can't move on, can you? I thought we were all moving forward. We had a lovely time at Greta's birthday tea. But you take one step forward and a thousand back. You need to stop this now, Mother.'

Diane sat down on the sofa. She looked down at the floor. She knew her son was right, but she couldn't let go of Zachery. It wasn't an option. 'I'm so sorry, Marcus,' she said, looking back up at him. 'I *need* to know.'

'Mum, you're going to make yourself ill.'

'I have no choice.'

'You do.' He crouched down in front of her. 'This is the perfect opportunity to put the past firmly behind you and move on.'

'I said that,' Hannah interjected.

'Mum, we all miss Zachery. There isn't a day that goes by when none of us here thinks about him, but he's dead. You need to focus on what's happening right now, today, with the people who love you, who are still here.'

Diane looked up. There were tears streaming down her face. She shook her head. 'I'm sorry.'

'So am I.' Marcus stood up to his full height. 'When you're ready to be a mother to me, and a grandmother to Zachery, give me a call. I don't want any part of this. I will not have my family be a part of this, either.'

'Marcus, please … don't go.'

'I'm sorry, Mum' he said, his voice breaking. He turned and walked away, slamming the front door behind him.

Diane was alone. Her mother went home soon after Marcus's outburst. She sat in the armchair, a framed photograph of Zachery in her hands, and cried. She felt exhausted, tired, sad. She felt exactly like she had twenty-five years ago when Zachery had first gone missing. Why was this so hard? Why could everyone move on when she couldn't? It wasn't fair. When she heard the sound of Alex's Volvo coming up the road, she placed the frame back on the shelf behind her and wiped her eyes. She went over to the window, waved at her visitors and went to open the front door.

Caroline looked at the boxes on the back seat. 'How do you think she's going to react to all this?'

'I've no idea,' Alex replied. He put everything into one box and carried it into the house.

In the dining room, they explained everything they'd been told by Lachlan Minnow but left out going to see Nick at his work.

'We've not looked at everything in this box,' Alex said, his hands firmly on top of it. 'But we've seen enough to know it's not going to be easy for you. Now, you don't have to look if you don't want to.'

'No. I'm all right,' she said, taking a deep breath. Her voice may have said she was prepared, but her face had lost all colour. She couldn't take her eyes off the cardboard box.

'Is everything all right?' Caroline asked.

'Yes. Fine. I have a good cry every now and then. It helps,' she lied with a false smile.

Carefully, Alex pulled back the flaps of the box and began emptying it onto the dining table.

Diane stepped forward and picked up a photograph of a young Jonathan.

'Is this Jonathan as a child?' she asked, holding the picture in a shaking hand.

'Yes.'

'He looks ... so normal,' she said. 'If you saw him playing out, you wouldn't think that he'd grow up to become ...' Her quiet voice trailed off. She placed it back on the table, turning it over. She wiped away a tear.

'Are you sure you're all right?' Caroline asked, placing a hand on her shoulder.

'There's no sign, is there? You see a child and you think they're this young, innocent little boy. And they are ... to begin with. Then they grow up, and look what people do to each other. It made me think of my grandson. What's he going to grow up to be?'

'Diane, from what you've told me, your grandson has two loving parents. He's going to grow up in a happy, stable environment. That's vital to a child's development,' Caroline said.

'I know. You can't help thinking of the alternative, though. When you've looked evil in the eye, it's difficult not to see it everywhere else.' She took a tissue out from her pocket and stepped away from the table to blow her nose.

'I've got your letters here, Diane,' Alex said, holding them up.

'He kept them? He probably read them every night and had a good laugh,' she said, taking the small bundle from him. 'Am I allowed to burn these?'

'I'd rather you didn't,' Alex said. 'They may help with the book.'

'Of course. Sorry. Who are the other letters from?'

Alex flicked through a few pages that had been held together with a rubber band. 'Somebody called Hannah Bridges.'

'That's my mother.'

'*Really?* Did you know she'd been writing to Jonathan?' Caroline asked.

'Yes. She told me after he'd died.'

'Do you want to read them?'

'No. Look, what are you hoping to find among all this?'

'I'm hoping I find something that will tell me where he took his victims,' Alex said, flicking through the pages of a sketchpad. 'It was the one thing I never found out. I asked him over and over again and he kept avoiding the subject. He used to look at me out of the corner of his eye and he had this smirk. The number of times I felt like giving him a backhander,' he said through gritted teeth. 'If we can find where he hid the boys, I'm sure we'll get a lot more answers.'

'But even if you do find where he took them, it was twenty-odd years ago. There'll be nothing left there, surely,' Diane said. She noticed the sideward glances Caroline and Alex shared and it suddenly dawned on her. 'Unless ... unless you think Zachery might be buried there.'

'I know we're working on the theory that Jonathan didn't kill Zachery, but we can't rule it out until we know for sure,' Alex said.

'I suppose not.'

Alex picked up another pack of photographs and began flicking through them. 'Oh, my God.'

'What is it?' Caroline asked, looking over his shoulder at the picture.

'This T-shirt. I've seen it somewhere before.' He showed them the photograph of a young Jonathan sitting on a beach. He was wearing a yellow T-shirt with a red-and-blue geometric print on the front and red shorts. He was holding a rapidly melting ice cream in one hand and flashing a wide smile to the camera.

'Where?'

'I think it was among his collection.'

'You saw his collection?' Diane asked.

He nodded. 'The police have it all in storage. I opened one box and this was lying on top. I need to make a phone call.' He left the room, taking his mobile out of his back pocket as he went.

Diane pulled out a chair and sat down. She picked up a sketchpad and slowly began to look through it.

'You don't have to do this, if it's too difficult for you.'

'I think I've become hardened,' she said. 'When you're surrounded by grief and horror, you sort of grow a shell. There are times when I burst into tears watching an advert on television of children running with the Andrex puppy, but then I can look through things like this and not bat an eyelid. He wasn't a bad artist, was he?'

'No. There's real talent there. His solicitor said he took a few classes in prison. There are a few of a house somewhere, which are really—' Abruptly, Caroline stopped when she saw tears streaming down Diane's face and a hand clamped to her mouth. 'What is it?'

'Zachery. He drew Zachery,' she struggled to say through the tears.

'Oh, shit, I'm sorry. I forgot that was in there.' Gently, Caroline took the pad from Diane, closed it, then held her firmly in her arms.

'Why is he torturing me like this? If he didn't kill him, why did he draw him? Why write to me? What's he trying to do?'

'I don't know, Diane. I wish I did,' Caroline said, putting her arms around her.

'What's going on?' Alex asked, entering the room.

Caroline nodded towards the sketchpad.

'Oh. Do you want me to leave you …'

'No,' Diane said, quickly, wiping her nose. 'It's fine. I'll just go and freshen up.' She left the room and ran upstairs.

'This is really taking its toll on her. Who were you ringing?'

'Siobhan Gardner. I'm almost one hundred per cent certain this T-shirt was in Jonathan's collection. She's going to have a look for me. She's asked if I can email her all the photos of Jonathan as a child so she can check other items. You haven't got a scanner I could use, by any chance?'

'Sure. I think we should probably leave Diane, anyway. I'll just go and see how she's doing.'

Caroline left the room and Alex sat in Diane's chair. He opened the sketchpad and looked at the pencil drawing of Zachery. It was a flawless depiction of the boy. Any parent would be happy to have such an elegant drawing of their son, if only it hadn't been drawn by a serial killer. He turned the page. There was that house in the middle of nowhere, again, a drawing of a gnarled tree, another one of a boy who looked familiar, probably another of his victims. The next page shocked even Alex. Quickly, before Caroline came back into the room, he closed the pad and returned it to the box, stashing it at the bottom. He was sure Caroline wouldn't want to see a drawing of her own son.

Chapter Forty-Nine

C aroline had hoped Jamie would still be out when she arrived home. She knew how long some of his golfing rounds could go on for and, as he was with Frank, they'd usually spend several hours in the club bar afterwards. So, when she saw Jamie's car in the drive and a light on in the living room, her heart sank. She didn't have a problem with Alex meeting Jamie, she was more worried about her husband asking awkward questions, or even blaming Alex for involving her in the first place.

She made the introductions and stood back while the two men eyed each other up. She hadn't realised how short Alex was before. Jamie towered over him. Alex put the cardboard box down on the floor and shook Jamie's hand.

'Can I get you a drink, Alex? I've just opened a bottle,' he said, his words slightly slurred.

'I think you've had enough,' Caroline said. 'Please tell me you didn't drive back.'

'Of course I drove back. I only had three in the club.'

Diane rolled her eyes and headed for the kitchen, Jamie in tow. 'I'll make us all a coffee. Make yourself comfortable, Alex,' she said, indicating their living-room door.

Picking the box up again, Alex entered the room. He saw a photograph of who he took to be Caroline's son, Dylan, with his wife on their wedding day in a silver frame on the windowsill. He picked it up. They looked happy. Dylan was the spitting image of his father, Alex noted. Further along the gallery of family photos, his eye fell on one of Dylan in his school uniform. He didn't look much older than ten years old. He immediately thought of the drawing in Jonathan's sketchpad. He'd captured the boy's likeness perfectly: the crooked smile, the soft smiling eyes, the spiky hair. How had he managed to make such an intimate portrait without ever having seen the boy? He wondered if Julianne Parker was behind it. Had Jonathan been manipulating her to keep tabs on Caroline and her family over the years?

'You won't find any of Jamie on there,' Caroline said, entering the living room with a tray of coffee. 'He hates having his picture taken. I've told him, he'd better not go missing or we'll have nothing to give to the police,' she joked.

'So, how's the case going?' Jamie piped up, having returned from the kitchen swigging from a bottle of lager. 'Have you decided which one of you is Cagney and which one is Lacey?'

'They were detectives,' Caroline replied, nonplussed.

'Ah. What was Poirot?'

'A retired detective,' Caroline said.

'Like you. So that would make you Hastings, then, Alex.' Jamie laughed.

Caroline took the bottle from him and handed him a coffee. 'You've had enough. Come on, Alex, I'll show you to the study.'

As they left the room, Jamie called out after them: 'The study's on the right. The bedroom's on the left. Make sure you stick to the right.' He laughed again, to himself, as he flopped down onto the sofa.

They were in the study around twenty minutes. By the time they returned to the living room, Jamie was still on the sofa, reading a letter. The cardboard box Alex had brought in with them was open on the coffee table.

'Jamie, that's private.'

'Who's Julianne Parker?'

'Why?'

'Well, her spelling may leave a lot to be desired but she's definitely giving *Fifty Shades of Grey* a run for its money,' he said with a laugh.

'What are you talking about?' Caroline asked, snatching the letter from him. She quickly scanned her eye down the page. 'Oh, my God, it's filthy. Where did you find this?'

'In that box, underneath a scrapbook of newspaper clippings. There's a whole load of them,' he said, pointing to the pile on the sofa next to him. 'She sounds like a complete whack-job.'

'Jamie, leave it,' Caroline said through gritted teeth. She looked over at Alex, who had slumped down in the armchair.

'Why?'

'Nothing. Just leave it.'

'Have I said something I shouldn't have?'

'Alex, do you want to stay for dinner?'

'No, but thanks. I think I'm going to have an early night. I don't feel properly recovered from sleeping on Diane's sofa the other night, I'm still shattered,' he said, standing up. 'It was nice to meet you, Jamie.'

'Likewise.' Jamie looked perplexed. 'Look, if I've said something wrong, I'm sorry.'

'Don't be. It's fine.'

'I'll show you out.'

Jamie watched as Caroline took Alex into the hallway. There was a closeness between them he would never have with his wife, a shared history. It might not be sexual, but they had a connection that he had been left out of, and he didn't like it. He picked up another item from the box Alex had brought in. It was a sketchpad. He began flicking through its pages.

'Hang on you two,' he called out.

'What is it?' Caroline replied from the hall, annoyance in her voice.

'Come and have a look at this.'

They both returned to the living room.

'This picture here, of the house – whose is it?'

'I don't know. He's drawn it several times. It could be something from his imagination.'

'No … I've seen this house.'

'*Really?*' Alex asked, surprised. 'Where?'

'I can't remember.'

'Thanks, Jamie. That's a big help,' Caroline said, sarcastically.

'Show me the other pictures,' he said.

Caroline and Alex rummaged through the box to retrieve the single pages of and other pads containing similar drawings of the same house. They all showed the house in the middle of nowhere. Sometimes, the sun was shining and casting large shadows, other times, it was dark and there was a single light glowing in an upstairs window.

'I definitely know this house,' Jamie repeated, scratching his head.

'Where?' Caroline asked, slightly exasperated.

'I don't know. Let me think.' He stood up and began to pace the room. 'Is it significant?'

'It could be,' Alex said. 'The place obviously meant something to him or he wouldn't have drawn it over and over again.'

'Look, why don't I cook us something?' Caroline said. 'We could all do with a break. Maybe then, it'll come to you.'

'Frank Barnes!' Jamie suddenly called out.

'Who?'

'Frank Barnes.'

'What about him?'

'He's got a painting of this house in his hallway.'

'Who's Frank Barnes?' Alex asked.

'A bloke I play golf with. He paints watercolours. He and his wife go on holiday and they spend days just painting the landscape. He's painted this house, I know he has, and it's in a frame in his hallway.' With that Jamie went into the hallway to call Frank.

Caroline disappeared into the kitchen to make them all something to eat, leaving Alex on his own in the living room. He picked up the letters written by Julianne Parker. Looking at her childish handwriting, the obsessive language she used towards the killer whom she thought was the love of her life, made Alex feel sick and angry. This woman, this girl, had destroyed his family. He put the paper to his nose and sniffed. There was a hint of cheap perfume. It took him back to the time when he was interviewing her in her flat, when she had tried to manipulate him. His beautiful, intelligent wife was a shell of her former self, thanks to this obsessive, useless piece of—

'He's going to text me a photo of it,' Jamie said, coming back into the room and interrupting Alex's thoughts. 'He said it's an old cottage in the middle of nowhere between Croft Marsh and Gibraltar.'

'Oh, so not in England, then?' Alex asked.

Jamie laughed. 'There's a place just south of Skegness called Gibraltar.'

'I've put us some pasta on. Is spag bol OK for you both?' Caroline asked.

Jamie's phone beeped an incoming text.

'That sounds lovely, thanks. I'm actually starting to feel quite hungry,' Alex said.

'Great! What are you looking for?' she asked as Alex rummaged through the box.

'When my book came out, Jonathan wrote to me. He said that although I'd covered his story well there was plenty more to be told. He mentioned that he'd write it all down one day before he died. I was hoping there'd be a diary or a journal of some sort in here.'

'Is there?'

'No. I always knew he was holding something back. Whatever it is, he's taken it to his grave.'

'Maybe it's the best place for it.'

'True,' he mused, biting his bottom lip.

'What are you thinking?'

'I'm just wondering … if there *is* a diary, Lachlan Minnow will have probably got his grubby hands on it. He'll know how much something like that is worth. I wouldn't be surprised if we saw it in the bookshops in a year or so.'

'Here we are. Does this match the drawing?' Jamie piped up.

They all gathered around Jamie's phone to have a good look at the photo of the painting that Frank had sent over.

'It certainly looks similar. Just more rundown than when Jonathan drew his pictures,' Alex said.

'Do you think this is where he took his victims?' Caroline asked.

'I don't know. But why keep drawing the same house if it didn't have any significance? Hang on, Caroline, do you have a copy of *The Collector*?'

'Yes. Why? Do you want to sign it for me?' She joked.

'Will you get it for me? I've thought of something I'd like to check.'

Caroline went over to the bookcase in the corner of the living room and picked off a paperback.

'Don't lose my page,' Jamie said as Caroline handed the paperback to Alex. Caroline looked at Jamie, startled. He looked sheepish.

'What are you looking for?' Caroline asked.

Alex scrolled down the index in the back, turned to the relevant pages, then skim-read until he found what he was looking for. 'Jonathan broke his leg at the age of seven, just before the school summer holidays. Obviously, that meant he couldn't play outside. His gran, to cheer him up, took him away for a week to their cottage by the sea. I actually wrote "their cottage" … look. Is this Gibraltar place by the sea?'

'Yes.'

'But how could his gran afford to buy a cottage? I didn't think she had much money.'

'No. That was one of the reasons Jonathan and his gran didn't get on. She did have money but she refused to spend it all on him. I remember her saying at the time that his parents should pay for his upbringing, not use her money.'

'But she took him in after his mother died. She chose to take on that responsibility.'

'I know. I remember saying as much to her,' Alex said.

'And what was her reply?'

'She said she'd already paid for *her* child, and what money she had now was for her old age.'

'Well, she sounds like a lovely woman,' Jamie said, sarcastically. 'I mean, I know Jonathan didn't turn out to be a model grandson, but she *was* his guardian. She was supposed to look after him.'

'She gave him a roof over his head,' Alex said. 'To her, that was enough. Anything else he needed, he had to provide for himself.'

'But when she died, everything she owned would have been in her will, including the cottage by the sea. Someone will have inherited that, surely,' Caroline said. 'It can't be the same one that Frank Barnes painted.'

'Actually, now I come to think about it, I don't think she did leave a will,' Alex mused. 'I wish I had all my notes with me. I'll give Shona a ring, she'll be able to look it up for me.'

Alex got through to his daughter on the third attempt – she'd been bathing Melanie. He apologised and had a hushed conversation in the kitchen about how she was coping. When Shona asked about his coming home, he quickly changed the subject, telling her he needed some information about Jonathan from his old notebook and asking whether she could go up to the attic to retrieve it. She said she would, and phone him back once her mother was settled in bed.

Sitting at the table in the living room, with the detritus of Jonathan's cardboard box strewn in the background, they ate in silence. It was a well-cooked meal – the hint of garlic and basil from the tomato sauce was subtle, the pasta al dente – yet none of them enjoyed it. It was just fuel to keep them going. The taste was irrelevant. Eventually, Jamie spoke up.

'Let's say this cottage is where Jonathan took his victims. And let's say Zachery is buried somewhere in there. Why?'

'What do you mean?' Caroline asked.

'Well, out of thirteen victims, why has he buried Zachery there when the rest he buried close to their homes?'

'If he's buried there, then he *is* close to home,' Alex said.

'But why bury him in the house where he committed his crimes and not elsewhere, like he did with the others?' Jamie asked.

'I don't know,' Alex frowned.

'Maybe Jonathan felt close to Zachery and wanted to keep him close. They were distantly related,' Caroline thought out loud.

'Or, maybe ... no,' Jamie stopped himself.

'What?'

'No, I don't want to think about it,' Jamie said.

'Go on, you've started now.'

'I remembered something from one of those programmes about strange crimes that used to be on late-night television. There was a man in America, years ago, and his wife died. She was the love of his life, childhood sweethearts. Anyway, instead of having a funeral, he kept her in the house, in their bed, and he slept with her every night. He couldn't accept that she was dead, you see.'

'So, what does that have to do with Jonathan and Zachery Marshall?' Caroline asked.

'Maybe, because they were related, Jonathan thought he and Zachery had some kind of a connection, and that's why he kept him at this cottage. Maybe he wanted them to always be together. *What?* You're both looking at me like I'm speaking a foreign language.'

'No, not at all,' Alex said. 'You could have a point.'

'But I thought we were working on the principle that Jonathan *didn't* kill Diane's son,' Caroline said, gripping the bridge of her nose.

'We are. Well … we were. Oh, I don't know.' Alex pushed his plate away. 'One minute, I think Jonathan *did* kill him, another minute I think it was someone else. The guy was such a manipulator. For all I know, thanks to Jonathan, my whole book could be a fabrication.'

They all fell silent again while they contemplated the fact that the truth may never be known.

Suddenly, Alex's phone rang, making them all jump. It was Shona. 'I've found your notebook, Dad. What do you need from it?'

'Something about Elizabeth Walsh dying and if she left a will.'

'Hang on …' Shona rustled through the pages. 'God, Dad, your handwriting is shocking.' There was a long pause while she read on to herself. 'OK … I think I've found something. It says here "there was no will when E died". I'm assuming you mean Elizabeth. It says everything was held up while next of kin could be located. Eventually, the house and all the possessions were sold after being inherited by a Paula Robinson, her sister in Eccles.'

'Is there any mention of a second property? A country cottage, maybe?'

There was another long pause while Shona flicked through

pages. 'I don't think so. Look, Dad, maybe you should come and look at this yourself, I can hardly make out your writing.'

'No. You've done great, Shona. Thank you. Look, I'll let you go now. Give your mum a kiss for me.'

'I will. Hang on, before you go, you've had a letter from the solicitor. I opened it like you told me to. He said we should be able to start with proceedings whenever you're ready.'

'Shit,' he said quietly.

'I know. What do you want me to do?'

'Nothing. I'll deal with it when I come home.'

'When will that be?' she asked, sounding agitated.

'Just … leave it with me. I have to go. Thanks again, Shona.' He ended the call before she could say anything else. With his back to Caroline and Jamie, he composed himself before he turned round to them. He hadn't realised his solicitor would be so on the ball. Typical.

'But how do we find out if this Paula Robinson inherited the cottage?' Caroline asked after Alex had relayed the information to them.

'Simple. We ask her,' he said with a smile.

'But if we mention there's a cottage out there, she's going to want to get her hands on it.'

'True. OK, I suggest we visit this cottage, have a look around and go from there. If it's as dilapidated as Frank's painting makes it look, then it's obvious Paula didn't know about it, and, if we find nothing, she's welcome to it.'

'I really hope we don't find anything,' Caroline said.

'Well, we'll find out tomorrow,' Alex said, standing up. 'Right, then, time I was heading back to my hotel room.'

'Look, Alex, would you like to spend the night here?' Jamie asked. 'We've got a spare room all made up for guests.'

'Yes,' Caroline agreed. 'You'll be coming back here tomorrow morning to pick me up, anyway. You may as well stay the night.'

'Well … if you're both sure you don't mind?'

'It's no problem,' Jamie replied for them both, Caroline nodding.

'OK. Thanks,' he said, flashing a genuine smile. 'I'll give Diane a ring, see if she wants to come with us tomorrow.'

Diane hung up the phone. She looked shell-shocked.

'Bad news?' asked Nick.

'No,' she replied staring at the phone. 'It was Alex. He was just giving me an update.'

'Oh. And?'

'I don't know yet. He and Caroline are coming over tomorrow morning. Sorry, I shouldn't have answered it.' Diane put the phone away in her bag and picked up her knife and fork. The lasagne had tasted delicious until her phone rang. Having heard from them that they may have found Zachery's final resting place, she felt sick. The pasta tasted rubbery, the meat was greasy, the cheese was bitter.

She looked up. She'd eaten in this restaurant many times in the past. She often brought her mother here when they fancied a decent meal but neither of them could be bothered to cook. She smiled at Nick. It felt strange being out for a meal with her ex-husband. It had been his idea. She'd thought they were just meeting up for a coffee and a chat, maybe to try to agree to be civil with one other from now on, for the sake of Marcus, Greta and baby Zachery. She had nearly dropped through the floor when he suggested having a meal. If she'd known she would be dining out, she would have put on a more glamorous outfit.

Nick was wearing a navy suit and white shirt with the top couple of buttons undone. He'd lost weight since they'd been married. She knew he went to the gym on a regular basis and jogged along the coast at the weekends. Diane felt self-conscious. She didn't go in much for exercising. She'd never been inside a gym. She knew she could do with losing a few pounds, a stone at the most, and she'd tried every fad diet going, but exercise wasn't high up on her list of things to do.

'You're looking well,' she'd said to him once they'd sat down and were facing each other.

'Thanks. So are you.'

Diane knew it was a lie. She didn't look well at all. She looked old, tired, defeated, lost.

'Does Beth know you're out with me tonight?' She hoped she'd said Beth's name without any disgust in her voice, but wasn't sure how it had come out.

'Yes. I told her we needed to talk.'

'And she's all right with that?'

'She knows we have a history, realises we have family in common. Now that little Zachery has come along, we're going to be in each other's lives.'

Diane smiled. It was warming to hear the name Zachery again without it being tainted by thinking of missing children and murder and Jonathan Egan-Walsh.

'He's a lovely baby,' Diane said. 'He looks just like Marcus did when he was born. No hair and wrinkles.'

Nick laughed. 'Zachery had a great mop of hair, didn't he? I couldn't believe it.'

'Those first few photographs; he looks like he's wearing a wig.' Diane smiled at the memory.

'Diane ...' Nick leaned forward and placed his hand on top of hers. 'Is this a good idea, going through all this again? Do you honestly think you're going to find him?'

She was tempted to pull her hand away but it felt warm, safe. 'I don't know, but look what Caroline and Alex have uncovered so far. We didn't know anything about Bryn Jones until they started digging. They've found a cottage where they think Jonathan went as a child with his grandmother. They're going to visit it tomorrow.'

'And what's that going to achieve?'

'Who knows? That's why we're going.'

'*We?* You mean, you're going, too?'

'Of course. Nick, I'm sorry, but I'm not letting this drop. I can't.' This time, she did let go of his hand, then wiped her mouth with her napkin. She pushed the plate away. 'I was angry at first, for you moving on, finding Beth, settling down, but, I sort of admire you for it. I wish I could move on. It's too late for me, now, though.'

'It's never too late.'

'It is. I've been on my own too long. Besides, I like to stretch out in bed,' she said with a laugh.

'I'm worried about you.' Nick tried to take her hand again but she pulled away before he had the chance. 'You look so sad.'

Her bottom lip wobbled. 'I am sad. As a mother, you want to protect your children, look after them, keep them safe. I failed in my duty. I let Zachery fall into that man's hands. I need to bring him back home. I need to give him a final resting place. It's the last thing I can do for him, the only thing I can do for him.'

'And what if you don't?'

'Then I've failed,' she said, and a tear fell down her cheek. She didn't brush it away. 'I should go.' She dropped her napkin onto her discarded plate and jumped up from her seat.

'No, Diane. Please. Don't go.'

'I'm sorry,' she replied, choking through the tears, running out of the restaurant.

Nick took his wallet out of his back pocket and threw three twenty-pound notes down on the table along with a business card. 'If it's not enough, you have my address and number,' he shouted to a waiter as he ran after his ex-wife.

Outside, the cold night air hit him like a slap across the face. He looked left and right, searching for Diane, before seeing her further down the street, at the side of the road, looking for a taxi.

'Diane, wait!' he caught up with her and grabbed her by the shoulders, turning her towards him.

'I'm sorry, Nick,' she cried.

'Sorry? What for?'

'I failed our son. I failed you,' she said, tearfully.

'You did nothing of the sort,' he said, pulling her into a tight embrace and held her firmly against his chest. 'You are a wonderful mother. You did everything you could.'

'I let him ...'

He shushed her and hugged her tighter.

Traffic passed them by. People walked past, giving them strange looks. Nick ignored them. His eyes were full of tears, too, but he didn't want to shed them in front of Diane. Eventually, she pulled herself out of his hold.

'Sorry,' she said, wiping his shirt.

'It's all right.'

'Nick ...'

'Don't say anything.'

He held her chin and lifted her head up before leaning down and kissing her firmly and passionately on the lips.

Chapter Fifty

'Did you sleep well?'

Caroline looked up as Alex entered the kitchen. He'd already showered and dressed. A clean smell of soap and deodorant radiated from him, yet he still looked like Columbo.

'I did, thank you. Very comfortable bed.'

'A bit different from hotel rooms, eh?' Jamie said from the breakfast table.

'You get used to them after a while. I think it's because they're all so generic and impersonal that I have trouble sleeping, though.'

'You should get a motorhome. Drive around the country for your stories and sleep in that,' said Jamie, smiling.

'Don't say that. His family see little of him as it is. Oh, shit, Alex, I'm sorry. I didn't mean ...'

'It's OK,' he said. 'What time are we setting off?'

'Let me just have a quick shower, first,' Caroline replied. 'Jamie, did you get the map out?'

He went into the hallway and came back carrying a large A–Z. He placed it on the table in front of them. 'It's a few years old but I doubt the area has changed much.'

'I know my car is ancient, but I do have a satnav,' Alex said.

'That'll be useless where you're going.' Jamie looked up from the map.

'This sounds like a trip ill-advised teenagers take in a horror film,' Alex said with a laugh.

'Wouldn't it be better taking my car?' Caroline said.

'Why?'

'Erm … well, four-wheel drive. We may come across some tricky roads.'

'You really don't trust my car, do you?' Alex said, with a hint of a smile.

'Not really,' she said quietly.

'Fine. We can take your car. But for that, you're doing all the driving.'

Jamie turned the map around so they could get a view of their destination. There was very little on the page, as it showed mostly fields and meadows.

'According to Frank, you're looking for a cottage somewhere around here,' he said, circling his finger over a large area.

'Can't you narrow it down a bit?' Caroline asked.

'Sorry, but I can't, really. Frank was very vague. All he said was, if you hit the sea you've gone too far.'

Caroline rolled her eyes. 'Did he say which sea?'

Alex laughed. 'I'm sure we'll find it. It doesn't look like there are too many roads, and I'm guessing Frank wouldn't have walked too far from the road to paint, would he?'

Jamie shook his head. 'Not with his limp – or his wife in tow.'

'I get the feeling we're going to have to pack distress flares,' Caroline said.

———

While on their way over to Diane's in Caroline's comfortable Land Rover, Alex received an email from Siobhan Gardner.

'Many of the clothes Jonathan is wearing as a child in the photographs match clothes in his collection,' Alex read out.

'So he saved his own childhood clothes and placed them among his victims' clothes? What does that mean?'

He thought for a while. 'I'm not sure. Unless ...'

'What?'

'Hang on, let me get it straight in my head first. Do you remember in court when Jonathan was on the stand, he broke down when he was talking about his childhood?'

'Crocodile tears.'

'He said he wished he was one of the boys. Remember? Maybe he put his own childhood clothes among his collection because, in his eyes, he felt like a victim.'

'A victim of what, though? His parents?'

'Possibly.'

'But he was still alive.'

'Maybe he wished he wasn't. His father walked out on him. His mother killed herself. He would have felt abandoned. His gran didn't like him. This is a man who didn't know what it was like to be loved. He was completely alone.'

'You're not justifying his actions, surely.'

'No. I'm trying to see it from his point of view. He's lonely, he's sad and he sees himself in these boys. That's why he put his clothes with theirs, because, to him, they were exactly the same.'

Caroline was about to turn into Diane's road when Alex stopped her and told her to pull over.

'Jonathan knew the Marshall family. What if he knew what Diane and Nick were like – they were both having affairs, putting themselves first? Maybe he thought Zachery and Marcus were unhappy, just like he was.'

'But what about the other boys? He wouldn't be able to know about their home lives.'

'Unless he was watching them. In his statements, he said that at weekends he'd often be out in his van, just driving around, going to different towns. He could have been stalking these families, seeing how unhappy the children were, before deciding whether to take them.'

'To punish the parents,' Caroline said.

'Or put the kids out of their misery. Like you said to Diane, we're shaped by our childhood. Jonathan could have thought these kids were going to grow up like him, and he didn't want anyone to suffer what he was going through.'

'It's a bit of a stretch.'

'I know. We need to find out what the home lives were like for the other victims.'

'You can't ask Siobhan Gardner that. It's too much work. She won't sanction it.' Caroline's face lit up. 'However, Diane said she knows everything there is to know about the victims. She's got files on them all.'

'We can't ask her without telling her why.'

'We can. We'll ask her while we're driving. We'll make it seem like we're gossiping.' She started the car and turned into Diane's road, where she was waiting for them on the doorstep.

'*You're* keen,' Caroline said, winding the window down.

'I couldn't sleep.' She climbed into the back of the Land Rover, sniffed and pulled a face.

'Don't worry about the smell. It's from when I take the dogs out.'

'Oh.' Diane opened her bag. 'I've brought a flask of coffee. I thought we might need it. It's freezing this morning. Going to get colder, too, if the forecast is to be believed.'

As Caroline reversed she looked at Diane. 'Everything all right? You look a bit brighter this morning.'

'I'm fine. I just feel like we might finally be getting somewhere with this.'

'Fingers crossed.'

It didn't take long for them to leave Skegness. Then, once they'd passed the deserted caravan parks and hit the open road and Caroline was able to put her foot down.

Alex looked across at her. He caught her eye and nodded towards the back. A massive hint for her to get started.

'Diane, have you told the other members of Thirteen what we're doing?'

'Oh, yes, they're all very supportive. Did I tell you they've set up a crowdfunding page to raise money so I can hire one of those ground-penetrating radar machines, if we need one.'

'That's nice of them.'

'They're a wonderful group. I don't think I'd have survived this long without them, especially Martha. She's got such an amazing spirit.'

Caroline looked through the rear-view mirror and smiled. 'And Martha's husband, is he supportive?'

'Leon? Yes. It was his idea to do these retreats we go on.'

'Are he and Martha still together?'

'Yes.'

'I heard a lot of couples can split up after the death of a child. The relationship breaks down.'

'They can, a few of us parents of Jonathan's victims have, sadly, divorced. We offer support as a group when we can. Strangely, the opposite was true for Martha and Leon. They were on the verge of splitting up before they lost their Peter. It was him being murdered that brought them together.'

'Oh. So they'd been going through a bad patch?'

'Yes. She's never gone into any details, but Leon had a one-night stand. When Peter was killed, she realised how petty she'd been, that there was more to life than being angry over silly things. She genuinely loved Leon and wanted to make the marriage work. They're closer now than they've ever been.'

'Hmm,' Alex said.

Diane continued: 'Jeremy and Alicia Burdon were already split up. They were going through a very bitter custody battle when their James was killed; back and forth to court. Poor kid. Then that happened to him.'

Alex looked across at Caroline and raised his eyebrows. Three couples who were going through hell, neglecting their children.

'Then there was Linda and Grant Schofield,' Diane volunteered after a long silence. 'She'd left him because he had a temper. He used to hit her. She took an injunction out, but he was adamant that he was going to see his son. He threatened her, hassled her, he even kidnapped poor Owen from school once. When Owen went missing, everyone thought Grant had taken him again. When his body was found, my goodness… Linda was inconsolable. She took it very hard.'

'How is she now? Linda?' Caroline asked.

'She's fine. She's remarried. She runs a bed-and-breakfast on the south coast. She always comes to the retreat, though, every summer.'

So, Jonathan had a method for choosing his victims, it appeared. Alex made notes on his mobile phone. He had been stalking his victims, watching their lives, seeing who was suffering the most, and he was taking the boys to end their pain – to stop them from turning into him. Diane and Nick fitted into the same pattern. They were both being selfish by having affairs, putting their needs before those of their children. Another box ticked for Jonathan being Zachery's killer.

'Ah …' Caroline said.

'What is it?' Alex asked.

'I think we may have driven too far.'

'How do you know?'

'I can see the sea.'

'Oh.'

'Is that bad?' Diane asked from the back seat.

'It is if it's the Atlantic,' Alex replied with laugh.

'Pass me the map.'

'Is there any coffee left?' Alex asked Diane as Caroline scrutinised the map.

'No. You had the last cup.'

He looked at the barren landscape surrounding them. 'You'd think Costa would have seen the gap in the market out here,' he said with a smile.

'I think I know where I went wrong. There was a turnoff a while back we should have gone down.'

'I didn't see one.'

'It's basically a dirt track. Just as well we didn't come in your Volvo.' She grinned.

Caroline performed a seven-point turn on the narrow road and headed back the way they'd come. They all remained quiet while they kept their eyes peeled for the hidden turnoff.

Diane, leaning forward between the two front seats, spotted it first. Caroline turned, driving slowly as they made their way down the bone-shaking track. Despite the suspension, they were all juddered about as the car hit potholes and uneven ground.

'Can you see anything?' Alex asked, squinting as he looked out of the window.

'Not yet … Hang on, what's that?' Diane pointed.

'Where?' he asked, not seeing anything.

'There. Oh, don't worry about it. I can see cows. I think it's a barn. Keep going,' said Diane.

'I hate to break it to you, but I'm starting to see the sea again,' said Alex.

'Shit!' Caroline looked ahead, her shoulders slumping as she, too, saw the sea looming in the distance.

Diane concentrated hard, looking left, right, straight ahead. '*Stop!*' she shouted.

Caroline slammed on the brakes. 'What?'

'There. Look. There's the cottage.'

'You're sure?'

'Hang on.' Alex got out his phone and looked up the photo of the drawing he had taken last night. 'Yes, I think we've found it.'

In the distance was a small brown building. It was miles from anywhere and at least an hour's walk from the sea. Why would anyone build a cottage here? Why would anyone come here for a holiday with a small child? There would be nothing to keep them occupied in such a bleak and desolate place. It was the perfect place to hide someone, though.

Caroline pulled over and turned off the engine. All three remained silent as they studied the building from the car. It was obvious nobody had cared for it for years, possibly even as long as Jonathan had been in prison. They were all thinking the same thing – was Zachery buried here?

'Well …?' Caroline asked.

Alex opened his door, stepped out, to be hit by the strong wind buffeting the open countryside, whistling through waist-high dried grass, in competition with the crashing of waves in the distance. He took his old beanie hat out of his pocket and pulled it down over his ears. He was glad of the walking shoes he'd bought and the thermal gloves.

The three of them set off over the field in silence. Their words would have been lost to the wind, but there was nothing to say anyway. The atmosphere between them was heavy. The closer they got to the isolated cottage, the more they knew this was the building in Frank's painting, and the one Jonathan had drawn many times while in his prison cell. He had drawn it from his memory when the cottage was quaint and postcard-perfect. By the time Frank and his wife found it, it had suffered from lack of care and whatever weather the east coast had to offer.

Many of the slates were missing from the roof, a couple of upstairs windows were smashed and the chimney stack swayed precariously in the stiff wind. This building should have been demolished years ago, but, judging by the overgrown landscape around it, nobody had been this way for a very long time. Maybe people who saw it from the road thought it belonged to one of the surrounding farms.

As they approached, they could hear the wind howling around the building. There was a wooden porch with two rickety steps leading up to it. The front door was solid wood and there was a name plaque next to it, but the weather had erased the writing long ago.

'Not very inviting, is it?'Caroline said.

'Do you want to stay out here?' Alex asked, turning to Diane at the base of the porch.

Her face was red where the wind had bitten her cheeks. Her eyes were watering, or were they tears? 'No. I'm coming in with you,' she said with determination.

Alex went first. He placed a hand on the rail next to the steps, which creaked threateningly under his weight with every step he took. Carefully, Caroline followed.

Alex pushed on the front door and it opened slowly, its rusty hinges groaning as the door was forced back for the first time in years. A fusty, unclean smell immediately escaped from the house. Damp wood. It was dark inside and, from the doorstep, Alex couldn't make anything out.

Taking a deep breath, he stepped over the threshold, his eyes adjusting to the darkness surrounding him. The two women followed. The ground floor was divided into two rooms: a large living room with stairs in the corner leading to the floor above, and a small kitchen at the back of the building. To his right was a large wood burner covered in dust and cobwebs. There were two old armchairs that looked brittle and moth-eaten. There was no carpet on the floor, just the odd faded rug scattered here and there over the floorboards. Every step they took tested the strength of the boards.

The kitchen at the back was small and dark. A door led to the backyard and was locked. The cupboards had no fronts on them, the shelves were exposed, but there was little on them apart from the odd can of beans and soup, well past their sell-by dates. There was an old gas stove, but Alex didn't dare try it to see if it still worked.

He turned in the doorway and looked back at Caroline. 'It looks as though nobody has been here since Jonathan was arrested in 1996.' Alex pulled a face. He could taste the dust and decay.

'Do we dare try those stairs?' asked Caroline.

'I don't think we have much choice.'

'I'll wait here,' Diane said from where she stood just inside the doorway. A look of fear had etched itself on her face as she slowly glanced around the room.

Alex wiped his sweaty palms on his jacket and held onto the banister. Slowly, he ascended the winding staircase. On the third step, his foot went straight through the rotten wood and he fell. Caroline screamed behind him and grabbed hold of him.

'Are you all right?'

'Yes. Fine.' He looked down into the hole made by his foot and saw nothing but blackness.

'Are you sure?'

'Yes. Just be very careful.'

The two-room layout upstairs was much the same as downstairs: a large bedroom and a small bathroom towards the back above the kitchen. In the middle of the bedroom was a brass double bed with knitted blankets covering the mattress. Tatty and with a thick layer of dust, they'd seen better times.

'Oh, my God,' Caroline said upon seeing the bed.

Alex was thinking the same thing. The wind outside caused the house to creak and groan, or was it speaking, moaning the names of the victims Jonathan had brought here?

'Should we have a proper look around?' Caroline asked.

'We don't want to disturb any potential evidence, though, do we?' Alex said, not able to take his eyes off the bed.

'We can't ask Forensics to come out here on the off chance this might have been Jonathan's hideaway. We need evidence,' she said.

Alex took his phone out of his pocket and started taking photographs of the bed, other furniture, the views from the broken window, the bathroom, the stains on the floor.

'I'm going back downstairs,' Caroline announced. 'I'm worried these floorboards might give way under the weight of two of us.'

There was a small bookcase containing classic children's books in the corner of the bedroom. Jonathan had told Alex he only really became interested in reading when he was in prison. So, if these books weren't for him when his gran brought him here, who were they for? He shivered at the thought of all the boys he could have brought here and held against their will.

On the windowsill in the bathroom was a small yellow rubber duck. He took a photo of it. There was something sad about seeing such an innocent childhood toy sitting on its own, its colour faded over time.

Alex started to feel sick. His mouth was dry with the dust and he couldn't swallow. He needed some fresh air.

At that moment, a loud crash came from downstairs.

'*Caroline?*' he called out. No reply. Then, after a few seconds, he heard a scream, which caused his blood to run cold.

'*Alex!*' Diane shouted from downstairs.

He turned from the bathroom and ran back down the stairs, taking care to miss the third step with the hole in it. Behind the stairs was a large hole in the floor that wasn't there before. Diane was standing over it. He took a torch out of his pocket and turned it on.

'Caroline … it just gave way,' Diane said.

Alex shone a light into the hole. Immediately, he saw Caroline on the concrete floor beneath the house.

'What happened?'

She looked up at him. Her face was filthy, her eyes wide and staring. She opened her mouth to speak but nothing came out.

'What is it, Caroline? Are you hurt?'

She couldn't move. Her eyes darted to the left, signalling Alex to point his torch in that direction. He bent down on his knees. There, underneath the house, were what appeared to be four small bodies, all wrapped neatly in white sheets.

Chapter Fifty-One

After being hauled out of the hole in the ground, Caroline barged past her rescuers and ran out of the cottage. She held onto the banister on the porch, which gave way as soon as she put any weight on it, but, thankfully, she managed to steady herself from falling. She took in a lungful of cold fresh air, then promptly vomited. She could taste the dust, the decay, the death.

She then dropped to her knees, continued retching but nothing more would come out.

She gasped for breath and looked up. The landscape should have been beautiful. Tall grass was swaying in the breeze, the sky was laden with grey clouds and, in the distance, the North Sea was crashing against the coast. Caroline had always found the sea relaxing. In the days after Jonathan's arrest and as the extent of his crimes came to light, she had often escaped the horror with a drive out to the coast, to stand in the middle of nowhere, looking out to the sea, breathing in the air and allowing her head to clear. Now, though, all she could think about was how she had been within a few feet of four small bodies. Were they more victims of Jonathan's depravity, another four young boys whose parents had been agonising over their whereabouts?

She stood up and walked away from the cottage, not looking back. She could still smell death. She wanted to go home. She wanted Jamie to put his arms around her. She wanted to walk her dogs.

Diane ran out of the cottage after Caroline. Catching her up, she put her arm around her.

'Are you hurt?'

Caroline looked up at her and shook her head.

'What is it? What did you see?'

Their eyes remained locked on each other. There was nothing Caroline could say.

Diane swallowed hard. 'You found him, didn't you? You found my Zachery.'

Still in the cottage, Alex angled his torch on the floorboards, pointing into the hole, lighting up the four carefully wrapped bodies that had been placed neatly in a row. He bent down as low as he could go and took several photographs on his phone. He wanted to pull open the white sheets and see the condition of what lay within, but he knew that would destroy any potential evidence. He would find out eventually. Or so he hoped.

He stood up and wiped all the dust from his clothes and made his way out of the cottage. In the distance, he saw Caroline staggering back to the car, aided by an equally wobbly Diane.

'*Caroline!*' he called out. Neither of the women looked back. Either his words were lost in the wind or they chose not to hear him. He shouted again and set off in a run.

When he caught up with them, he saw that Diane's face was expressionless. Her eyes were wide but didn't seem to be focusing on anything. She was looking directly through Alex. Caroline had tears running down her face.

'Oh, Alex,' she cried. 'How many more victims are we going to find?'

He took her in his arms and held her to his chest. He could smell the dust in her hair. He could feel it on her clothes.

'I don't know. We'll need to call the police.'

'Do you think one of those is …?' she asked, stepping back, wiping her nose.

'I really don't know,' he replied, looking back at Diane's still-frozen stance. He took out his mobile and looked up the number for DI Siobhan Gardner. 'Take her back to the car. Put the heater on.' He waited until they were out of earshot before he made the call.

———

After he'd phoned Siobhan and explained what he had found, Alex called Jamie, filled him in on what happened, and suggested he come out to the cottage to comfort his wife. Jamie didn't need any persuading. He sent him a text with a screenshot of their location on Google Maps. He knew Diane could do with some company, too, but he didn't know who would be able to help her. He didn't have her mother's number.

Jamie arrived before Siobhan. He must have broken the speed limit on every road to get there so quickly. He parked haphazardly behind the Land Rover and ran towards them. Caroline was sitting in the front passenger seat, her legs dangling out of the car. Jamie stopped when he saw how distressed his wife was. She looked at him with tears in her eyes. Her face and hair were covered in dust. Her clothes were dirty and torn from the fall.

'Oh, my love,' was all he said, concerned for his wife.

Caroline opened her mouth to speak but she couldn't say anything. She cried. Jamie grabbed her and lifted her up, holding her in a tight embrace. He looked towards Alex with a worried expression. Alex gave him a sympathetic smile.

Caroline pulled out of her husband's arms. 'I don't know why I'm reacting like this. I was a detective for years. I've seen much worse than that.'

'What exactly have you found?' Jamie asked.

'We've found four more bodies,' Caroline said. She sat back down in the car and wrapped her arms around herself.

'I told you not to get involved,' Jamie chastised. 'I knew something like this would happen.'

'Jamie,' Alex said and shook his head. 'Not now.'

'Who's this?' Jamie asked, quietly, looking into the back of the car.

'Zachery's mother.'

'Have you found him?'

'We don't know, yet.' Alex replied. 'I'm guessing this is Siobhan Gardner,' he added, as a black Ford Focus drove erratically down the country lane. Behind her were two marked police cars.

Siobhan pushed open the door and struggled to climb out., then waddled over to Alex. 'I knew you'd cause me trouble as soon as I set eyes on you.'

'Nice to see you again, too.'

'I see you have company this time.'

'This is former DI Caroline Turner and her husband Jamie.'

'DI Turner?' Siobhan asked. 'I've heard a lot about you. Nice to meet you,' she held out a hand for Caroline to shake.

Without hesitation, Caroline stood up to do so. 'Likewise. Shame it's under such circumstances, though.'

'Can't be helped. And who's ...?' she asked, nodding to the back of the Land Rover, where Diane was sitting, motionless, clearly in a deep state of shock.

'Diane Marshall.'

'Diane Marshall? Zachery Marshall's mother? *Jesus, Alex!* I always knew journalists were insensitive, but I didn't think you'd bring her here to find ...'

'We're working together. As a team,' he said loudly. 'If you'd put just one officer on this to look into the letter, do a bit of digging, none of us would be here!'

'Is now really the time for finger pointing?' Caroline asked.

Siobhan winced as the babies kicked her. 'You're right. I can blame Alex another time. So, come on, then, ace reporter, tell me what you've uncovered.'

Once Alex had explained about how they came to track down the cottage, and then stumbling, literally, upon the bodies, Siobhan Gardner told them to stay by the car while she and her team investigated. They watched in silence as she and her officers approached the cottage. Standing outside, Siobhan looked up at the building, turned to say something to her team, then carefully navigated the steps and disappeared inside.

'What are we going to do now?' Jamie asked.

'Well, Alex and I will have to give statements,' Caroline replied. 'Would you do me a favour? Would you take Diane home? Take her to her mother's. She shouldn't be left alone.'

Jamie bent down to look into the car. 'What do I say to her?'

'You don't have to say anything. I doubt she's going to want to talk about golf. Just drive her home,' she said, slightly impatiently.

Caroline carefully took Diane by the hand and helped her out the Land Rover before putting her into Jamie's.

'I've told her we'll call around as soon as we know anything. Drive safely,' she said, kissing Jamie on the cheek. 'I've said you'll take her to her mother's.'

'Where does she live?' he asked. He looked frightened at the responsibility of driving Diane home.

Caroline gave Jamie Diane's address so that he could put it into his satnav. She then moved over towards Alex, who was transfixed by what was happening at the cottage.

'Jamie looked petrified, bless him. He's never been very good at handling other people's emotions.' She laughed faintly.

'How's Diane?'

'In a daze. I don't think it's sunk in yet.'

'I suppose it won't until we find out who is in there. How are you?'

'I'm fine,' she replied. 'I wasn't expecting ...'

They both shivered as a strong gust of wind slammed into them.

'I don't know if I want one of those bodies to be Zachery or not,' Alex said.

'What do you mean?'

'Well, if it is him, he's been here since the early nineties. Diane's been searching for him for twenty-five years and he's only been a few miles away from home. It will devastate her.'

'If he isn't among those, then the alternative is, she'll be living in limbo forever more. This really is the last chance. We've no other leads left to chase,' Caroline said.

Four more bodies took Jonathan's toll up to seventeen. Was this it, Alex pondered, or would there be more? Either way, he would definitely get his second book now. Repositioning himself slightly, he took out his phone and took a photograph of the cottage. He didn't zoom in. He wanted to see the isolation, the stark landscape, the dying sun in the background. Whoever had been held in this house against their will, they could have spent days, weeks, months screaming for help, and nobody would have heard them. A tear fell from Alex's eye. He hated himself for thinking it, but this was the money shot.

Chapter Fifty-Two

Alex stood in the shower. The water was hotter than he could cope with, but he needed to feel the pain. He needed to wash off the death and decay he had been breathing in. The water was now running clear down the drain, but he still felt dirty. He turned off the shower, wrapped the too-large dressing gown around him and went into the bedroom, where he flopped down on the bed. He looked at his phone for the time. It was almost midnight. There were four texts from his daughter, which he hadn't read, a few emails he'd ignored and two missed calls.

He turned over and looked at the mirror. He saw the message, the threat from Julianne Parker taunting him. The hot shower may have helped to suppress his tension, but it rose to the surface once again. Knowing that sick, twisted, psycho had been in his hotel room made him angry.

He turned back again, away from the mirror, and winced as he rolled on something hard and painful. He dug under the duvet and found a small bottle of Scotch. He couldn't remember how long it had been in his overnight bag, but it was there for when times were hard, when he was crying over his broken life, what he was putting Melanie through and forcing Shona to endure. He was a terrible husband and a bastard of a father. He broke the seal of the bottle and took a long slug. It felt good as the warm liquid slid down his throat. He had another drink then looked at the bottle. There was just over half left. Was it enough to dull the pain, the agony, the torment he was putting himself through? Probably not. But for one night, hopefully, he would have an uninterrupted sleep.

'How are you feeling?'

Jamie came into the bedroom, closing the door behind him. He'd performed his nightly check of the house, making sure all windows and doors were locked, plugs were unplugged, and the central heating timed to come on, and then came up to bed.

Caroline was already waiting for him. She'd had a long shower, fish and chips from the takeaway around the corner, and poured her heart out to her husband while a repeat of a detective drama played out silently on the television.

'I feel like I could sleep for a week,' she said.

'Nothing to stop you.' He climbed in next to her and held her close to him.

'Thank you,' she said after a long silence.

'What for?'

'For being so understanding.'

'I know I've been a bit … you know … about all this, but it's just because I'm worried about you. I love you,' he said, kissing the top of her head.

She smiled. She snuggled further into his arms. She closed her eyes and drifted off into a deep sleep.

Outside, Caroline's Land Rover was parked on the road, since Jamie's car was in the driveway. A figure dressed from head to toe in black walked slowly up the close and stopped behind the car. The house was in darkness, Caroline and Jamie were obviously in bed. There were no lights on in any of the neighbouring houses. From the rucksack on their back, the figure pulled out a small canister of petrol, unscrewed the cap and poured it over the top of the Land Rover. The sound of the liquid hitting the roof resounded around the quiet neighbourhood. The smell of petrol filled the cold night air. Once it was empty, the person returned the bottle to the rucksack, then took out a lighter, pausing to look up at the house before flicking open the lighter. The flame was bright and illuminating, and, if anyone had been looking out of their window, they would have had a good look at the would-be arsonist. In the living room of the house next door to the Turners' home, a light suddenly went on. This was too risky.

The lighter was quickly pocketed, and the figure turned and ran down the street.

'Where are you going in your dressing gown?' Caroline asked her husband as she descended the stairs. Jamie was at the front door, unlocking it.

'I forgot to put the blue bin out last night. It won't be long before they're here.'

'It completely slipped my mind. Coffee?'

'Please.'

Caroline headed for the kitchen while Jamie, in his pyjamas, dressing gown and walking boots, headed outside. The blue recycling bin was heavy as he struggled to push it down the driveway. As he did so, the bin lorry was coming up the road. He had caught them just in time. He shivered in the morning cold and headed back to the warmth of the house.

The lorry slowed down and several bin men jumped out. The driver performed an expert three-point turn in the narrow road and the workers began collecting the bins to empty. One young worker took the opportunity to have a crafty smoke. He lit the cigarette and went to collect the Turners' bin. He emptied it then returned it to the kerbside.

'You've been warned about that, Scott,' the driver shouted at him from the open window.

Scott rolled his eyes. He removed the stub of the cigarette from his lips and tossed it to the ground.

Everyone stopped in their tracks as a whoosh of flames engulfed the Land Rover.

'*Jesus Christ!*' Scott screamed as he ran for the safety of the bin lorry. He'd almost made it when the explosion threw him to the ground.

Chapter Fifty-Three

Alex opened his eyes. He expected to feel like death. Surprisingly, he wasn't hung over. His mouth was dry, and he was cold from passing out on top of the bed wearing only a dressing gown, but he felt fine. He showered, changed, ignored the most important meal of the day once again, and drove back to Croft Marsh. The spot Caroline had parked in yesterday was taken by unmarked police cars and a coroner's van. He parked well back and took his camera out of the glove box. He wished he'd brought it with him yesterday but, thankfully, the photos he took using his phone were of a good enough quality. For what he planned on photographing today, however, he would need a decent zoom.

Alex shivered as he opened the car door. As much as he had been putting off going home, he was now looking forward to the relatively mild winter that London offered. He wasn't made to endure a northern winter.

He hunkered down and slowly walked through the long grass towards the cottage.

There wasn't much to see. A large white forensic tent had been erected in front of the porch. Alex held up the battered camera, selected a wide angle to get in the whole of the cottage, the surrounding landscape and a hint of the sea, and ran off a few shots. He zoomed in, focusing on the forensic tent, and clicked the shutter a few more times.

He sat back and tried to make himself comfortable while he waited for something to happen. He was in for a long wait.

Eventually, the flaps of the tent were pulled back and a heavily pregnant Detective Inspector Siobhan Gardner stepped out wearing an ill-fitting forensic suit. Alex couldn't help but smirk as he raised the camera and fired off a few pictures. She would hate him for it if they ended up in the finished book.

Siobhan stood back while a trolley was wheeled out by two similarly dressed officers. On the trolley was a small body bag, which, from this angle, looked empty. He zoomed in and kept his finger on the shutter, taking as many pictures as he could.

'Well?' asked Caroline.

'She's been too busy with everything we've found. She's getting someone on it right now.'

As soon as Caroline had called Alex and told him about what had happened to her car, he left Croft Marsh and went straight round. After surveying the damage, he got on the phone to Siobhan and asked her to locate Julianne Parker as a matter of urgency.

Jamie stood at the window looking out at the ruined Land Rover. 'We could have been killed! What if the car had been on the drive? Or worse, what if it had been in the garage and she set fire to the house, instead? This has gone on long enough. I've been tolerant, but it stops *now*.' His voice was shaking with anger and fear.

'What did the police say?' Alex asked.

'There's not much they can do,' Caroline replied. 'There were no witnesses, no fingerprints. Someone's going to come and take the car away but it's obvious how it started. I've taken some photos and contacted the insurance company. They're going to sort out a replacement.'

'How was the bin man?'

'Fine. They took him to hospital as he knocked his head when he fell, but he should be OK.'

'A small consolation, I suppose. Speaking of photos, I went back to Croft Marsh this morning and ran off a few shots.' He handed her the camera.

Caroline scrolled through them. 'You take a good picture.'

'Thank you. I took a few of Jonathan for *The Collector*. That was a very strange shoot. He was actually treating it like he was having his photo taken for the cover of *Time* magazine or something. I had a few drinks that night, I can tell you.'

'I'm sorry, are any of you listening to what I'm saying?' Jamie asked, annoyed, turning from the window. 'I don't want any more of this in my house. You can take that box out for a start. I don't want to hear Jonathan's name mentioned ever again. Do you understand me?'

'Jamie ...' Caroline began.

'No,' he said firmly. 'I mean it now, Caroline. This is too much. It's over. You get a replacement car and you get back to walking dogs.' He stormed out of the living room, every angry step up the stairs resounding around the house.

'I'd better be going,' Alex said, eventually. He went over to the dining table and picked up the box of Jonathan's effects.

'What's happening now with the bodies?' she asked.

'Maybe Jamie's right. This is getting too close, too serious.'

'Alex, please,' she said, lowering her voice. 'I can't back out now.'

Alex sighed. 'According to Siobhan, the bodies are going to be taken to a special digital autopsy suite in Sheffield to be scanned so they can see if there are any clues as to how they died. Then there'll be a full post mortem. In the meantime, Siobhan and her team are searching Missing Persons and will see if anything matches.'

'Are you sticking around?'

'No. I'm going back to London,' he said, looking dejected. 'I've got a meeting with my publisher to pitch my new book and a few other things to take care of. Siobhan has promised to keep in touch and let me know of any developments.'

'Will you keep me informed, too?'

'Caroline!'

'Alex, please,' she practically begged.

'Yes, I'll keep you informed. Actually, I'd like to interview you for the new book.'

'Well, let me know and I'll get my hair done,' she said with a smile.

'Listen,' Alex said, leaning forward, 'will you keep an eye on Diane?'

'Why?' Caroline frowned.

'Insurance. On the off-chance one of those boys isn't Zachery Marshall, then we'll be back to square one.'

'Good thinking.'

Alex turned to leave and looked back out of the living-room window at the destroyed Land Rover again.

'I'm sorry about your car.'

'Thanks.'

'I can lend you a Volvo if you need it.'

Caroline smiled. 'I'd be better off taking the dogs on the bus.'

Alex had just turned the corner when his phone started ringing. When he saw it was Siobhan calling, he pulled over and answered.

'I've got some news for you. You may not be too happy about it, though.'

'Listen, I haven't actually had any good news for years, a bit more bad isn't going to hurt.'

'We've found Julianne Parker.'

'That sounds like good news to me.'

'Well, it isn't. To be more accurate, we've found her grave.'

'*She's dead?*'

'She killed herself in 2001. I spoke to her sister. She couldn't get over the Jonathan's rejection of her.'

'Bloody hell! So, if she hasn't been doing all this vandalism, who has?'

'I've no idea.'

'Does the sister have an alibi?'

'Yes. She lives in Gloucester and works in a care home. She hasn't left the area since she went on holiday last summer. I'm going to have a team look into all this. We should have taken it more seriously, Alex. I'm sorry.'

'Don't be. Although, when you find out who's responsible, let me know. I've got a bill from the hotel to replace a mirror that I'd like to pass on to them.'

Alex ended the call and continued on his journey back to London. He wasn't sure if he should tell Caroline and Diane that Julianne wasn't responsible for the damage to their property. Fingers crossed, Siobhan and her team could find the culprit before any more harm was done. He certainly hoped so. Just how far was this going to escalate?

Chapter Fifty-Four

Three weeks later: Wednesday, 14 March 2018

Alex Frost was dressed smartly, for a change. He stepped out of the solicitor's office and held the door open for his daughter. They were both wearing sensible, almost funereal clothing, and their faces matched their outfits. They walked along the busy street, side by side, in total silence.

'Drink?' Alex asked.

Shona nodded.

The pub was quiet, which was what they both wanted. Shona sat in the corner while Alex went to the bar. He brought a pint of beer and a large vodka and tonic to the table and sat opposite his daughter.

'Should we tell her?' Shona asked after taking a sip. She didn't look up from the table.

'Yes. We'll tell her tonight.'

'I feel sick.'

'I know you do, sweetheart. I do, too,' he placed his hand on top of hers. 'It's for the best, though. She's not living. You're not living. I'm not living. We're all of us trapped.'

'I'm killing my mum.' Shona looked up and a tear ran down her face.

Alex moved to her side of the table and pulled her into his arms. He kissed the top of her head and tried to comfort her but he couldn't find the words. It was difficult to think of it as anything else. They were killing the woman they both loved. As much as Alex had told himself his wife was no longer there, that she was just a body in a bed, she was still his wife. She was still the woman he had vowed to love and to cherish for the rest of his life.

Shona didn't want to stay for another drink. She kissed her dad goodbye and said she would be home for around six o'clock so they could speak to Melanie together. Alex remained in the pub and ordered a second pint. He'd have a third, too. And a fourth.

His mobile rang. He looked at the display and saw it was Siobhan. He'd been expecting this call for the last three weeks.

'Good morning, Alex, how are you?' she asked in her usual sing-song voice.

'I'm fine thanks,' he lied. 'You? Have you had the babies, yet?'

'Not yet. I am on maternity leave, though, supposed to be resting with my feet up, but I'm so unbelievably bored. I can't wait to get these things out of me. Kicking day and bloody night.'

'You'll not be having any more, then?'

'Absolutely not. Anyway, the reason I'm calling is because we've identified all four boys from the cottage.'

Alex took a deep breath. 'And ...?'

'None of them are Zachery Marshall.'

'You're sure?'

'One hundred per cent. I'm sorry.'

'Do you know, I'm not totally shocked by that. I had a feeling he wouldn't be among them. So, who are they?'

'I can't let you have the details. However, they all disappeared between June and October 1994.'

'How sure are you that they're victims of Jonathan Egan-Walsh?'

'They all match the MO of his other victims. We've also had their parents look at Jonathan's collection and they've identified some of the clothing as belonging to their children. Forensics have been over the cottage with a fine-tooth comb. They've found hair samples from Jonathan in the bed, and semen stains, too. There's no doubt.'

'Have you spoken to Diane Marshall?'

'I haven't, but one of my team has. Apparently, she broke down when she heard the news. She was getting her hopes up that Zachery would be coming home.'

'Shit!' Alex uttered. 'Well, thank you for letting me know.'

'You're welcome. Like I said, I'm on maternity leave but I'm still a member of the human race, so if you need anything, let me know.'

'I will. Thanks, Siobhan.'

Alex ended the call and frowned as he bit his bottom lip. His publisher had been hoping Zachery was one of the four bodies, as it would all tie up neatly for the second book. Now, that book would be in serious doubt. He downed what was left of his pint. He was feeling lightheaded, but his thoughts were still clear.

'Where the hell is Zachery Marshall?' he asked himself.

Chapter Fifty-Five

Three weeks later

Caroline was on the beach as two golden Labradors, a Dalmatian and a Jack Russell stretched their legs. She threw the ball as far as she could and waited until one of them brought it back. Surprisingly, it was usually the nippy Jack Russell who reached the ball first.

The sun was shining and the sky was blue, but the wind was strong, and it was still chilly, so Caroline was dressed in thick waterproof trousers, a fleece, scarf, gloves and a beanie hat. Her cheeks were red as the freezing wind bit at her exposed flesh.

The Jack Russell brought the ball back and dropped it at her feet. She picked it up and waited until the other dogs joined her. She told them all to sit, which they did, then looked at her with their eyes wide and their ears pricked. 'This is the last one, OK? And I mean it this time,' she said, for the fourth time. 'Are you ready?' She lobbed the ball as far as she could. 'Go fetch it.' The dogs turned and hurled into the distance to claim the prize.

'You've got quite a throw on you.'

Caroline jumped and turned around. She thought she had the

beach to herself. 'Alex,' she said, surprised. 'It's lovely to see you.' She leaned forward and kissed him on the cheek. 'What are you doing back up here so soon?'

'I came to see if it's any warmer.'

'Well, as you can see, I'm in my summer clothes,' she said, stepping back and holding her arms out. 'You've had snow in London, too; I've seen it on the news.'

'Yes. Fortunately, I'd had my Arctic training up here,' he smiled. 'How have you coped with the bad weather?'

'We lost power for a couple of days, but we managed. We're made of sterner stuff up North.'

They both knew the chat about the recent bad weather was just a cover for what they really wanted to talk about. One of them was going to have to bring it up soon.

'I'm guessing you heard about the identification of the bodies,' Alex said.

'I did,' she said, dropping her smile. 'Diane's devastated.'

The dogs all came running back and they patiently waited while Caroline attached leads to them all.

'Help me with these and I'll treat you to a coffee. I've got something to tell you about Diane.'

Alex, not used to walking a dog, struggled as the Jack Russell pulled him towards Caroline's courtesy car. She tried to hide her smile but couldn't.

'He loves going for a walk but he knows when he's had enough,' she called after Alex as the Jack Russell moved closer towards the car.

'Have you got your breath back yet?' Caroline asked as they sat down in the tastefully decorated coffee shop. She took off her hat, scarf and gloves and draped them over the radiator behind her.

'Just. It's the most exercise I've had in years.'

The elderly waitress (this place wasn't modern enough for them to be called baristas) brought them a tray laden with coffee cups and matching saucers and two of the largest chocolate-chip muffins Alex had ever seen. He was looking forward to biting into that. He was pleasantly surprised when Caroline received change from a ten-pound note, since in London there wouldn't have been any.

'So, you were going to tell me about Diane,' he said, taking the wrapper off his muffin and sinking his teeth into the soft sponge.

Caroline leaned forward. 'She's having an affair.'

'*Another one?* Who with this time?'

'Nick.'

'Nick. Her ex-husband, Nick?'

'Yes.'

'Since when?'

'About three weeks or so, it seems. Apparently, her mother isn't best pleased.'

'I'm not surprised. When did she tell you this?'

'I went round to her house when DI Gardner phoned me to see how she was. She was in a right state. Anyway, I let her pour her heart out and she just told me she's been seeing Nick again.'

'Is he going to leave … what's her name?'

'Beth? I don't know.'

'How's Nick taking the news of none of the bodies being Zachery?'

'I don't know. She didn't say.'

'Hmm …' he mused.

'So, what's the real reason for you coming back up to the cold North?'

'I'm going to see Siobhan. I'm hoping to gather some information from her about the dead boys.'

'Really?' Caroline frowned. 'Why is she being so helpful?'

'Because of my warm charm,' he said, smiling.

'If you want to believe that, then go ahead,' she said,

sarcastically. 'Did you manage to get in touch with the sister in Australia?'

'Yes,' Alex sighed. 'A big dead end, there. It's all above board, why they moved. From what she was telling me on the phone, they sound like the most boring couple in the world. I'm dreading my next phone bill.'

'Are we really back to square one, then?' Caroline frowned.

'Maybe square three.'

'Siobhan said they were releasing a statement in the next day or so to the media.'

'Yes. It's going to be big news – four more bodies found after twenty-four years. If only we could find where Zachery Marshall is.'

Caroline picked up her mug and took a lingering sip. 'Do you think, perhaps, that there's the slightest possibility he's still alive?'

'I would love to say yes.'

'But …?'

'But, after all this time? I seriously doubt it.'

'It would make a lovely happy ending.'

'There's no such thing as a happy ending,' Alex said, his voice dropping.

'That's a very cynical thing to say.'

He turned to look out of the window. The blue sky was bewitching, suggesting it was a warm summer's day outside, when in reality there was a bitter easterly wind blowing and the temperature was hovering in the low single figures. Alex's eyes prickled with tears and he tried so hard to keep them at bay but he couldn't.

Caroline leaned forward and touched his hand. 'Alex, what's wrong? Has something happened? Is it Melanie?'

'We've been granted permission to stop feeding her,' he said quickly, his bottom lip quivering.

'Oh, Alex, I'm *so* sorry.'

He shrugged.

'What happens now?' she asked.

'A couple of doctors are going to come around to assess her one last time; see if there's any chance of her life improving. If not, then, that's it.'

'How's your daughter taking it? I'm sorry, I can't remember her name.'

'Shona. She's been very quiet, but knows it's for the best. We both know that.'

'If there's anything I can do,' she said.

'That's kind of you, thanks.'

'Shouldn't you be at home with Shona?'

'No. We've got a carer in looking after Melanie for a few days. Shona's gone away with a couple of friends. I told her to have a break before ...' He stopped himself from putting his final act into words.

'I think you need a break, too.'

'I'm having one. I've come up here to lovely, sunny Skegness.'

Caroline laughed. 'You have a warped sense of what a holiday is.'

'I'm supporting the British economy,' he said with a smile on his face.

Caroline offered to go with Alex to see Siobhan but then remembered she had a new client to see who had a Great Dane puppy. Alex promised to visit her and Jamie in the evening and have a late supper.

Siobhan lived in a quiet, leafy cul-de-sac on the outskirts of the town. In the distance, the sound of waves crashing on the shore could be heard. He was almost jealous. He could think of no better sound to listen to at night when he couldn't sleep. For the first time, the thought came to him that perhaps he should move once Melanie was gone.

The front door was opened by Siobhan, who had grown even bigger since the last time he saw her. She looked tired, stressed, and ready to give birth at any moment.

'I'd ask how you are but I don't think I need to,' he said, taking in her red face and harassed expression.

'Would you believe I still have two weeks left?' she said, rubbing her huge stomach. 'I'm dreading what's going to come out: two, three, a whole rugby team? Come on in. I can't be on my feet for too long.'

She slowly trudged into the living room. A black-and-white film was playing on the widescreen television on the wall. On the coffee table was an empty box of chocolates, a part-packet of biscuits and a large *open* bag of Kettle Chips.

'I'd offer you a cup of tea, but my back is really killing me today.'

'Do you want me to make it?'

'Please. That would be lovely. There's some Bakewell tarts in the cupboard above the kettle; bring those in, too, will you?'

Alex made them both a mug of tea each and took it and the Bakewells into the living room. Siobhan had slumped onto the sofa, her legs up on a footstool. She looked as if it would take a crane to lift her out.

'Thanks, Alex,' she said, snatching the tarts from him. 'You know, nothing seems to be able to fill me up lately.'

'Siobhan ...' Alex began as he sat in an armchair next to her, 'why are you giving me information for my book so readily?'

She smiled. 'Because I saw you taking photographs of me and my team while we were at the cottage. You're going to use them, so I thought I'd supply information rather than have you write about how unhelpful we were.'

'How did you see me?'

'Here's a tip – the next time you're sneaking around a field taking pictures, remember your surroundings. Fields are generally green, and a red coat stands out a mile,' she said, laughing.

'Well, I didn't have my commando gear with me.'

'See that file under the coffee table?' She pointed. 'That is everything you need to know about the four boys found under the cottage.'

Alex picked up the thick file. He didn't wait to open it. He'd grown used to seeing photographs of happy smiling schoolboys posing in their uniform in one picture and laid out on a mortuary slab in the next.

'The four boys are Shaun Paisley, aged seven, from Norfolk; James Hambleton, aged six, from Mablethorpe; Kevin Watts, aged seven, from Friskney; and Craig Mosby, aged eight, from Bridlington.' Siobhan reeled their names and details off without having to check.

'Cute boys,' Alex said, looking at the photographs supplied by their families.

'They were,' she said.

'That's seventeen victims,' Alex said, subdued. 'And I can't help thinking there's more out there.'

'I know. I've been thinking the same, too. And there's nobody left to pay for these crimes. Jonathan has got away with four more murders.'

'How have the families reacted?' Alex asked, after letting an awkward silence build.

'Relief, mainly. After twenty-four years, they'd more or less resigned themselves to the fact that their children were dead. Now, they finally have a body they can bury and a place they can visit. That's what they've wanted.'

'That's all Diane Marshall wants, too.'

'I'm not a religious woman, but I was praying so hard for one of these boys to be Zachery Marshall.'

'Are you going to visit her while you're up here?'

'Yes. I'm still going to keep looking for him.'

'Do you think you'll ever find him?'

'Definitely. Every story has an ending. Someone knows what happened to Zachery and I'll get them to tell me. Eventually.'

'I wish you all the luck in the world.'

'I'm going to need it.'

Diane sat at her dressing table with a large pink bath towel wrapped around her. She had showered and was now choosing which lipstick would go with the dark-pink dress she had bought earlier that day.

She felt happy. At first, she was devastated that none of the four boys was Zachery. She had spent days crying. Fortunately, Nick was there to support her, something he hadn't done all those years ago when their son first went missing. Now, he had refocused her attention. It really was time for her to move on. For the first time in as long as she could remember, she had a reason to get on with life. She and Nick had poured their hearts out to each other over the past couple of weeks. It was like they were meeting again for the first time. She tried not to think about Beth. After all, Beth hadn't thought of Diane when she was having an affair with Nick.

She hummed along to the radio as she applied eyeliner and lipstick. She didn't want to look like mutton dressed as lamb – she was pushing sixty, after all – but she wanted to make a good impression. She tried telling herself it was just a bit of fun she and Nick were having, but she couldn't help feeling a flutter of something inside her. It was like she was dating all over again.

Once dressed, Diane looked at herself from all angles in the full-length mirror. She didn't like her body at all. There were lumps and bumps where there shouldn't be, her bum was dropping, and her waist was expanding, despite a strict diet she'd been following recently. The ravages of age. Thank goodness for modern technology and the invention of underwear to hold you in exactly where you needed holding in. Her stomach looked flat and firm, her bum was almost pert. She smiled at her reflection. She saw a different woman looking back at her – a happy, confident woman.

The doorbell rang and Diane ran down the stairs with all the excitement of a sixteen-year-old on Prom night. She pulled it open to find Nick on the doorstep holding a bunch of flowers.

'*Wow!* You look amazing,' Nick said.

'Thank you. You're looking very smart yourself,' she replied, taking in his new designer suit, before taking the flowers and inviting him in.

'Do we have time for a drink before we go to the restaurant?' she asked.

'Yes. The table isn't booked until eight.'

They went into the living room. There was a hint of underlying tension in the air. Diane had felt it the day after she had first slept with Nick again. She wondered if it was because they were rekindling something they had thought confined to the pages of history, but the more she analysed it, the more she realised it was this house. If she and Nick were to have any kind of a future together, they would have to move. There was too much sadness embedded in the walls for the couple to make a happy life in them.

She poured them both a small drink. They clinked glasses and sat next to each other on the sofa. Nick was about to say something when the doorbell rang again.

'Are you expecting someone?' he asked.

'Not that I'm aware of.'

'It won't be your mother, will it?'

'God, I hope not.' Diane replied before heading to the front door. When she looked through the spy hole, she visibly relaxed: Alex Frost was on the other side.

'Alex, nice to see you,' she said through a small gap in the door. 'I'm just about to go out, actually.'

'I won't stay long. I just wanted to see how you were doing after … you know.'

Diane's face saddened. 'It was a blow, but I've had them before when there's been sightings that have come to nothing. I'll be fine.'

'You have my number if you want to talk or if anything new comes up.'

'I do. Thanks for everything, Alex.'

'I won't give up, Diane. I want you to know that I'll keep asking questions. I'll keep searching. We will find your son, I promise you.'

Diane choked back the tears. She opened the door further and stepped outside, then grabbed Alex and hugged him tight. 'Thank you,' she whispered tearfully into his ear.

'You look nice,' he said when she released him.

'I'm just taking my mum out for a meal; get us both out of the house.'

'Well, I'll let you go, then. I just thought I'd pop round while I was in the area.'

'Thanks.'

Diane stepped back into the house and closed the door firmly behind her. She went into the living room and saw Nick sitting in the middle of the sofa.

The ice cubes in his glass were rattling.

'It was Alex Frost,' she said.

'I heard.'

Alex stood on the garden path looking at the closed front door. As he turned away and headed down the drive he looked at the Citroën Picasso parked in the road. He was sure it was Nick's car. He looked back at the house, at the living-room window, but couldn't see anything as the curtains were drawn.

He climbed into the Volvo, turned the key in the ignition and drove slowly to the end of the road, all the time looking in the rear-view mirror at Diane's house, though he had no idea what he expected to see. He indicated left, turned and pulled into a tight parking space between two Fiat Puntos. He turned the engine off, hunkered down in the seat, and waited.

Less than ten minutes later, there was movement in the mirror. The silver Citroën Picasso turned left from Diane's road and passed his car at speed. He stole a glance and saw Nick in the driver's seat. Diane wasn't with him. Either he had just popped around to see her and she really was taking her mother out for a meal, or Alex's presence had caused them to change their plans.

Chapter Fifty-Six

'Once a cheat, always a cheat,' Hannah said from the kitchen table.

'Yes. You've said. Thank you, Mother,' Diane said tartly.

'I knew this would happen. I told you it would, but would you listen?'

'Mum, can we change the subject, please?'

Diane hadn't seen Nick since he abandoned their meal out when Alex unexpectedly called. She had sent him many texts and left several voicemails, all of which had been ignored. At first, she didn't tell her mother, but, mothers being mothers, Hannah knew exactly what had happened and revelled in her 'I told you so' speech.

'I went to the optician this morning,' Hannah said.

'Did you? You didn't mention it. I'd have taken you.'

'I told you last week. You said you were working this morning.'

'Did I?'

'Yes, you did. I knew you weren't paying attention at the time. You were too busy with Nick, I suppose.'

'I thought we were changing the subject? How did you get on?'

'Fine. A slight change in my right eye, but that's to be expected at my age. I've ordered some prescription sunglasses, too, for the summer.'

'It seems to have been a long winter,' Diane said, looking into the distance.

'It's March now. We do the clocks in a couple of weeks. I do enjoy light nights,' Hannah said with a smile. She looked at her daughter, at the wistful expression, the sadness in her eyes and the downturned mouth. 'Why don't we rent a cottage somewhere?'

'What?' Diane asked, not paying any attention.

'We could go to the Lake District or maybe to Devon. They have lovely beaches down south. What do you say?'

The phone rang. Diane snapped out of her reverie and went into the living room to answer it. She hadn't paid the slightest bit of attention to her mother.

'Diane, it's Beth.'

'Oh.' Diane couldn't think of anything else to say. She had never spoken to her ex-husband's wife on the phone before.

'Is Nick with you?' Beth asked. She sounded strange, her voice seemed higher than usual.

'Nick? No. Why? Should he be?'

'I just thought he might be, that's all.'

'Why?'

'I can't find him.' She nervously laughed. 'He's not answering his mobile. I called his work and he didn't show up today. He didn't even ring.'

'Oh.'

'That's why I thought he might have been with you. He's been very quiet lately since those four boys were found. I think he's taking it hard that one wasn't Zachery.'

'I haven't seen him, Beth,' Diane said, an icy tone to her voice.

'You don't know where he might be, do you? Any old haunts, or something?'

'No. I can't think of anything, I'm sorry.'

Diane put the phone down without saying goodbye or asking to be kept informed. She looked up and saw her mother standing in the doorway.

'What's happened?' Hannah asked.

'Nick's gone missing.'

'Oh,' she said, not sounding very interested. 'Do you want another cup of tea?'

Diane frowned. Nick had changed suddenly on the night Alex came round – he suddenly said he was going home instead of to the restaurant with her. He had claimed he didn't feel well, but she knew that was a lie. Nick had told her of his previous run-ins with Alex. He said he didn't like him.

'Mum, will you be all right here for a bit?' Diane called out.

'What? Why? Where are you going?'

'I'm going to pop out.'

'Where?'

'I don't know,' she said, picking up her car keys and mobile phone from the coffee table.

'You're going to visit Beth, aren't you?'

'No.'

'Then you're going to try and find Nick. Diane, why are you getting involved? They've probably had a row and he's stormed out. You know what he's like. He never could face responsibility for his actions. He'll go back home when he's calmed down.'

Once again, Diane ignored her mother. She was in the hallway putting on her jacket and a pair of comfortable walking shoes.

'If he wanted to talk to you he would have come round. Maybe he just wants to be on his own for a while,' Hannah said.

'No. There's something wrong. I can feel it.'

'It's probably wind.'

'Mum, leave it. I won't be long.'

She grabbed her scarf from the hook by the door, wrapped it around her neck and went out into the cold night air, leaving Hannah alone in the hallway.

Diane had no idea where she was going. As she drove through the dark streets of Skegness she realised that she no longer knew her ex-husband. When they were married, Nick would often go with friends to the pub to play pool, go to watch a football match or, occasionally, go to the park for a run. She always knew where he was. But that was almost twenty years ago. What were his hobbies now? Did he still play pool? Was he still in contact with his old friends? She had no idea where she should be looking for him.

She wondered if she should contact Marcus, ask him about his dad's habits, but she didn't want to worry him and she also didn't want him to wonder why his mother was suddenly so concerned for his father. No, Diane was on her own with this.

If he hadn't been to work that morning, then where would he have gone when he left the house? What direction would he have headed in? If she had wanted to get away from everything for the day, where would she go? Probably the coast. She had no idea if she was on the right track but there was nothing else she could think of. She performed an illegal U-turn and headed for the coast.

It was past eleven o'clock and the streets were quiet. There wasn't a cloud in the sky and the moon was full and bright. An infinite number of stars helped to light up the black sky. Diane kept looking at every silver car she passed in case it was Nick's, but she couldn't keep her eyes off that bewitching moon. It looked huge.

Before the dual carriageway, she looked to her right and saw Barrett International where Nick worked. There, in the centre of the car park, as if it wanted to be found, was the silver Citroën.

Diane smiled as, once again, she performed an illegal manoeuvre and entered the car park.

Nick's car was empty. Diane cupped her hands over her eyes and looked into the darkened car. There was nothing there of interest. No note left for anyone, no discarded clothing. She looked around her and shivered as a stiff breeze picked up and chilled her bones.

The large building behind her was in darkness. She didn't know which floor Nick worked on in the six-storey building but he wasn't in his office, unless he was sitting in complete darkness. She went to the main entrance. The doors were automatic but stayed closed. There was no keypad to type a code in or swipe a card on, so how had Nick gained access to the building out of working hours? Unless, that is, he had a key, which was highly unlikely. He didn't own the company and he wasn't an MD or anything.

She stood back and looked up at the imposing building. That's when she saw Nick, sitting on the roof, his legs dangling over the side.

Diane wondered if she should call out to him. He didn't look as if he had noticed her. He seemed to be staring into space. Deciding against startling him, she went around to the back of the building, looking for any way to get up to the roof. There was an iron ladder screwed to the building that acted as an emergency fire escape.

Diane hated heights. Even standing on a chair to change a light bulb made her feel sick. She closed her eyes and took a deep breath. She had no choice.

Carefully, she placed one hand on a rusted rung, then the other and pulled her heavy legs up one at a time. She held herself close to the ladder, not wanting to risk slipping, and slowly ascended. Whenever the wind picked up and a gust howled around the building, Diane stopped and held on for dear life until it died down. Then she started climbing again. It seemed to take an age and she didn't dare look down. She looked up instead and saw she wasn't even halfway to the top, despite feeling like she had been clamped to this bloody ladder for days.

She bit the bullet and moved faster. Eventually, she made it to the roof, though she had no idea how she was going to get down. There was no way she was going to attempt the creaking ladder again.

She stood up, dusted herself down and looked ahead. Nick was still sitting on the edge of the roof.

'Nick,' she said softly so as not to startle him. He didn't respond. She stepped forward and called out to him again, a little louder this time.

Nick turned around. He had a look of surprise on his face, and there were tears in his eyes. 'Diane. What are you doing here?'

'Looking for you.'

'How did you know …?'

'Beth called. She said you hadn't been to work today and nobody knew where you were.'

'Oh,' he said, turning back to the darkened Skegness landscape.

'What are you doing up here?' she asked, stepping closer.

He said something but his words were lost on the wind.

Diane went over to him. She risked looking down over the side of the building. They were only six storeys off the ground, but to Diane, it felt like they were on the top of Blackpool Tower. Her stomach was turning somersaults. She felt sick. Carefully, she sat down on the cold concrete and swept her legs over the side, dangling into the void below.

Her teeth were chattering as the cold enveloped her. The wind seemed stronger, so high up. She hoped she wouldn't be blown off the roof. It would be a tragic yet entirely pointless end. She budged up closer to Nick until they were touching. He acted as a windbreak from the breeze coming from the east.

'Nick, what's going on? What's the matter?' She looked at him, at the torment etched on his face. Tears were falling from his eyes and the wind was blowing them away.

'I can't live like this. It's killing me.'

Diane linked arms with her ex-husband and leaned into him. 'I know, Nick. It's a nightmare not knowing what happened to Zachery, but we can't give up. And this is no way out. Think of your other children. Think of how devastated they'd be without you.'

'They'd be better off without me. Everyone would.'

'Why do you think that?'

'Diane.' He turned to look at her. 'It was me. I killed him. I killed Zach.'

The wind stopped blowing. The world stopped turning. Diane saw Nick's lips moving but didn't register a single word he spoke. Surely she had heard wrong.

'What did you say?'

'I killed our son.'

'You can't have. It was Jonathan.' She removed herself from him and edged along the building.

'No,' he said, shaking his head. 'It was me.'

'But ... I don't understand.'

She looked out at the lorries and cars driving on the dual carriageway and at life carrying on as normal while hers was crumbling. The petrol station across the road was lit up in gaudy neon light. Staff and customers were going about their business, unaware that a few feet away, a woman's life was being chewed up and spat out.

'When I left British Gas on the Sunday, I was going to visit Beth. On my way, I saw Zachery riding his bike. I pulled over and asked where he was going. He said he was going to the park. I told him to be careful, then I carried on. I didn't think to look behind me. I didn't realise ...'

'Realise what?'

'How fast he was on his bike. He was following me. I arrived at Beth's. She answered the door and kissed me. Zachery saw everything. He waited for me. He stayed outside the house all the time I was in there. I came out, got in the van and at the bottom of the road, there he was. He looked so disappointed in me.'

'Where was Marcus in all this?'

'Francesca had taken him into the house. She loved to play with him.'

'Who the bloody hell is Francesca?'

He took a deep breath. 'Beth's daughter.'

She looked at him, saw his eyes darting from side to side. 'Your daughter, too?'

He nodded.

'Quite the happy family you had going on,' she said with scorn.

'It wasn't like that.'

Diane tried to speak but her mouth was too dry. She swallowed hard. 'So, what happened?'

'I got back out of the van and asked him what he was doing. He told me he'd seen me with Beth and asked who she was. I panicked. I'm never good at thinking quickly on the spot. He was a lot like you, Zachery. He saw straight through me, and my lies.'

'What did you do?' she asked, wiping a tear away.

'I asked him not to tell you. I wanted him to promise to keep what he saw to himself. All he kept saying was that he was going to tell you when he got home. I grabbed him. He tried to break free but I just grabbed him and shook him. He pulled free and staggered back. He lost his balance and fell. I can still hear the sound when he hit the pavement,' he said, closing his eyes.

'But Marcus was in the van with you. He would have seen, surely.'

'He was asleep. He'd been playing hard and was bang out before we reached the end of the road.'

Diane was numb. None of this was happening. It couldn't be.

She was hearing Nick's words but none of them were making any sense. Why was he saying this to her?

'So, what happened?'

'I picked him up, but he was limp. I knew he was dead straight away. I put him in the van with his bike and just started driving while I thought what to do.'

'But what about Marcus, didn't he wake up?'

'He'd been running around Beth's house for hours. He didn't wake up until we got home and saw all that commotion in the street.'

'I don't understand any of this,' she flustered. 'You came home. You started the search. Where did you take him?'

'I didn't take him anywhere at first. I left him in the back of the van.'

Diane's mouth fell open. Tears fell down her face. 'You mean, all the time I was in the house, screaming, begging for you to find him, all the time you were searching, he was in the van on the driveway?'

Nick looked up at her. 'I'm sorry,' he choked.

'Sorry?' she asked, incredulous to his words. 'What are you actually sorry for, Nick? Killing my son, hiding his body, lying to everyone for all these years? *What are you actually fucking sorry for?*' she screamed. She was physically shaking as the full horror of her new world began to take hold.

His mouth opened and closed a few times but no words came out.

'So, where is he? Where did you eventually take him?'

'There's a small patch of woodland off the A158 Skegness Road near a small caravan park on the Ingoldmells Road. I buried him there. I planted a rose bush so I'd always be able to find him. I visit him every week.'

'Hang on a minute. What you're saying, it doesn't make sense. His clothes were found … it couldn't be you … why are you saying this?'

'I undressed him. I kept them in the van for weeks, not knowing what to do with them. I was in a daze. My head was all over the place. I took them along the cliff top. I was going to throw them into the sea. I got back to the van and I didn't have them with me. I couldn't remember throwing them but I must have done. I don't know what I did with them. I must have just left them somewhere.'

'You bastard! You complete and utter bastard. You've ruined my life. You've ruined my relationship with Marcus. You've ruined his life, too. You make me sick. You're as evil as Jonathan, do you know that? You allowed us all to go through all that heartache, thinking someone else had taken him, when all along it was you.'

Nick cried. 'I know. I'm sorry. I thought it would be easier if I allowed Jonathan to take the blame. Diane, there isn't a day goes by when I don't regret everything. I've never forgotten Zachery. I loved him. I still love him.'

'So, was it you? The brick through the window? Breaking into Alex's hotel room? Pouring petrol on Caroline's car?'

He nodded. 'I was frightened of what would happen if you found out. I thought if you were scared, you'd put a stop to it all.'

She looked at her ex-husband and she saw what her mother had been telling her all these years – a pathetic excuse for a man. The anger inside her reached boiling point.

'You piece of shit.'

'Diane ...'

'No. Don't say anything. Don't say my name. I don't want to hear any more of your pathetic excuses.'

They fell silent, looking out into the dark night sky.

'You just buried him,' she said eventually, breathing heavily. 'You threw him in the ground like he was nothing. You buried him on his own. He must have been so scared,' she said. A solitary tear fell down her face. She could feel the warmth on her cold skin, but she didn't react to it.

'Diane, I am *so* sorry. I don't know what to say.'

'Say? There's nothing you can say. Every word that comes out of your mouth is like a knife in my heart. You're a sick, evil bastard,' she seethed.

'What do we do now?'

Diane took a deep breath and tried to compose herself. She turned to look at him and felt sick to her stomach. She couldn't think of a word vile enough to call him. The contempt she felt for him was limitless. He was a useless father, a hopeless man, a failure as a human being. As she looked into his watery blue eyes she realised what she felt for him was pure hatred. He had made her live a life in limbo for twenty-five years, thinking up every conceivable scenario about what had happened to her son. And all this, taking her out for meals, worming his way back into her bedroom, was just his twisted way of trying to find out how close Alex and Caroline were to uncovering the truth.

'Diane, say something.'

There was nothing Diane could say. She couldn't find the words, and even if she could, she wouldn't waste them on this useless shit sitting next to her.

'Jump,' she said quietly.

'What?' he asked.

'I want you to jump.'

'You want me to kill myself?'

'Nick, if you don't jump, I'm going to push you off this building. Now, for once in your pathetic life, do the right thing, and jump.' Diane's whole body was shaking. She was angry, frightened, shocked and cold.

'I'm so sorry, Diane.'

'Don't say anything,' she said, looking straight ahead. 'Don't say another word.'

Nick looked down at the empty car park below. Tears falling off his face were picked up by the wind. 'I can't.'

'Only one of us is getting off this roof alive, Nick. What you did to my son, what you've put us all through for twenty-five years, is unforgivable. You don't deserve to live to be an old man. You don't deserve a family and happiness. It's you who should be buried alone in an unmarked grave, not my Zachery,' she cried. 'Now, for once, do the right thing.'

Chapter Fifty-Seven

Alex had decided to stay in Skegness an extra few days. Shona had called to say she was staying with friends in Brighton until the weekend and the carer was fine to look after Melanie.

Alex should have gone back to London. He should have taken the opportunity to have some alone time with his wife. Soon there wouldn't be any more chances left for them to be on their own. However, he couldn't face it. He booked into a Premier Inn and spent his days on the laptop, working on his book, or on the beach, walking the dogs with Caroline. In the evenings, he either went to the Turners for a meal or he ate alone in his dull hotel room.

After four days, he realised he should be in London. He decided to drive overnight to the capital. The motorway would be quieter. He could put his foot down on the accelerator and stay in the fast lane for the majority of the journey.

He said goodbye to Caroline and Jamie, promised to stay in touch and was leaving the built-up area of Skegness when his mobile rang. He answered and put the phone on speaker.

'Alex. I don't know what to do.'

'Diane? What's wrong?' he asked, genuinely concerned at the panic in her voice.

'Nick disappeared. I went to look for him and found him sitting on the roof where he worked. He was crying. He told me he killed Zachery and then he jumped. He just jumped off the roof.'

Alex slammed down hard on the brake and jerked forward. The seatbelt cut into his neck and pulled him back into the seat.

'Are you serious?'

'Yes,' she cried.

'Where are you now?'

'I'm at Barrett International. I'm still on the roof. I can't get down. I don't know what to do, Alex.'

'All right. Stay where you are. I'm on my way.'

He ended the call and looked around him. He had no idea whereabouts he was in relation to Barrett International but he knew a woman who did. As he performed a three-point turn, he called Caroline and told her as much as he knew. She was in as much shock as he was. By the time he arrived at her house, she was already waiting for him at the side of the road.

'What the hell?' she asked as she climbed into the passenger side.

'I really don't know.'

'Why would Nick kill his own son?'

'I've no idea. And why confess now, after all this time?'

Caroline opened her mouth to reply but nothing came out. She looked stunned.

Alex thought for a moment. 'When I went round there to tell her I wouldn't stop looking for Zachery, Nick was there. He must have overheard and knew I'd get to the truth eventually.'

'I can't believe this.'

'Not the happy ending you thought, is it?'

Caroline shook her head in disbelief.

Caroline directed Alex to Barrett International. He pulled up, not caring about parking correctly in the allotted bays. They both jumped out and immediately saw the broken body of Nick Marshall in front of the main entrance.

'*I'm up here!*' Diane called out.

They both looked up.

'Diane, you need to come down.'

'I can't. I don't like heights. I'm scared.'

'How did you get up there?' Caroline asked.

'There's a ladder around the back.'

'I'll go and get her,' Caroline said to Alex.

'I'll give Siobhan Gardner a call. Fingers crossed she hasn't gone into labour yet.'

While he waited for the call to connect, Alex crouched to the ground and had a good look at Nick's body. He was lying on his front, his head twisted away from him. His limbs were at an unnatural angle. There was a jagged pool of blood around his head. Alex stood up to full height and took a step back, looking up at the building then down at the body again.

Alex didn't speak to Diane. By the time Caroline had helped her down from the roof, Siobhan's car, driven by her husband, was pulling up. A marked police car soon followed, and Diane was placed in the back of it, then driven to the police station to make a full statement about what had happened. There was nothing more for Alex or Caroline to do. They would also have to make a statement, but not tonight. It could wait until morning.

Alex drove Caroline home in silence. They were both in shock at the abrupt ending. Jamie was waiting for them with a large whisky each. They sat by the fire and soon began to warm up – the alcohol helped.

'What will happen to Diane?' Jamie asked.

'Nothing. She'll give a statement. The coroner will rule the death as suicide, and that will be it,' Caroline said.

'I wonder if he told her where he'd buried their son,' Jamie asked.

'I hope so. For her sake,' Caroline said. 'She needs to know where he is in order to move on. You're very quiet, Alex. What's on your mind?'

'What? Oh, nothing. I was just thinking,'

'What about?'

'Why did Nick wait until now to kill himself, after all this time?'

'Well, it's like you said: he obviously heard you telling Diane you wouldn't give up looking for Zachery. Maybe he saw no way out.'

'But why didn't he kill himself when we started all those weeks ago? He must have known we'd come up with something. I should have seen this coming.'

'You weren't to know.'

'Remember when we went to see him at his work? I saw marks on his wrists. He'd obviously attempted to take his own life before. If I'd questioned him about it, maybe I would have uncovered this sooner. I could have saved Diane from all this heartache.'

'You can't blame yourself, Alex.'

He took a long slug of his drink and started biting his thumbnail. 'I just don't see why he waited until now. It doesn't make sense.'

'Maybe he thought he'd covered his tracks enough.'

'Then I'm back to my original question: why wait until now?

What has happened in the last couple of days to make him realise he has to kill himself now?'

'You'll have to ask Diane that; she was the last person to speak to him.'

'Oh, I will,' he said firmly. 'You can count on that.'

Chapter Fifty-Eight

Alex stayed the night at Caroline's. He had called Shona, who was having a lovely time with friends in Brighton. She sounded happy and there was a lightness to her voice he hadn't heard in years. Despite the fact it was painful, he knew he was doing the right thing in ending Melanie's life. For all their sakes.

The next morning, the sombre mood continued as he sat on the sofa, not knowing what to do with himself, while Caroline and Jamie tiptoed around him. It was early afternoon when the doorbell rang. It was Siobhan Gardner.

She collapsed into the armchair and accepted the offer of a cup of tea.

When offered a slice of cake, she almost snatched Caroline's hand off. She had developed a serious sweet tooth since becoming pregnant. Between huge bites of Victoria sponge and drinks of tea, she filled them all in on what Diane had told her. The police were heading out to Ingoldmells Road that afternoon to dig up Zachery Marshall, if they wanted to go along.

It took less than an hour to drive to the woodland where Nick had buried his son. Twenty-five years he'd been missing, and he had been lying less than an hour's drive away. It seemed incredibly cruel, somehow.

By the time they arrived, a forensic team had already gathered. Diane was sat in the back of a marked police car with a female officer keeping her company. She looked out of the window as Alex and Caroline passed. She gave them a slight smile. Caroline nodded in sympathy, but Alex remained impassive.

They walked carefully over the rough terrain to where the team were waiting for them, shovels at the ready. In between two large oak trees there stood a small, unkempt rose bush. It looked out of place, but nobody had questioned its existence. Had people walked through here and thought it a miracle of nature that a rose bush should grow in such rugged surroundings?

The three stood and looked down at the unmarked grave.

'It's a beautiful spot,' Caroline said.

'Yes. Quiet,' Siobhan agreed.

'It's almost a shame he has to be disturbed.'

'He can't stay here,' Alex said. 'He needs to go home.'

The digging began. Alex took a few photographs on his mobile phone and stepped back as the forensic team went about their business. They dug slowly and carefully, making sure they didn't put their shovels through any bones.

Alex looked back at the waiting police car. Diane was looking. She had her head down. 'Isn't she going to get out?' he asked Siobhan.

'No. She said she wants to be here but she doesn't want to see him.'

'That's understandable,' Caroline said.

'Her son, Marcus, wanted to come with her for support but she said she wanted to be alone.'

'I can't believe what Nick did,' Caroline said. 'He destroyed his family and went on to have more children with Beth. That's two families he's wrecked.'

'Ma'am,' the call came from behind them.

All three looked at each other, then went back towards the makeshift grave. The hole wasn't deep – a few feet, if that. They looked down and saw the unmistakable sight of the side of a small skull.

'Keep digging,' Siobhan instructed. 'I'll go and tell Diane.'

Caroline wiped away a tear. 'That poor boy.'

Alex remained silent.

Chapter Fifty-Nine

Three weeks later: Thursday, 19 April 2018

The day after Alex buried Melanie, he headed back to Skegness for another funeral. The inquest into Nick Marshall's death had been completed and the coroner ruled he had taken his own life. The Crown Prosecution Service had been satisfied with the investigation's conclusion that Nick had killed his son and buried him unlawfully. Zachery's body had now been released and Diane was finally getting the closure she had been waiting a quarter of a century for. She would finally have a place to visit to mourn her eldest son.

Alex knocked on Diane's front door. He was wearing the same suit as yesterday; the same tie, the same shoes, the same sombre expression. Diane opened the door. She, too, was in funeral clothes.

'Alex, I'm *so* sorry,' she said, holding out her arms to hug him. She held him tight. 'How are you doing? Sorry, silly question.'

He gave her a weak smile.

'Is Shona with you?'

'No. She's gone to stay with friends for a couple of days. We're going to sort the house out, then put it on the market. Too many memories.'

'Do you want to come in?'

'Shouldn't we be going to the church?'

Diane looked at her watch. 'You're probably right.'

It seemed like the whole of the town had turned out for Zachery Marshall's funeral. It was a cool day. The sky was a brilliant blue and the sun shone, but there was a stiff wind coming in off the sea. Outside the church, with the sea in the background, people lined the roads as the hearse carrying the wicker coffin crawled slowly up the road. In the car behind, Diane stepped out, turning back to help her mother. Marcus and Greta followed. They waited, expressionless faces staring straight ahead at the small coffin. As the pallbearers pulled the coffin out of the hearse, Marcus stepped forward to help carry his brother up the steep incline to the church.

Alex and Caroline waited until family and friends had entered the church before they went in. They took a booklet each from someone at the door and went to sit at the back of the small stone building. Caroline looked down at the booklet and into the smiling eyes of a seven-year-old Zachery Marshall looking up at her. He had his whole life ahead of him. He could have been anything he wanted to be, but he was killed by the one person he should have been able to trust most.

The service lasted for thirty minutes in which the vicar said a few words before a hymn was sung. Marcus stepped up and made a statement about what a funny, loving brother he had known. He made the congregation laugh with his stories, but the laughter turned to tears when Marcus began to cry as he said his older brother, who would permanently be younger than him, had missed out on so much – college, university, marriage, a family of his own. When he became inaudible because of the tears, Greta stepped up, took her husband by the hand and led him back to their pew.

Another hymn was sung, a prayer was uttered, and the coffin was carried out of the church to the graveyard at the back.

Alex and Caroline stood well back. This part of the service was for the family only.

Members of Thirteen were in attendance, showing solidarity to one of their own. Alex was surprised to see Lachlan Minnow leaving the church. He had his head down and looked genuinely sombre. When he looked up, he caught Alex's eye and quickly turned away.

Caroline was crying as she watched the coffin sink into the ground. Her tissues were wet and torn.

'Are you OK?' Caroline asked Alex, putting her arm through his.

He nodded. He wasn't crying. He had spent the whole of the past thirteen days crying – as feeding his wife ended and he watched as she slowly died. It took eight days. He and Shona had spent the whole time by Melanie's bedside watching her fade away. They told stories of the happier times, but they didn't seem real. It was as if they had happened to other people. They had laughed at the stories of Shona growing up. Alex had told his daughter all about meeting Melanie and falling in love with her at first sight.

When Melanie died it was almost a relief. The funeral was a sad affair and Alex hid his emotions behind sunglasses as he stood by the graveside, holding firmly onto his daughter. They were numb with grief.

Now Caroline asked, 'Do you want to go?'

'No. Let's wait a little while longer.'

They moved over to a bench and sat down to watch as Diane picked up a handful of earth and tossed it into the grave.

'How's the book coming along?'

'Slowly.'

'I hope you'll take ten years off me.'

'Of course.' he smiled.

'And make me thinner and taller, too,' she chuckled.

Alex smiled. 'Listen, where Nick died, there's a petrol station across the road from Barrett International. I spoke to the staff who were working there on the night he died, and they heard him scream.'

'Well, they would. It was night and there was very little traffic around.'

'The point is, why would he scream if he jumped?'

'Oh ...' Caroline said, her mouth wide open. 'You'd only scream if you fell, or ...'

'You were pushed.'

Caroline nudged Alex. They looked up and saw Diane walking down the pavement with her mother by her side, Marcus and Greta, carrying baby Zachery, behind them. Nobody said anything. Diane gave a weak smile, which Alex returned.

'You don't think ... do you?' Caroline asked once they were out of earshot.

'I don't know what to think.'

'Alex, you can't start throwing accusations around. Not without proof.'

'I know.'

'What are you going to do?'

'I'll know when I get to that part in my book,' he said. He headed towards the open grave to pay his final respects to the boy he never knew.

Caroline looked at Alex then turned to the retreating Marshall family. As Diane opened the back door to get into the car she looked up to the cemetery and made eye contact with Caroline.

A cold wind blew and chilled the former detective to the bone.

Acknowledgments

It's always scary writing something new and *The Seventh Victim* is a marked change from my police procedural series, but it was a story I wanted to tell and not have a criminal investigation as the main focus. I wanted to deal with the aftermath of a murder and how the lives of those who are grieving the loss of someone they love are changed for ever.

In the researching of this book, I came across a charity called SAMM (Support After Murder and Manslaughter). They help the families of people who have died through murder. It's an incredibly sad fact that marriages don't always survive when a child is murdered, and friendships end as grief takes over people's lives. SAMM is there to help those left behind. Nobody should have to deal with the pain of grief alone. For more information, please visit samm.org.uk

I would like to thank my first agent, Tom Witcomb and the people at Audible including Victoria Haslam and Josephine Lane. I'd also like to thank Joanne Froggatt and Mathew Horne for their amazing performance in bringing *The Seventh Victim* to life on audio.

The reason you're reading this paperback or ebook is thanks to my current agent, Jamie Cowen at Ampersand and the wonderful people at HarperCollins and One More Chapter including Jennie Rothwell, Charlotte Ledger and the talented marketing and publicity team. I couldn't be happier or prouder to be working with such an amazing group of people.

Technical information including details of post-mortems,

medical matters and police procedure are thanks to Philip Lumb, Simon Browes, 'Mr Tidd' and Andy Barrett. Any inaccuracies are down to me.

Lastly, thank you to the usual suspects: Mum, Chris Schofield, Kevin Embleton, Jonas Alexander, Chris Simmons and Maxwell Dog for their continued friendship and support.

Introducing the brand new series featuring Dr Olivia Winter

Dr Olivia Winter finds serial killers. Her job is to talk to them and understand their motives.

Now a serial killer wants to find her.

But Dr Winter has a secret. One she thought was hidden firmly in the past. And one that is about to disrupt her future.

If it takes a killer to catch a killer, is she ready to face a deadly game where there can only be one winner…

COMING SPRING 2024

Matilda Darke will return in Autumn 2023...